A HOT TIME IN THE OLD TOWN . . .

"Beacon ahead," Merlo noted. "Read it."

I looked up at the screen and punched for higher magnification. The printed words on the sign grew larger, until I could read:

NO SMOKING!

I stared. "What in the name . . . ?"

Just then, a klaxon blared from the speaker. When it stopped, a stern voice grated, "Welcome to New Venus. For your protection, absolutely *no smoking* is permitted. Smoking is a capital crime, punishable by death."

"They're *serious*!" I turned to Merlo. "What's the matter—was New Venus colonized by health nuts?"

"No," Merlo answered. "A petroleum company. And with ninety percent of the planet surface covered with petroleum derivatives," Merlo nodded to the red letters burning on the screen, "the only thing they're afraid of is a lighted match."

WE OPEN ON VENUS

VENUS

Book Two of Starship Troupers

Christopher Stasheff

A Del Rey Book

BALLANTINE BOOKS • NEW YORK

A Del Rey Book
Published by Ballantine Books

Library of Congress Catalog Card Number: 93–90709

ISBN 0–345–36891–6

Manufactured in the United States of America

First Edition: February 1994

1

I was out of my acceleration couch and into the "down" lift before the first strangled moan finished coming out of the intercom. I called out, "B deck!" and the door closed behind me while Barry was still calling into the audio pickup, "Ogden? Ogden, old friend! What is the matter? What is wrong, Ogden?"

What was wrong? I knew damned well what was wrong! I fidgeted as the door closed and the lift sank at a sedate and leisurely pace. I had heard that kind of groaning too often, way too often, when I had "volunteered" for our local ambulance squad—Sensei had said it would do me good to see what kind of agony I could inflict if I wasn't careful. I did see some damage from fighting, but I saw a lot more of other kinds of human misery, too, and I began to develop a greater degree of compassion—and a very strong stomach. I think Sensei had that in mind, too. And along with all the rest, I learned real fast to recognize the kind of sound a person makes when he's just had a heart attack.

What was wrong? Sixty years of hundred-proof lunches and two hundred pounds of fat slammed by the hammer blow of a spaceship's takeoff, that was what was wrong!

The lift door opened. I shot down the hall and swerved toward Ogden's stateroom, then came to a skidding halt. The door was open, and Susanne was bending over the old ham, giving him what had to be the deepest kiss I'd ever seen from the outside. Jealousy tore through me, and it was

1

all I could do to stand still until the surge had passed, even though I knew damn well that it wasn't passion I was watching, just CPR.

Then the jealousy ebbed, and I yelled at the intercom, "Bridge! McLeod! Where's the first-aid kit on this tub?"

"On the wall by the door to the companionway, *ensign*," the old captain's voice snapped.

I took the emphasis on the last word as a rebuke, but I took the robo-doc out of its recess, too; I think I remembered to open the little door first. Then I ran around to Ogden's far side and knelt down, to start clipping leads onto his wrists and head and, when Susanne wasn't pumping his chest, onto his breastbone. Then I taped the little hollow tube right over the vein on the inside of his elbow—and sat back . . . All I could do was hold my breath and twiddle my thumbs, while Susanne blew air into the old actor's lungs and the robo-doc diagnosed Ogden's condition, then injected the appropriate pharmaceuticals.

It took about thirty seconds.

Thirty very long seconds—I was surprised to find out that I was actually caring about Ogden, about this man I had only met a few days before—that I was hoping in an agony of impatience that he'd be all right. I realized I had come to like the huge old coot, in spite of his grandiose manner and his boozing.

Then his color began to come back, and he started to breathe on his own. Susanne sat back with a gasp of relief and wiped her mouth. I went limp myself, then realized what she'd just been through and jumped up to get a glassful from the autobar. I took it back to her and she looked up, surprised, then smiled and said, "Thanks, but I think I've had enough alcohol for the time being—secondhand."

"Mouthwash," I said.

She stared at me a minute, then grinned and took the glass. She took a tiny sip and sucked on it as she watched

Ogden. He was breathing steadily, and opened his eyes again as we watched. "Th ... Thank ..."

"Shhh." Susanne pressed a finger over his mouth. "You need to save your energy now. Anyway, you're welcome."

The robo-doc hummed and issued a strip of paper. I tore it off and read it.

"Diagnosis?" Susanne asked.

"Minor heart attack," I answered. "Just as we thought—but only a small one. It says we don't have to turn back to Terra, but we should have him checked out by a human doctor when we get to New Venus."

"It knows our destination?"

"No, it says, 'next port of call.' I was interpreting freehand. Then there's a list of pills, two a day each, two days' bed rest—and absolutely no alcohol."

Ogden groaned.

"There, there." Susanne took his hand. "It must have been horrible for you—the pain, the fear ..."

"Worth it," Ogden croaked gallantly. "Worth every agon of angst. Go through it again in an instant, m'dear, for the pleasure of such devoted attention from one so beautiful."

Susanne actually blushed. "You need to rest now, Mr. Wellesley."

"Of course, my dear—after just a small dram, eh?"

"No!" Susanne said firmly. "You heard what the robo-doc said—absolutely no alcohol!"

Ogden groaned again, even more loudly.

"Such noise!" Susanne scolded. "I thought you said you'd go through agony for me!"

"Well, yes, my dear, agony—but not temperance!"

She gave him a slow and roguish smile, which I swear did him more good than all the drugs put together. "You're very gallant, sir—but it just makes me more determined to keep you alive." She looked up at me. "Get the stretcher, will you, Ramou?"

"Sure." I got to my feet, considering the advantages of

having a heart attack myself. I turned to the door, calling out, "Bridge! Captain, where do I find a stretcher?"

"End of the companionway," McLeod said into the audio pickup. "That's the hall, to you. Can't miss it—the door's got a red cross on it."

"Gotcha," Ramou's voice came out of the speaker. "I mean, 'Aye, aye, sir!' "

"And don't you forget it," McLeod grumbled, then sat back. "Guess he'll live, gentlemen."

"Praise heaven," Barry sighed. "Eh, Horace?"

"Amen." I agreed. The sweetest sound I had ever heard had been Susanne Souci's voice saying Ogden was breathing again. When I had heard his groan of revival, his voice had never sounded so melodious.

We heard Ramou's footsteps retreat and come right back. Merlo frowned. "Maybe I should go down there and help Ramou get the old guy onto the stretcher. He's no lightweight, you know."

"Neither is Ramou," I pointed out.

McLeod said, "The stretcher slides in under him and inflates around him, Mr. Hertz—you know that. The two of them are certainly enough to rock him from side to side. You stay right here, First Officer."

"Aye, aye, sir," Merlo sighed.

Then all I heard for the next few minutes was a deal of grunting and panting, until Ramou said, "Okay, he's secure. Sick bay, now?"

"Certainly," Barry said. "Then one of you stay with him, if you will—but we'll need the other at the meeting."

I sat back in my acceleration couch, cursing myself for a fool. I had known the risk—known Ogden's addiction to alcohol, and his obesity; he weighed at least twice what he should have—but had deluded myself with the notion that he would rather die attempting to tread the boards of a stage one more time than to wither away in some fetid and obscure tenement, unknown and miserable. I still thought I had been right, but I wished devoutly that I hadn't tried to assist, if I had only helped my old friend to his death.

"He will be all right, Horace," Barry assured me, though he looked rather doubtful himself.

Captain McLeod nodded. "The automated sick bay aboard this ship has full resuscitation equipment—even an exterior pacemaker, if he needs one. He'll be okay now, as long as it's only a cardiac arrest."

"Only a *cardiac!"* I protested.

"Only," he assured me. "Any modern ship is equipped to take care of heart attacks."

"But this ship is scarcely modern," I demurred.

"It's younger than that Lazarian kid. Its sick bay will also take care of strokes, seizures, even kidney and liver failure. Anything more exotic, though, such as bubonic plague or a timed genetic disorder, we'd have to make planetfall for."

"Well, it's certainly nothing of that magnitude." But I wasn't all that thoroughly reassured.

Barry saw, and tried to distract me. "Whatever it is, he is in the care of the automated sick bay, and there's nothing we can do about it."

Ramou's voice came suddenly from the speaker. "The robo-doc says he'll live—it was only a hiccup, not an explosion. He's not supposed to get up for two days, though—and no alcohol!"

I heard another groan from Ogden, much louder than the last. I smiled, relieved—if he could suffer withdrawal, he would survive.

If he could.

Barry's voice became a bit more brisk. "We must get on with business, after all."

"Yeah, sure, Mr. Tallendar. Let's go, Susanne."

Barry keyed the intercom to "all stations." "The emergency seems to have passed, friends. Ogden is well, in spite of his stirrup cup. Now, as I was saying before I was so rudely interrupted, everyone please report to the lounge immediately. We must discuss the situation. Respond, please."

He had said those exact words before—but the first response had been a strangled, gurgling groan from Ogden's cabin. Apparently Susanne had heard it, too, along with everyone else—it must have been picked up by Barry's microphone. Between herself and Ramou, I was sure Ogden was as well as possible.

There was a staggered chorus of assent, including a few "aye, ayes." Barry keyed off the intercom and rose, wiping his brow with a still-shaky hand. "I find I could do with a dram myself, though at the moment it seems somewhat less appealing than usual. Well! Shall we go, friends?"

"You have my permission," McLeod said, in a slightly frosty tone.

Barry looked up, surprised, then remembered where he was. "Of course. Thank you, Captain. Forgive my overlooking the proprieties."

"Certainly, Mr. Tallendar," McLeod said, with a stiff nod, "though as with any proprieties, these have a reason underlying them—especially when we're talking about who can be on the bridge and who can't, and whether or not all hands can assemble without hazard."

Barry had the grace to look abashed. "I hadn't thought . . ."

"I know," McLeod agreed. "You didn't know the ship might not yet have been safe for landlubbers to walk around, or to talk with each other without brewing panic. But as it happens, the artificial gravity did phase in as the acceleration eased up, just as it was supposed to, and panic would be most easily averted just now by your answering everybody's questions—so carry on, Mr. Managing Director."

"Thank you, Mr. Captain." Barry was the soul of politeness as he inclined his head, which was in itself a rebuke.

"Merlo, you'll come, of course? Er, beg pardon, Captain! May the first officer be released from his duties to attend the company meeting? He is the scenic designer and technical director, after all."

"Then he can attend the meeting in all three capacities." McLeod nodded toward a sliding panel in the wall. "Take the repeater console with you, will you, Number One? And tell me when it's plugged in, in the passenger lounge—I intend to get in on this meeting, too!"

I confess that I was rather nervous, looking up at the dais at the end of the room, where Barry sat right next to the grand synthesizer—and the remote-control console with Captain McLeod right behind it. Merlo was muttering something to him, and McLeod gave him a curt nod. Merlo straightened up, stepped back, and sat down beside me. "Says it's working just fine," he confided.

"What in heaven's name is it for?"

"All the basic functions of the ship, Horace," Merlo answered. "He's got the four main viewscreens, the sensor scopes, and the attitude jet controls right there. If anything goes wrong, he can take care of it long enough for me to get to the bridge and take over. Not that anything's going to go wrong, of course," he added as an afterthought.

"Of course not," I agreed, "as long as we're prepared for it. I wish I could say the same for the personnel." I glanced around at my fellow actors, each one highly, shall we say, individualistic, and very energetic.

"Don't worry about them," Merlo said, with amazing confidence. "Just wait till McLeod gets through."

I looked up with sudden apprehension. It hadn't occurred to me that the captain was there for any purpose other than observation. Surely he was nothing but the driver of a very elaborate taxi! But I recalled reading certain novels by C. F. Forster during my salad days and found the muttered conference between McLeod and Barry somewhat unnerving, even if it seemed to be only a sentence or two, ending with Barry's nod.

Then he stood up and called out, "Your attention, please, my friends! This meeting is called to order!"

"Called to order?" Marnie Lulala's lip curled with scorn. "Come now, Barry! What is this—the grade school student council?"

"No, Marnie," Barry said with grave courtesy, "it is the first full business meeting of the Star Repertory Company. Never before have I had all the actors together at the same time—I have done my best to make sure that each of you is only in three of our four plays, so that although each of you has met most of the other players, none has yet met all. And, of course, this is the first session at which both our scenic designer and costume designer are in attendance."

Marnie gave a very loud, very martyred sigh and sat back in her lounge chair. "Shall we endure a roll call? Or shall we stand up and introduce ourselves?"

"I don't think . . ." Barry began, but just then something huge came in the door, and he broke off, staring.

Everyone turned to look, myself included. Then I looked again, amazed. I hadn't known stretchers came in so large a size.

"Ogden!" Barry cried. "Ramou, are you out of your mind?"

"I did not offer him a great deal of choice, Barry," Ogden Wellesley said from his recumbent position on the floating stretcher. "I insisted. After all, I simply couldn't have one of these excellent young people missing out on this first meeting because of my infirmities."

His voice had only an echo of its usual richness, but his color was good, and he seemed to be speaking without undue effort. For myself, I was delighted, if apprehensive.

To judge by Barry's expression, he shared my feelings. "Ogden, you mustn't! Ramou! Susanne! Take him to the sick bay at once!"

"Oh, well, if you must." Ogden signaled to Ramou to turn the stretcher around. "I'm sure I can persuade the beverage dispenser there to issue some bourbon . . ."

"On second thought, perhaps you *should* attend the meeting," Barry said, never missing a beat. "After all, if the full company should be assembled, the *full* company should be assembled, eh what?"

"So good of you, Barry." Ogden waved Ramou away. "I would hate to think that my misfortunes had dampened the festive spirit of this initial occasion."

"Festive!" Marnie was on her feet. "Frenetic, perhaps, but scarcely festive. Here we are, leaving Earth in a panic, just scarcely time to grab my jewelry case and a totally inadequate sampling of my wardrobe . . ."

"All right, that'll do." McLeod's voice wasn't really all that loud, but it cracked like a gunshot. Marnie spun to stare at him, shocked that any mere mortal should dare to interrupt her.

McLeod met her glare with a look that could have pierced steel as he said evenly, "Would you introduce me, please, Managing Director?"

Marnie recovered and took a breath.

"Why, yes, of course," Barry said easily. "The first order of business. Ladies and gentlemen, may I present to you our captain, Gantry McLeod."

"Captain!" Marnie cried. "Barry, if you think this overgrown rocket jockey is going to—"

"Thank you, Director Tallendar." McLeod overrode her voice as he came to his feet. "Just keep it right up, Ms. Lulala. If you prefer to spend the rest of the trip in the brig, I'll be glad to accomodate you."

"Brig! Just who do you think you are, you annoying little man?"

Gantry was considerably taller than any of us except Merlo and Ogden, but they both knew that was not the matter of which Marnie was speaking. McLeod pressed something on his console and said, "Maintenance Unit Number Three, enter the lounge."

The doors opened, and a robot with rubber-padded pincers and a huge waste bin rolled in.

Marnie stared at it, then whirled back to him. "You wouldn't dare!"

"Wouldn't I just." McLeod measured out a small smile. "Not that I'd have to, of course—I'd command you to report to the brig, and you'd go."

"Go! Why, you—"

"And if you didn't, I could command any of your fellow passengers to put you there. If any of them disobeyed, they'd be tried for mutiny as soon as we made planetfall. So would you, for that matter."

Marnie started a hot retort, then caught herself in one of her rare moments of uncertainty.

"Now hear this." McLeod looked around at us all, his face stony. "This is the dictator speaking. Also the king, emperor, lord of the castle, and general monarch of all he surveys. The laws are the same as they were in the days of sailing ships, folks—a captain aboard a vessel in space is the last of the absolute tyrants."

"Not the only one, if the LORDS party gets its way," Marty interrupted.

"Belay that," McLeod snapped.

Marty saluted. "Aye, aye, sir!"

" 'Yes, Captain,' will do," McLeod growled, glaring at him. "You don't have the right to say, 'aye, aye, sir,' unless you're registered as crew. Right, Mr. Hertz?"

"Aye, aye, sir," Merlo answered.

Somehow, that made us all more nervous than anything McLeod had said. We all knew Merlo Hertz as our scenic designer—and to have him suddenly emerge as McLeod's assistant was disconcerting, to say the least.

"For those of you who don't know it," McLeod said,

"Mr. Hertz is first officer of this ship and has the master's papers to prove it."

Uproar. Fast and loud. Barry looked gratified; I believe he was reassured that all his actors could project.

"Terran law requires a minimum crew of three for any space vessel," McLeod called over the uproar, and everyone stilled, waiting for the rest of the bad news.

"Mr. Lazarian has signed on as ensign," McLeod informed us. "He doesn't have any papers yet, but he'll have qualified for his basics by the time we reach New Venus."

"Ramou?" Lacey cried, and swung around to stare at him as if he were a jellyfish who had just sprouted legs and come ashore for a stroll. She wasn't alone—everybody had turned to have a look at the turncoat.

Also the sudden crown prince.

I stood frozen, caught between a sudden rush of embarrassment that urged me to duck under Ogden's stretcher—and a flush of pride that made me want to strut. The upshot was that I froze, which fortunately seemed to pass for standing at attention. Susanne was looking at me in a whole new light—one that I wasn't sure I wanted.

"If either of these men tells you anything, it comes from me," McLeod said, loud and hard. "If they give you advice, take it. If they give you orders, obey them—fast! Sometimes, in space, there isn't time to explain."

The stares became a little harder.

"Of course, they *will* explain whenever possible," McLeod qualified, thawing just a little. "I pride myself on having a polite and attentive crew. If you have any complaints about them, tell me. If you have any complaints about me, tell the Space Authority—on New Venus. Till then, you'll do as you're told."

"You can't get away with this!" Marnie stormed. "I'll tell Valdor, and he'll have your hide! He'll nail you to the wall and see to it that you never leave Earth again!"

"Fine," McLeod shot back. "You can tell him anything you want—as soon as we get back to Terra. You can tell the authorities on New Venus anything you want, too—but not until we get there. We're traveling much faster than light, Ms. Lulala, and that means we're traveling faster than radio, too. Nothing yet invented can travel faster than a ship in H-space—which is why the captain has to be the sole and total authority aboard ship. He can't call a planet station for advice, and he can't receive orders. He can't call the cops, he can't call the marines, he can't call anybody. Once we shifted into H-space, we lost communication with every planet in the galaxy. That means we're outside the jurisdiction of every government there is—and that's why I have to *be* the government."

" 'As it was in the days of Nelson's fleet,' " Horace murmured, " 'as it was in the days of old.' "

"How's that again?" McLeod peered sharply at him. "Mr. Burbage, isn't it? 'The Ballad of the Good Ship Clampherdown,' was it? My sentiments exactly, Mr. Burbage. That's the way it is, so that's the way it's got to be. I like the power, but I don't like the responsibility. Not much I can do about it, though—and neither can you."

"Mutiny," Winston Carlton suggested.

"Don't even think about it." McLeod glared at him. "The penalty for mutiny is still death—though it's much quicker and less agonizing than it used to be."

I swallowed, feeling like the enemy. We all knew what McLeod was talking about. In the days of sailing ships, they strung you up by the neck and let you choke to death. Now they just shove you into a conversion chamber, punch the button, and let your constituent atoms instantly unconstitute. Quick and painless, they tell me, though I don't know of anybody who's been through it and has really said anything to confirm that.

You couldn't blame McLeod for jumping to conclusions—Winston Carlton looked like the most sadistic villain that ever counted blood drops. Horace tells me he's the gentlest soul alive, but he sure doesn't look it—and he's one of our few genuine stars, having made a fortune playing bad guys.

"I won't," Winston promised, "but I did think the issue should be aired."

"Spaced, if they try to do anything about it," McLeod growled. "I just might not wait for planetfall. For some things, I'd rather take my chances with a Board of Inquiry."

Myself, I wasn't about to argue.

McLeod suddenly smiled, warm and friendly. "Of course, I've never imposed any punishment harder than short rations—and the individual in question needed to go on a diet, anyway."

Ogden blanched under his pallor.

"Of course, there's always extra KP and scrub patrol," McLeod amended, "but that's not so bad—or even a night in the brig, until the perpetrator sobers up."

Ogden blanched again; I had trouble telling where he ended and his sheet began.

"On the other hand!" McLeod snapped, his stare nailing each one of us to his or her chair. "I've never been one to let myself be limited by past performance, either."

He held the glare a moment longer, then suddenly relaxed and straightened up. "Well. That's all I have to say for now. Hopefully, you won't have to hear from me again until we're about to land on New Venus. In the meantime, take a few minutes to read that little card in your bedside drawer that says 'Rules Aboard Ship,' and make sure you live by them tighter than the Bible. There'll be a lifeboat drill every now and then—not that we think we'll need them, but neither did the *Titanic*."

"But," said Larry Rash, "how are we to know when we're talking to Ramou as gofer, or Ramou as ensign?"

You could tell he cared by the way he said it. That kind of thing meant a lot, to Larry. He was one of the youngest members of the company, like me, and was very anxious to know whom he could kick and whom he couldn't.

"When he's doing his theater job, he's . . ."

"Technical assistant," Barry muttered.

". . . technical assistant," McLeod finished, with only the slightest hint of a pause. "Any other time, assume he's crew—and treat him accordingly."

Larry's eyes burned, and his throat convulsed—it was an awfully hard fact for him to swallow—but he kept his mouth shut. Not that I was worried—Larry and I had already had our little talk. I had to admit, the kid had guts. Not much else, but he did have guts.

"Any questions?" McLeod rapped, in a way that implied there had better not be any—and there weren't, though there were an awful lot of stiletto glances. The points glanced harmlessly off the armor of his self-assurance, though, and he nodded crisply. "Very good. I'll turn the meeting back to your director, then. Mr. Tallendar?" He sat down.

Barry rose, trying to suppress a smile. "Thank you, Captain McLeod. Now then, my friends, let me discuss our schedule for the next few weeks."

2

"As you know," Barry said, "we had originally planned to open our first season on New Venus anyway, since it is the closest to Terra of all its colonies. Then, due to the gratuitous publicity provided by Elector Rudders . . ."

There were a few chuckles, most notably from Winston, who was the only one of us in a position not to be concerned about cost. It was true enough that the elector's publicity had been free, but it certainly had not been intended to be favorable in the slightest. Could we help it if a condemnation from Rudders was a com*men*dation, to most of the theater-going public?

"So we moved our opening date up a bit," Barry went on, "and, to maximize the benefits of this unexpected notoriety, we determined to begin our season on Broadway, rather than ending it there. The good elector, however, moved to prevent our leaving Terra at all, and since that was the purpose for which we were formed, we had to rush to leave the planet before his new law was passed."

"Has it been?" Lacey Lark asked.

"We haven't quite had time to check the broadcasts," Barry told her. "We only lifted off half an hour ago, after all."

"But we *could* have had a successful Broadway run!" Marnie stormed. "Really, Barry, how shortsighted of you! Why, you've sacrificed us all on the altar of your asinine dream!"

15

There was a mutter of agreement, most notably from Lacey Lark and Larry Rash. We older actors, though, looked skeptical.

"A run," Barry agreed, "and with luck, we might have broken even. With great luck, we might have run more than one season. But what then, Marnie? When the rush of publicity had passed, what then?"

"The company would have had to dissolve," Winston murmured.

The younger folk saw his point—no company, no paycheck. But that would have been a blessing, to Marnie. "What of it?" she ranted, in true prima donna fashion. "Who says the publicity would have ended?"

"Elector Rudders," Barry said, "for he is the one who generated it. After all, we were controversial only because we intended to leave the planet and take live theater to Terra's colonies all across the Terran Sphere. No lift-off, no controversy—and with no controversy, we would have had no publicity."

"What of it?" Marnie scoffed. "With a successful run behind us, surely we could have mounted another new play! Honestly, Barry! To have given up the Earth, and all that's in it!"

"That was the purpose for which we formed," I noted.

"Oh, be still, Horace!" Marnie blazed. "Just because a silly old man like you has become disenchanted with Terra does not mean we younger souls have!"

I stood up slowly, letting my shock and anger show just enough. "Ms. Lulala, New York City has been my home, my world, and the mother of my soul. She beguiled me in my youth and formed me in maturity. She has occupied a place in my affections far stronger than any woman's, and I would have wished no greater blessing than to have died in the city I love. But where there is no money, there is no life. Roles were coming more and more rarely, and I was forced to face the fact that this Star Company was my final opportunity to be sure of a chance to tread the boards for the score or so years that are left me. In the final analysis, I had to choose between my beloved New York, and my mistress, the theater. I deeply regret that the choice was so clear and so drastic, but such is life—and I could not abandon the stage."

The look Marnie gave me would have steamed a pudding, but she had no answer. What could she have said—that faced with the same choice, she would have chosen New York? We all knew that, but she could scarcely have admitted it. And she certainly could not have admitted that for her, at least, the demise of the Star Company would have been no tragedy, for if there had been no company, there would have been nowhere for Valdor Tallendar to send her in exile, as is the fate of many a mistress who has become importunate. No, of us all, only Marnie had been joined to the company by force, rather than free will. All she could say was, "Perhaps you are willing to waste the rest of *your* life in the rustic provinces, Horace Burbage, but I am not!"

"Hey, Captain, stop the ship!" Marty cried. "She wants to get off!"

He earned a burst of surprised laughter, and he made his point—we were committed now, whether we wanted to be or not. The first chance to "get off" would be New Venus, and I didn't much think Marnie would care to walk the four light-years back to Terra.

Marty also earned a glare from Marnie, a look that would have shriveled him from the insides out, if she could have had her way. It was a look that fairly promised him that he would never work in the theater again—but Marty only smiled brightly back at her, then deliberately turned to gaze up at Barry, all innocence. The point was well taken—if he had made an enemy of the leading lady, he had made a friend of the producer.

For Barry had been watching the whole episode with a

look of covert amusement. He was quite content to let Marnie make her enemies for herself, though he was too much the gentleman to have attempted to do it for her.

I could have cheered when Marty scored on Marnie, and I damn near applauded when Horace sat down. Not quite, though—I realized it would have embarrassed Marnie to the point where she would never be willing to cooperate again, and I knew enough of human groups to realize it was important that we become a company, a unit, in the fullest sense of the word. Going through the motions wasn't enough—we would all have to be committed, or we'd fall apart. Barry knew that, too, and I wasn't about to make his job any harder for him.

Still, it made me nervous hearing all those actors calling question after question at him, not giving him time to answer a single one.

"But weren't we acting illegally in lifting off, Barry?"

"Just why was Elector Rudders watching us so closely?"

"What is the real reason the LORDS party didn't want us to take theater to the stars?"

"Don't worry, Ramou," Ogden wheezed.

I looked down, startled. He was touching my arm with a feeble attempt at a reassuring squeeze, and was very pale— but the huge old bear was smiling! Sort of.

"Don't let it bother you," he said again. "They're all actors, you see, and can never quite remember when they're offstage. There's an audience available, so every one of them must have his or her say." And he managed a ponderous wink.

I stared, amazed that a man who had just had a heart attack could spare that much consideration for a tyro like me. Beside him, Susanne beamed and gave his arm a much more effective squeeze. He got a little color back in his face and managed a wink at her, too.

"In sequence, please, my friends, in sequence!" Barry

pleaded, hands upraised—but the uproar grew louder, if that were possible.

Until Captain McLeod stood up and roared, *"Now hear this!"*

Instant and total silence answered him, the actors staring in shock—as much in horror at what such a shout must have done to his larynx as in amazement that any mere nonactor could equal them in volume.

I shared the horror, at least. It was horrible voice production, really—the man blasted, he didn't project, and I winced at the calluses that must have formed on his vocal folds, if he'd been doing that all his life. But it *was* loud, as good as Ogden in his long-ago prime.

Then the actors recovered and were just about to begin another round when McLeod nodded, satisfied. "Good. That's very good. Thank you. Now, as your director was saying, he needs your questions one at a time. Mr. Tallendar?" And he sat down, turning to look at Barry as he did. I had never seen a more deliberate yielding of focus.

"Thank you, Captain McLeod," Barry said, and meant it. "Now, I believe the first question referred to the legality of our departure from Terra. We were perfectly legal in what we did, since no law prohibiting our enterprise had yet been passed."

"But what of the court order, Barry, eh?" Ogden wheezed.

Susanne repeated it for him: "What about the court order that was supposed to restrain us, Mr. Tallendar?"

"What court order, Ms. Souci?" Barry said, with bland innocence. "Oh, I must admit that I had heard rumors . . ."

"From a very reliable source," Winston murmured, and Marnie made an exclamation of disgust; the source was Barry's brother Valdor, who had recently proved to be anything but reliable, for her. Never mind that he had been so for more years than she cared to remember . . .

"A rumor," Barry said firmly, "that such a court order was being prepared. However, I must classify it as nothing but a rumor, since no such paper has been served on us."

"How about the man in the gray suit on the grav-scooter, hey, Barry?" Ogden wheezed.

Larry pressed, "Wasn't he bringing it?"

"Since the unfortunate gentleman never arrived, we shall never know his mission," Barry said with pious regret.

"No doubt hunting for autographs," Marnie said with withering scorn. The company laughed, as much in surprise at hearing Marnie deliver a witticism as in appreciation of it.

"Quite possibly," Barry agreed. "After all, half our company are established stars."

Or have been, he might have added—we were all over forty, and the only one still in the headlines was Winston. Except for Marnie, of course, who was frequently featured in the scandal sheets—but that was for her actions, not her acting.

The other half were only beginning. Larry was fresh out of school, and I do mean fresh; Marty had graduated from the same institution a year earlier, but had already gained a few small comic appearances in off-off-Broadway productions and one off-Broadway; Lacey Lark had been making the rounds for a year longer, with similar results; and Susanne Souci was a veteran of five years, in regional theaters and summer stock. Her roles in New York had been few, but she already had the air of a trouper. Fascinating, with her air of innocence, which I think Ramou had noted.

Ramou was our technical assistant, not an actor, and had left college without finishing his degree. In fact, he had apparently left in considerable haste, due to a young lady's allegation that he was linked by blood to her unborn baby. He swore it was impossible, of course, and from what he had told me of her, I didn't doubt it.

"As to the reason for close surveillance," Barry went on,

"none but Elector Rudders can know for sure. However, I surmise that we were only the latest, and most defenseless, of his targets for public indignation, allowing him to curry the favor of the masses."

"That scarcely seems adequate cause for such concentrated venom," Ogden wheezed, and Susanne obligingly repeated it for him.

Barry shrugged. "If he had any ulterior motive, I have no knowledge of it—not even enough for an educated guess. As to the real reason the LORDS party did not wish us to take theater to the colony planets, I can only point out that Elector Rudders is one of their leaders, and the move may have been completely his own."

"But they are such hidebound reactionaries, Barry!" Marnie protested. "Isn't such a move in keeping with their policies?"

"To cut the newer colony planets off from Terra, in order to save the expense of their maintenance?" Barry nodded. "Yes, we could be regarded as a tie to the mother planet, and the Latter Order of Republican Democracy would surely wish to sever that umbilicus."

"They should be apprehensive about the fate of the negligent parent when the child grows up," Ogden rumbled, and Susanne did not have to repeat it for him. Everyone laughed—except Ramou. I remembered that his father had left his mother before he had been born, and that his resulting attitudes might most mildly be termed "bitter." It sent a chill down my spine, thinking what the colony planets might do to Terra one day, if they reacted with the same intensity as Ramou did. Fortunately, he had no idea where to find his errant parent—but the colony planets would know where to find theirs.

Charles Publican finally spoke up. "I might add that the LORDS have shown a great desire to control the flow of information to the colonies."

"The colonies!" Marnie exclaimed with indignation.

"Why stop there? They want total censorship on Terra itself!"

"I wouldn't debate the notion for a moment." Publican
inclined his head in acknowledgement of the validity of
Marnie's view. "However, since they haven't said so, we
can only surmise."

"And while we surmise, they take over," Marty added.

Publican chuckled along with the rest, then continued.
"We are certainly a channel for the flow of information, and
one they can't control once we're off-planet. I submit that
they would see us as a wild card, an unpredictable force that
might be turned against them."

"Only if we get the chance," Merlo muttered.

Publican smiled equably. He was an odd one—had no
professional experience at all, but was obviously well ac-
quainted with the theater and quite adept at character roles.
Besides, he was willing to work for a scandalously low
wage. Barry thought him an aspiring actor who had been
aspiring for twenty years, one of the dogged few who keep
auditioning and auditioning even though they are never
cast; his employment record as a weekend bartender
seemed to corroborate this. Myself, I placed him as a professor in midlife crisis, trying to make a change to the life
of adventure and romance from which he had turned away
in his youth. We were both probably wrong.

"As to the question from Ms. Lark, that every performance on a colony planet might violate a law passed on Terra
in our absence," Barry resumed, "I can only reply that we
cannot *know* that, since the fastest way to take news from
one planet to another is by spaceship and, for some reason
I can't understand, there is no way for any ship to travel
faster than any other, in H-space."

He glanced at Captain McLeod, who nodded and explained, "Everything travels at maximum there—all, or
none. Of course, there's a chance that a courier ship might
drop out of H-space a week behind us, but still overhaul us

in normal space. I wouldn't put money on it, but it's possible."

"Thank you, Captain." Barry was obviously no wiser than he had been before the captain spoke. "For that reason, I expect that we will stay ahead of the news throughout our tour—so that we may find out at the end of the season, when we return to Terra, but not until."

"A convenient fiction," Winston said. "What if Elector Rudders decides to confront us with reality?"

The company was very quiet, each one of us picturing a homecoming resulting in arrest and prosecution.

Merlo looked up at McLeod, and the captain nodded. Merlo rose and turned to the rest of us. "*United Spaceways v. Biederman et al*, 2356. A package-tour ship was returning to Terra. They were holed by a meteor shower as they were dropping out of H-space to visit Haldane IV. The passengers all survived, but they had to sleep in shifts and go on short rations because the ship only had one lifeboat for every forty people. When they were returned to Terra, they found out that a law had been passed requiring one lifeboat for every twenty people. They sued. United Spaceways won, because the law hadn't even been proposed when the ship left Terra." He sat down again.

"Precedent," Publican murmured.

"Yes, a legal precedent." Barry nodded. "Even if they pass the law today, we won't be bound by it. They will not be able to imprison us."

"They could try," Marty pointed out.

"They could," Barry admitted, "but they would fail. The company would, of course, assume the cost of your bail, and of your legal defense."

Everyone relaxed, ever so slightly. They knew that "the company," in this case, was Valdor Tallendar, who quite possibly had more money than all the colony planets combined.

"Of course, it would be excellent publicity for us," I

pointed out. " 'The Star Company returns from its triumphal first season. All members arrested for the high crime of entertaining the pioneers! Indicted for the offense of playing to packed houses!' Oh, yes, we would have an immensely successful Broadway run!"

"An excellent point, Horace," Barry said, with a grateful glance.

But Marnie countered, "*If* we play to packed houses. You're assuming these barbarians even know we exist."

"Publius Promo will assure that for us," Barry replied. "I don't believe you've met the man . . ."

"He ran the box office at the theater where I played my first summer season," Marnie said, her voice hard. "Surely you haven't hired that inept flack as our advance man, Barry!"

"He was available." Barry sighed. "And he has a successful, if modest, employment record. He was scheduled to meet us on New Venus for a single day, before he departed for Haldane IV—but we are arriving almost a month ahead of schedule, now, so our stays will overlap for a longer term. I will tell him of Elector Rudders' attempts to silence us, and of our courageous insistence on bringing the benefits of sophistication and culture to the hinterworlds. He will leave as soon as he has seen to the local publicity, so that when we land on Falstaff, we will find the populace already agog."

"A nine-days' wonder," Marnie said sourly.

"True," Barry agreed. "On the tenth day, we'll have to manage on the quality of our production."

Marnie glared at him, and I spoke up again. "As to New Venus, we can plant a few rumors ourselves. It should only take a day or two before the population knows that the government of the Interstellar Dominion Electorates attempted to silence us, and that in itself will guarantee a large house. Nothing is quite so appealing as forbidden fruit."

"I didn't know we had any in this company," Marnie said acidly, and Marty glanced up in surprise.

"Of course," Barry said, "once they have sampled the fruit, they will not come for a second helping if they do not find it tasty. Ultimately, it is the quality of our performance, and the appeal of the plays we choose, that will determine the size of our audience."

"Not that we've much choice about the plays," Marnie said. "You've chosen the first season!"

"True," Barry agreed, "but we could make additions to the bill, if we find enough audience demand."

"Demand!" Ramou snorted, and I looked up in alarm—as the most junior member of the company, his wisest move was silence. He realized it, too; he had clapped a hand over his mouth and was staring in horror.

He had reason to; Barry had begun to gain a substantial opinion of him. No wonder—Ramou had proved himself quite capable and thoroughly reliable.

Before this, that is. Now, though, Barry had heard his exclamation. "You question the choice of plays, Mr. Lazarian?"

"Uh . . . no, sir!" Ramou swallowed, and seized a metaphorical shovel to attempt to dig himself out of his own figurative hole. "Just the audiences!"

Larry's eyes were glinting as he followed the exchange; nothing delighted him so much as someone else's discomfiture—especially Ramou's.

"In what way?" Barry asked, as gently as possible.

"Well—from what I hear about these frontiersmen, their taste isn't exactly highbrow," Ramou explained.

"Surely you don't mean we should lower ourselves to their level!" Marnie said, with massive indignation.

"No, ma'am!" Ramou said. "I just mean we'll have to settle for small audiences—at least, at first. The only way we'll pull a big audience out there is if we do plays that are damn near pornographic."

"Oh, don't worry, little man." Marnie's lip curled in scorn. "By frontier standards, our plays are quite pornographic indeed. To be any worse, we'd have to do Shakespeare."

Ramou stared. "Shakespeare is pornographic?"

"Let us say, 'earthy,' " Ogden rumbled.

"Earthy indeed!" Marnie said, with savage amusement. "Read *The Taming of the Shrew*, young man—Act II, Scene I. That will please your frontiersmen almost as much as a striptease."

"You're not suggesting we do *Shrew*!" Lacey cried, then bit her tongue, eyes huge.

Marnie turned to the sweet young thing with a smile that fairly dripped venom. "And why not, dear?"

Lacey swallowed, but she was in it now. "It has to be the most sexist work in the English language!"

"It does offer a massive rationalization for the oppression of women," Susanne agreed.

"It does that," Marnie admitted, much against her will, "though I can think of a novel or two that might be worse."

"On a frontier planet," Barry said, "the Shakespearean play that will draw the largest audience is the one they teach most often in their schools."

I had to admire the man. Somehow, he had turned a protest meeting into a debate over the season's bill.

"Schools?" Larry Rash looked up indignantly. "Are we going to let secondary school teachers determine our repertory?"

"Of course we are, you idiot," Marnie said with contempt.

Larry went rigid, but didn't dare talk back to the leading lady.

"It's a better standard than the prurient interests of middle-aged men," Lacey agreed.

Winston looked up, interested.

"Oh, the old dears are perfectly harmless," Susanne said

with airy disregard. I was considering whether or not to take offense when she added, "If you handle them right."

"I'd rather not handle them at all!" Lacey snapped.

"I do agree that soft-core sadism is not in the best of taste," Barry said, "though I can imagine a production of *Shrew* which would be a virtual parody of itself."

"So can I," I said, "but I would rather write that parody myself than twist Shakespeare's words to a purpose he didn't intend. He, too, has a right to be heard, after all."

"He has been heard," Marnie said dryly, "for a millenium and more."

"All things considered . . ." Ogden began, but his statement ended in a groan.

"Just rest, Mr. Wellesley," Susanne said, and bent over to put her ear near his lips. "Whisper it to me and I'll repeat it."

Lacey was giving her a very stony look, and Ramou's eyes were riveted to her—no doubt because of the angle of his view; he was standing across from her—as Ogden whispered hoarsely in her ear.

Susanne nodded, lifting her head. "He says he thinks we had better go with the English teachers. He said something about 'ruffled feathers,' too, whatever that means."

"He means that we should toady to the local powers," Marnie said.

Ogden frowned, but Barry said, "We must deal with realities, my friends. If we wish to be welcome for a second season . . ."

". . . or even be allowed to finish out our stay," Winston qualified.

"Even so," Barry agreed. "If we don't wish to be run out of town on a rail and poured back into our ship in a stream of tar, well coated with feathers, we must consider local taboos."

"But I thought being run out of town was a mark of distinction," Marnie said sweetly.

"Only when Elector Rudders is the power source," Marty said.

Marnie turned to him. "Young man, your career could be very short indeed."

"I thought you only said that to your lovers," Marty shot back.

Marnie's eyes narrowed. "Your career may not be all that is short."

Marty slapped his jaw, snapping his head to the side. "Score one for the champ! I shouldn'ta led with my chin."

"And your chin isn't what you led with," Marnie said sweetly.

Marty snorted. "Lady, if I were an elephant with you around, the only thing I'd pack would be my trunk."

"An elephant?" Marnie's eyes gleamed, and with a shock, I realized she was enjoying the exchange. "Don't be conceited, young man. Possibly a tapir . . ."

"Tapering off is exactly what this exchange should do," Barry said firmly. "Could we return to the curriculum?"

Marty pointed to the little door at the side of the room and opened his mouth, but Barry said quickly, "*Thank* you, Mr. Kemp. Now, there are two plays that are studied by almost every English-speaking secondary school—"

"Not *Julius Caesar*!" Marnie was horrified, quite properly—there are only two women's roles in the saga of Caesar's assassination, and neither is terribly long. Winston looked gratified, though—Cassius is a fascinating role for the resident villain.

"I'm afraid so." Barry strove for a sympathetic tone. "But there is another."

Ogden paled to the color of parchment and gasped, "Not . . . the Scottish play!"

The hall was deathly silent.

"I fear we must consider it," Barry said.

Marnie wore a small smile, and her eyes were glowing.

"I beg your understanding, friends," Barry pleaded. "If

we perform a standard from the secondary school curriculum, every English teacher on the planet will send his students to see it. Their parents and guardians will be dragged along, of course—so we are virtually guaranteed a viable box office."

"Censorship by English teachers!" Ogden groaned. "And who will I be—the ghost?"

"Yes—you really will be, if you don't relax," Susanne said. "Please, Mr. Wellesley—won't you let us take you to the sick bay now?"

"Not before the issue is decided, child," the huge old actor rasped. Then his voice ran out, and he crooked a forefinger.

Susanne bent down to listen, and Ramou caught his breath. Then she straightened up and called, "He asks for the courtesy of a vote."

"This really falls within the province of the managing director." Barry sighed. "But no prince can rule without the consent of his people. Which will it be, my friends—*Julius Caesar*, or the Scottish play?"

There was a silence.

"All in favor of *Julius Caesar*," Barry said.

Marty raised a hand. Marnie glared daggers at him, and he yanked it down.

"None," Barry said. "The alternative is to rehearse both *Julius Caesar* and the Scottish play, then to perform whichever is taught in the local curriculum. All in favor?"

There was a long pause, then reluctant hands began to rise.

"A majority." Barry nodded. "We will rehearse both, then, as well as *Vagrants from Vega*, and perhaps one or two others. Blocking tomorrow—think positively, friends. But for this afternoon and evening, I think we deserve to celebrate—by your leave, of course, Captain," he added as a too-obvious afterthought.

But McLeod nodded. "A lift-off party is traditional aboard a passenger ship, Director. Proceed."

"Meeting adjourned," Barry said quickly, just barely managing to get it in before the massed cheer broke loose. Then he turned to the captain and began to converse in a low tone.

The actors were on their feet and heading for the beverage dispensers, laughing and clapping one another on the back, and debating the merits of the various plays as they moved toward the food and drink synthesizers. None of them seemed to notice that Barry had totally ignored Shakespeare's other thirty-three plays. I was sure they would eventually, but the only one who was likely to cause difficulties was Marnie, and she seemed quite happy with the results.

3

"All right, my dear," Ogden rumbled, "if you insist."

"I'm afraid I really do, Mr. Wellesley," Susanne said firmly. "You've run out of excuses—the meeting's over." She looked up at me. "Would you give me a hand, Ramou?"

"Sure," I said. I was about to ask her where she wanted it, but caught myself in time. I also managed to hold back the offer to let her have any other part of my body that she wanted. Instead, as we maneuvered the stretcher toward the door, I asked, "What's this business about 'the Scottish play'?"

"It is bad luck," Ogden wheezed, and Susanne nodded. "Such very bad luck that actors don't even mention the title when they're in a theater. That's why they call it 'the Scottish play.' "

"But what's so bad about *Brigadoon*?"

"No, dear." Susanne shot me an affectionate smile.

Ogden wheezed, "The one with the man who meets three witches."

"*Macbeth*?" I stared.

"Shhh!" Susanne glanced frantically around to make sure no one had overheard my gaffe.

"Quite so," Ogden said, his tone iron, "and I'll thank you not to use that word again, outside of rehearsals."

Well. That explained what Marnie was so happy about.

* * *

I found out later that actors have a lot of superstitions. No, I can't call them the most superstitious people on Earth—or off it, for that matter. They're definitely in the running, but I've run into people in every walk of life who have things they're funny about. Even computer programmers worry about gremlins and glitches, and we engineers hang up joking signs asking St. Vidicon to protect us from Murphy. Actors just have a tradition of superstitions that's a little longer—like about a thousand years. Horace tells me there's a rumor that Thespis wouldn't wear his makeup outside the theater.

For instance, it's bad luck to whistle in the dressing room. It's bad luck to wish an actor good luck. It's bad luck to throw your hat on a bed. That last one made sense to me—the last time I'd done it, I'd wound up leaving town one foot ahead of a paternity suit. Believe me, it was impossible—but that never stopped a lawyer. As they say, you don't have to be able to win to be able to sue.

The nervousness about *Macbeth*, though, seemed really silly to me. I mean, a play is just a play, right? Words on paper, then words spoken aloud—how could it cause bad luck?

"Skeptical you may be," Ogden warned me, "but the Scottish play has never been performed without at least one casualty, and frequently a fatality."

"Aw, come on!" I scoffed. *"Never?"*

"Never," he solemnly averred.

"Laugh while you can," Susanne warned me. "You're about to be part of it."

I wasn't worried. After all, I wasn't going to be onstage.

"What do you mean, I'm going to be onstage?" I stared at Merlo, appalled. The laughing and conversation were all around us, but not loud enough to have drowned out his threat. "You want to see jelly? Look at my knees if you get me in front of an audience!"

"*You* are scared?" Merlo jibed.

I flushed. Just because you have a black belt in karate, people think you aren't scared of anything. Not true at all—you just don't let fear stop you. I mean, if some guy is pointing a laser rifle at me, damn right I'm going to be scared. It's not going to stop me from trying to take the blasting thing away from him, but I'm going to be scared.

And going up in front of an audience had absolutely nothing to do with physical courage.

"Too right I'm scared!" I pointed to the holo of a scene from *Macbeth* that someone had already hauled out and tacked to the wall. "You'll never get me up there on one of those things!"

"It's not as if you had to deliver any lines, Ramou." It was Barry, coming up behind Merlo. "I'm only asking you to come onstage carrying a spear, step aside to guard the entranceway, then follow Duncan off. Nothing difficult there."

"Yeah, except the thousand people looking at me!"

"Only if we're fortunate." He sighed.

"Besides," I said, "I've got to be offstage, running the console."

"Only when I'm onstage," Merlo told me, "and when I come off, you can go on. How else are we going to do an army with only twelve people in the company?"

"Even *I* am carrying a spear, Ramou," Barry said gently.

"Yeah," Merlo said, "and that's after he's finished playing Duncan."

"It's easy for you," I said, "you've been doing it all your life!"

"Only since my teens," Barry corrected. He turned to Horace, who had drifted over, looking interested. "Could you?"

"I'll certainly try," Horace said, and stepped forward.

I braced myself; I liked Horace, and I owed him a lot—including my being here in the first place.

"Now, see here, Ramou," he said, "you signed on to help provide scenery, didn't you?"

I frowned. "Yeah—that's what you told me the tech assistant did, in addition to going for coffee, and a lot of other odd jobs."

"Well, carrying a spear is another odd job." He raised a hand to forestall my protest. "Besides, all a spear-carrier is is moving scenery. Is there so great a difference between *making scenery* and *being* it?"

They had me convinced—*Macbeth* was bad luck. I mean, "the Scottish play."

Meanwhile, the party raged on around us. Well, maybe "raged" is too strong a word—or maybe it was the drink that was too strong. I do remember chatting with Susanne, who was very receptive and cuddly, but somehow I remember snuggling up with Lacey, too, and in between there, I seem to have a memory of dancing with Marnie, if you can believe that. She moved smoothly as silk on even the most inane college-fad dance that I knew, then insisted on teaching me an antique she called the samba, and how those movements made her body look should be decidedly illegal. I also remember some loud and shrill arguments with Larry—Lacey with Larry, Susanne with Larry, Merlo with Larry, me with Larry, and Marty always managing to work his way into the quarrel somehow and turn it into such a rip-roaring farce that the quarrelers always had to break off gasping for air. For example:

"Modern shet dezhign?" Larry hiccuped, and stubbed out a cigarette. "Your idea of 'modern' is Robert Edmund Jones!"

"Hey, he had a history course!" Merlo jibed. "Did they teach you to act?"

They were both a bit more intense than the lines maybe seem like. This had been going on for five minutes.

"Of course they did!" Larry snapped.

Marty was between the two of them, nodding and saying, "Yeah. Yes."

"Then you probably think 'the new stagecraft' meant an improved way of making flats," Merlo sneered.

Marty nodded at Larry. "Flats. Right."

"They haven't used flats in a century!" Larry retorted.

Marty said, "Century," to Merlo.

"Don't tell me your college was still using wood and canvas!" Merlo said. "Well, that explains your acting style."

"He's got style," Marty agreed.

"How would you know the tiniest thing about acting?" Larry stormed.

"Know any tiny things?" Marty asked Merlo.

Merlo tried to ignore him. "Tiny things! I'll bet you think 'Stanislavsky' is two names."

"Yeah, Harry Stanislavsky!" Marty said brightly. "I worked under him in Cleveland!"

"When were you in Cleveland?" Larry demanded.

"Not likely, kid," Merlo said. "He's been dead a few centuries."

"That's Constantin. I'm talking about his great-great-grandnephew, Harry. We worked summers as ushers at the Cleveland Festival. I worked the ground floor, and he—"

"Was in the balcony," Merlo finished for him. "Right. Look, do you mind if we have an argument here?"

"Do you have enough mind for an argument here?"

"I should say we do!" Larry snapped indignantly.

"Then have another drink . . ."

That was the way Marty was. I noticed the older folks were just holding up the wall and talking at first, till he started making the rounds with the dozen or so practical-joke props he usually carries with him. Somewhere toward the middle of the party, I realized that Winston and Marty were shooting it out with water pistols. Then a little later, I realized that Barry and Horace were holding a knife fight with rubber daggers, and some yells that would have won an award at the county fair, in the pig-meat preserving contest. Marnie was actually teaching the girls and Marty how to do the conga, and a bit later on, I saw a bemused Charlie trying to figure out which one of Marty's buttons to push in order to get some light out of the lamp shade he was wearing over his face. I never figured out where he got it—all the lights were set into the ceiling.

Of course, when Larry actually managed to start a fight with Marty, it was another matter. He raged at our comic for ten minutes, telling him to stop trying to buy his way out of trouble with cheap jokes, and Marty finally got angry enough to start answering back. The epithets flew fast and hard for a few minutes, with remarks about low comics and large heads, so I figured I'd better do for Marty what he'd done for the rest of us. I co-opted Lacey and strolled over to the shouting match.

"Doing it very well, aren't they?" I said.

"Oh, I don't know," Lacey said. "Larry hit his energy peak five minutes ago, and he hasn't flagged since. He really needs a bit more variation."

"True." I nodded. "And now that you mention it, Marty's getting way too red in the face. That shade of mauve just doesn't go with his socks."

Marty broke off fighting to glare at me.

"Actually, he needs to yell a bit," Lacey informed me. "This low, intense vituperation just won't project at all."

"But Larry really lacks sincerity, when you think about it. Doesn't sound as if he believes a word he says."

"Sincere!" Larry turned on me, his face white. "How dare you!"

" 'Cause I'm getting bored," I said. "I just heard you use the same insult that you'd used on Susanne an hour ago."

"Originality never was his strong suit," Lacey agreed. "Larry, just because I said you should practice improvisation more often, doesn't mean you have to do it all through the party."

Marty grinned, and I knew we'd won our case. "Yeah, it is getting boring," I told Lacey. "Let's go see if we can get Marnie to teach us how to waltz."

"I already know how to waltz, I'll have you know!"

"Yeah, so do I." I grinned.

"Really?" Larry snarled. "I'm very surprised, since you don't know how to conduct yourself in polite society."

I turned back slowly, and that was when Marty had to get me laughing.

We laughed best as we were carrying Larry back to his stateroom. Lacey followed along with a tall glass in her hand, giggling and bouncing off the wall every three steps.

We tucked him away and came back out. "So what did you put in his drink, Ramou?" Marty asked me as we closed the door.

"Me? Nothing," I said. "It was the beverage machine that did it. Think they've worked their way up to the bossa nova yet?"

A door clicked open behind us. I turned just in time to see Lacey vanishing into Larry's room. I was about to object, but the door clicked shut behind us.

Marty's hand fell on my shoulder. "So she needs to crash, too. That should dampen our good time?"

The tension ebbed. I hadn't even realized it had been building—but my body thawed, and the rush of sobriety went away. I hooked an arm around Marty's shoulders, leaned against him, and staggered back toward the lounge.

I remember making it back to the party. I remember trying to back Susanne into a corner, and winding up backing her all around the dance floor instead. I remember saying something to her that seemed extremely smooth and romantic, but I couldn't figure out why she was giggling all the way through it. And that's about all I remember. Fortunately, I'd set my alarm clock for daily buzzing.

4

Now, if there's one thing I hate more than the sound of an alarm clock going off in the morning, it's the sound of an alarm clock going off when I'm hung over. Admittedly, Sensei taught me to avoid intoxicating substances, because the Way of the Warrior insists that a fighter always have his wits about him—but he also taught me that you have to really let yourself go now and then, when you're sure it's safe and somebody else is guarding your back. And you can't be much safer than aboard a spaceship, with a captain who's a determined teetotaler on duty, and gruffly insisting you go and have a good time at the lift-off party with everyone else. That's even more remarkable because the captain in question was an alcoholic—but Gantry McLeod had informed us that whenever he stepped aboard a space wagon as captain or first officer, he went on the wagon in more ways than one. However, he did admit that it was easier if he didn't even think about alcohol, which is why he preferred to be alone with his books and computer and antialcohol beverage. How it satisfied the craving for booze without getting him drunk, I didn't understand, but centuries of use had proved that it did, and without any harmful side effects, either. In fact, Antihooch was so tasty that everybody drank it now, which made things a lot easier for the recovering alcoholic in public—he only had to endure some ribbing about having sissy drinks when he was a grown man.

So on captain's orders, I had gone off and gotten stinking drunk along with the rest of the party—though I did seem to have some sort of hazy recollection of helping Marty drag Larry Rash back to his cabin, with Lacey following along behind, which had given me hopes—but when Marty and I had tossed him into his bunk and left, she had lagged behind to tuck him in—and locked the door behind us. It left me miffed, but not very—much good might he do her, in *his* condition! Besides, I was feeling no pain myself, nor much of anything else, either. I had some notion of Marty going with me sometime later as far as my cabin and holding my thumb up to the print plate—but I had staggered in on my own and fallen into bed, which is about all I remember. I wondered which of us had locked the door.

Fortunately—or not, depending on how you look at it—I had set my chronometer to wake me every day at the same time, so here it was, announcing that it was "Ten A.M. and all's well!" in the soothing tones of Beethoven's *Pastorale*. Thank Heaven for musical wakers.

I staggered out of my bunk and over to the beverage dispenser. I was about to punch for some hair of the dead dog when I noticed a dram glass of dark, syrupy fluid on the table in front of it, with a notecard leaning against it that read:

> You deserved it, kid!
> —Merlo

I wondered which way he meant that.

Either way, I decided he was right, but that I deserved that glassful even more—it was his patent hangover cure. I held it up to my chin, took one last breath of clean air, and chugged.

It tasted vile. It tasted like the Nile at high tide. It tasted like black molasses with sulfur and vinegar added.

It worked.

I gasped for breath and staggered back against the wall. I could almost feel that horrible concoction shivering through my every neuron and cleaning off the dendrites with steel wool. It was like a tide of electricity flowing outward from a bomb in my stomach, outward and onward, past my extremities . . .

And gone.

So was my hangover.

I set the glass down with a silent prayer of relief. Nice to know the boss looks after the hired help. I lifted the card in fingers that scarcely trembled, and happened to notice a set of numbers in the lower right-hand corner. Could it be that my boss had programmed the beverage-dispenser system with Gran'ma Horrhee's Home Hangover Remedy?

I decided to try punching it in later. Right now, my muscles still felt like water, but there was gelatin in that solution, and it was firming up fast. I turned to the beverage dispenser and punched for some orange juice to get the taste of Merlo's potion out of my mouth. My finger hovered lingeringly near the "vodka" button, but I decided the only screwdrivers I needed were in my toolbox, so I took my vitamin C straight. I followed it with a cup of coffee, half milk to cool it for convenience, then headed on up to the lounge to punch dispenser buttons for those too weak to do it for themselves.

Marty was my first customer, stepping up to my table array of coffee and doughnuts to peer closely at me. "Only slightly the worse for wear. Hi, Ramou."

"Hi, yourself," I said, ever the master of the snappy comeback, "and thanks for getting me through the door. What did I do last night?"

He stared at me in surprise. Then a slow grin spread over

his face from ear to ear, and he said, "Buddy, you did it *all*."

I hid my face in my hands and groaned.

"Don't worry," he said. "I think Lacey took it as a compliment, and Susanne was having more fun than you were. I think you picked the wrong one to take home, Ramou."

"You mean Larry? Definitely. Can't think what got into me."

"Lacey's request. She played on your sympathies and your sense of duty shamelessly, pal, and I think your hypertrophied sense of responsibility got the better of you. He did need the help, though."

I snorted. "That part, I remember. He needed a stretcher."

"Good idea!" Marty held up a forefinger. "Too bad we didn't think of it. Uh-oh!" He stepped aside. "Here comes the lady in question."

Lacey staggered into the lounge, pale and wan, and holding onto the wall for support. She took one look at the doughnuts and turned away, swallowing hard. I snatched up a cup of black coffee and brought it over to her. "Try this first."

She sniffed it suspiciously, then accepted it as if she were Socrates taking the hemlock. "What did you put in it?"

"Nothing, yet. When you're feeling up to it, I'll dial you a potion that will take the hammer off that anvil that's beating in your head, or at least turn it to rubber."

"I'll take it!" she exclaimed with fevered need.

"You won't like it," Marty warned.

"What does liking have to do with it?" Lacey snapped. "I need medicine."

"Coming right up." I punched in the secret code—secret only because nobody else had ever bothered to look it up after Merlo put it into the dispenser system—and took out a small glass of oily dark liquid. I realized that was a mistake and poured it into an empty coffee mug.

Too late—Lacey had seen it. "What *is* that villainous-looking gunk?"

"Gran'ma Horrhee's Patent Drunk and Hangover Remedy," I said helpfully. "Drink it down, and you'll feel right as rain in two minutes." I carefully didn't say how she'd feel in between.

"It helps if you hold your nose," Marty supplied.

She paused with the rim at her lips. "You've tried it already?"

"Not this morning," Marty said, sidestepping the question.

"Then you have absolutely no right to be sounding so damn cheerful," Lacey muttered.

"Cheerful?" Marty said, wounded. "I haven't even made one pun this morning! It *is* morning, isn't it, Ramou?"

"By the chronometer, yes," I assured him, "and someplace on Earth, definitely. Other than that, it seems to be an academic matter, aboard a spaceship."

"It's morning." Lacey grunted. "It feels way too early." She closed her eyes, held her nose, and tossed the mug-full back, swallowing mightily. Then she slammed down the mug and leaned on the table, eyes bulging and cheeks puffing out, turning a lovely shade of maroon.

I knew about the minor explosion that was going on inside. "Swallow," I recommended.

She gulped, then opened her mouth and started panting. Her color slackened to normal as she made some sort of hissing sound.

It resembled words. "What's she saying?" I asked Marty.

He leaned his ear close, then straightened up and looked at me. "Sounds like 'assassin.'"

"It only feels that way for a moment," I assured Lacey, and held out a glass of orange juice.

She took it, swallowed it all in one breath, then set it down, panting again. Her breathing slowed, her mouth closed, and she looked up at me in wide-eyed wonder. "It worked. I feel . . . well, okay, at least."

"Knew you would." Secretly, I felt relieved.

"Thanks, Ramou," she said, as if the words felt strange on her lips.

"Just goes with the service." I held out the filled mug. "Ready to try the coffee again?"

"Yes, thanks." She took the mug, cradling it in her hands to absorb its warmth by osmosis as she looked up at Marty. "How come you're feeling okay without tasting that stuff?"

I swiveled to look at him. Come to think of it, that *was* a good question.

"I cheated." Marty looked abashed. "I didn't get drunk."

"How low!" Lacey cried. "You watched the rest of us totter around rolling under the gale, and you weren't even three sheets in the wind?"

"Well, maybe three," Marty allowed. "But I had a hangover once, and it made me very cautious."

"Must do wonders for your sex life," Lacey muttered, and turned away to find a soft, a very soft, chair.

Marty looked after her, and for just a split second, his face was bleak. It was over so quickly that I would have missed it if I'd blinked, but I hadn't. When he turned back to me, though, the old grin was back in place. "Last I heard, sex was better when you could remember it afterward."

"Only when it's your own idea," I assured him.

"Good morning, all!" a gravelly basso cried, and we turned to see Ogden sailing into the room in his floating stretcher.

"Ogden!" I yelped. "What're *you* doing out of the sick bay?"

"The same as I was doing last evening, young man—or attempting to do, at least: live." His voice was still slow and feeble, but his enthusiasm was high and strong. "No, don't worry, when Barry realized there was no stopping me, he gave in and told me that I might attend rehearsal this morning."

"Well," I said doubtfully, "in that case . . ."

"In that case, I qualify for liquid refreshment, eh? Don't stint, there's a good fellow—but just a drop of something invigorating in it." He looked around elaborately, to give me time to put something in his cup without his noticing. I wondered if he was old enough to have invented the term "legal fiction."

Instead, he seemed to have the patent on early riser's cheer. "Ah, what a splendid morning! Fit as a fiddle and ready to rehearse, eh?"

Lacey looked daggers at him from the safety of her chair.

He took up the mug I handed him, steadying it with both hands. "The oddest thing, Ramou. I became dreadfully sleepy after the second Scotch."

It hadn't been Scotch, just tasted like it—but I wasn't about to let him know that.

"I just barely remember Susanne tucking me into bed," Ogden said. "Wouldn't know anything about that, would you?"

"About Susanne tucking you into bed? No, but . . ."

"Come now, come! You know very well I was referring to my sudden sleepiness!"

"Oh, that," I said. "Yeah, sure. All the excitement—it was a big day. The dash to Newark Spaceport, the takeoff, the heart attack—follow all that with a party, and it's amazing you lasted as long as you did." I frowned. "How'd you get out of the sick bay, anyway?"

"I floated. Didn't think I would willingly miss out on a one-time-only party, did you? Though I must admit to having waited until everyone was sufficiently intoxicated not to remember I wasn't supposed to be there. So it was all the more disappointing to fade so quickly."

I nodded, commiserating. "I've gotten sleepy after the second drink myself, sometimes."

"I don't doubt it," Lacey said dryly.

"Of course, it always follows high stress," I said.

"Nicely said." Ogden nodded judiciously. "Did you have the words memorized, or just the gist?"

My stomach sank, but I spread my hands. "Would I lie to you?"

"Yes, if you thought it was in my own interest." But the old man smiled and reached for a doughnut. "Your pastries are excellent, though, so I believe I'll forgive you." He trundled off to Lacey with his plate and mug, foghorning, "Good morning, Miss Lark!"

Lacey pulled herself together with only a small groan and prepared to be nice to the company's most senior member, in age if not in authority.

Marty cocked an eyebrow in my direction. "You did know something about that early beddy-bye, didn't you?"

"Hey, come on," I said. "Whoever heard of a beverage dispenser having a drink code for a Mickey Finn?"

"Only the guy who did the programming," Marty retorted.

There was a thump at the doorway, and we both looked up in time to see Susanne stumble against the jamb. I was over to her like a shot, but Marty beat me anyway. "Good morning, beauteous damsel! Allow me to lead you to the pavilion of refreshment and resuscitation!"

"Marty . . . please." Susanne raised a hand to fend him off. "Not so early in the morning." She looked up at me, squinting against the pain of the lights I'd carefully lowered. "It *is* early, isn't it?"

"Relatively," I assured her.

"The penalties for trying to create a pleasant ambience for others," Marty sighed, taking her arm gently and walking her slowly toward the coffee table. "Set the lady up with a glass of the cure, would you, Ramou?"

I eyed Susanne carefully, for some reason unwilling to

risk getting onto her bad side. "Maybe some hair of the dog . . .?"

"I tried," she said. "It bit back. *Please*, Ramou?"

"Well, since you ask." I turned away and punched up Merlo's special. After all, she'd asked for it.

She took it and knocked it back so fast the aroma was just registering in her nose as the bomb went off in her stomach. Marty steadied her through the frog eyes and the bulging cheeks and the red face while I seethed with jealousy. Then she went limp, and Marty had to set himself to hold her up. "My lord! What a relief!" She turned wide eyes to me and, for a miracle, they were almost as clear as usual. "Thank you, Ramou."

"Ever the knight to the rescue of the damsel in distress." I handed her the glass of juice, secretly marveling at the contrast with Lacey. "This for the taste, then a mug of black coffee to set you up."

"Just keep me away from the bowling ball that hit me last night," she said.

I was about to ask who he was, jealousy ready to rip into mayhem, when I remembered that she had been one of our merry little troupe of homebound alcoholics and had dropped off at her own door. I also seemed to remember volunteering to see that she got to her bed okay, and being turned down with a kiss. Yes, I definitely remembered it—the spot on my cheek flowered into tingling.

"Front row, on the left," Marty said, ushering her away from the table and off to a lounger a quarter of the way around the lounge from Lacey. I thought he was being too cautious—after a night like that, neither of them was apt to be on speaking terms, period.

But Lacey knew a break when she saw one. She looked up, smiled sweetly, and called out, "Good morning, Susanne dear!"

"Susanne?" Ogden turned his stretcher toward the new

arrival. "Excuse me, Miss Lark! I must thank my valiant nurse!"

"Go right ahead," Lacey purred, and Ogden floated over to Susanne, who blanched for only a split second before she forced a tired smile. "Good morning, Mr. Wellesley."

Footsteps, slow and dignified. I turned to the doorway and saw Barry and Horace coming in arm-in-arm—or leaning against each other, whichever way you wanted to look at it. Their dignity was draped around each of them like an iron toga, but their faces were rigid. I seemed to remember a quartet still going in the lounge as Marty and I steered what was left of Larry out, and I had a notion they'd gone through at least two more musicals after I'd finally left. After all, they had only worked their way through Rodgers and Hart and Rodgers and Hammerstein, and had just barely begun work on Lerner and Loewe.

Barry stopped, hip leaning against the table, not looking, and held out a hand. I put a cup of hangover remedy in it. He passed it to Horace, and the hand came back, cupped for another one. I filled it.

Horace sputtered and gagged. "Ramou! What *is* this stuff?"

"Gran'ma Horrhee's Hangover Remedy," I said, giving it the short form. "I thought you knew."

"I assure you, I did not. *Phaugh!* That is positively the worst thing I have tasted since the crew substituted pure vanilla extract for the elderberry wine in *Arsenic and Old Lace*."

"I am sure it will be good for us, though," Barry said, with iron determination, "I think. Come on, old fellow, drink up."

Horace still hesitated, eyeing the fluid in his cup as if it might pull itself together into some sort of obscene parody of an anthropoid shape and reach out to bite him.

"I've got barf bags," I supplied.

He nodded grimly and tossed back his glass-full. So did Barry.

I wasn't prepared for the reaction in men of their age. Apparently it hit harder than with us young'uns—their knees buckled, and they both grabbed at the table. I jumped to lean down on the back edge, to keep it from tipping and drenching them with hot coffee, and Marty leaped over to catch Horace's arm. I reached across the table to grab Barry's elbow before he sagged all the way, but he dropped the cup and waved away my hand, straightening up slowly and sucking in a very, very long breath. "Yesssss," he hissed, and hauled up on Horace's arm. "I dare say that will help us get things off to a good start. Shall we, old fellow?"

"By all means," Horace croaked, and they turned away, still leaning on each other, heading for the chairs.

"Think they'll make it?" Marty muttered to me in a low voice.

"To the chairs, yes," I whispered back. "Through the whole morning? That's another guess completely." I handed him two cups of black coffee. "Here, take these over as a cover and make sure they're okay."

He took them, but asked, "Don't you want to yourself?"

"Yes," I hissed, "but I have another customer coming."

He looked up at the doorway and saw Marnie feeling her way along the wall, her head very high, her back very stiff, wearing dark glasses. Indoors. In dim light.

Marty nodded and whispered, "Bye, Ramou!" and hurried away to Barry and Horace.

"Good morning, Ms. Lulala," I muttered, careful to keep it soft and sad.

"Don't be so impertinent, young man!" She tried to snap, but her heart just wasn't in it. "*I'll* tell you whether it's good or not—and I assure you, it's not."

"Yes, ma'am." I won't say I didn't feel like arguing, but now was not the time. It would have been like picking on a hamstrung hamster. "Coffee, ma'am?" I knew better than to mention the doughnuts.

"Is there an alternative?" she groaned.

"Yes, ma'am. Gran'ma Horrhee's Patent Hangover Cure."

Marnie stood very still for a moment. Then she said, "Anything is worth a try—well, almost anything, anyway. Give it to me, young man."

I handed her the glass-full and stood back. Warning? Why should I have given her a warning? "It works best if you just drink it straight down in one breath, ma'am." Otherwise, she would have had to smell it.

"Don't tell me how to drink!" she growled, and knocked the dose back as if she were a Russian with a shot of vodka. Then she froze, and the glass fell from numbed fingers.

I waited, holding my breath. And waited. And waited.

She just stood there in rigor mortis, with her arm in the air and her head tilted halfway back. And stood. And stood.

Finally, I started getting worried. I came around the table and reached out, but didn't quite dare touch her. Instead, I positioned my arm under hers, ready to grab, and asked, "Ms. Lulala?"

"Hm?" Her head swiveled around toward me, and I could have sworn I heard something snap.

I breathed a sigh of relief. "Could I recommend a short orange juice now, ma'am? It kinda helps with the aftertaste."

"Yessssssss," she said, with an expulsion of long-held breath. "I can see that it might."

I reached over and set a new glass in her hand. She set it to her lips mechanically and drank it off in one straight draft, then lowered it. "You missed your calling, young man."

"My calling?"

"Yes; I can see you were trained by the Borgias. Now fetch me some coffee!"

"Yes, ma'am." I took the cup from her fingers and replaced it with another, warmer, one. As she sipped, I reflected that, like so many women, she really wanted to be a spoiled little girl. Problem was that Marnie had been in a position where she could get away with really being one, and still thought that's what she was.

No, strike that—if she really had been able to behave like a spoiled brat, she wouldn't have been here with us.

"That will do," she said regally. "Ordinarily I would censure you for making coffee strong enough to make the flag itself snap up and salute—but this morning, it is just what the physician fizzed. Now show me to a chair."

"Yes, ma'am." I figured she meant it, considering that I had the lights set low and she was wearing dark glasses. "If you'll just rest your hand on my arm, ma'am . . ."

She hooked her fingers through my elbow, and I played seeing-eye 'bot for her, guiding her to a very soft chair. "We're here."

She stepped back gingerly, feeling for the edge of the chair with her calf. "Take the cup."

I did.

She sat, slowly and carefully, then held out a hand again. "Cup."

I gave it back to her.

She sipped, then said, "Keep it filled."

"Yes, ma'am."

"You may go."

"Yes, ma'am."

"Can't you say anything but 'Yes, ma'am'?"

But I had gone. After all, Winston had just come in the door, and I couldn't favor one star to ignore the other, could I?

He was walking extremely erect, carrying himself carefully, but that was the only sign of hangover. Other than

that, he wore his usual polite smile—I was beginning to realize that was what it was, though on his face, it looked
like a sarcastic smirk. Just the way he was put together,
apparently—the eyebrows slanting in over the nose, the
black mustache and goatee, the raven hair . . .

"Good morning, Ramou." His voice sounded only a little
rusty. "I believe coffee is in order."

"Yes, sir." But it was Gran'ma Horrhee's torture syrup I
lifted. "Unless you'd consider the alternative. Takes the top
off your head, but when it settles back on, the hangover's
gone."

He just stared at it for a minute. Then he said, "Interesting."

"It works," I said helpfully. "I'm living proof."

"So am I, though it's closer to a hundred proof than living. However, if you're alive, you're a testament to its effects."

"I know it looks villainous . . ."

"Then it's sweets to the sweet." He took the little cup,
passed it under his nose twice, grimaced, then knocked it
back.

I ran around the table to stand at his elbow.

I hadn't needed to; he stood ramrod straight, totally immobile, but his eyes widened enormously, and he drew in
a very, very long breath.

I waited.

He exhaled slowly, for a very long time. Then he went
loose and gave his head a shake. "Quite a kick, hasn't it?"

"Like a chorus girl straight out of Toulouse-Lautrec, sir."

"I assume you refer to his paintings. Yes. I'd just as soon
experience Montmartre in other ways than this. Could we
see about that coffee, now?"

"Yes, sir!" I bustled around behind my table again. "Unless you'd like to try the orange juice first—it cleans the
taste off your tongue."

"Along with the skin, no doubt. Still, what have I to

lose? Though it's not my general rule to be healthy." He took the glass of juice, sipped, rolled it around on his tongue, and nodded. "Not bad. Must have been a good year."

"It's very fresh, sir." In fact, the synthesizer had just put it together out of scrap molecules a half hour before—but I didn't see any reason to mention that.

He set down the empty glass. "Very well, I've served my penance. Now about that coffee?"

"Thick and dark, sir." I handed him the cup. "Don't suppose you'd be interested in cream or sugar?"

"Only academically—and organic chemistry never was my strong suit." Winston turned away toward the chairs. "If you don't mind, I believe I'll go sit down, now."

"I've never been one to argue with a man's beliefs, sir."

He glanced back to see if I was being sarcastic, but I kept a perfect poker face, so he just nodded. "There may be more to you than meets the eye, young man—a certain pawky vein of humor, as Holmes said of Watson."

I would have thought he would have been more familiar with Moriarty, but I didn't think it was polite to say so.

He was just sitting down as the final few came in, one after the other. Larry was the last, which surprised me—I'd had an even bet going with Marty that we'd have to half carry him this morning, too. But he staggered in, glared at me through eyes that were mostly red, and snarled, "What did you do to me last night, Ramou?"

There you go. That was Larry, in a nutshell. Couldn't even accept the blame for his own drunks. I thought he'd make somebody a horrible wife, some day.

"I hauled you back to your own room, Larry," I said, "with a little help. If you woke up in bed, you have me to thank. If you woke up alone, you have you to blame."

"Alone?" He turned fierce, but there was a strange sort of panic under the viciousness. "What the devil do you mean, 'alone'? Who should have been with me?"

I chose my words with care. " 'Should have'? Why, no one, of course, Larry. No one at all."

He glared at me, but he couldn't hold it. "Glad to hear you say it," he muttered, dropping his gaze—but only because he couldn't keep his neck stiff. "Couldn't face me this morning, hey?"

I didn't have the faintest idea what he was talking about. "Larry," I said, "sometimes I don't have the faintest idea what you're talking about, and I'm always glad. How are you feeling this morning?"

"How do you *think* I'm feeling? Haven't you eyes?"

"Eyes, and a quick touch on the keyboard." I held out a ceramic medicine glass. "Have an eye-opener."

"I don't think I want my eyes open," he mumbled, but he took the cup anyway.

"Drink it straight down," I warned him.

Bad idea; it made him suspicious. He sniffed the drink suspiciously, then took a tentative sip.

"Okay, suffer." I sighed.

He coughed and spat. "Poisoner! What the hell is in this brew, anyway?"

"A fabled hangover remedy," I told him. "But it doesn't work it you don't drink it."

He stared into the glass. It shook.

"Drink it," I coaxed.

"I can't," he whispered.

I sighed and came around the table. "Sure you can, Larry. You just hold it to your lips, like this . . . then tip your head back, like this . . . then tilt the glass, like *this* . . ."

The fluid rolled down his throat. He coughed and tried to jerk his head out of the way, but I held him clamped to my side, and his throat worked, swallowing. When I was sure it was all down, I let him go. He staggered into the table, clutching at the edge, coughing and gasping . . . then suddenly looked up, wide-eyed. "It's gone!"

"A little pain to prevent a greater," I assured him.

"I didn't believe it," he said reluctantly, then, as if it were dragged out of him, "Th . . . thank you, Ra . . . Ra . . ."

"My pleasure," I assured him, and I meant every word. "Orange juice, now? It helps with the aftertaste."

He took it, then took a cup of coffee, picked himself up, and wobbled to a chair, just in time for Barry, almost fully recovered, to beam around at his gelid company and say, "Good morning, all."

"I move we put it to a vote," Winston groaned.

"I'm afraid the clock is immune to our opinions, Winston. Since none of us is, this morning, really quite himself . . ."

"Or herself," Marnie corrected.

"Actors never really are," Ogden rumbled.

"What?" asked Marty. "Himself or herself?"

"Speak for yourself, young man. Actors are never quite themselves. In fact, some members of our profession have completely lost sight of who they are. One thinks of Junius Brutus Booth, swordfighting Laertes off the stage, through the wings, and out the stage door . . ."

"Got too far into character." Marty nodded sagely. "And couldn't get out. My professors warned me about that."

"With you, they had reason," Larry muttered.

"If the conversation could become a little less philosophical, and a bit more practical?" Barry asked pointedly. "We are met to discuss rehearsals of the Scottish play."

He was answered by a unanimous groan. I glanced at Horace, but he nodded to me, as if to reassure me all was normal, and I had done my job well.

Ramou no doubt thought the groan to be a comment on his preparations—he had a knack for taking blame that was not his by rights. He could not have been more mistaken, of course, for he had prepared the lounge for rehearsal as well as could be. He had assembled the easy chairs into an open square and hovered by a table at the side, right next to the food and drink synthesizers; he already had an assortment of pastries and several cups of caffeinated beverages set out. The actors were busily absorbing them.

Barry had decided that it would be less hazardous all around to allow Ogden to attend on a stretcher, rather than argue with him about staying in sick bay and watching his blood pressure soar—so he was reclining at table like a Roman, seeming suspiciously satisfied with the potation Ramou had provided him. I mentioned this to my protege, but he assured me, "Only amaretto extract, Horace. All the flavor, but only about half a percent of alcohol." Born diplomat, that boy.

I wasn't the only one who had suspicions—Susanne was watching him with concern. Ogden beamed at her, but she did not seem especially reassured.

"Ogden will, of course, play Duncan," Barry informed us, and a muted sigh of relief went about the table—after all, Duncan makes his final exit at the end of Act I and dies offstage at the beginning of Act II. Ogden would be that much less tempted to overextend himself, but could not complain of inactivity.

He also could not complain about the casting—as the oldest member of the company, he of course should play that good old king. As Lady Macbeth points out, she would have murdered Duncan in his sleep herself had he not so resembled her father.

"Marnie will play Lady Macbeth," Barry went on, "and Winston will undertake the part of the evil king."

There was a stir of surprise, and Winston said, "Are you sure, Barry? I mean, I'm flattered and delighted, of course—but as managing director, the lead should go to yourself."

"I would prefer to stay away from the focus as much as possible, Winston, the better to observe the progress of the production and the overall picture," Barry explained. "Also, this is one of the few plays in which the villain is also the lead. It is yours by rights."

"Well! Thank you." Winston looked quite gratified.

"Grudy, I'm afraid you are drafted as one of the three witches," Barry said apologetically.

"Oh, dear!" our costumer said. "So that's why you wanted me to attend rehearsal! Barry, it's been years!"

Lacey looked up, not quite managing to hide her contempt. On second thought, perhaps she wasn't trying.

"I'm afraid it is necessary," Barry commiserated. "In so small a company, everyone will have to help out."

"What's Ramou doing?" Larry said with scorn.

Barry frowned at him, but answered, "I have prevailed upon him to carry a spear. I will appreciate your giving him your support, Mr. Lash—it will be his first time on stage."

Larry wasn't quite so quick as he might have been to assure Barry of his willingness to cooperate. After all, having left Terra behind, it was going to be rather difficult for Barry to replace him.

I, however, knew that for the fallacy it was. Barry was quite capable of training any reasonably talented young man—and Larry was scarcely the veteran he seemed to think himself.

"You, however, will undertake Malcolm," Barry went on.

Larry drew back, afronted. I was amazed—surely he had not thought he would have MacDuff?

Fortunately, he had better sense than to say so.

"I shall undertake the part of MacDuff," Barry said, "and Ms. Lark will be his lady." He turned to Lacey. "But you will also have to double as a witch."

"It sounds delightful." Lacey smiled, no doubt relishing the thought of being able to show up one of the Old Guard, even so minor a one as the costumer.

"Ms. Souci, you, too, will be a witch," Barry said, "and will double as Donalbain."

"Malcolm's *brother*?" Susanne glanced at Grudy, wide-eyed. "But, Mr. Tallendar . . ."

"Yes, my dear?" Barry said with a bland smile, totally unperturbed by the magnitude of Susanne's encumbrances in seeking to portray a male.

"Don't worry, dear—I'll make you a plastron," Grudy assured her. "It will be snug, but we won't have to bind you."

Susanne looked only slightly reassured. Lacey gave her a vindictive smile. Out of the corner of my eye, I saw Ramou frown, and rejoiced within—he was having a difficult time deciding between the ingenue and the soubrette, but Lacey was certainly giving him factors for consideration.

Of course, I'm sure Ramou would have preferred not to choose—as which of us would not?

"Mr. Kemp, you will be the drunken porter, of course," Barry went on, "as well as Fleance, the bloody sergeant, and several other assorted minor parts, which I'll assign as we come to them."

Marty tried to look gratified—but the drunken porter is one of the unfunniest comic roles Shakespeare ever made, and has only that one scene. One would think Marty would have felt that the abundance of bit parts would have compensated him for the lack, but I could see the comment in his eyes: "They aren't funny!" I felt leaden apprehension sink within me—surely he would not attempt to make every minor part amusing?

"Mr. Burbage will essay Banquo."

I was gratified, though amazed. Banquo is usually protrayed as tall and lean; I was short and, ahem, "stocky," and my face is naturally far too kind for a warrior. However, I would endeavor to make it hard.

"Merlo," Barry went on, "I'm afraid you will have to undertake Ross in addition to carrying a spear."

Merlo nodded. "That's why I keep my equity membership up to date."

Larry looked up at him, startled. I'm afraid the poor young man was rapidly losing all of his preconceptions.

"I'm stage manager, right?" Merlo asked.

"Yes. Thank you. Mr. Publican will undertake the first murderer, as well as Old Siward, and any other spare parts left lying about," Barry summarized, "and I believe that completes the cast list. Now, if we could begin? Ladies, if you will?"

"When shall we three meet again? In thunder, lightning, or in rain?" Grudy cackled.

Everyone sat up ramrod stiff—except for myself, Barry, and Ogden, of course. We remembered the days when Grudy had taken small parts in summer stock, just to help out. In fact, I'm sure we were the only ones who knew she had double membership in both actors' and costumers' unions.

But her delivery of that simple opening line had knocked the smile off Lacey's face and left her staring in shock. Fortunately, Susanne had the second line. She recovered from her surprise within two beats, and came in: "When the hurly-burly's done, when the battle's lost and won."

Lacey gave her head a quick shake and croaked out, "That will be ere the set of sun."

"Where the place?" Grudy demanded.

"Upon the heath."

"Excellent vocal quality!" Barry cried. "Certainly that will establish a clear separation from Lady MacDuff! But can you sustain it, Ms. Lark?"

"I'll try, Mr. Tallendar," Lacey said, and went on to do the croak deliberately.

It was an excellent stroke, of course—Barry saved face for her, but reinforced the acknowledgment of Grudy's skill by giving Lacey direction that followed Grudy's lead. This was more pointed by his not commenting on Grudy's work. After all, she had the experience to sense what was required—but Lacey hadn't known that.

We must forgive the poor young ones. It had never occurred to them that costumers did their jobs by preference, not by force. I thought it might be quite enlightening for Lacey Lark to discover that Grudy was an artist in her own right, working in the field that was her first choice, not a failed actress who was seeking to be near the stage in any way possible. The fact was that Grudy regarded acting as a great deal of fun, but scarcely a medium for artistic endeavor. The same was true of Merlo, who was capable of undertaking several small parts at once, himself—he felt that acting was stimulating, but did not give him adequate scope for his creativity. To each his own medium—and Lacey had just begun to realize the fact.

Merlo's enjoyment of performance was fortunate, since he was needed onstage as well as off, in this production— but that is why stage managers are members of Actors' Equity.

Lacey and Susanne managed to pull abreast of Grudy's unabashed overplaying as they took turns saying, "I come, Graymalkin!"

"Paddock calls."

"Anon!"

Then all three joined to chant,

> "Fair is foul, and foul is fair!
>   Hover through the fog and filthy air!"

"Here we will have a trumpet," Barry said, "and Duncan and his entourage will enter. That will include Misters Lazarian and Publican, plus whatever holograms Merlo can conjure up, or perhaps some local lads who are in an adventurous mood."

Out of the corner of my eye, I noticed Ramou scribbling on a notepad. I wondered why, but was struck by the irony of a computer genius resorting to stylus and paper.

"Ogden?" Barry prompted.

"What bloody man is that?" Ogden rumbled. Within the confines of the lounge, it sounded impressive, but I knew what that pipe-organ voice had done in ages past, and shrank within myself. Even the young ones, who knew only the remnant they had heard during rehearsals on Terra, recognized this; you could tell by the sudden neutrality of their faces and the downcast eyes as they listened to the rest of his line.

Marty saved the situation by picking up right on his cue. "Doubtful it stood, as two spent swimmers that do cling together and choke their art."

We all looked up in surprise. The voice was a deep, resonant baritone, without the slightest hint of the comic in it. Marty met the concerted gaze with an apologetic shrug. "Sorry, but that's what the part calls for."

"No, no, Mr. Kemp, that's fine, that's fine!" But even Barry seemed surprised, though pleasantly so. "You are here to be a character actor, as much as a comic one. Please do go on."

Marty tried to keep the glow off his face, and did manage to keep it from being too obvious. I realized, with a start, that Barry had probably been one of the heroes of his adolescence—then realized again, with a sinking stomach, that I had probably been one of the heroes of his childhood. Drat Morty the Milkman! Though he *had* provided the income that had allowed me to seek more challenging parts.

The scene played on, until Ogden finished his final line, then went limp, exhausted by even this slight effort. Susanne glanced at him with concern, but met Ramou's gaze from across the room and changed the concern to a wink, then turned quickly back to the scene. I was amazed at Ramou's insight, then reflected that a man trained as a warrior would certainly understand the necessity of another man's pride—or "face," as it was called by the Orientals in whose arts he had been trained. It was a shock to think of Ramou as a man, too—I had unwittingly been pegging him as "the kid," even though he had saved my withered old hide from a trio of muggers, and perhaps my life.

But Grudy was gathering up her misbegotten chicks with one of the highest and most grating cackles I had ever heard. I made a note to remind Barry that we should do *The Wizard of Oz*; the children's audience can be lucrative, too, especially since the younglings give their parents an excuse to see the old plays that they secretly revel in.

"Where hast thou been, sister?" Grudy cried, with so much ham that I found myself wishing for pumpernickel.

"Killing swine," Susanne said, with a low and croaking tone. I swear she hit tenor.

Barry looked up in concern.

"Sister . . ." Lacey began.

"Ms. Souci," Barry said, "can you sustain that? Without injury to your vocal folds, that is."

Lacey's face flamed in outrage at having been interrupted, but Susanne smiled, pleased. "Oh, yes, Mr. Tallendar! I learned it for Halloween, and used it for children's theater when I was a teenager."

Lacey eyed her with suspicion.

"Well, if you're certain," Barry said, frowning, "but at the slightest discomfort, mind you, you must stop. No false heroics, please—we need your voice intact for a full year at least."

Larry muttered something about vocal mugging, but Susanne ignored him and sailed blithely on.

"Sister, where thou?" Lacey demanded, a little more loudly than necessary, and they were off, each having great fun with parts that allowed full scope for an actor's worst instincts. Each gave way to temptation with delighted abandon, vying to see who could overplay the most. I would have said they were ready to perform right there, but the touch of reserve in Barry's gloating smile said they needed to be toned down a trifle. Still, I'm sure he intended to thank Grudy privately for having spurred the young ladies into a competitive frenzy. They all wound up with a howling chorus of:

> "The weird sisters, hand in hand,
>   Posters of the sea and land,
>   Thus do go about, about!"

"Thrice to thine," Lacey said to Grudy.

"And thrice to mine," Susanne said.

"And thrice again," Lacey responded, "to make up nine."

"Peace!" Grudy cried. "The charm's wound up!"

"A drum, a drum!" Lacey squealed. "Macbeth doth come!"

Ramou made another note, and this time I caught a flash of light from his pencil. I realized, in surprise, that it wasn't a pad of paper he was writing on, but a sort of computer scanner in the same shape. Where had he found it? I knew quite well that he had possessed nothing of the sort when I met him, back on Terra—and he certainly had not had time and money to buy one. One or the other, yes, but never both at the same moment.

"So foul and fair a day I have not seen," Winston complained.

I looked up in surprise. It had been so long since I had heard Winston do anything other than Standard Villain Number Three that I had quite forgotten the man could act. I recited my speech describing the witches—rather mechanically, I fear. Winston demanded of them, "Speak, if you can. What are you?"

"All hail, Macbeth!" Grudy cried. "Hail to thee, thane of Glamis!"

"All hail, Macbeth! Hail to thee, thane of Cawdor!" Lacey started to cackle the line, but realized halfway through that Grudy had moaned hers, and shifted to mourning in time for "thane." That settled the issue; from then on, Lacey and Susanne followed Grudy's lead in the parts—not that she made any attempt to establish her primacy, of course, nor tried to coerce them in any way. She merely outdid them.

After all, this was closer to her age range than theirs.

Winston stood up and stepped toward the ladies, looking suddenly and immensely threatening. Barry frowned—this was only a read-through, after all—but deferred to Winston's own experience.

It was serving a purpose, after all—Lacey and Susanne jumped up and scurried to crouch beside Grudy, who put her arm protectively about Lacey's shoulders as she held her script in the other hand, declaiming, "All hail Macbeth, that shall be king hereafter!" The movement did add a certain zest to the readings.

So they played out the scene, Winston moving only a few steps from his chair, though I stepped up behind him. Then all three women united in a cascade of cackling, and Susanne and Lacey darted back to their chairs.

Merlo rose, Ross stepping up to tell Macbeth of his promotion, saying, "The king hath happily received, Macbeth, the news of thy success . . ." Then something snapped and Merlo fell, with a howl of pain, quickly bitten off. Susanne was at his side in a second, and Ramou was right behind.

5

I was off that stool and over to my boss in a sprint that would have qualified me for the Olympics—but Susanne was closer, and she got there first. "Where, Mr. Hertz?"

"Nothing, just a stumble," Merlo ground out as he struggled to get up—but his face was white.

Susanne pressed back on his chest firmly. "I'm sure it is, but I'm going to ask you to lie still until I'm certain."

"Look, it's just . . ." Then Susanne probed, and his face went whiter. He gasped.

"Ramou?" Susanne looked up and saw me. Her eyes widened in surprise; then she flashed me a smile of gratitude. "Make sure he doesn't get up, okay?"

"Sure," I agreed, but I remembered that nobody was watching Ogden, and I gave him a quick glance to make sure he was okay. I wouldn't have put it past him to have another heart attack, just to keep from being upstaged. But his gaze was fixed on our little tableau, too, and he nodded impatiently, so I turned back and dropped down, holding a hand out toward Merlo's chest.

Merlo got a look of foreboding in his eye, but he tried bluster anyway. "Look, who's your boss any—*yiiii!*"

Susanne took her hand away from his ankle, nodding with grim certainty. "It's a sprain at least, and maybe a break. No, Mr. Hertz, don't try to get up until we're sure."

"But all I did was get out of a chair!" Merlo protested.

"Okay, I stepped across my own path to get around Charlie's chair—but I was still just stepping!"

"It was an odd move, though, and you came down on that foot at just the wrong angle," Susanne explained, "and I'll bet you were off balance, too, and came down a little hard?"

"But not hard enough to cause a break!" Merlo protested.

"Freak accident," I said, to give him an out. After all, what engineer wants to feel clumsy? "Just bad luck."

The room was suddenly very, very quiet, and I realized I had made a very bad mistake. I glanced from face to face, and nobody had to say it: *the curse*.

Susanne let me off the hook. "Ramou," she said, "would you get another stretcher?"

"Sure," I said, wondering how many we had. As I turned away, I decided I'd better check the inventory.

I also noticed that Lacey was looking extremely peeved. At a guess, she didn't like Susanne getting the notices as angel of mercy—but she still wasn't making any move to help.

And, as I went out the door, I wondered when Charles Publican had become "Charlie" to Merlo. After all, it had only been one day since we took off.

As to "the curse," it had evolved. "*Macbeth* is bad luck" had turned into "There's a curse on *Macbeth*." I was never too clear as to who had put on the curse, or why, but it did kind of make sense—if you believed in superstitions.

After all, if that first rehearsal was anything to judge by, *Macbeth* really *was* bad luck. Of course, that could all be autosuggestion—if people believe something bad is going to happen, they subconsciously *make* it happen. Sometimes.

But sometimes it happened all by itself.

I decided that one of my goals in life was going to be tracking down the records of every performance of the Scottish play ever done and programming them into a computer. Then I was going to have it give me a statistical analysis of accidents, injuries, maimings, and deaths. After that, I'd run the same kind of breakdown on a representative sample of some other plays and see if it really did rate as all that much more dangerous.

Well, no, of course it would, if it were in there with drawing-room comedies and talk plays like *Uncle Vanya* and *Waiting for Godot*. I'd have to select my sample from other war plays, like Shakespeare's *Henry IV* and *Henry V*, maybe including some murder mysteries like *Ten Little Indians*, where there's a gun that's supposed to be loaded with blanks. After all, if you've got a bunch of big muscular guys hauling around claymore swords and fake spears, you have to expect a few more accidents than if you're just having a maidservant wheel in a tea cart. And if the script calls for a great flashing broadsword duel to the death, you can't be surprised if somebody slips a little . . .

Come to think of it, maybe the play *was* more dangerous than the average.

Nothing supernatural about it, though. Just probabilities, and the right conditions for accidents. So I decided to make the atmosphere as accident-proof as possible.

"Hey, look, I'm the tech assistant, right? Why should you have to do all the drudgery of grinding all those props out of the holoform? Just show me the designs and turn it over to me!"

Merlo looked tempted; he was gazing at the three-foot screen-top of his drafting table, moving the square bar and drawing lines with the light pen. I knew he'd much rather be designing than building, and that was my in. Out, rather—but he shook his head. "I brought the main swords with us—I'll have to distress them, but they're fine. For the extras, though . . . No. Like as not you'd get safety conscious and program a change in the materials, like making the swords out of a ceramic compound."

"Would I do that?" My tones of offended righteousness were sharpened because I'd been planning exactly that.

Merlo looked up and gave me an appraising glance. "Maybe you do have some talent as an actor."

I shifted tacks. "Look, even if I did churn out ceramic broadswords, what difference would it make?"

"Sound," Merlo said succinctly. "They wouldn't clang."

"All right, so I'll metalize them!"

"Good." Merlo nodded with satisfaction. "Then you've got something that's just as dangerous as the real thing. Very good, Ramou."

"I'll dull the edges," I suggested, "make them mushy."

Merlo was still nodding. "So all they can do is bludgeon each other to death. Nice improvement."

"It does lower the risk," I pointed out.

"No, it doesn't," Merlo contradicted. "You didn't think I was going to put an edge on those swords, did you? Cold rolled iron won't be any more hazardous than those metalized putty-edges of yours, and they'll be a darn sight more reliable."

"Look, just because it's been done that way for five centuries—"

" 'Doesn't mean it has to be done that way now.' " Merlo gazed off into the past with a nostalgic smile. "I remember when I used that line."

I reined in my rearing temper. "So now it's my turn. What have you got against innovation?"

"It's unreliable." He went back to designing. "We have people's lives riding on this, Ramou, whether you believe it or not. Better the old dangers we know than new ones we don't."

"I never pegged you for a conservative."

"Responsibility tends to do that to people."

"But—"

"No, Ramou." Merlo drew the line on his screen. "I program the designs onto read-only cubes, you punch the buttons to grind 'em out. That's it."

I sighed. It was some gain, anyway. After all, if I couldn't put in a modification between cube and holo, I didn't deserve the degree I hadn't finished. "Okay, boss. Any way you want."

"Glad to hear it." Merlo nodded, satisfied. "What's going on in the cargo hold?"

"Oh, I'm building." I sighed. "How come a passenger ship had a cargo hold, anyway?"

"So the company could make an extra profit off the trip." Merlo drew another line. "No spaceship ever carries just passengers, or just cargo either, for that matter. They'll carry anything that pays—and sometimes, even on a liner like this, the cargo brought more than the passengers. How's the stage coming?"

"I've got almost all the platforms formed," I grumbled, "but I still don't see why."

"Because we must have a dress rehearsal, Ramou." Barry gestured to include the whole cavernous space. "When we've earned enough to afford it, this whole cargo hold will be modified into a theater—a small one, yes, only five hundred seats, but large enough for the average audience we'll be hoping for in most of the colonial capitals."

I stared. "Where are we going to perform till then?"

"In any space big enough that we can rent," Horace told me. "If we're very lucky, there may be a genuine theater for a local amateur group . . ."

"Otranto and Falstaff," Barry sighed. "None of the other colonies has any such endeavor, according to the current word from the embassies. Of course, that information may be out of date . . ."

"But probably not," Horace finished for him. "Barring that, there may be a school auditorium that's not too badly equipped."

"No information on that," Barry murmured, "other than that New Venus's educational facilities are of the best and most modern."

My stomach sank. "Gymnasiums."

Barry nodded. "And militia armories, and union halls."

I shuddered. "You mean if it's big enough, we've got to find a way to perform in it."

"It won't be so bad as that," Barry assured me. "After all, Ramou, any theater is only an empty space." He turned, indicating the rest of the hold with a sweeping gesture. "Even this hold, that will one day be a theater, fully equipped, is only a void. We will fill it with artifacts arising from our imaginations—yes, by way of solid-forming machines, but products of our imaginations nonetheless. We will have a thrust stage that can be converted to full proscenium, or even arena, and you will lay rails that will let you paint sets with light, just as Grudy Drury will program costume designs and pull finished garments out of her Fabriccator; the actors will put on their finery and paint their faces, and fill the stage with lunacy, drama, and poetry, which will draw both laughter and tears from our audience. But when all is said and done, all our wonderful machinery, all our paints and costumes, can only stimulate the audience to use their own imaginations, and the world we shall evoke and the characters who people it must come as much from their minds and hearts as from ours. For that is the magic of the living theater, that it is living indeed for both actor and audience, that it is the creation of a wonderful illusion in which both must participate. And this vast dark cavern, like any other theater, is only an empty space, and we must fill it with our imaginations."

I stared around at the gloom about me, and the confounded emptiness did seem suddenly magical and imbued with all sorts of potential.

"So build the stage, eh, Ramou?" Barry smiled down at me. "At least we will be able to have a proper dress rehearsal, for the time being—but someday, a theater complete."

"Yes, sir," I muttered, and blast it if he didn't make it all sound genuinely mystical.

I did it, of course. It's not that you don't say no to Barry Tallendar—it's just that after five minutes talking with him, you don't *want* to.

Of course, I could have been much more efficient about it. I could have put everything together a lot sooner if I hadn't had to keep running off to attend rehearsals—but what the hey, I was still gofer as well as carpenter.

I know, I know, the planks were made out of plastic, and the forming machine did most of the detail work—but I still had to join the units. I sawed 'em and nailed 'em and clamped 'em as if they were genuine, organically grown cellulose. I know, 'cause I did a little work with real, actual, fallen tree limbs and dead trunks at Scout camp now and then.

But I had to get up early to put in a couple of hours of work before rehearsals started. Oh, sure, they could have gotten along without me—but I didn't want to let *them* know that.

Besides, Susanne and Lacey were there, too.

Marnie? Yeah, she was there. Every now and then, something about the way she moved made me realize that fifteen years ago, watching her must have been almost as much fun as watching Lacey or Susanne was now. It was a shocking thought, but it explained how Valdor got involved.

I could not help but notice that she was still a very beautiful woman. Of course, she caught the look in my eye and snapped, "At your age, Horace, aesthetics should be divorced from experience."

Well, who was I to quarrel with her about divorce? If experience counts for anything, Marnie Lulala was an expert on the subject. Still, she did seem to walk with a little more arrogance after the exchange.

Of course, I doubt that I was as limited as she seemed to think—though I must admit that I hadn't had occasion for experiment in recent years. Even at my age, however, feminine pulchritude still gave a lift to my soul, almost as much as when I turned a corner at the Metropolitan Museum of Art and came upon Van Gogh's *Sunflowers* without warning—the original, blazing there in static splendor. Marnie still had that quality, when she chose to display it. I understand that she always chose not to, as soon as the ring was on her finger, which may have explained why she had had three husbands, none for longer than a year.

However, as leading lady, the opportunities for her to slink and to snuggle were much more limited than when she had been a starlet. I remember her well, even though she very obviously thought of me as a doddering old fool even then, and took every opportunity to belittle me—until she learned that Morty the Milkman also played character parts on Broadway. Then she became surprisingly civil, if not complimentary. Never one to turn away a possible friend, I responded with courtesy, and a hint of warmth. Apparently she assumed that the silly old fool had been captivated by her youthful charms, and forebore any attempt at closer association—which was quite a relief, I must say. I understand that black widow spiders are lovely to behold, in their way—but I prefer to admire from a distance.

Of course, that made her the perfect Lady Macbeth. Good thing, too—at least that gave her one Shakespearean role in which she was competent. I had a notion that might have influenced Barry's choice of play. After all, we *could* have done *Julius Caesar*, and were still planning to rehearse it.

* * *

In the meantime, Merlo was out of action for the heavy stuff. So guess who that left trying to get the stage together?

Oh, Merlo was more than willing to guide me. "Right, Ramou, but we need another six-by-forty unit."

I turned and stared. "You mean I got the dimensions wrong?"

"No," he said, "forty by twenty is what I had on the drawings. But Barry took a look and told me he needs another six feet in front of the proscenium line, for a deeper forestage."

"I thought you told me we weren't going to use a picture-frame opening!"

"We're not, but some of the performance spaces we use will probably be municipal theaters, and the locals will have gone to a lot of trouble to build in a proscenium, just like in the encyclopedia articles on theater. They'll be real proud of it, too, so we'll just have to cope with it."

"So we *are* going to build a proscenium," I said, trying to check the exasperation.

"No, we're just going to put six more feet into the fore-stage."

I threw up my hands. "Look, wouldn't it be easier to just feed those platforms into the vat and set the extruder to make new ones, twenty-six feet deep?"

"Waste of time. Besides, the crack between the six-footers and the stage will give the actors a great idea where the proscenium line is." Merlo levered himself up onto his good foot and his Canadian crutch. "Look, I'll show you how. You just set the horizontal for—"

"I know how to operate the machine!" I rushed over to him, to ease him back down into his chair. "You know the robo-doc said you should stay off that ankle unless you're walking, and you have to watch how much you do of that!"

"Oh, all right," Merlo grumbled, and let me ease him down. I turned away to punch the codes into the Constructor, seething. He was manipulating me, the louse—he knew I'd do what he told me, rather than see him hobble around and stand still on that damn crutch.

Besides, why not? It would take a little less time.

I reconsidered that question while I was underneath the platforms on my back, wearing the oxygen mask and holding the heat gun.

"Meld 'em every meter," Merlo's voice said, muted by the depth of the platforms.

"I didn't bring a measuring stick with me," I called out.

"It doesn't have to be exact—just *about* a meter." His chair scraped, and the crutch thumped on the floor. "Here, let me show you . . ."

"No way!" I bleated. "You sit back down, damn it!" I pointed the gun and pressed the thumb patch. The aiming laser stabbed out at the resin, showing me where the heat was concentrated. Of course, there was a fair amount of spillover; I began to sweat. When I saw the surfaces of the two platforms flow and mingle enough to eliminate the crack between them, I let up on the trigger patch—but not quite soon enough; a single drop of resin spattered onto my hand. I swore.

"Hey, look," Merlo called, "this is the boss's job, at least until you've seen it done once." That damn crutch thumped again.

"Sit down," I roared. "I'll get it!"

And I did—cursing every inch of the way. After all, labor has its rights.

I stared at the parallel rows of light cables on Merlo's sketch. *"Why?"*

"So they'll look like the old wing grooves from the eighteenth and nineteenth centuries," Merlo explained. "We lay the rails out in two-meter segments, parallel to the upstage wall, each one a meter closer to the center line as you go upstage."

"If you say so." I sighed, and began lugging rails. After all, he was the boss—and I was learning real quick not to argue. "But why does Barry want to make it look like two hundred years *after* Shakespeare?"

"He's decided to recreate the Scottish play the way Garrick did it."

I frowned. "Who's Garrick?"

"A famous actor and manager from 1700s England," Merlo said, "the most famous of his day. They were still naming theaters after him a century after his death."

An actor-manager? Something connected. "And Barry identifies with him, huh?"

Merlo pursed his lips. "Let's say he's aware that he's following in Garrick's tradition."

I nodded. "So he wants to do the Scottish play the way Garrick did. Makes sense."

"In a way," Merlo admitted, but he was looking at me as if he'd never seen me before. "I still say his good judgment will overtake his sense of history. He'll probably take one look at this layout and change his mind, but it's not all that tough for us to move the rails, now is it, Ramou?"

"No," I said, "but we'll have to connect each rail to the light board separately this way, and we don't have that many cables."

Merlo frowned. "You sure? I thought I laid in plenty of everything!"

"Not one for each rail, no. Oh, we've got twenty hundred-foot rolls of cable—but I'll have to attach connectors at each end, and that'll only leave us about a dozen spares."

"Then we'll have to splice the pieces if we need to make a really long run later." Merlo frowned. "Well, we'll buy more cable on New Venus. Here, let me give you a hand . . ."

"No, I'll bring them to you," I said quickly.

* * *

As we sat there attaching connectors to pieces of cable, I said, "Why did the eighteenth century techies lay out short walls parallel to the back wall?"

"To give them the illusion of depth," Merlo explained. "Each of those 'walls' was a flat, of course, and they called 'em 'wings.' The Italians invented them when they discovered perspective, and—"

"Each wing was a little shorter than the one before it, and a little closer to center!" I looked up, wide-eyed. "Just like a perspective drawing! Yeah, sure, that'd give it one hell of an illusion of depth!"

Merlo grinned. "We call it the 'wing and drop' system now. They could change it really easily, because they laid out their rails two by two, so they could just slide one set of wings out as they slid another set in. Meanwhile, one backdrop was being raised while another one was being lowered—and voila! You had a new set. There were even theaters where you just turned one master windlass, and the whole set changed."

"Talk about presets!" I said. "But wouldn't that kind of limit you? I mean, it'd be great for outdoors, in a city, but how about a forest? Or what if you had to have a scene inside, say, a castle?"

"That did look a little contrived," Merlo admitted. "Probably one of the reasons why they switched to counter-weighted fly systems and freestanding flats—and the main reason why I don't think Barry's gonna like the look of this. The Scottish play just has too many scenes that don't take place in cities or forests."

I stared. "Then why are we going through all this?"

"Because directors have to be shown." Merlo sighed. "Pass the soldering gun, Ramou."

Barry gazed at the scene with a happy sigh. "It's absolutely splendid, Merlo."

Merlo flushed with pleasure. "Just a quick sketch, really, Barry. I didn't even debug it."

"Still, it's a marvel." Barry turned to him. "Take it down."

Merlo stared at him, then managed to heave a sigh that ended in a grin. "Didn't figure you'd like it once you saw it."

"Oh, I love the effect! And make sure you keep the system intact—we'll do *School for Scandal* next season. But it would be just too limiting for Shakespeare."

I thought of all those hours crimping connectors onto cables and ground my teeth.

"So what are we looking for?" Merlo pressed. "A uniset that will play all of Shakespeare?"

"Heaven protect me from another reconstruction of the Globe Theatre!" Barry shuddered. "No, start with the interior of a castle's keep, would you, Merlo? Before they thought of dividing walls. Then we'll see how we can adapt it to the exteriors."

I stared, and bit my tongue just in time.

Merlo nodded. "I'll see what I can rummage up."

"Thank you, old boy. Sorry about all the wasted effort." Barry smiled, then turned the same beam on me. "So good of you to humor me, Ramou—but sometimes, the director does need to see his ideas realized, in order to recognize his mistakes."

And somehow, I felt as if all the effort had been worth it. What the hey, it had just been busywork, anyway, and I'd had a nice chat with Merlo while we'd been doing it.

After he had stepped into the lift, I turned to Merlo and let it out. "One big chamber? How to modify it for exteriors? Doesn't he realize we can change the whole set to a forest in five seconds?"

"Of course he does," Merlo said, "but Standard Shakespeare Set Number Four has deeper roots in him than that. Right, too—the action can flow better in a uniset, and you can have simultaneous scenes that don't distract from the poet's language. Most importantly of all, you can give the audience scope to use their imaginations, and that involves them more in the play."

"So we're starting from scratch, huh?"

"Not quite." Merlo turned away to his drawing board and pressed a key. The board lit up; he typed in a code, and a picture appeared, absolutely realistic, of a huge open hall built of granite blocks. At one side, a stairway curved against those stones, widening out into a landing halfway up, then again at the top. There was a dais in the center with a smaller dais on top of it, and a lower stairway at the other side, its landing disappearing into a doorway. There were a lot of doorways.

I stared. "When did you come up with *this*?"

"Had the basic idea about ten years ago," Merlo said. "So as soon as Barry said we were doing the Scottish play, I pulled it out and did some developing."

"But why? If he told you he wanted wing-and-drop!"

"Because I knew he'd change his mind once he saw it." Merlo grinned. "Go set up the rails in a semicircle, Ramou."

"How is Ramou progressing, Barry?"

"Oh, quite well, Horace—he's finished with Introduction to Theater, and is well into Theater History I. Really, he's so avid to learn that he's a joy to chat with. Merlo says so, too, and Ogden—and I haven't solicited opinions from Susanne or Lacey, but from what I've seen of their conversations, they would say the same."

"Team teaching is so effective," I said, with a smile of amusement. " 'The best school is a log, with a motivated student at one end and Mark Hopkins at the other.' Too bad we can't always keep that student-teacher ratio. What is next in his curriculum, Barry?"

"Introduction to Acting," Barry answered grimly, "and I think we may finally encounter some learning resistance."

Y'know, you don't realize how much work there is in putting on a play, when you're just sitting out there in front watching. Okay, it occurs to you that someone had to build and paint the set, and someone else had to construct all the costumes—but you never stop to think about all those little things they pass from hand to hand, like drinking mugs and swords and spindles. Somehow you don't realize that some-body had to make them all, or go out and find them.

"Somebody" was me.

Granted, it's a lot easier than it used to be. Back in the Stone Age, Merlo tells me, the prop master had to go visit all the junk shops to find what he could, then look up pic-tures of the rest and build it out of papier-mâché or a kind of cloth impregnated with plastic—or out of the real mate-rials, if they had the money.

I had it easy. All I had to do was look up the pictures—which was no problem with the complete historical data base Merlo thoughtfully ordered—then feed the program into the Constructor. It would mulch up the data, let it soak in, mull it over a while, then grind out a chunk of plastic and carve it with laser beams inside—and bingo! It would serve me up a completed goblet. Or bowl. Or shield.

Of course, I had to write the program that describes the item, first.

The most common items in the catalogue came with ready-made programs, and all I had to do was make a few adjustments—but the rare stuff, like standing cups and snuffboxes, I had to do from scratch. It took a hell of a long while the first time I tried, but Merlo showed me a few techniques, and where to look up subprograms for orna-mentation, and I picked it up fast enough. Fortunately, for the Scottish play, almost everything had a premade pro-gram.

Including the swords.

I carved out a sample and showed it to Merlo. After all, it looked a lot better than the beat-up old things he'd scrounged up and brought along. But would you believe it, he told me it didn't look as if it had been used enough?

"Now, this broadsword," he said, taking one of the cold rolled iron things out of its packing case, "this looks as if it's been through the wars."

It sure did. The blade was nicked and gouged so bad you would have thought metal-loving gophers had been at it. The flat of the blade had these ridges of metal on them, as if the iron had melted here and there and run like wax, hardening in a bead at the end, and the pommels were so worn they looked like advertisements for saddle soap.

"The wars it is," I agreed. "I could modify the program a little, for some wear and tear . . ."

Merlo grinned and handed me the sword. "Heft that. Then take a swing at me." He brought out another one.

Me take a swing at him? I wondered if Merlo knew what he was asking. Then I remembered that this was supposed to be just pretend, so I swung the sword the way I would have chopped at a beginning student. Merlo grinned wider and swung his blade down overhand—none of this pussy-footing around with parrying, I guess—and slammed his blade against mine with a clang that echoed off the bulk-heads far away in that dim and cavernous hold. The pommel jolted against my hands, but I'd been expecting it. "See?" he said. "You can't get a heft like that with a syn-thetic sword—and you sure as blazes can't get that sound!"

"You sure can't," I agreed. I had this sinking feeling in the pit of my stomach; I was beginning to understand why *Macbeth* had a high accident rate. Excuse me, "the Scottish play." The back of my mind started trying to figure out a program for a material that would look, sound, and perform believably.

"Now that's a stage sword." Merlo patted it and put it away, then held out his hand for mine.

I handed it to him pommel first. "Did the medieval knights really swing their swords to block each other's blows like that?"

"Probably, if they didn't have shields. You can't stop a sword with this kind of mass by a parry."

"Yes I could." I frowned. "And you left a hole a mile wide with that counterslash. I could have driven through it with a thrust, easy as pie."

Merlo frowned and took the swords out again. "Show me."

I didn't like doing it without protective clothing, but after all, they were blunt—square edges, and the tips were really more rounded than pointed. I took the sword, and Merlo said, "Ready?"

I nodded, holding the sword at guard. He swung, and I half stepped and swung from the elbow, not the shoulder, with English. His sword rang like a chime, jolting aside, and I riposted to touch his chest with the point. "Like that."

"Oh, you're talking about *real* sword fighting," Merlo said with disgust.

I frowned. "What other kind is there?"

"Stage fencing," Merlo answered. "See, the object of real fighting is to kill your opponent—but if we tried that in the theater, we'd run out of actors awfully fast."

I thought of saying that the Romans hadn't, then remembered that the gladiators probably weren't all that good as actors. They also weren't willing. "That makes sense," I said judiciously. "So what *is* the purpose?"

"To put on a good show. So we use big movements, that show up well from the back row in the balcony."

I frowned. "Isn't accuracy a factor?"

"No, not really." Merlo grinned. "Just fun."

"Fun," I echoed, and sighed. "I'm beginning to understand why you want the swords to ring."

"Yeah—it sounds great." Then his brow creased at a thought. "But where did you learn to fence, Ramou?"

"Huh? Oh. From Sensei—I'd learned enough so he thought it was safe to teach me a few weapons." I said it absentmindedly; I was staring at the swords, trying to figure out how to make them showy but safe.

"A few?" Merlo's tone had become guarded. "Like how many?"

"Oh, just the staff, the spear, the sword, nimchuks, shuriken, and sais."

"Oh, that's all, huh?" Merlo was looking a little nervous. "Well, do me a favor, Ramou—just pretend you don't know anything, and let us teach it to you from the top. Safer that way."

"Yeah, it sure will be," I agreed. "I mean, I wouldn't want to goof up in front of an audience, and make it look like nothing." Then I remembered that I was going to have to be in front of an audience, a couple of hundred pairs of eyes all staring at me, watching for the tiniest mistake, and I shuddered. "Audience!" I felt the churning in the pit of my stomach, but this was a different kind. What good is fear if you can't fight the enemy?

"He'll take on half a dozen armed men without batting an eye, but he quakes at the thought of an audience." Merlo shook his head, mystified. "You're amazing, Ramou."

I was amazed myself. How had I ever let Barry talk me into this?

The granite and mortar might have been illusions painted by light, but the steps the actors were going to climb had to be real. Merlo punched in the programs on the Constructor, and I took the gleaming white units as they extruded out of its delivery port.

"Here, I'll help," he offered.

"No!" I hollered. "You go take that game leg of yours and sit on it!"

"That would break it all over again," he said with great practicality. "Look, Ramou, it's immobilized and covered in plastic. I'm not gonna hurt it by carrying a little weight."

"That's not what the robo-doc says—and immobile or not, it's not exactly as maneuverable as it would be if you were only wearing a shoe on it. You're much more likely to trip and fall—so how about you just step back and tell me what I'm doing wrong, eh?"

"Oh, all right, nursie," he grumbled, and sat down in the folding chair again, his cane near at hand.

I set up the post-and-lintel unit; the posts were plastiform, tall and straight, but L-shaped if you looked at 'em in cross section, which was what I did as I pulled 'em out of the extruder. Then I stood them up.

"You don't have to stand there ready to catch them," Merlo told me. "They're self-supporting."

"Then they'll earn my praise." I turned back to catch the next section as it came out. "Y'know, we *could* program the machine to make 'em any color we wanted."

"That's what I did. We're projecting colored light in front of them, remember? Any color but white will dim it down."

"When they're in *back*? Of laser beams?"

"You'd be surprised. Besides, why take chances?"

I set the unit up next to its mate. "I'll need the ladder for the next one, right?"

Merlo shrugged. "You could lay the platform top-down, then stand them upside-down on it."

"Probably easier." I turned to catch the platform as it came out.

"Here, you'll need four hands on that."

"*No*, I won't." He was right, though—I just barely managed to get under the platform and balance it. The weight didn't bother me—it was foamed, and very light, though it was rigid enough to be very, very strong. But it was awkward. I took it over by the posts, flipped it, and laid it top-down, then turned the posts over and set the lintels on top of the platform. "Why did I turn it upside down? It's solid—what's the difference between the top and the bottom?"

"The top is textured to give the actors traction."

"Oh." I felt dumb. To cover it, I pulled out the heat gun and started melting the lintels into the platform. "You sure these are going to come apart easy? We have to pack them in a truck and take them to a theater, don't we?"

"If we're lucky. More probably a gymnasium or a field house. And yes, they'll come apart like a dream. You just use the heat gun again, and push on the leg; the seam will melt, and the post-and-lintel units will peel right off."

"If you say so." I stood back, surveying my handiwork, and gave it a dubious nod. Then I racked the heat gun and came back to flip it right side up. I toppled it over easily enough, but when I went to lift the platform, the legs skidded. It was top-heavy, and that top didn't want to go up.

"Now you *have* to let me help." Merlo grinned as he levered himself onto his foot.

"*No*, I don't!"

"Oh, but all I have to do is this." Merlo put the toes of his good foot against the end of one post with his cane against the other. "Now lift."

I did, and the legs didn't skid, of course—Merlo was blocking them.

"That's called 'footing,'" Merlo explained to me.

The unit settled with a soft thud. I looked up at it and nodded. "I guess that didn't strain you too much."

"Not so's you'd notice it, no."

I frowned up at the underside of the platform. "What's that bas-relief melted in there?" It was a pentagram made up of wedges.

"That's the IATSE 'bug,'" Merlo explained, "the insignia of the stagehands' union. I'm a member there, as well as in the Designers' Guild—though neither of them is all that happy about it." He grinned.

" 'Stagehands' comes out to 'yatse'?"

"I-A-T-S-E." Merlo spelled it out patiently. " 'The Interplanetary Association of Tridimensional and Stage Employees.' "

"Interplanetary?" I stared. "I thought we were going to be the first ones!"

"We are, the first stagehands," Merlo soothed. "But the union includes a lot of public 3DT projectionists and engineers, and they're already out there on every planet where there are people. We'll have to check in with each one of them as a courtesy."

I hoped they'd be courteous.

"Well, let's get the stairs up," Merlo said.

I turned around and touched the circle that started the machine cycling out the next piece. The stairs were a bear, but I just backed up as they came out, then let the end drop down onto the floor by itself.

Merlo nodded approvingly. "I was wondering how long it would take you to think of that."

"I'm not always dense." I lifted the unit and carried it over to the high platform. "Neither is this."

"Sure, amazingly light," Merlo said, eyeing me strangely. "Ain't modern materials wonderful? Now you'll need the ladder."

"And you need your chair again," I retorted. I felt a glow of satisfaction as I watched him hobble back to his portable recliner and sit down, grumbling about overattentive nannies. Then I set up the ladder and climbed up with the heat gun, to melt the top step into the unit. "You sure that'll hold?"

"Like iron. Now shove the whole thing into place."

His voice echoed; I looked up and saw he was sitting at the scene board. Well, that didn't look too strenuous, and at least he was sitting, so I pushed the unit into place. It com-

pleted the stairway down from the highest level—
presumably where the ramparts would be when we had the
exterior set on, and the bedrooms in the interior.

"Okay, step back," Merlo called.

I stepped. I have a healthy respect for lasers, even when
they're set to be cool light, not heat rays. I kept stepping,
too, all the way back behind Merlo—I wanted to see what
he was doing at the board.

He dimmed up the exterior set, and I saw that the top of
the illusory granite blocks was an inch below the landing,
leaving a strip of gleaming white plastic showing.

"Sometimes you get the dimensions to match exactly on
the first run through the sequence," Merlo said, "and sometimes you don't." He punched a patch on the keyboard and
nudged the joystick just a hair. The wall rose. Merlo
frowned. "Go check that and make sure I didn't overshoot,
will you, Ramou?"

"Yes, sir!" I ran back and peeked. "Half an inch high,
Merlo. Too far . . . there! Right on the nose!"

"Only time I ever want to be accused of being on the
level." Merlo punched another patch.

"Don't we have to write a correction for the program?"

"No, it's self-correcting. It just reads the new information
from the joystick and adjusts itself."

I wondered why I'd bothered to learn programming.

Merlo sat back. "Not bad, if I do say so myself."

I ran back to look at it from his angle. "Damn good!" I
breathed. It wasn't a set, it *was* the castle, age-darkened
granite, streaks of dampness, and all.

"Now for the outside." Merlo pressed the "change"
patch, and the scene dissolved into the bailey, looking toward the curtain wall. Sure enough, the battlements were up
there at the top—and the platform didn't show at all.

Merlo frowned. "I think it's a little high."

So was I. Too high—I was still standing there, thrilling
at the sight of something so magnificent that I had helped

make, when Merlo stepped up onto the set, hobbled up two steps, and said, "Yeah, it's two centimeters off. Tap the 'adjust' patch, Ramou, and touch the joystick down about . . ."

About two steps. Merlo, that was. The cane slipped, and he toppled backward with a yelp.

"Merlo!" I was up beside him before I even thought of running.

His face was white again. "I'm okay, I'm okay!" He struggled to stand up, but his face went white again, and he gasped.

"There is no further damage to the foot," the mellow female voice informed us, "but his wrist is badly sprained."

I breathed a sigh of relief, and Susanne told Merlo severely, "There, now. You heard it from the robo-doc itself. You'll have to keep that wrist taped for a week, Merlo—and absolutely no physical work, you understand?"

"Yes, nursie," Merlo grumbled, but his eyes weren't exactly sour as Susanne fastened the clasp on the broad bandage around his wrist. "Thanks, kid," he said. For a second, I thought he was going to kiss her, and my glands revved up for jealousy—but he only smiled and hobbled out the sick bay door.

Susanne rounded on me. "Really, Ramou! You were supposed to keep him from doing anything more strenuous than laying his finger on a pressure patch!"

"I got carried away," I said humbly, "admiring the set—and he wanted me to have a chance to trim the program, so he went out to eyeball it for me."

"Don't let him be so generous again." But she had thawed; Susanne understood the kind of people you couldn't turn your back on for a second. "He's a very bad patient."

"And you're a very good nurse. Did you have a second career, too?"

She blushed and looked away. "An actress always has to

have some kind of a job to put bread on the table while she's waiting for one of the auditions to pay off."

"I can think of a lot worse," I said. "Just make sure Barry pays you for both."

"Oh, I couldn't ask that!"

"Yes you can," I told her. "Just try a little. Or I'll do it for you—you've just made my job a lot easier."

Susanne frowned. "How?"

"Because Merlo can't try to do any manual labor now." I grinned. "Not with his right hand taped up."

But he did, of course. He was left-handed.

6

While Merlo and Ramou were constructing the sets, rehearsals went on unchecked. Truthfully, I suspected that Ramou wasn't putting in as much time on the set as he should have—I saw him far too frequently at rehearsals. Admittedly, in the mornings, he was there to supply coffee and doughnuts—though we could all quite easily have operated the food and drink synthesizers by ourselves, of course. I could understand why Ramou and Susanne might not have wanted Ogden operating the beverage dispenser for himself, but surely Susanne could have managed that little task, as she seemed to manage all the rest of Ogden— and to be sure, Ramou could plead that, since he was actually going to have to appear onstage in this production, he had to become fully familiar with it in rehearsal. Merlo accepted about as much of that as you might suspect, and was growing more than a little exasperated with his assistant. I assured him that if he truly objected to Ramou's absence, Barry could probably be persuaded to manage without him, except for the scenes in which he had to appear, especially those in which he and I were to lead an army of local hirelings to battle. But Merlo only grumbled some nonsense about adolescent hormones and not wishing to deny the lad the innocent pleasures of youth, which more or less confirmed my own conjecture—that it was not the blocking and positioning of actors he wished to witness, but the movements of the actresses. I could hardly blame him—

Lacey and Susanne were both delights to watch in daily life, but even more pleasurable onstage, especially if the role called for the exercise of feminine charms. Since Barry had them in competition to see which would be allowed to play her witch as young and seductive, the rehearsals allowed them more than adequate scope for the most enticing of their skills.

Then, too, I was delighted to see that Ramou had come to realize that the alluring developments onstage were entirely artificial, and that the charming and enticing airs the girls so proudly displayed in performance, they counted demeaning in real life.

Barry made another try at rehearsing *Mac* . . . excuse me, the Scottish play. Everything went well at first; the upheavals were limited to disagreements between actor and director. For example, Barry found it necessary to say, "That is excellent, Marnie, but we need a bit less of the seductress and a bit more of the demon."

"A *femme fatale* can't be *fatale* without being *femme*, Barry," she returned. "My conception of the part is intensely feminine."

Barry knew what that meant—that Marnie couldn't accept being onstage without doing her utmost to make the male members of her audience drool. But all he said was, "I believe you have a line that tells the demons to 'unsex me here.'"

"True," Marnie riposted, "but she goes on to say, 'Come to my woman's breasts, and take my milk for gall.' She is obviously referring only to her maternal nature; when it comes to leading a man to his doom, she will use whatever means prove most effective."

Barry pursed his lips and became rather thoughtful. "A point, a telling point. Well, if it was good enough for Ellen Terry, it should be good enough for us. Just keep the strumpet within, will you? Very well, proceed."

There were similar discussions of characterization, and I

could feel the company beginning to develop the first faint stirrings of enthusiasm as they saw how seriously they were each taking the play.

"Knock, knock!" Barry called, and Marty shambled out into the center of the lounge, the very picture of a man who has been awakened in the middle of the night. "Here's a knocking indeed!" he grumbled. "If a man were porter at Hell Gate, he should have old turning the key."

"Bang, bang," Barry called.

"Knock, knock, knock." Marty looked up in surly resentment, and I was galvanized. I was suddenly reminded that this young man had it within him to play serious parts well, perhaps even with the same inspiration he brought to things laughable.

Indeed, he was being quite serious. "Faith, ere's an English tailor come hither, for stealing out of a French house! Come in, tailor!" Then he broke off. "Doggone it, Mr. Tallendar, it just ain't funny!"

There was so much of the ludicrous in his indignation that we all laughed; we couldn't help ourselves. Marty looked surprised, then looked around him with a slow grin. Barry smiled, too. "Come now, Mr. Kemp. It has the reputation of being the only moment of comic relief in the whole play."

"Yeah, right after they've killed a king and gone running off with some bloody daggers! Great comic lead-up, oh, sure! And why doesn't the porter do something about that knock on the door, instead of prosing about sinners? You sure this playwright shouldn't have stuck to making gloves?"

"I assure you that he poached plots far better than he poached game," Barry returned. "But you must understand, Martyn, that he grew up watching the Miracle Plays—yes, they were still being performed during his youth, and the fact that they only came once a year made them all the more fascinating to a young child. Which of the stations

would have most vividly impressed itself on the mind of a
ten-year-old boy?"

"Hell-mouth," Marty said instantly.

"Precisely. And this porter, being from an even earlier
time, would have grown up seeing those same cycles of
plays. When he mentions the porter at Hell-mouth Gate, he
isn't thinking of an abstract religious concept—he's thinking of—"

"The character from the play!" Marty exclaimed, with
the look that accompanies the flash of insight.

"Precisely," Barry said, "and he's alone in the great hall,
so this is his opportunity to mimic the players in their fa-
vorite bit of overacting. So he adopts their posture . . . probably hunchbacked . . ."

Marty pulled his head down and hunched his shoulders
up, grinning.

"Deformed," Barry prompted.

Marty shrank his arms up against his body like a tyran-
nosaurus, the hands hooked into claws.

"Bowlegged."

Marty's knees bent and turned outward.

"Delighting in his own evilness," Barry said.

Marty's face twisted into a wicked leer, and his eye
gleamed with demonic glee.

"But even more, delighting in seeing human souls cor-
rupted and twisted even more than he, to the point at which
they sink to hell and become his toys!"

Marty gave a low, gloating laugh that chilled me to the
bone.

"Then the porter proceeds to ham it up unmercifully,"
Barry said, "as Shakespeare has him recite, not the list of
accepted cardinal sins, but his own catalogue of crimes that
should send a man to hell—at least, in the eye of an Elizabethan gentleman."

Marty crowed with delight and hauled open an imaginary
door. "Come in, come in!"

And he proceeded to go through the most wonderful drunken porter I had ever seen; he could scarcely say a single line without rendering us all helpless with laughter. He grew and blossomed at the sound, until finally he was pantomiming the opening of the real door, and saying to Banquo, "Remember the porter!" and holding out a hand cupped for a tip in exactly the fashion of the porters at the less luxurious hotels in New York, a fashion that sent us all into gales of laughter again.

"Oh, my abdomen!" Barry gasped. "If you can run it that well in performance, Marty, we will all be unable to finish the play! For now, however, let us attempt to continue the rehearsal."

Banquo stepped up, but before he could utter a syllable, the lounge rang from wall to wall with the applause of the whole company. Marty looked up in flattered surprise, then took a very elaborate and ceremonious bow. Even Larry was clapping his hands, though slowly and with a bad grace.

"Awww, thanks, folks," Marty said, drawing a circle on the carpet with his toe. "It's just 'cause I finally got it 'splained to me, that's all."

"Don't be deceived; your English professor probably would not countenance my interpretation," Barry assured him. "Now, however, you must think of your exit while we resume the play."

So, all in all, it was turning into an excellent and very productive rehearsal—until Ramou and Charlie came in with Marty, presumably in another costume, to murder Banquo.

"Hark! I hear horses," Ramou said, with all the expression of a length of two-by-four. Well, it was his first attempt.

"Give us a light there, ho!" I called, ostensibly offstage.

"Then 'tis he!" Marty said with grim anticipation. "The

rest that are within the note of expectation, already are in the court!"

"His horses go about," Charlie pointed out.

Marty took Ramou's lines, out of pity: "Almost a mile— but he does usually. So all men do, from hence to the palace gate make it their walk." Then he gave his own line, *sotto voce*, to Ramou: "A light, a light!"

"A light, a light," Ramou repeated obligingly. Then, " 'Tis he!"

"Stand to it," Charlie advised.

"It will be rain tonight," I said as Banquo, coming between the two chairs that represented the platform sides of the set with Larry a step behind me as Fleance.

"Then let it come down," Charlie said.

"Now, gentlemen!" Barry called. Charlie and Marty sprang out from the chairs to grapple with me, while Ramou descended upon Larry. I was amazed how deftly Charlie managed—he gave me a knee in the back and an arm around the throat with just enough pressure so that I knew when to bend backward and gargle, "O treachery! Fly, good Fleance, fly! Thou mayest revenge! O slave!"

In response, I heard the sound of a blow, followed by a heavy thud. The arm around my throat disappeared miraculously, and I straightened up to see Ramou stretched out cold on the floor with Larry staring down at him in horror.

For a moment, it was a frozen tableau. Then Larry came alive, turning and running for the doorway—but Merlo blocked him and clapped an arm about his shoulders, saying in soothing tones, "Now, hold on, Larry, hold on. It was just an accident, could've happened to anyone—he'll understand that."

But Larry still struggled, eyes wide with panic.

Charlie, meantime, had dropped to one knee beside Ramou, but Susanne was somehow there ahead of him. She clasped Ramou's wrist; then, satisfied of the pulse, she reached for his head—but Charlie held up a hand to stop her. "Wait a moment, Ms. Souci. Let's wait till he comes to, and make certain he doesn't have a major pain there; we don't want to move his neck until we're sure." He looked up at us all, and his gaze singled out Larry. "A glass of water, please."

Larry stared, wild-eyed; then he seemed to snap back to his senses, nodded once, quickly and abruptly, and streaked over to the beverage dispenser.

"That takes too long." Susanne bent down and kissed Ramou very soundly, her long blond hair hiding his face for a moment. His body stiffened, and his arms came up to go around her. She straightened up with a self-satisfied smile. "Natural reflexes. You're not too badly off."

Behind her, Lacey burned.

"Not too much, no," Ramou agreed, his voice slow and rough. He started to lift himself off the floor, then froze. "Ow!" He reached for the back of his neck.

"Lie down." Susanne's hands were on him instantly, lulling.

"No, no, it's not that bad." Ramou started to massage the injury. "Believe me, I'd know." But his face was still taut with strain.

"Please lie down," Susanne entreated.

Charlie said, "We really should have the robo-doc give you an X ray and a diagnosis, just to be on the safe side, Ramou."

Ramou's face tightened with annoyance. "Hey, I really appreciate the thought, Charlie, but I've had a lot of experience with injuries, and believe me, if there were anything broken, I'd know it. I might have a sprain, though."

"Please," Susanne entreated, "Just for my peace of mind."

"And mine, Ramou." Barry stepped forward.

I was right behind him. "Yes, Ramou, please."

"Oh, all right," Ramou grumbled, "but you make me feel

like a baby." He was looking decidedly less annoyed, though. "What happened, anyway?"

Susanne started to answer, but Charlie held up a hand again. "What do you remember?"

Larry stepped up with the drink just then, white showing all around his eyes, tense as he waited for the answer. Ramou took the glass from him. "Thanks, Larry." He sipped, then said to Charlie, "I remember jumping out and grabbing Larry. He struggled, just the way Barry had said to, while I pantomimed putting a knife across his throat . . ." He looked up at Larry, frowning. "How the hell did you ever manage to give me a rabbit punch with your elbow?"

"I don't know!" Larry said, almost in a panic. "I was just struggling, Ramou, and all of a sudden, I felt this shock in my elbow, and you collapsed!"

Ramou's frown turned to a scowl of concern. "How's your elbow?"

"Well, it does hurt a little, but . . . Oh, that's ridiculous! How's your *neck*?"

"About like your elbow, I expect," Ramou returned. "Right on the funny bone, huh?"

Larry gulped and nodded.

"Musta hurt," Ramou said sympathetically. "I've had it done to me—but deliberately. This was just an accident."

"Yes, surely." Barry nodded. "It was just an accident. It could have happened at any time."

Especially in this play. The unspoken thought hung there in the air between us, not needing voice to carry it to everyone's mind. We all exchanged glances, then looked away.

Ramou pushed himself up, but Susanne and Charlie were there to help him, protesting every inch of the way.

"Ramou, we'll bring a stretcher—"

"You really shouldn't move until—"

"Hey, I really appreciate it." Ramou seemed rather be

mused by their solicitousness. "But I'm okay, really. If I had a broken neck, it would sure as hell hurt too much to move."

Susanne clung to his arm as if to hold him up, completely missing Lacey's glare. "Mr. Wellesley, if you could move to a chair and let Ramou take your floater . . ."

"Of course, my dear." Ogden steered himself over to an armchair, but Ramou said firmly, "No! I can walk! I damn well better be able to walk, or Merlo will try to finish the set by himself, and you know what'll happen *then!*"

"I promise," Merlo said instantly.

"We can all turn to and help, Ramou," I added. "Union rules allow for emergencies."

"They don't have to." Ramou started to shake his head, then winced and clapped the sore spot. "Ow! I can walk just fine—I just can't turn my head!"

Susanne started massaging again. "All right, all right, we'll let you walk! But walk to the sick bay, will you, Ramou?"

"Yeah, sure," Ramou muttered as he headed for the door. "You sure your scene isn't coming up, Charlie? I don't want you to stop rehearsal just because of me."

"All things considered, I think it's just as well we adjourn for the day." Barry was looking rather unsettled himself. "We'll begin again tomorrow."

But we didn't.

7

It hadn't exactly been an exuberant afternoon, but by dinnertime, everyone seemed to have shrugged off the effects of my accident. So even the evening was cheerful enough, with talking, and singing around the keyboard as people took turns playing. I indulged in a little light flirtation with Lacey, and a little heavier flirtation with Susanne, and everyone had a very pleasant evening. Even Larry didn't manage to get anyone mad, so we all retired to bed at a more or less respectable hour—somewhere between midnight and two A.M., everyone remembering the 9:00 call Barry had announced. So everyone was awake and in the lounge on time, and I did a bonanza business in coffee and doughnuts, but almost none in Gran'ma Horrhee's syrup. We were all in rather good spirits, too—which was why Barry's announcement really took us by surprise.

"In view of the situation," he said, "I think any further rehearsal of the Scottish play is somewhat premature—so let us begin with *Vagrants from Vega*. We have already blocked the first act; let us commence with the second."

There were murmurs of surprise, but no one really objected. Larry wore a look of scorn for everyone else's superstitious fear—but I noticed he didn't complain any, either.

There was a rustle as everybody put away their *Mac* . . . excuse me, Scottish play scripts, and riffled through the stack to find *Vagrants*. They must have been hoping he'd change his mind. Only Larry said, "If you'll excuse me, Mr. Tallendar, I left my *Vagrants* script in my stateroom."

"Of course; this isn't as scheduled. But do be quick, Mr. Rash." Barry didn't look as gracious as he sounded, though, and Larry left looking sulky. "Now, then," Barry went on, "beginning with Act II . . ."

"Ah well, if we must, we must." Ogden set his hands on the arms of his floater and began to rise.

" . . . with you seated, of course, Ogden," Barry said quickly. "I am sure you will be hale and hearty by opening night—"

"I am now," Ogden grumbled.

"—but I'd just as soon have you save your energy for that felicitous occasion," Barry finished. "Now, let me refresh your minds as to the first scene. As the second act begins, Brinker the Thinker is leading our doughty crew to his village. It is a small city, actually, filling the air with spires of crystal—Merlo has shown me a preliminary sketch, and I really think it will be quite lovely."

"That hammer-handed grease monkey?" Marnie must have been feeling well this morning, too—back to her old self, in fact. "Merlo couldn't draw a poker hand!"

My gaze snapped over to her, and I frowned. I felt as if an attack on my immediate boss was an attack on me. Irrational, I know—he hadn't chosen me, Horace had—but I respected him and was trying to learn everything he could teach me.

"I'm afraid I must ask you to keep personal opinions out of the discussion, Marnie," Barry said, "or we'll never get beyond the first line."

"Neither can Merlo!" she snapped.

"We'll try to keep you as far from the set as we can." Barry sighed.

"You know you won't go near the upstage wall anyway," Winston reminded her.

"Not unless she's talking to someone else who's in danger of attracting attention," Ogden muttered to me.

"Yes, but I'll have to be seen against it!"

"Against it? You certainly are," Winston rejoined.

"It isn't as if you knew anything about beauty, Winston Carlton!" Marnie turned on him. "If you had any taste at all, you wouldn't perform in those horrible 3DT soggies!"

For a moment, I thought she meant "sagas"; then I realized she was talking about Winston's five-year stint as resident heavy on a soap opera.

"If I had taste," Winston retorted, "you certainly wouldn't be able to perceive it. In fact, come to think of it, I have—and you don't!"

"Company, please!" Barry cried.

Barry looked faintly shocked. I didn't blame him; I had scarcely ever heard Winston say an unkind word, myself. Of course, the one occasion on which I had, certainly had been memorable; I still winced at the recollection. I put this morning's lapse down to the remnants of his condition; he was the only one who had needed Gran'ma Horrhee's remedy this morning.

Marnie, unfortunately, lacked such perspective. She was just drawing breath for another blast, when Barry said, loudly and firmly, "Now! They discover Brinker's home city and immediately fall to arguing among themselves as to whether or not they should proceed into the town."

"I think we can manage that," Winston said. Marnie glared at him.

"Brinker resolves the question," Barry said hastily, "by pointing out that the city is abandoned. He then sings a delightful little ditty explaining why." He keyed the recorder beside him, and a synthesizer rippled out a light, amusing tune, doing a fair imitation of a full orchestra; then the voice of Arbuthnot, the composer and lyricist, came in over it, explaining, with interior rhyme and amusingly erratic meter, how Brinker's race had virtually killed itself off, due to an excessive fondness for material goods and artificially induced states of ecstasy, combined with a growing distaste for children, resulting in an expanding and eventually total use of birth control.

When it was finished, Lacey asked, "Isn't he editorializing a bit there?"

"Thoroughly," I replied, "and has every right to. He is not a journalist, after all, but a playwright, and has no obligation to be objective. He makes no pretense at fairness or lack of bias; he is stating his opinion. He is doing so in a very entertaining way, but is nonetheless very definitely stating his opinion."

Lacey frowned. "I don't know if I can endorse that."

"You have no need to," I assured her. "You need only deliver your lines well."

"But that's an implied endorsement!"

Barry sighed, leaning back in his chair. "Ms. Lark, you had the opportunity to read the play before we left Terra, and you had the opportunity to resign from the company without contract penalty before our ship lifted off. Now, however, if you refuse the part in which you are cast—"

"Oh, no, I didn't mean anything like that!" she said quickly. "I just meant . . ." She floundered, at a loss for words.

"I assure you," I said with some asperity, "Arbuthnot has as much of a right to freedom of expression as you do, and has perhaps earned considerably more. Not every play we do will agree with your own convictions."

Ramou was staring at me, and I really couldn't blame him; it was not like me to be so testy. I was rather surprised at myself, but I had become somewhat tired of the young folks' presumption, and felt the need to correct some of the misapprehensions their professors had impued in them.

"Some may grate on your sensibilities," Barry agreed, "though many will be quite acceptable to you. This company will not be restricted by ideology. Our only requirements for a play are that it be good theater and affordable to produce."

"Precisely," I agreed, "but if we are not to be bound by any particular ideological viewpoint, we each must occasionally appear in a play that contradicts our own opinions. In this instance, we are extremely fortunate that so renowned a playwright team as Cant and Arbuthnot should have allowed us to produce the out-of-town tryouts for one of their new works. If the whole play were detestable, or even its overall theme, you would be in a crisis of conscience and would have been wrong to join a company that planned on producing it. But if only this one barbed comment in this one scene is deplorable to you, I would say that your attitude is highly unprofessional."

Lacey was red-faced by this time, whether with anger or embarrassment, I could not tell. "Are you saying that just because I'm an actress, I don't have any right to my own opinions?"

"Not at all," I replied. "It is merely that the time for acting on those opinions is past—and that your freedom of expression must not eliminate Mr. Arbuthnot's. If the play was not so abhorrent to you as to make you leave the company before we lifted ship, then it should not be so abhorrent as to induce you to comment now."

"I see," she said bitterly. "So by joining the company, I committed myself to expressing whatever opinions our scripts present."

"Quite so." Really, the poor child was learning in a very rude fashion that the real world was not like college. Though I'm certain I did her an injustice—Lacey was usually so very careful about currying favor, that she must have felt sure of support that had not materialized. I glanced at Marnie out of the corner of my eye, but she was only looking interested in the exchange, not partisan.

It was quite unlike me to take so hard a line with a

child—but I had lost patience with the spoiled brat that had begun to emerge as soon as she had set foot upon the deck of this ship. She had thought, no doubt, that once in space, we could not replace her and were committed to suffering her whims. I wondered if Barry had a budget for tickets home.

"It really is quite unprofessional," he said quietly. "But Ms. Lark is not the only one to react strongly to Brinker's words; Mr. Malfeasance is instantly suspicious, and demands to know why Brinker has brought them to an empty village."

That easily and that smoothly, he had moved us away from the quarrel and back to the rehearsal. I subsided, feeling ashamed.

"Brinker replies that he has brought them here to give them an abundance of shelter," Barry explained, "but Mr. Malfeasance demands to know the ulterior motive. Brinker reveals that he has recorded the personalities of his dearest friends, dead now for centuries, but able to come alive again if transferred into the minds of sentient creatures with sufficient brain capacity. Mr. Malfeasance is of course shocked, and commands his troops to turn away and return to the ship—but Brinker calls out a command, and gun turrets open in the rocks about them, covering the whole group."

"Constrained against their will," Lacey said bitterly.

"Quite so." Barry let it breeze by him.

"Otto Hand to the rescue, of course," Ogden rumbled.

"Of course." Barry looked up at the sound of a footstep and saw Larry coming into the room with the correct script loosely in hand. Barry rose. "Let's just try that much, shall we?" The subtext was: *I've stalled long enough.* He walked over to the side of the lounge, where the keyboard sat in remembrance of song-filled nights and the intoxicating atmosphere of bygone days, when our ship had been a luxury cruiser, and the lounge's main purpose had been that of helping affluent individuals while away the ennui of enforced idleness and confinement during the weeks between stars. I had shipped as an entertainer on such a vessel during my salad days and could attest to the intoxicating atmosphere—indeed, stepping in the door and drawing breath had almost been enough to make one heady. There had been nights when it had been all I could do to remain sober long enough to perform my act.

No longer. The dance floor by the keyboard was small, but large enough to represent the inadequate staging space we would probably have to deal with in a colonial theater—if we found any theaters at all.

"Are we supposed to block this play on *that*?" Marnie demanded. "It's scarcely large enough for a tête à tête!"

She exaggerated—it was easily large enough for six singing waiters, side by side.

"Future rehearsals will take place in the ballroom," Barry said, "but I thought that for these few, we would do better with easy chairs."

"I've had a look at the ballroom." Winston frowned. "I'd scarcely call it capacious."

"Alas, no. Merlo and Ramou are cobbling together a rehearsal space in the cargo hold, which will be adequate for an extravaganza—but until it's ready, the ballroom will have to suffice. Even at that, we may have to condense our action to its size—or expand it to the playing space in the hold. I'm afraid we will have to be very flexible, since our playing spaces are apt to vary considerably. Now, you'll come filing on from stage left, along the upper platforms, then down the stage-right steps, and you will see the city through a sort of archway under a natural bridge."

"*Under?*" Ogden frowned. "How are we to come walking in on platforms that have no supports under . . . Oh. The light rails will project the scene in front of the wall."

The dear old chap had already spent ten years as a professional before light rails and holographic staging came in;

he was still accustomed to thinking in terms of scenery as coming from video projectors and actual sculpted units.

"Quite so. Now, Mr. Publican, if you will lead the party in? And the rest of you line up behind him in the usual straggling formation, or lack thereof . . . Good. Very well, enter, please."

Charles Publican led them in, capering in a flex-kneed step that managed to convey a comic alien who was absurdly pompous. Really, the chap's ability amazed me; he must have toiled long in the groves of academe, for me not to have encountered him in the profession. Winston, Lacey, Susanne, Larry, and all the rest followed him, with myself between Marty and Ogden, who was bringing up the rear on his floater. We curved around down to the edge of the dance floor, Charles chattering,

> "Come, my city will delight you!
> Nothing there would ever fright you;
> Many chambers there will house you!
> Lilting music will arouse you!
> All will seem
> A splendid dream!"

"And nothing will be what it seems," Otto Hand muttered.

"There she stands!" Brinker stopped, bent-kneed, leaning back against the direction he was pointing—upstage right. "Towers of light, that dazzle sight! Spires of hue, inspiring you!"

I half expected to see the city glow into existence right there.

"Splendid!" Marnie exclaimed.

"Fantastic!" Marty echoed.

"Beautiful!" Lacey breathed.

"Majestic!" Ogden rumbled.

"It is our humble abode," Brinker said modestly.

" 'Our'?" Winston peered at it, frowning. "I see no other beings moving among those towers ..." He turned to Barry. "What does this man have for eyes—binoculars? If the city's far enough distant to be seen as a whole, how could he possibly make out individuals?"

"A salient point." Barry punched a note on his noteboard. "Presumably it's the lack of traffic he's noticing, or the movements of large masses of aliens. I'll send a list of these discrepancies to Cant and Arbuthnot."

"But we can't get an answer before we open," Lacey protested. "Not if radio waves can't even go as fast as we can."

"Quite so; it will have to go by courier mail, as all interstellar communications do, and we certainly won't hear back until we've arrived at Falstaff, if then."

"So we go with the line as written?" Winston sighed.

"I'm afraid so. To do else would be to violate the playwright's confidence. But be certain your delivery is as if the line had been rewritten to include those evidences of life, old fellow."

" 'Is as,' rather than 'as is,' " Winston sighed. "Very well, Barry. We'll do wonders with the subtext." He turned back to Brinker and repeated, "I see no other beings moving among those towers. Where are the millions of denizens such a city might house?"

"Fewer dwell here than when the last of those towers was built," Brinker admitted.

"Oh?" Winston elevated the famous arched eyebrow. "Why?"

"Country living became very popular," Brinker noted.

"Understandably. What about those who preferred the amenities of the city?"

"They delighted in the ambience," Brinker said evasively. "Now, let us go to find your dwellings!"

"Everyone may start moving forward," Barry instructed,

"but Winston will hold out his arm, and Marnie will come up against it as if it were a wall. Everyone else . . ."

"Will slam into each other like a train stopping abruptly," Marnie finished for him. "Yes, Barry, we know the bit. Feed us the line, Brinker."

Barry frowned at her insolence, but didn't protest. I nearly did, then withheld comment. But really, we had so little time to rehearse a full bill that we could not afford to waste time in personal acrimony.

"Hold!" Winston cried, throwing out an arm. Marnie stepped up against it and snapped her head and arms as if running into a low wall. Larry slammed into her, and Lacey into him, and Susanne into Lacey . . .

Lacey yowled. "You clumsy elephant, get off my foot!"

"Oh, I'm sorry!" Susanne backed up hastily—just in time for Larry to slam into her, knocking her against Lacey again.

"I said get off!" Lacey shoved back, very hard. Susanne jolted rearward, and Larry yelped as a spiked heel drove into his toe. He yanked his foot up to cradle in his hand, just in time for Ogden to yell, "Look out!" and slam into him—floaters have difficulty with abrupt stops. So did Larry—he went flying into Susanne again, who lurched up against Lacey, who unfortunately saw her coming and pushed back before she was even hit.

"Ouch!" Susanne cried. "Look, I said I was sorry! It's not the easiest thing in the world to stop when—"

"I wouldn't expect you to be able to stop at all, dear," Lacey said sweetly.

Susanne's eyes narrowed. "Spoken as one who knows, *darling*. Or can't you even get started?"

As insults went, these were from the bargain basement, and surely neither of the young ladies would have stooped to answering such crudities under ordinary circumstances— but these circumstances were scarcely ordinary, and Lacey shot back, "When the spirit moves me, dearie, not the land-lord."

"Oh, is that why you live in hotels?"

Lacey laughed, but it was strained. "Darling, you're so open about your background! The Plaza is scarcely a mere hotel!"

"What does the Plaza have to do with you?" And before Lacey could answer, "Oh, you mean *near* Central Park! I thought you lived *in* it!"

"Ladies . . ." Barry murmured, but Lacey overrode him.

"Of course not, dear, but didn't I see you there—with the baboons?"

"Oh, is that who you were walking with! I thought they were your boyfriends!"

Lacey forced a superior smile, looking down her nose at Susanne. "Perhaps a person of your class has boyfriends, darling, but in my milieu, one is only seen with gentle-men."

Susanne smiled, amused. "Anyone seen with you, sweet-heart, could scarcely be a gentleman."

"Indeed? I distinctly saw your last suitor, swinging by his tail."

"Ladies," Barry said, a little more loudly, "if we could return to—"

"Of course," Lacey said, "there's the matter of sensitiv-ity, darling—at least enough to tell the difference between the floor and my foot."

"Well, now that you mention it, dearie, they *are* equally flat."

"I wear flats because I don't feel small, love," Lacey purred. "Is that why you wear spike heels to rehearsal?"

"No, it's closer to the reason why you wear leotard and tights when there's no dancing. Of course, dear heart, there isn't that much to watch when you do."

"Quality over quantity, darling," Lacey said, with more

than a bit of an edge this time. "Don't you ever feel top-heavy?"

Susanne smiled, secure on her home territory. "Not in the slightest—it's worth developing good posture. But I must admit that you're a credit to your plastic surgeon, dear."

"Really? Wasn't it you I saw on that last silicone commercial? You know, the one with the—"

"Girls!" Marnie's voice was the smallest of firecrackers, but Lacey and Susanne spun around toward her, wide-eyed. The leading lady advanced like a cheetah, purring, "I'm delighted to learn that you both have a minimal talent for improvisation after all—but you really must restrict it to the stage."

The subtext was, of course, that only the leading lady was entitled to throw tantrums during rehearsals. Lacey's face flamed red, but she swallowed thickly and said, "Of course, Ms. Lulala. Please pardon the lapse."

"Yes," Susanne said in a strange, absentminded tone. Her face was its normal tint and wore a slight frown. "I'm sorry."

"Of course," Marnie said, with the tone of an indulgent empress—but she cast a quick frown at Susanne.

The soubrette broke into a sudden, sheepish smile, gave an apologetic shrug, and turned back to her place in line. "Don't shove quite so hard this time, Larry."

"We'll bypass the pileup for the moment—" Barry sighed, "—and move along to the question. Winston?"

"Hold! . . . No, we did that," Winston said hastily, then, "Step no farther, friends, until we know the truth of it! Brinker, say—what is the true reason no more of your kind dwell herein?"

Brinker sighed. "Because, honored visitor, there *are* no more of my kind."

Susanne began to talk in a whisper, turning from Lacey to Larry and back. "Oh! Isn't that horrible! Really, how could he have deceived us so?"

Marty was whispering, too. "He lied to us! Just like a human!"

"What could have happened to all his friends?"

"Use your imagination, darling," Lacey whispered sweetly, and not at all in character. Larry just stared at her blankly.

"If you will look closely at your scripts," Barry said, with iron politeness, "you will notice the comment, 'The characters discuss the matter in shocked and horrified tones'—known in the trade, my friends, as 'rhubarb.' Could you attempt a bit of improvisation, now when it is appropriate?"

Larry flushed, and so did Lacey, but she started hissing at Susanne, "Rhubarb-rhubarb-rhubarb-rhubarb!"

Larry took the cue from her and began reciting a whispered, "A-B-C-D goldfish? L-M-N-O goldfish!" to nobody in particular.

Heartened, Susanne began to whisper, too. "Such an idea! Deceiving poor simple tourists like us . . ."

"Speak for yourself dear," Lacey hissed back.

Marty was muttering to Ogden in shocked and incredulous tones, and the huge old actor was muttering back.

"Let it die," Barry said.

The whispers faded out quickly, leaving Ogden's voice alone saying, "You mean, 'just like an *alien*,' don't you?"

"No, 'just like a *human*,'" Marty answered. "Otto was assuming aliens were ethically superior."

"A fascinating insight into character," Barry said, "but interior monologues should remain so. Not that I begrudge Ogden his curiosity, or you the benefit of discussion with so expert and experienced a member of your profession, Mr. Kemp—but could you manage it on your own time?"

"Oh! Sure, Mr. Tallendar!" Marty turned back to Brinker. "So what happened to them all?"

Barry stabbed at the player, and melancholy strains of music began softly.

"They died," Brinker mourned. "They passed away, like summer hay."

"Bit of an odd simile," Ogden rumbled.

"Like blades of hay before the scythe," Brinker explained. "Their lives were gay . . ."

Winston dropped character, frowning at Barry. "Odd choice of adjective."

"Perhaps not, in context," Ogden mused. Winston turned to him, puzzled, but Brinker was saying, "Their deaths were blythe" to finish his lead-in, and the music began a sweeping progression with a syncopated beat. Brinker began to dance the old soft-shoe, chanting,

> "They lived a life of grace and ease,
>   They partied, dined, as each one pleased!
>   Their lives were gold-set, glittering jewels!
>   Unbridled license, reft of rules!
>   They lived in pleasure, free from cares—
>   But when they died, they left no heirs!"

I was astounded; I hadn't known Publican had it in him. Really, the man was quite startling. How could it have taken him so long to land his first professional role?

Perhaps he had needed to wait until his chronological age matched those of the parts that fit his gift. Physically, he was limited to character roles, of course—plump, round-faced, and balding, he was the perfect image of a fatherly wood-carver or a country general-store keeper, but he would never have been suited to juveniles or romantic leads.

He finished as the music did, with a flourish. Susanne waited a beat, then cried, "Oh, the poor people! Are there none of them left, then?"

"I alone am returned to tell the tale," Brinker pontificated.

"What tragedy is that?" Marnie demanded. "They lived lives of joy and leisure, the sort that everyone dreams of, unfettered by the demands of squalling infants or scurrying brats! What point is there in pitying them? Do you honestly think they could possibly care about our pity? No, their ghosts are laughing themselves silly!"

"But their race is dead!" Susanne protested.

"Everything must die sooner or later, child," Marnie said, with saccharine sarcasm, "so that doesn't matter. What *does*, is how good a time they had while they were alive."

"A point," Winston said. "Therefore, if this race wished to commit racial suicide, who are we to quibble? But that does raise a point, Brinker."

"I could think of several," the alien replied with a bland smile.

"And already have, I don't doubt," the captain rumbled.

"Nor I. But the most pertinent one at the moment is: why have you brought us here?"

"Why, so that you could find shelter. There is an abundance of it here."

"I should think so, in an abandoned city," Winston said.

"It is very kind of you and all that, Mr. Brinker," Marnie added, "but I am nasty enough to suspect an ulterior motive."

"It takes one to know one," Larry muttered.

Marnie turned slowly, seeming to swell with outrage, and everyone braced for the blast.

8

Barry, though, tried to avert it. "Really quite an impertinent remark, Mr. Rash! I'll thank you to keep your weakened witticisms to yourself in the future. Now, Marnie, if we could take it from 'I should think so, in an abandoned city'?"

But he was Canute forbidding the tide to roll in, and everyone knew it. Marnie continued to swell, and Larry gave her his nastiest smile, and we all waited with bated breath.

Marnie began quite softly, turning a stony gaze on Larry and hissing, "Children should be seen and not heard, Mr. Rash."

Larry gave his script an elaborate glance, then looked up with a vacuous smile. "Sorry. I thought it said 'rhubarb' again."

"When there isn't the slightest sign of a stage direction at this point in the script?" Marnie's lips curled in cruel anticipation. "Can't you even find the correct page, boy?"

It was the "boy" that did it. Larry reddened and snapped back, "I may be getting ahead of the script, Ms. Lulala, but at least I'm not so advanced in age as to remember the whole text before it was written."

Marnie whirled and paced toward him, nostrils pinched, pale-faced. "You little curmudgeon, the only reason you can dwell on the benefits of your supposed youth is because you're still on the pacifier—or do you think those noxious things you smoke are *mature*? Who is changing your nappies these days?"

"Certainly not you," Larry retorted. "I fairly shudder at the thought."

"He doesn't mean it, Ms. Lulala," Lacey said hastily. "He's just feeling so —"

"If I might interrupt—" Barry began.

Marnie ignored him, turning her fury on Lacey Lark. "Stay out of this, young lady, or your poor little ego will be a mass of quivering jelly spread out for an audience of thousands to trample underfoot!"

Lacey stared, shocked and affronted, but Marnie scarcely noticed her as she thrust her face within an inch of Larry's and snapped, "You haven't the slightest ghost of talent, young man, and I shudder to think how you went about getting passing grades in your college acting classes! A favor for a favor, was it?"

"I would certainly never seek favors that are past history," Larry answered.

"Now really," Barry cried, "this is getting out of hand—"

But Lacey had recovered and snapped back at Marnie, "Just because you could teach Medieval Theater History from personal experience, Ms. Lulala, is no reason to vent your spleen on those of us who are still vital and fresh!"

"Entirely *too* fresh," Ogden rumbled. "Young lady, you should speak with some respect to your betters!"

"I will, Mr. Wellesley—when I find one."

Marnie turned on Ogden. "I can fight my own battles, thank you, Ogden! Really, when you can't even support your own weight, let alone pull it, you certainly shouldn't be taking sides in a quarrel!"

"The play—" Barry tried, but Ogden's face darkened. "Pull my own weight? Child, you forget your place!"

"Don't judge me by your own condition," Marnie snapped. "*My* place isn't so long past as to be forgotten."

Ogden turned beet red and drew breath for a blast, but Susanne gasped, "Mr. Wellesley! Your blood pressure!"

"Don't worry, my dear," Marnie said. "He hasn't any."

Susanne stared at her, shocked in her own turn, and Barry took advantage of the lull to storm, "Now this is really the outside of too much! I demand that you all—"

But Susanne had recovered from her shock, and her whole form seemed to solidify somehow. Her fists clenched, and her eyes narrowed.

Alarmed, Ramou stepped up behind her.

It was time, and past, that I took a hand. "Marnie, I realize you're rather young to have acquired a true sense of professionalism, but might I ask that you set the neophytes an example by returning to the script?"

She turned on me, ignoring the two covert compliments and subtle rebuke of Larry and Lacey. "When I need your advice, Horace Burbage, I shall know how to ask for it! Don't patronize me by purveying so blatant a lie as to tell me I'm young!"

"You are, to me," I returned. "You may be a mature leading lady now, Ms. Lulala, but I'm afraid I shall never shake my initial impression of you as the razor-edged child who played the ingenue to my judge in *Ten Little Indians.*"

Her lip curled. "A considerable amount of time has passed since then, Horace."

I began to feel my own temper rising. "But you have changed so little, my dear! You are still so frantically concerned with superficial sophistication, without having gained an ounce of the genuine article!" Really, the woman could have angered a koala.

"Superficial!" she cried, stung, and I noticed that Lacey Lark was listening with unusual interest. "Why, you declassé old *ci-devant*! If you weren't so dowdy and common in your own tastes, you might be able to appreciate true class when you see it!"

"I can," I said crisply, "and I don't."

"Hear now, Marnie," Ogden put in, gliding toward her on his floater. "Horace is the soul of courtesy! You've no call—"

"I have no call for you, Ogden Wellesley!" Marnie turned on him with unwonted savagery—but succor appeared from a most unexpected quarter.

Charlie Publican stepped between them and said, "Ms. Lulala, if you really are so discontented with the script, you should say so, rather than taking it out on your fellow actors."

Marnie jerked to a halt, eyes wide, at a total loss for a moment—and that was all Publican needed. "Surely a grande dame of your eminence is above the petty slights and clumsy insinuations of we mere beginners."

"Speak for yourself," Larry began, but a hard hand clamped on his shoulder from behind—Ramou, sensing a possible resolution. Larry tried to turn, winced, saw who it was out of the corner of his eye, and subsided.

Marnie tossed her head, a gleam of satisfaction in her eye. "Beginners at acting, Mr. Publican—or insulting?"

"Yes," Charles said. "Quite so."

Marnie took a step closer to him, head tilted to the side, the gleam in her eye changing quality. "You intrigue me, Mr. Publican. I think you have more experience than you claim."

"In acting? No, surely only as an amateur," Publican protested.

"No," Marnie said, "in insulting."

Publican answered with a slow smile. "Well, I've never been paid for it."

"Noooo," Marnie mused. "You were paid for concocting mixed drinks, weren't you? But surely, in that capacity, you became accustomed to sustaining insults—without responding."

"Madam!" Publican protested. "You wound me! Surely I mixed better cocktails than *that*!"

Marnie laughed and touched him lightly on the arm. "Well, then we shall return to rehearsal, as you said. Surely I would not wish to deny you the opportunity to shine in so focal a role at last. But perhaps over lunch, we might discuss the matter further?"

"I would be honored," Publican said gravely and without the slightest sign of being flustered, as you might have expected of a man of so humble a rank as he professed, being approached by so famous an actress—and one who was still damned attractive and extremely alluring, though I would have wished to deny it if I could have.

"You shall have the opportunity sooner than that." Barry sighed, closing his book with every evidence of relief. "Let us retire to refresh ourselves, friends, and we will attempt to begin anew in the afternoon. Good morning to you all."

It was a dismissal and a rebuke, so the younger folk murmured in hushed tones as they turned away. Marnie, however, shed the implied criticism with a toss of her head and turned away to take the arm Charlie offered her.

"Publican?" Ogden tugged at my sleeve, whispering up at me. "Marnie and *Publican*?"

"Don't make more of it than it appears," I admonished, though I was quite sure Marnie would. "Any of us is eager for the homage of a true fan."

"Well, there's something in that," Ogden admitted, "though she certainly has the look of desiring something more than praise."

"At her age, Ogden, I suspect homage is the greater pleasure." Though I did not say so to Barry; instead, as the rest filed out and he began to pack up his papers, I said, "I think we may have made a very fortunate choice in the Publican chap."

"Yes," Barry said. "He bids fair to prove a major asset to the company. Amazingly talented fellow—though perhaps not in acting."

"I wouldn't be sure." I reflected that any grown man

who knew Marnie for what she was and could still wish to dine with her, must have been either completely dazzled by glamour—or excellently skilled in dissembling. In Publican's case, perhaps a bit of both—but I suspected it was far more the latter than the former.

Barry gazed after Marnie and Publican as they retreated through the door, sighing, *"Honi soit qui mal y pense."*

"It doesn't bear thinking about," I assured him.

I didn't want to seem too obvious, but nobody said, "Come on, Ramou, let's get lunch"—not even Marty. He was trying to have a last few earnest words with Ogden, but Susanne was hovering over the old actor like a mother hen, scarcely giving Marty room to get a word in edgewise. Lacey was hurrying out the door beside Larry, the two of them commiserating in harsh, angry undertones—so I sighed, gave up, and turned away to cleaning up my morning buffet. It only took a few minutes, by the end of which time Ogden seemed to have managed to convince Susanne that he was well, calmed down, and not about to collapse from emotional upset.

"But really," he said to her, "the arrogance and rudeness of these young people is quite appalling!"

Marty and Susanne nodded earnestly, apparently not including themselves with "these young people."

"I swear I shall have to study Zen Buddhism," Ogden huffed, "to be able to maintain my equanimity in dealing with them!"

"That really might be a good idea," Susanne said slowly. "I mean, not the religion itself, of course, but its philosophy and meditation techniques could be just what you need to keep your blood pressure normal."

Ogden flashed her a quick smile. "I assure you I learned them in my youth, Susanne, and I've found them to be of monolithic reassurance at various rocky times during my career. Yes, perhaps it is time to schedule a daily session of *za-zen* again." His lips quirked in a sardonic smile. "Not much else I can do, is there? But I do thank you for all your care." He laid a gnarled old hand over her smooth one. "You're an immense comfort to an old codger—but you mustn't waste all your time looking after others. Have a care for yourself—and a better afternoon than this morning."

She smiled. "Thanks, Mr. Wellesley." She glanced at Marty, finally admitting to herself that the old man was actually looking forward to a conversation with somebody else, then turned away toward the door.

I came up behind her. "You really ready for lunch so soon?"

She looked up, startled, then flashed me a quick smile. "No, and there must be something else to do. Think we can find a gym aboard this tub?"

"Probably," I said slowly, "but I wouldn't want to bet on the equipment being safe, after all these years."

"Well then, we'll just have to go check it out, won't we?" she said, and tossed her head toward the corridor outside. I grinned and followed.

Behind us, Ogden was saying to Marty, "Yes, Harlequin is a sound model for Otto Hand, Mr. Kemp, but I trust you do not restrict his psychological development to a character mask."

"Oh, no! Not at all!" Marty said hastily. "It's just the first point of departure that came to mind when I read the script. I'm going to broaden it out as we go along through rehearsal, of course, and deepen it."

"Ah, I'm glad to see you've included both . . ."

I caught up to Susanne. "He's in good hands."

"Which 'he'?" She smiled. "Good to see someone else among 'these young people' has the common sense to realize what a treasure trove he is."

"Of knowledge?" I asked. "I thought he was just a nice old guy."

"Oh, he is that! But he's wise, too, with the garnered wisdom, the residue, of more triumphs and tragedies than I can really imagine. And he's a positive well of knowledge about acting. A very deep well."

"Eighty years deep." For a second, I tried to imagine having lived that long. When Ogden was ten—that was enough to daze me by itself, the notion of that huge mound of bone and blubber being a little boy! When he was, though, the Falstaff colony was still very raw and new, the Wolmar lost colony had just been rediscovered, the last two sovereign nations, the Ukraine and Switzerland, had finally succumbed to pressure and joined the Dominion of Terra, like it or not, and theatrical designers were still using holograms without light rails, according to Merlo—in spite of the severe limits the sets put on the actors' movements that way; he says it was like performing in a straightjacket. I asked him how he knew, and he just got red in the face and muttered something about historical displays in a museum and impertinent apprentices. I was just pulling his chain, really—I couldn't imagine actually having *lived* through all of that!

But Ogden had.

It made my brain reel, and a kaleidoscope of the professional history Merlo had been teaching me reeled through my brain—the Embrasionists, Woodenists, the 3DT explosion, the split between musical theater and "legitimate" theater, the Skeinists, the Dissonists, the Contortionists—and through it all, the steady stream of commercial theater with its well-made plays filled with rich, deep characters and stinging caricatures, and musical plays that continually sought and sometimes achieved the ideal synthesis of music, drama, and poetry.

At least, so says Merlo.

And so would Ogden say, too, I was sure, if I ever had the time to get him started—and wait an hour or two till he ran down. Which I did have this afternoon, technically—

except that I did have to spend that afternoon technically; if it was afternoon and we weren't rehearsing the Scottish play, Merlo would expect me to show up in the cargo hold and get to work turning it into that rehearsal space Barry had mentioned. Which meant that if I was going to get any time in with Susanne, I was going to have to go for it now. Too bad, Ogden. I'll catch you another time.

In the meantime, I had already caught Susanne, and I was enjoying it to the fullest. Mind you, I didn't really care what she was saying as long as she was saying it to me— but it was pretty interesting. I was getting quite an education out of this job.

Was I really such a louse that I would have enjoyed listening to Lacey just as much? Sure. Or, well, almost. A patron in an art gallery can get a thrill off of admiring any number of paintings. Of course, some may give him more elevation of spirit than others, but all of them are worth looking at.

Didn't I care about them as women? Sure—what do you think I was looking at? Why do you think I was getting such a high off of talking with them? What you really mean is, didn't I care about them as people? Again—sure. It's just that I cared more about Susanne. I was beginning to realize that Lacey's company could pall very quickly, at least on me. I'd still care about her as a person, of course—as a human being, as a member of the company, as a worthwhile person in her own right—but all things considered, I'd rather spend my free time listening to Susanne. Not that I was really that picky, of course.

There's where I'm a cad, right? Not really dedicating myself to either one of my true loves.

But they weren't my true loves. They were friends and, being female friends, I enjoyed being with them in ways that I didn't enjoy being with men. That wasn't sex, it was just the side effect, the spillover. To get that kind of thrill, I didn't have to be anything more than a friend, or even maybe just an acquaintance. No law said I had to be, legal or moral. No law said I'd be damned if I was.

Maybe literally.

9

We were gathered in the semicircle of folding chairs in front of our brand-new makeshift stage in the cargo hold, undergoing the ritual of notes. As Barry gave each of us comments, we would punch them into our noteboards, so that we would have them to review before rehearsal on the next day.

"Now, Ogden," Barry said, "coming in to swing a spear in the final battle is all well and good, but I must ask you to stay in your floater until we've landed on New Venus and are certain of your health. I'd really rather not have to stop rehearsal again to remind you."

"Oh, very well," Ogden grumbled, "though I hate to slow everyone else down so. It's not as if I were a complete invalid, you know."

Everyone maintained a tactful silence on that point as he dutifully jotted it down. Ogden was the only one of us who persisted in the use of paper and stylus. No one complained, of course—it was a harmless affectation. Larry's was not—he was the only one who smoked, thank heaven, and his reward was a place of honor next to the smoking lamp that devoured his uncombusted carbon-and-carcinogen mixture as fast as he produced it. I suspect the lad thought it made him appear more sophisticated; heaven knows he needed something along that line, but tobacco wasn't it. He only looked like the callow youth he was, flirting with a forbidden vice. He needed to *be* sophisticated, not merely to appear so—but that could come only with time, and a deal of absorption of knowledge, which I fear he was too lazy to undertake.

Barry keyed his noteboard to save and file, then turned it off as he tucked it under his arm. "Now, friends. We will start rehearsal at a later hour than usual tomorrow—Captain McLeod assures me that we will reach the breakout point sometime in the morning."

A murmur of excitement went through the lounge. We had only been three weeks in H-space, but everyone was already seized with cabin fever—or an excess of companionship. We were all becoming socially claustrophobic after too long in one another's company, even those of us who were seasoned troupers. It takes practice, you see, to endure such intimate contact with so many for so long. It was amazing that we had had so few squabbles.

And, of course, the younger folks, who had toured before only briefly or not at all, were quite unaccustomed to so long a stint of confinement. I could scarcely blame them— even on the road, we were not accustomed to more than a day on the bus or train or rocket, and usually only a few hours. Of course, a monorail travels at hundreds of kilometers per hour, and Terrestrial cities large enough to support a theater-going population are never more than a few hours' apart by rocket, so even those of us who counted ourselves seasoned were quite unused to being together in so small a space for weeks at a time. Barry's stringent rehearsal schedule had helped quite a bit, but I couldn't resist wondering what would happen when all five plays we were working on were polished and done.

I believe that was when I began to realize that Barry would never be done having us rehearse.

"So," Barry finished, "upon the morrow, please return to your cabins immediately after breakfast. Captain McLeod will tell you when to web yourselves in, and Ramou will be around for the safety check."

Larry muttered something about Ramou's being totally unnecessary, but he had an apprehensive look as he said it. Ramou merely kept his gaze fixed on Barry; we all knew that Larry had been his largest problem during takeoff, what with refusing to web in and raiding the autobar.

"But the productions are still far from ready for an audience," Ogden protested, "the Scottish play least of all."

"Peace, old friend." Barry smiled. "Do remember that we still have five days in normal space—and the Scottish play is the only one still in need of major work. The other five are rough, but could certainly withstand the scrutiny of a provincial audience if they had to."

"Speak for yourself, Barry," Marnie said sharply. "I, for one, would shudder at the thought of having to appear in *Vagrants* without further rehearsal."

"As would I," Barry assured her. "But the show must go on—and if it had to, it could. Now I'll leave you all to your evening's relaxation, and we will begin with *Ramble* an hour after breakout."

I wondered why he planned to wait so long, and was rather apprehensive as a result.

The company rose with a deal more chattering than usual, and the move toward the beverage dispensers began.

Ramou appeared at my elbow, looking rather nervous. "Should I turn 'em off before they can get totally plotzed, Horace?"

"It would be wise," I agreed, *sotto voce*. "I haven't experienced breakout myself, but I doubt that it goes well with a hangover."

Ramou nodded, turning grim. "I'll tell 'em the bar is closed after the third round."

"Oh, nothing so drastic, dear fellow!" I shuddered at the thought of the mutiny that would ensue. "Simply visit them with a tumbler full of Merlo's hangover cure when you come to check their webbing in the morning."

Ramou shuddered. "I don't much like the thought of

what they're gonna say when they have to take another glass of that stuff, Horace. I can hold their arms, but who's gonna keep their mouths open while I pour it down?"

"A point," I agreed. "Perhaps a strategic and localized power outage might be the wiser course."

Ramou nodded, looking relieved. "I'll talk to the computer about it." He glided away.

One less problem for me to worry about. I realized that I was coming to depend on Ramou more and more, and felt the old habit of caution raise its wary head within me. I had learned what happens when one human being comes to depend excessively on another, and that other suddenly ceases to be dependable—or is simply gone. I reminded myself sternly that I mustn't trust the lad to the point of exploitation.

On the other hand, I also needed to trust him enough so that he would still feel vital to the welfare of the company as a whole. Not difficult—he already was.

The lads and lassies were becoming quite jubilant. Emotionally, they were thinking of the voyage as nearly over—but four days could scarcely be described as "nearly," especially when they included a technical rehearsal. Ah well, time enough for them to face facts tomorrow.

Time enough for me, too. I let the long-withheld smile wrinkle my face and made my way toward the nearest dispenser.

"Web in, Ensign Lazarian," McLeod said. I did, surprised that he seemed so calm. Okay, so a landing was routine for him—but it had been six years at least, and he'd been savoring his liquid assets for most of that time. Roaring drunk, in fact. Wouldn't he be feeling the teensiest bit nervous about his first landing in so long?

If he was, he didn't show it. "Courses of navigation beacons, Number One?"

"Closing at fifty thousand kilometers, Captain." Merlo

was gazing intently at the screen of his G-field-disturbance sensor. "They're at the Lagrange points in the satellite chain . . ." He stiffened. "Bogie astern! Eight o'clock!"

"Bogie?" McLeod frowned and glanced at the screen. "Approaching, too. That's one fast puppy, whatever it is. Try for visual."

"Visual, aye." The image on the main screen blinked a few times, stars wheeling dizzily across velvet, then stabilized with a brighter star in its center. "There she is, Captain."

"Magnify," McLeod snapped, eyes glued to the screen.

Merlo touched patches, and the bright star grew brighter as other stars swam off the edges of the screen. Finally, the zooming halted. "Magnification limit, Captain."

"It's enough." McLeod glared at the screen. "It's a discernible silhouette." He raised his voice. "Computer! Rotate it to profile!"

The image on the screen turned so that it was sideways to us—a long, lean shape, like a barracuda.

"Streamlined to minimize solar wind resistance at near-light velocities," McLeod growled, "and atmosphere, too, of course. That baby is built to travel *fast!*"

Behind him, Barry asked, "A courier ship?"

McLeod nodded. "For very important mail. Probably diplomatic."

"It will bear a message from Elector Rudders to the government of New Venus," Barry said, "advising them to turn us away as a disrupting influence. Captain, we *must* land before they do!"

But McLeod shook his head. "Not a chance, Mr. Tallendar. If that courier can gain on us astern, we can't possibly land before he overhauls us. On the other hand, he won't beat us in by all that much—certainly not enough to give him time to chase through the amount of red tape it'd take to get them to deny us permission to land."

"Perhaps, but there is no point in landing if we cannot perform!"

McLeod shrugged. "So we dawdle and give them time to tell us no. That way, if they do let us land, they'll be so curious they'll want to see you perform something. This is where you find out whether or not you were right about the colonists being really hungry for live theater, Director."

"Yes, I suppose it is," Barry sighed. "Very well, Captain. How do we 'dawdle' in space?"

"Throttle down, Number One," McLeod said, and Merlo lowered a slider. "That'll let us coast in past the L-point beacons." McLeod peered at the sensor screen. "Should time out nicely; we'll get a visual look at them as we slide by. Courier will land a couple hours ahead of us, if he maintains his pace."

"Why do I feel that we've just had the trip for nothing?" Horace wondered.

"Not nothing, old boy," Barry said. "Haldane's Star is only a little further in this direction."

"Yes, about fifty light-years," Horace sighed. "Well, I suppose our lessons in peaceful coexistence might as well be a crash course."

"Approaching craft, identify yourself," the speaker said.

I reached for the communicator, but Merlo laid a hand over mine. "He's talking to the other guy."

Looking up, I saw a silver dart flash across the visual screen. "He really is traveling!"

"IDE courier *Mercury* to New Venus ground control," a raspy voice said. "Permission to land."

"Right, *Mercury*," ground control said instantly. "Touch down in the northwest quadrant, Target Fourteen."

"Northwest quadrant it is," the raspy voice confirmed.

"And we all know what message that courier is carrying," Merlo growled.

"Oh, I'm sure there will be several," Barry murmured. "After all, the LORDS party itself is not officially part of the government, and cannot commandeer a courier. But Elector Rudders could, of course, place a personal message in with official dispatches."

"Entirely too personal," Horace agreed.

"Whatever they're carrying, they've got five hours at least on us." McLeod glared at the viewscreen, where the courier was already only a brighter disk of light that seemed to be just barely moving toward the dimmer but larger disk that was New Venus. "How much trouble can they make for you in that amount of time, Mr. Tallendar?"

"Officially, none, Captain," Barry answered; neither of them seemed to be getting tired of the formality. "Unofficially, of course, they can . . . shall we say, create an atmosphere of hostility? We may find that we need a permit to perform."

"On New Venus? You *bet* you'll need a permit! The whole planet's one big company town, Mr. Director! You damn near need a permit to *breathe*!"

I thought he was joking. Turned out he wasn't; there was no free oxygen on New Venus. They had to manufacture it, and everybody was allotted just so much per week. Management got more than labor, of course; rank hath its privileges. I found out that the managers insisted on having it written into their contracts.

"Beacon ahead," Merlo noted.

I looked up at the screen just in time to see a bright button swell to the size of a dinner plate. It slid smoothly toward the side of the screen, so quickly that I almost wasn't sure I'd seen what I thought I'd seen.

"Merlo," I said, "that isn't a signpost sticking out from it, is it?"

"Sure is," Merlo grated. "Read it."

I punched for higher magnification, maneuvering the direction buttons to keep the beacon satellite centered in the screen. The printed words on the sign grew larger and larger, until I could read:

"NO SMOKING."

In five languages.

I stared. "What in the name . . . ?"

Just then, a klaxon blared from the speaker, and blinking red letters stamped themselves across the screen: "Absolutely *no smoking*! Of any kind!"

The klaxon stopped, and a stern voice replaced it. "Welcome to New Venus. For your protection, absolutely *no smoking* is permitted. This ban applies to private rooms, bathrooms, and hallways, as well as public places. All chambers of any sort are equipped with smoke detectors. Tampering with smoke detectors is a crime punishable by five to ten years imprisonment. Smoking is a capital crime, punishable by death."

The blinking letters changed to Russian, and the voice stated, *"Ne kooreetye!"* and went on to what I assumed was the same message.

I stared. "They are *serious*!" I turned to Merlo. "What's the matter—was the planet colonized by health nuts?"

"No," Merlo answered. "A petroleum company."

I squeezed my eyes shut, gave my head a shake, and opened them again, but the red Cyrillic letters were still there. "Why would a petroleum company colonize a whole planet?"

It was Merlo's turn to stare. "What did they teach you in that college—basket weaving?"

"Electronics," I snapped. "Of course they didn't teach me history—I wasn't in the humanities."

"And they call that an education," Merlo said, with the fine disgust of the self-taught technician. "But I shouldn't criticize—this was high school stuff. Didn't you learn about the history of colonization between bells?"

"Well, sure, about the brave pioneers facing the void for the sake of freedom. They told us New Venus was colonized by people dedicated to preserving free-market economics."

"Some truth to that," Merlo said with a cynical smile. "The Founders were out to make a profit."

I frowned. "I thought it was bold pioneers, looking for space to live and freedom from rules."

"Not on New Venus," Merlo said. "The whole atmosphere is helium, and you can't go out without a helmet and air bottles."

"Helium?" I stared. "Enough for a whole *atmosphere*? Where did that come from?"

"The Company put it there," Merlo explained. "It's to keep the gasoline from exploding."

"Gasoline? *What* gasoline?"

"The ocean of gasoline that the Company exports," Merlo explained. "Ninety percent of the planet's surface is covered with petroleum derivates."

I stared at the viewscreen. "No *wonder* they don't want anyone smoking!"

"Which, they claim, is why they have to maintain the tightest dictatorship any government ever managed," Merlo agreed. "Like the scarecrow in *The Wizard of Oz*, the only thing they're afraid of is a lighted match."

"We're trying to land, Number One!" McLeod snapped. "Ensign Lazarian, give me a channel to ground control."

I keyed the communicator.

"Liner *Cotton Blossom* to ground control," McLeod rapped. "Come in, ground control."

Out of the corner of my eye, I saw Barry cross his fingers.

"Ground control to liner *Cotton Blossom*," ground control answered. Barry heaved a sigh of relief and uncrossed his fingers.

Beside him, Horace nodded. "I was afraid of that, too, Barry. Apparently, though, the pilot of that courier ship does not know the contents of the documents he carries."

"I was afraid that he did," Barry admitted, "and might

have tried to prevent ground control from giving us permission to land."

He had a very suspicious nature. It made the hair on my neck stand on end. Not his paranoia—the fact that he was probably right. As one of my psychiatrists told me, a *little* bit of paranoia is a pro-survival factor. A lot of it can kill you, but I didn't have a lot—just enough to help me live longer.

Apparently, so did Barry.

"State your owner's name and business," ground control demanded.

"My owner is the Star Repertory Company," McLeod returned, "and their business is theater."

"A 3DT distributor?" ground control snapped. "You've wasted your water; we have an exclusive arrangement with the Lackland Features Syndicate."

I felt a stab of sympathy for the New Venusians. I'd seen the kind of epics Lackland stocked—all bland, mildly educational, and guaranteed harmless. Of course they were harmless—they scarcely had any content!

"Not 3DT," McLeod was saying. "Live theater. Real live actors, right there in your own auditorium."

Horace winced; "auditorium" was a dirty word.

"Live?" ground control blurted in disbelief.

"Live," McLeod confirmed. "We're carrying a dozen actors with costumes, lighting, and scenery."

"I never heard of such a thing!"

"You never saw anything like it, either," McLeod agreed. "And you won't, if you don't give us permission to land."

"I—I'll have to check with management . . ."

"Anything in the rules against it?" McLeod said with an edge to his voice.

"Well, no—but . . ."

"You'll never forgive yourself if you miss this chance," McLeod promised. "It's just like those shows on Broadway. In fact, half the actors have *been* on Broadway." He didn't

bother mentioning that they couldn't get jobs there anymore.

"Clearance granted!" ground control said quickly.
"Northwest quadrant, Target Fifteen."

I could fairly hear him drooling into the mike. I frowned;
I'd heard of dedicated theatergoers, but this didn't sound
like quite the right attitude.

Barry, however, was smiling. "It sounds as if we were
right, Horace. They're starved for theater."

"It does indeed," Horace agreed, but he was looking at
me. "You seem troubled, Ramou."

"Just wondering why that guy went into heat when the
captain mentioned Broadway," I said.

"Bright lights and glamour." Horace smiled with gentle
amusement. "See the Star Company, and you don't just see
a show—you participate in the experience of being on
Terra, in one of the greatest cities humanity has ever
known. Not since Nineveh."

I found out later that it was more a matter of "not since
Babylon." For these provincials, the word "Broadway" con-
jured up visions of luscious ladies with almost nothing on,
performing in decadent plays about passion and depravity.
Needless to say, they were doomed to disappointment.

Barry was nodding. "I rather like that, Horace. 'See the
Star Company, and share in the experience of Broadway!'
Yes, I'll have to remember that. It might do nicely on a
poster."

"Confirmed, ground control. Northwest quadrant, Target
Fifteen." But as I disconnected, McLeod looked as if he'd
just bitten a bad lemon.

Barry saw. "What's the matter, Captain?"

"He's got us right next to that courier ship," McLeod answered. "I can think of happier berths."

Horace said, by way of reassurance, "At least, this way,
we can keep on eye on him."

Which is why, as the ship grounded, I saw a man in a

gray *complet*, with matching gray narrow-brimmed hat, riding away in the landing taxi, toward the ground control tower.

"What's the matter, Ramou?" Merlo asked.

"That guy." I pointed at the screen. "I could swear he's the same one who was in the crowd, that night the reporters ambushed us. He was there when they jumped Marnie, too, and he was the one who was coming out on the scooter to deliver the restraining order as we were trying to take off!"

"The same one in all three places?" Merlo looked up at the screen, shaking his head. "Hard to believe. Besides, how could you see his face at this distance?"

"All right, so maybe he's triplets, and they all dress the same! But I saw him all three times, I tell you!"

"And we all saw him tumbling hat-over-scooter in our backwash, as we took off," McLeod agreed. "Not much we can do about it, though."

"Except keep an eye on him," I muttered under my breath.

"Not a favorable sign." Barry was watching the screen, too. "At the worst, I would say he was a bird of ill omen."

But Horace was watching me. "Don't be tempted to try any auguries, Ramou."

"I won't give in," I promised him, "but I can't help being tempted."

Merlo turned to me, eyes wide with alarm. "Hey, Ramou! Remember, no throwing the first punch!"

"Yeah," I said, "but I can be watching for it. Paranoids live longer, Merlo."

"Perhaps," Horace said, "but they haven't much pleasure in it."

Horace had hit the nail squarely on the head, of course. Which did I want—a short life and a merry one, or a long life looking over my shoulder and waiting for the ax to fall? I mulled it over as McLeod went through the postlanding check with Merlo, then leaned over to the intercom and announced, "We're down."

I could almost hear the massed cheer through the steel of the hull.

"They're going to want to get out and stretch their legs, Mr. Tallendar," McLeod advised. "Shall I tell them they can, or would you rather do the honors?" He gestured toward the microphone patch.

"I believe I would, Captain," Barry said slowly, "but let us observe the formalities—publicly. Ramou, if you would give me all stations?"

I pressed a patch.

Barry stepped up beside McLeod, bent over a little to make sure he was within the pickup pattern, and asked, "Permission to go ashore, sir?"

"Permission granted," McLeod said. "Four-hour leave, Director—I think we'd better rendezvous back here for dinner."

"An excellent notion. After all, we have no idea what hotel facilities are available. Everyone will return to the ship at 1800 hours. Everyone going ashore, meet at the aft air lock—you know, where we came in—in twenty minutes." He nodded to me to end the call, and I punched out. "Why so long, Mr. Tallendar?"

He looked up, amused. "Eager, are you? Well, I can't say that I'm any less, after three weeks closeted inside a hotel without windows, no matter how luxurious it is."

Merlo let out a short laugh before he clapped a hand over his mouth, and McLeod snorted. "Three weeks? Mr. Director, that's just a warm-up!"

"I'm well aware that we will have months in space on some of our longer expeditions, Captain," Barry sighed, "and I'm not looking forward to the effort of keeping this group of egomaniacs from killing one another. However, at the moment, I am looking forward even less to confronting the powers that be about permission to perform. Still, it will be good to feel fresh air on my face again . . ."

"Uh, Barry . . ." Merlo said.

Barry looked up in mild surprise. "Yes, Merlo?"

"The only fresh air here is helium," Merlo told him. "If you go outside a dome, you'll have to wear a breather."

Barry just stared at him, his face growing longer and longer.

"At least," Horace said, "there will be a bit more space about us."

"The official domes are pretty roomy, yes," McLeod agreed. "They even have transparent walls."

Barry smiled and squared his shoulders with a sigh. "Well, at least I shall rejoice in the illusion of room—and, I hope, in a kind reception."

"I hope so, too." McLeod held up a hand, showing no sign of getting out of his couch.

Barry started to turn away, then paused, looking back. "Aren't you coming with us, Captain?"

"No, not just yet. Someone has to mind the store—and I've seen New Venus. Too often. I might get out to stretch my legs now and then, when Merlo's here to stand watch— but right now, I think he's got a bit of cabin fever himself. In any case, you'll need him to play tour guide for the older folk. I suspect the younglings will want to go exploring on their own."

Barry looked up in alarm, and Horace said, "Won't they supply guides for us?"

"Not officially," McLeod said, "though I'm sure the young folk can find somebody willing—if *they're* willing to spend the money. That's after you all get through customs, of course. Have a good trip."

10

Since all the planets in the Terran Sphere of colonized space are members of the Interstellar Dominion Electorates, we didn't have to worry about passports—we were still in territory controlled by the same government. On the other hand, each planet is semiautonomous, so we didn't have to worry about being arrested for having left Terra against Elector Rudders' wishes—especially since his process server never did manage to get the hard copy to us.

But we did have to worry about customs. Transporting illegal goods is a crime on any planet, and customs searches are still very effective ways of holding down on that particular crime. Besides, the Company had a few items it didn't want brought in, either—such as books. Not all books, mind you—just certain ones. They had a list. Two lists, one bad, one good—and if it wasn't on either list, it was impounded while the censors thought it over. I know, because I tried to bring along a copy of *Torrid Flame Girls of Altair*, to read just in case the trip got boring. It was a recent release, so it wasn't. Released, I mean. The customs agent impounded it, and I never did see it again. Presumably, the censorship committee was still debating its literary merits. Of course, they all had to read it first. What can I say? Maybe they were slow readers.

Of course, there was the mean and nasty suspicion that maybe the agent never turned it over to the committee in the first place, just kept it for his own personal edification and moral improvement—but I wouldn't say a nasty thing like that, would I?

All of that was still ahead of me, though—about an hour ahead of me. Before we could worry about the agents, we had to get to their counters. They were way over there, halfway across a huge enclosed space with the girders showing up at the top of a very high ceiling; I think it was a converted rocket hangar. There was a vast expanse of beige plasticrete floor, roughened enough for good traction, with a few improvised booths selling refreshments to a half-dozen empty tables and hard chairs. There was a ticket counter way over there at the other end, past the tubular fences that herded people up to a gate that was empty at the moment. We were looking at it from the back, so I assumed it was for outgoing passengers. It had a duplicate over on our side of the huge echoing building, only this one we were seeing from the front. The gate was a scanner booth, adept at detecting secret weapons or any kind of contraband that could be hidden on a person and wasn't made out of flesh; presumably, it couldn't pick up pork sausages being smuggled in, if anybody had a mind to try it. Anything else, vegetable or mineral, it could pick out with no trouble. Apparently they had set it to ignore the cloth of our clothing, which opened up great possibilities for smuggling in contraband underwear.

On the other side of the scanner was the counter with the customs agent behind it, looking harried, weary, and rapidly turning sullen.

How we could all have been stacked up six deep when there were only a dozen of us, I'll never know. Thirteen, counting McLeod, but he wasn't along just then. The customs agent wasn't dragging his heels, either—he was just handing out a form, waiting while the person filled it out, then asking a couple of questions and waving him or her through the sensor door. Of course, he could have handed out the forms to all of us at the same time, or maybe even have had them waiting on a table—and he certainly didn't have to take a fifteen-minute break every fifteen minutes. At least, I assume that's why he had to go through that little door every so often, though I suppose his boss might have been there to cross-examine him about what the last three people had said. After the first half hour, we started getting impatient; after the second, we began to gripe, and Marnie tended to gripe very loudly. "Really, this is ridiculous!" she confided to the nearest hundred people—and there were only eleven in sight.

"Be patient, young lady," Ogden advised. "He wasn't even searching anybody's suitcase."

"Only because none of us *brought* a suitcase! After all, this was just supposed to be a short walk around town."

"On the other hand, if this is what we're going to have to go through every time we get off the ship," Lacey opined, "hotels begin to look good."

"A hotel room would even look good just as a change of scene," Marnie snapped. "Really, this is insupportable!"

"No worse than the average technical rehearsal," Ogden said affably. "Do strive for patience, Marnie."

We all knew what Marnie's patience level was, and everybody was dreading going through the next tech rehearsal with her.

"It's all right for you, Ogden," Marnie sneered. "You don't have to stand. Give me a floater to sit in, and I wouldn't mind waiting, either."

Ogden's face hardened, and he set a foot down on the floor.

"Oh, no you don't!" Susanne was beside him in two quick steps. "You heard what Mr. Tallendar said—you're only supposed to get out of that chair for your exercises!"

"Yes, listen to nursie," Lacey purred.

Ogden scowled up at her. "Since she is the only one to show a bit of compassion, I will."

"Oh, I don't mind," Susanne said. "I'm proud of what I am, Mr. Wellesley."

Lacey reddened. I wondered why, but made a mental note never to ask.

"And don't forget," Susanne said, "that as soon as we're past those customs gates, you're going straight to the nearest doctor!"

"Unnecessary," Ogden grumbled, though you could see he appreciated the attention. "And I'm rather curious to see the town."

"I'm afraid we can't, Ms. Souci," Barry said gently.

"Can't?" She looked up, startled. "*Mr.* Tallendar! You don't take chances with a coronary!"

"Quite right, but the New Venus medical service does. Merlo called from the ship, but when he told them the robo-doc's readouts, they said there was no emergency, and the soonest they could squeeze him in would be tomorrow at thirteen A.M."

Winston frowned. "You mean 'thirteen hundred hours,' don't you?"

"No, Winston, noon is fourteen o'clock here; the planet has a twenty-eight hour rotation period. Just enough to cause a whole panorama of medical problems, apparently, and the clinic is both understaffed and overloaded. Under the circumstances, tomorrow is really a concession on their part."

"I suppose so," Susanne said, with a glance at Ogden, "but it does seem negligent."

"Not at all, not at all," Ogden said, relieved. "The robo-doc warrants me as stable, young lady. I really don't feel that the floater is at all necessary . . ."

"You'll stay in it until a real live doctor says you're fit enough to walk!" Susanne snapped, then immediately moderated her tone. "I'm sorry, Mr. Wellesley, but . . ."

Ogden had looked surprised, and the first signs of hardening had shown in his face—but now they melted again,

and he took her hand to pat it. "I know, my dear, I know.
It's wonderful to see that someone cares. If you value my
comfort, though, you might sneak me just a small bottle
of—"

"*Mr.* Wellesley!"

Ogden laughed wickedly and patted her hand again, then
turned away, chuckling—but I think he had really been
hoping to get a bottle out of the deal.

Meanwhile, Marnie had been growing more and more
exasperated as she saw that somebody was getting attention, and it wasn't her. "Really, if there were some shred of
efficiency to this operation," she said, rather more loudly
than was necessary, "we would have been out that door
long ago!"

The customs agent snapped her a glare that said he
would have liked to have put her through a door, all right,
but not the one she had in mind.

"They need a management consultant," Marnie
orated—to no one in particular, since everybody was busy
looking the other way. "They need a whole team! Really,
you'd think they didn't want to be favored with the company of real live actresses!"

The customs agent cocked an eyebrow at her and gave a
single, slow nod.

That gave Marnie blood in her eye. She turned on Barry.
"Really, Barry! There must be something you can do to
speed up this incompetent!"

The customs agent very slowly and deliberately stood up
and stepped away from his desk.

"And just where do you think you're going?" Marnie all
but shouted.

"Some place where there's a little peace and quiet," he
retorted, and went off toward his little door again, leaving
Marnie fuming and sputtering behind him.

Lacey edged over to me. "Ramou—if I get to be a rich
and famous actress, do I get to throw tantrums, too?"

I didn't answer—mostly because I think she meant it.

Fortunately, Barry saved me from responding, and the situation from deteriorating—any further. "Come now, Marnie, you know the mind of the petty bureaucrat. How else can he know he has authority, other than by exercising his limited right to say no?"

"By saying yes," she snapped.

"But if he did," Horace pointed out, "nobody would be inconvenienced, and if nobody were inconvenienced, nobody would become upset—and if nobody became upset, he would have no proof of his own modicum of power."

Marnie narrowed her eyes as she glared at him. "Are you trying to say that I'm rewarding this imbecile for his interminable delay?"

Horace nodded judiciously. "A vivid way of stating the issue. Yes, quite vivid. Not how I might put it, certainly . . ."

"Yes, Horace, but the way you might put it, nobody would know they'd been criticized!" Marnie snapped, then turned away, settling down to a simmer. "Oh, very well. I'll be good—but it galls me, Barry, it galls!"

"We all appreciate your nobility and spirit of self-sacrifice, Marnie," he murmured, and she looked mollified, at least a little. I glanced at Lacey, her face filled with resentment, and at Larry, who was allowing his contempt to show—though actually, I thought he only looked envious—and counted, on one hand, those who were really appreciating Marnie's nobility.

Of course, Merlo, Grudy, and Winston were already through—they'd been the ones to hurry down from the bus that brought us in from the ship. Now I knew why—but they were looking pretty impatient, too. I wondered whether they were irritated with Marnie, or with the customs agent.

That worthy came sauntering back and handed a form to Susanne, deliberately bypassing Marnie. She almost exploded. "I was next, young man!"

"No you weren't." He was anything but young, and the smile he gave her wasn't all that pleasant. "You're last." And he went back to his desk and started discussing Ogden's form with him.

Marnie turned red and took a breath—and Barry, with impeccable timing, murmured, "How good of you to keep us two old codgers company, my dear! It would be quite tedious without your presence to lighten our burden."

Marnie paused on the verge of a scathing remark, then closed her mouth, still simmering. "Don't you try to sweet-talk me, Barry Tallendar!"

"But why not?" Barry asked innocently. "Certainly it is no more than is due a beautiful lady."

"You are unscrupulous and a scoundrel." Marnie glared at him. "But you are also charming."

"Indeed!" Barry gave her his most debonair smile. "It has been so long since we conversed merely as friends. Tell me, do you think the weather will be fair?"

"Oh," Marnie said archly, "does this planet have weather?"

And on they chatted, just like two old buddies. You'd never guess Marnie was constantly at Barry's throat—but she needed salve for the ego that the young clerk had wounded, and a face-saver for the humiliation imposed by the petty bureaucrat. Barry was willing to supply both—for the good of the company. If he hadn't, we might still be standing in that line, since Marnie, so adept at antagonizing the customs agent, would have done the same to his replacement, too, when the first one went off duty. My respect for Barry went up yet one more notch—I admired his ability to sacrifice himself for the general good. He chatted and chuckled, and doggone if Marnie didn't start flirting with him.

"Why, he's flirting back!" Lacey gasped next to me.

"You don't suppose he's actually enjoying it, do you?" Larry asked, wide-eyed.

I was wondering myself. After all, Marnie had been the mistress of Barry's billionaire brother for five years. Maybe that sort of susceptibility ran in the family.

Then I realized what I was thinking and gave myself a shake. How could I harbor such unworthy suspicions?

The customs clerk kept casting dark glances at Marnie, but she seemed blissfully unaware of him now, having a regular party with Barry and Horace, who was joining the Conversation Society now, too. That seemed to nettle the clerk, but there wasn't much he could do about it except take more frequent breaks, and he was up to the maximum by now, I was sure—so pretty soon, he was cross-examining me about my form and confiscating my book.

"Any lethal substances?" he asked.

"No," I said, discounting Marnie.

"Any currency in excess of fifty kwahers?"

I stared. "You folks don't use kwahers?"

"Of course we do," he said, with an impatient twist of his head. "It's just that the Company prefers to issue its own bills, representing IDE currency."

Oh. So they had found a way to make their own scrip. Which meant it was probably worth a lot less than an IDE bill. Interesting.

"How much?" he demanded.

"Ten kwahers." I took out my wallet and showed it to him.

"No, that's all right, I don't have to look." But he was peering pretty closely anyway. "Any cigarettes or other recreational alkaloids?"

"Never touch the stuff," I assured him, and he nodded me on through. I went to join Ogden, Susanne, Grudy, Merlo, and Winston, and the clerk beckoned Larry over.

Larry didn't do too well, either—he stepped into the scanner booth, and it screamed like a wounded banshee.

The agent was over beside him in a tenth of a second

with a handgun leveled. "Okay, out of the booth, hands on the wall. No funny stuff."

Larry went pale. "But this is ridiculous. Why, I would no more—"

"Do it." The gun twitched.

Larry swallowed, set his palms against the wall, and endured the agent's groping hand. He didn't have to grope very far—he pulled a carton of cigarettes out of Larry's inside coat pocket, another from his left coat pocket, and a third from his right-hand pocket. "Three *cartons*? You're trying to bring in not one cigarette, but six *hundred*?"

"I'm a heavy smoker," Larry said lamely.

The customs agent narrowed his eyes. "Thought you were only going to be here for four hours."

"I'm a *very* heavy smoker."

"What, with only one mouth?" But the agent wasn't done; he started patting Larry's pants pockets, then froze. "Empty 'em."

With trembling hand, Larry scooped a dozen permatches out onto the counter.

"Fire-makers!" the agent gasped. "What are you trying to do—blow us all to kingdom come?"

"No," Larry said, "just light the cigarettes."

The agent pulled out a set of handcuffs. "Importing matches is a capital offense, mister. You can hope for a quick trial."

"You can't mean it!" Larry started to tremble.

"Certainly," Barry said, "ignorance of your law—"

"Is no excuse. We have a satellite system that tells all incoming ships that tobacco and matches get the death penalty. One side."

"But he *hasn't* smuggled them in!" Barry said desperately.

The agent hesitated.

"He was merely carrying them on his person. Would he

have carried them so plainly if he was knowingly trying to bring in contraband?"

Well, he knew, and we knew, that the answer was yes—Larry really was that dumb. Very intelligent, but not a shred of judgment. The customs agent didn't know that, though. He only glowered at Larry, looking doubtful.

"He did not know about your laws," Barry pressed. "All the members of the company were confined to quarters during landing, and we did not relay the feed from the communicator to their cabins. Only those of us on the bridge saw the warning."

"You should have told the rest," the customs agent snapped.

"Yes," Barry said. "Quite so. We should have, indeed. I beg your pardon."

The agent still stood, glaring at Larry. Then he shrugged a millimeter and said, "Okay. This time. This one time."

And he turned, went behind his desk, and handed Larry the form.

I was standing with Merlo. My boss was livid and muttering under his breath. "Barry should have let him twist in the wind!"

"Be charitable," Winston murmured. "Perhaps he was having visions of trying to train some local to do Larry's parts."

Larry came through, and Merlo clapped him on the shoulder with a mile-wide grin—and shoved him into the center of our little group, hissing in his ear, "You half-brained wet-eared puppy, you could have gotten us all jailed!"

"Why?" I demanded. "Why would even you make such a stupid move?"

His face darkened with anger, and it gave him some of his poise back. He gave me a glance of withering contempt and said, "Because I read the traveler's guide before I

boarded the ship, and learned that cigarettes are worth their
weight in gold here."

As soon as the old United Nations had changed itself
into the IDE, right after the Jerusalem Crisis, it had es-
chewed all precious metals as a basis for currency—but
gold was still in great demand for jewelry, and greater demand for circuitry. It was worth more than when it had
been used for money, if anything.

I just stared at Larry for a few moments. Then I said, "I
never figured you for a black marketeer."

"You don't figure very well at all," he sneered. "You'll
never be rich."

"I won't get stuck in jail, either," I retorted, but I crossed
my fingers; there was always the chance my temper might
get me in worse trouble than any lawyer could get me out
of. Much less chance than if I hadn't gone through martial
arts training, but still a chance.

Winston wasn't about to give Larry even that much of a
chance, though. "Money?" He gave Larry the cold-eyed
stare that had chilled so many 3DT viewers. "Milled and
minted dross? You would have sold us all into bondage for
your own piddling gain?"

Larry tried to lock glares with him, but he had grown up
watching the Mordant Emperor on 3DT, too, and even
without the makeup, Winston looked so sinister and malevolent that Larry quailed and turned away, trembling.

The clerk took one more break before he was willing to
work on Marnie, and Barry and Horace loyally stayed with
her until the moment she walked up to the counter. The
clerk started grilling her, but her answers were downright
civil, maybe even pleasant. He frowned; you could see he
couldn't figure it; but I noticed Barry's closed eyes and silent moving lips, and knew our managing director had flattered her into such a good mood that even the clerk's
rudeness couldn't quite throttle it. Close—but no tantrum.

She'd lost her smile by the time she came through to join us, but her eyes were glittering, and there was a certain swing to her step that stated her triumph—and not without reason; the clerk's gaze followed her every inch of the way, until she joined our happy throng, at which point he reluctantly wrenched his attention back to Horace. He was glowering with hostility, but the old trouper's charm and grace had him mollified within two questions, and Horace strolled through to join us with only Barry left to face our human Cerberus. The clerk looked as if he would have liked to pin Barry to the wall—after all, the "tourist" had spoiled his fun by reconciling Marnie to the vicissitudes of bureaucracy—but the aging leading man was so damned pleasant to chat with that the clerk forgot his hostility by question three and actually wound up telling Barry what life was like on New Venus for a few minutes, before he remembered himself and waved Barry on through.

Our leader came out with a jaunty step and a flourish of his hat. "Well done all! Now, let us be off to see the sights!"

The sights he was planning to see, as it turned out, were the posters our advance man, Publius Promo, had pasted up to announce our arrival, and the theater he had booked for us to perform in—or whatever passed for a theater on New Venus.

"There will be some difficulty," Barry explained, "since we are coming considerably sooner than Publius expected. It is really too bad that radio waves cannot travel faster than light—it would have been so much more convenient if we could have sent word on ahead about our change in plans."

"It certainly would have," Horace said, "but until someone invents a system that allows communication more rapid than a spaceship, we will have to make do with the consequences. So, then, you and I shall seek out our stalwart Publius."

"I don't envy you the task," Marnie said. "Disgusting little man!"

"He *is* rather common," Barry allowed.

"Why anyone would take the news of the ability to cure lung cancer as permission to begin smoking such horrendous cigars, I shall never know," Horace said.

"Still, he is effective at his chosen occupation," Barry said, "or was, until his wife left him . . ."

"Small wonder, with those cigars about." Marnie wrinkled her nose.

"Under the circumstances, I thought an opportunity to begin anew might prove salutary," Barry said, "especially with his first assignment being in a location that forbids smoking."

"It is likely to win him a salutary prison term," Marnie declared. "Really, Barry, your preoccupation with charity will be your undoing! Business was never well mixed with altruism!" She said that with the confidence of somebody who knew she wasn't a charity case—just a burden imposed on Barry, one that he really had no choice about. That was the price of his rich brother's underwriting—taking Marnie off his hands.

"Perhaps," Barry allowed, "though he was willing to work for expenses and commission . . . Well! For good or for ill, we must seek him out! I do not, however, expect you to accompany me."

"Small worry about that," Marnie returned. "I shall willingly devote myself to sight-seeing—though what there is to see on this dreary planet, heaven knows!"

"Valleys and hills," Winston suggested, "without walls around them. Buildings high and low—from the outside!"

"You have a point," Marnie admitted. "After all those weeks aboard ship, open space of any sort will be welcome, no matter how dreary!" She started for the door.

A piece of the gray wall detached itself from the plasticrete and stepped forward, holding out a face mask with a tank on a shoulder strap. "Gotta wear a mask, lady. Regulations. And suicide if y'don't."

Marnie slowed and regarded him as if he were a particularly offensive piece of litter. Not surprising—he wasn't exactly dressed to the teeth and had seen so many better days it was a wonder he had any left. His face was leathery and wrinkled; his mouth had the slightly pursed look that old people get when their dental implants aren't quite as long as the teeth they grew up with; and his jumpsuit seemed to have been handed down from a larger man. I found out later that it had—himself. Those jumpsuits were made out of a cloth that wore like the pyramids, and when he shrank, it didn't.

Horace stepped in adroitly between this ancient specimen and Marnie's repulsion. "Yes, I do think we had better each take one." He reached out for the mask, but the oldster pulled it back just beyond his reach and said, "Fifty BTUs."

"Fifty?" Marnie gasped.

Horace pursed his lips. "Local, or IDE?"

"Local, of course," the man snapped. "Think I could take anything else, right in here where anybody could see me?"

" 'Anybody' being the police, of course," Horace mused, in a very low voice. "Why so much, friend?"

The oldster eyed him with suspicion. "I ain't your friend."

"I should hope you are not my enemy," Horace returned. "Why is the rental so high?"

The oldster shrugged. "It costs to import these things, y'know, and it costs to make the oxygen. B'sides, I gotta earn my cut, don't I?"

Larry pounced on it. "You mean they allow you to?"

"It's part o' the job," the old guy said impatiently. "Salary plus commission—and believe me, the salary ain't nothin' to write home about. You want 'em, or not?"

"Of course, of course." Horace pulled out his wallet and

slipped out a few bills. "May I ask why you undertook this job, if it pays so little?"

The old guy shrugged, irritated. "You get too old for the pumping stations, the Company finds you something you can still do."

"Semiretired?" Horace hazarded.

"To a semiuseless job," the old guy agreed, "renting out air masks to the tourists, which there ain't very much of—maybe once er twice a month. Maybe. What's it to you, anyway, old man?"

" 'Old man'!" Horace stiffened. "Rather indelicate of you, isn't that? Just how old are *you*, may I ask?"

"Fifty-two," the decrepit one said.

Horace put on his mask.

We all did; we filed out the three-meter-wide door in silence. As the panels closed behind us, Marnie gusted out a "Well!"

"Only fifty-two?" Lacey's eyes were wide. "And he looks *that old*?"

Their voices came muffled through the grilles of their masks. They sounded thin, too—not with the falsetto that you get from breathing helium, but with the attenuation that comes from thin air.

Susanne's eyes were huge above her mask as she looked about her. "It's rather ... odd, isn't it?"

It sure was. Start off with a very pale sky, and a completely barren expanse of hard-baked mud for miles around, frozen in the contours of flowing. It had been like that ever since the rain dried up, and the last of the runoff trickled past on its way to the sea.

"Kindly put," Marnie said grimly. " 'Dreary' comes to mind."

"Bleak," Larry opined.

Marnie nodded. "For once, Mr. Rash, I find I could agree with you."

A man of that ageless look you think of as being between forty and sixty slouched up to us. "Taxi?"

Barry opened his mouth, but somebody on his other side said, "Taxi?" And before he could answer, they were coming at us from all sides. "Taxi?" "Taxi?" "Taxi?"

Lacey looked around as if she couldn't believe it. "What do they do—wait around here day in and day out, hoping for someone to come out this door?"

"I didn't think they had unemployment here," I ventured.

"We don't, Jack."

I looked up, startled. The guy who said that was maybe a little older than I was, hair plastered into the nautilus shape that was popular with the teens when I was a brat trying to work my way up to juvenile delinquent. He wore a jacket with the sheen of plastic to it—and a grin with a toothpick in it.

I knew about those toothpicks, and what they were flavored with. "My name's not Jack."

"No, a 'jack' is what you are." One of the older guys was glowering at the kid. "That's what we call a tourist, somebody coming in from off-planet."

I frowned. "Odd slang. Where's it from?"

The kid shrugged. "Who can say? Slang just bubbles up like methane out of pitch."

I didn't like the sound of that, especially since I had an idea about that term—but the kid was right, he couldn't have known where it came from. He'd never seen any live animal bigger than a dog, much less a donkey. Besides, Barry was nodding graciously. *"Autre temps, autre moeurs."*

"Outdoor moors? Yeah, we got plenty of 'em." And the senior cabbie started detailing the wonders of New Venus to our august veterans.

I sidled over to the kid and said, "So if they don't have unemployment, what are you doing here?"

"Trying to pick up a little extra tucker for my bag, Jack,"

he said. "Got the Company car, too, so you know it's comfy."

I stared. He mistook it for skepticism, not surprise, and waved me over to the last car in line. "That's my roller. I'm Chovy, by the way."

It took me a second to realize he was giving me his name, not his description. Then I nodded and stuck out a hand. "Ramou. Nice car."

He gave my hand a shake, then let go to let me take a look at the vehicle. It was a little smaller than the others, but not much different in shape—streamlining is streamlining, after all, and the only question is whether it's shaped like a dolphin or a fish, and which kind of scale. It was transparent on top, like all the others, but opaque below—who wants to see the motors sitting behind each wheel, or the big central box of the battery? Admittedly, the look's been nice and clean, since they started putting on bottoms that only let the wheels stick out. Oh, there are some people who really get a thrill out of seeing the insides of machines—but I'm very much aware that we're in the minority, and most people would rather see a sleek, smooth shape with maybe some interesting flares and sweeps, like the ones on Chovy's car, and with a pretty color, like its glittering gold and purple design.

"That bloke up at the head drives for the Company." The kid jerked his head toward the older driver who was doing all the talking—at the moment, a very polite conversation with Winston and Marnie. "I mean, that's all he does for a living—drives managers around. So he's got the upscale bus."

It was, too—wide but long, sort of like a small whale. The kid's car was more like a trout.

"You mean the Company sent a car to pick up Barry?"

"Not likely, Jack." The kid chuckled. "Old Bomey takes private passengers in his off hours. Company doesn't mind, so long as there's no sign of use."

"The Company lets you use their cars for taxis?"

"Blazes, yes. They want to give the boost to private enterprise, now don't they? Long as it doesn't get out of hand. Keeps us off the streets, y'see, Jack."

I nodded. "What happens if you start hanging around under lampposts?"

"No chance, Jack. When we're through with grammar school, we're outfitted with jobs—'less we qualify for high school."

I nodded again. "Never laid off?"

"Blazes, no. Too much to do, Jack, and not enough hands." He grinned wickedly. "Though if you're a bad boy, they send you to the tar pits."

I didn't want to ask. "What kind of a deal can you cut us here?"

He shrugged. "What you want? Just a ride into town, or the whole flaming tour?"

"The whole flaming tour," I said, "and back."

Just then, Larry came over. "Here now, Ramou! *You're* not making a deal for us, are you?"

"No, just for me, Larry," I said slowly, "and anybody who wants to come along with me."

He looked suddenly uncertain, but Marty overheard and stepped up with a joyful yip. "Hey! Free ride? Count me in!"

"Well, you could share the cost," I qualified.

"But you wouldn't charge a lady, would you?" Lacey batted her eyelashes under my nose.

"Be my guest," I said gallantly, though I could have wished she had volunteered to pay her own expenses.

Chovy glanced around at them, losing his smile. "How many you booking me for, Jack?" Then he took a look at Susanne, and the smile came back, slowly.

I counted noses. "Four, so far." I looked up at Susanne. "Coming?"

"I'd like to." But she glanced anxiously at Ogden. "Mr. Wellesley, would you care to join us?"

Chovy stared in alarm.

"No, I think I'd prefer to tour with members of my own generation—or closer to it, at least." At the look of anxiety that crossed her face, Ogden leaned over from his floater with a smile and patted her hand. "Don't worry, Susanne, they'll care for me well enough, if need be. After all, you can't go dancing attendance on me every minute of your young life, can you? No, of course not. You must have some time to yourself—really, all of it; I appreciate your attentions deeply, but I won't rob you. No, now, not a word! Go along with your young friends and have a lovely time."

"What, have the young folk made arrangements of their own?" Winston looked up with a smile.

"Uh, well, we're negotiating," I hedged.

Winston nodded. "A splendid idea! Especially since we don't seem to be able to find a limo, and none of the cabs can hold all of us. In fact, we, ah, veterans, will have to take two cabs."

"You gentlemen go ahead with Marnie and Grudy, Winston." Barry dismissed the issue with a wave of his hand. "I'm afraid Horace and I have a rather more demanding task ahead of us just now."

Winston frowned. "So soon? Really, Barry, you should take an hour or two to soak up the feeling of the milieu of your audience."

"It would be desirable," Barry admitted, "but I'm afraid it is rather more necessary to ascertain the current status of preparations."

"Meaning, that you must find Publius Promo," Winston said.

Barry nodded. "We will have to see the sights at a later date."

"If at all," Winston said, with sympathy. "The penalties of being in management."

Every single one of those cabbies looked up, tensed; then they sort of grinned sheepishly and relaxed a little.

"We shall survive," Barry promised.

"Barry!" Marnie cried. "Surely you are not leaving me alone between the villain and the octogenarian!"

"You have Grudy for chaperone, my dear, and she has you," Barry said, not without sympathy. "Winston was never less than a perfect gentleman, and there is Merlo's strong left arm to lean on."

"And his broken ankle to trip him up," she said darkly.

Merlo shrugged. "What can I say?"

"The less, the better," she assured him.

"You are certainly welcome to accompany Horace and myself, my dear," Barry said slowly, "but I doubt you will find it at all interesting."

Marnie stood motionless for a second, then sighed and turned back to Winston. "Well, let's see if we can manage something moderately interesting as conversation, shall we?"

"The topic of your choice," he promised, then turned to me again. "Is your group accommodated, then, Ramou?"

I looked over at Chovy, who was busy admiring Lacey this time. "Okay, fifty kwahers for the five of us. Suits?"

"It's a tight squeeze," he said, "and fifty was the price when I thought it was just you. Seventy-five."

"Sixty," I said.

He grinned. "Seventy."

"Don't push it, Ramou," Lacey said nervously.

I paused in midhaggle and sighed. "Okay, seventy." I turned to my little troupe. "That's fourteen apiece. Okay?"

"I'll take the front seat," Marty volunteered.

Chovy looked nettled, but Larry gave a reluctant nod. I lifted an eyebrow in Lacey's direction, and she nodded, too. Susanne, though, gave Ogden another anxious glance, so I stepped over to her and said softly, "He has to learn how to manage on his own some time, Mama."

She looked up at me, startled, then gave a rueful little laugh. "I am being ridiculous, aren't I? Sure, Ramou. I'm in."

"Then step," I invited, waving toward the car, and Chovy popped the top right on cue. She gave him a bat of eyelash and stepped in.

Lacey frowned and stepped hard after her.

Susanne slid over to make room for her, and Larry stepped in quickly before I could. I took the hint and went around to the other side. All things considered, I'd rather sit next to Susanne, anyway. Close choice, I'll admit, but there it is.

Chovy slid into the driver's seat and set his thumb against the ignition plate. The roof folded down around us like a clamshell closing—automatic, I guessed. Then he nudged the joystick forward and to the side, and the car pulled away from the curb.

"Where to?" Chovy asked, toothpick sticking up at a jaunty angle.

Well, I figured the little bit of upper in that wooden splinter couldn't be enough to louse up his driving, and it sure would speed up his reflexes, so I said, "Wherever there's something to see. But just to be on the safe side, keep it slow, okay? We want to see what we're driving past."

"Nothing to see, Jack," he said, "just mud flat after mud flat."

"We want to get the full impact," I explained.

He shrugged. "Suits me—you're paying by the hour. Off we go, then."

And we went.

11

Chovy twisted around in his seat to ask, "Which one—the Gulf of Oil or the Bay of Benzene?" By some coincidence, his gaze fell on Susanne. She lowered her eyes demurely, and alarm bells went off in my head.

"Don't you need to keep your eyes on the road?" I asked.

"My eyes? Not a bit," Chovy answered. "Car's got auto-pilot. She'll follow the road just fine, 'cept maybe when a turn comes in sight. Then she'll beep me, and if I don't turn around, she'll slow down, nice and easy, and stop."

"Why is your car a girl?" Lacey asked.

I didn't think I wanted to hear the answer, but I had a hunch the best way to distract a guy like Chovy was to get him talking about his car, so I cut in with, "How come your cars run on wheels? Wouldn't it be easier and cheaper to build 'em ground-effect?"

Chovy switched his gaze to me, looking interested. "Y'know, Jack, I've wondered that myself many's the time. But we build roads pretty cheap here—a few big machines and big men, and the job's done, ten kilometers a day or more. I suppose there's more chance of sparks from ground-effect, but no one's been anxious to try the experiment."

I could see why.

"There's this, too," Chovy said. "It's easier to keep people from going where they're not supposed to, if they have

157

to have roads—but I'm just guessing there. Nobody in management is saying."

Susanne and Lacey were looking irritated that Chovy's interest had shifted from them to cars. "Would you still think of them as female if they could be so wayward as to leave the road?" Lacey asked.

Chovy switched back to her with a wide grin. "No, we call 'em 'she' because . . ."

I cut in fast; I was interested in the answer, but I didn't think the ladies would really want to hear it—and I wanted to get Chovy pointed back front fast, so I said, "Just show us the sights—right, folks?"

"I'm looking," Chovy answered.

"Maybe you should have warned us about him," Lacey told me.

"Maybe he should have warned us about himself," Marty returned.

Chovy gave Marty the raised eyebrow. "Come on! That's not in the rules of the game!"

"Yeah," Marty said, "but we're not playing."

I told Chovy, "He's got an odd sense of humor."

"We could use it around here." Chovy turned back to the road and cut out the autopilot.

"Just think, a whole new world!" Susanne said, breathless with anticipation.

"I can't think it will be much different from the old one, dear," Lacey sighed—but I think she had to work at it.

"Once you've seen New York, you've seen everything, right?" I asked, thinking of the Rocky Mountains. "Okay, Chovy—what's new?"

"Nothing, to me," he rejoined, "but we'll start with the docks."

"Docks?" I looked up, startled. "You *sail* on the stuff?"

" 'Sail' is the word," he confirmed. "A whole flaming planet full of gasoline, and they won't let us use combustion engines."

"Why not?" Larry frowned.

"'Cause they have sparks inside," Chovy answered, "and we don't really want to see a whole flaming planet."

"But doesn't that take oxygen?" Susanne asked.

"Too right it does, sweetheart."

"I thought there wasn't any in your air." Lacey eyed the outdoors nervously.

Chovy glanced back with a frown. "Can't hear you—ah, I see, then. You can take off your masks in here. Interior's pressurized."

"Oh," I said. "So when you open the top . . ."

"A bit of oxygen escapes, yes. Oh, the vacuum comes on automatically and sucks the oxy-nitro back in—but there's always a little bit leaks out."

"Yes, but surely such a small amount couldn't cause any problems!" Larry protested.

"Couldn't it just!" Chovy grinned, showing very white teeth that didn't quite fit. "That 'small amount' adds up like you wouldn't believe, when a million people let a little bit leak every day. And it all sinks down, you see."

"That's right." Susanne nodded. "Oxygen's heavier than helium. So's nitrogen."

I looked at her in pleased surprise, but Marty was staring in surprise, period, and Larry and Lacey were looking at her as if she were some sort of alien monster.

"Indeed it is." Chovy's smile broadened. "And the oceans are lower than the land—what you'd call 'water level,' back on Terra, but it's 'oil level,' here. And there's wind, so the wild oxy-nitro goes out over the seas."

Lacey's head snapped up in alarm. "Isn't that dangerous?"

"Too right it is, love, if a spark flies loose."

"Lightning?" I asked.

"What's that?"

"Huge electrical sparks. Natural ones." But Chovy was looking at me with blank apprehension, so I said, "Skip it."

"Oh, *storms!*" Chovy's face cleared, and he nodded.

"Right—I seen 'em in the 3DT. No, we don't have 'em, here. But some fool's always trying to puff some weed, or a lorry hits a flint stone wrong down by the docks, and *blooey*! There it goes."

Lacey turned pale, Larry got the shakes—guilty conscience—and Marty wasn't looking any too hale himself. "You mean this has actually happened?"

"Every year," Chovy affirmed, "once or twice, at least."

"But how come the whole planet doesn't just burn to a cinder?"

"'Cause when the oxy's used up, there's no more fire." Chovy chuckled, turning back to watch the road. "But it always turns a thousand barrels into smoke, maybe more. Filthy stuff, that smoke—and stinks to high heaven."

"Sure," I said, "because heat rises. Wouldn't it be safer for the Company to send someone out to burn off the oxygen every month or so? I mean, this way, they're risking a really *big* explosion."

"Too right they are, and there's not been a fire this two years past, so it's building up for a biggie, right enough."

"But how foolish!" Lacey protested. "If they would just burn it off every month, they'd have nothing to fear!"

"If," Chovy agreed. "But the blighters can only see profits going up in smoke along with the petrol. No, a fire deliberate's the last thing they'd do—obscene, they'd call it."

I suddenly understood why all his swear words were connected with fire.

The car slowed, turned ninety degrees, and stopped. "There she is," Chovy said, "the Gulf of Oil."

The land curved away toward the horizon on both sides, like arms holding a bowl—a bowl full of roiling, greasy liquid, undulating heavily shoreward in wave after wave that broke in a dark froth and spattered the shore with a black film, then receded.

Lacey shuddered. "That's all oil? Really *oil*?"

"Raw petroleum?" Susanne echoed.

"No, lubricating oil," Chovy answered. "There's no raw stuff here, love—it's all refined out."

"All refined?" Lacey turned about to stare at him. "Lying here open to the air? Oceans of it, already *refined*? How could that be?"

"The wonders of nature," Chovy crooned, and went on to explain.

The first probe to Alpha Centauri identified four planets, and found that the second planet was shrouded in clouds, just like Venus in the Sol system. It was about the same size and mass, and looked like a pearl in the ocean of night, just as old Venus did. But the second probe found that the clouds were made of hydrocarbons, with a pretty complex ring structure. It took a sample, analyzed it, and sent the findings back to Terra. It was almost indistinguishable from . . .

Petroleum. Petroleum vapor.

There was a huge flurry of interest, and the petroleum conglomerates got hyped to start a black-gold rush—until they did their arithmetic. After all, petroleum had been limited to the production of plastics for five hundred years, ever since the last oil wells in Siberia went dry. Methane, alcohol, and electricity had filled in the gap, and really efficient and comfortable public transportation companies boomed and made huge profits. Private cars were a convenience and a luxury, and electricity was generated by wind, water, Sun, and Earth.

So who needed petroleum anymore?

After all, even the plastics industry was busily finding substitutes. When the petroleum companies estimated the cost of gathering all that petroleum vapor, it was competitive with the homegrown product wrung from the shale. When you added in the cost of transporting it from Alpha Centauri to Terra, the price per barrel became . . .

Astronomical.

So New Venus just sat there, an untapped treasure for

twenty years, until the Falstaff colony was started on the fourth planet of Haldane's Star—and the pioneers realized that they needed energy. Low-tech energy—when a colony's just beginning, it doesn't have the resources to make high-tech gadgets like fusion reactors and thousand-hour storage cells. Oh, it can import them from Terra, but that costs a hideous amount, and a brand-new colony can't generate that kind of money—all it can do is export raw materials, and interstellar freight costing what it does, the only exports that make a profit are small-bulk, high-value items, such as gems or furs or pharmaceuticals. So most of what they need, they have to make. That's why frontier farmhouses still tend to be log cabins or sod huts—very big sod huts, more like sod mansions, but sod nonetheless. Their big industries tend to be farming, logging, mining, and refining—and any tools they need, they make themselves. A village smith's factory can make shovels and plows from the steel turned out by the nearest mill, and shipped out on railroads. The engines are powered by steam, from burning coal if they have it, or wood, which is plentiful in the early years of a colony . . .

Or they can be powered by diesels.

The colony brings out the dies for internal-combustion engines, and within five years, they're making their own. Then all they have to do is find oil and drill.

But Falstaff didn't have any oil.

I know, I know, all the rule books said a planet had to develop oil during its evolution—but Falstaff hadn't quite developed any native dinosaurs when the colony got there. That meant no coal, either—only peat. So the petroleum companies quickly cliqued together to form Amalgamated Petroleum and started selling New Venus fuels to Falstaff—or bartering them, rather; they swapped oil for gems and some exotic plants whose juices could be distilled into wonder drugs.

Then the explorers discovered Otranto and found out that

the development of life is not inevitable. Otranto was a world almost exactly like Terra, and a million years older; its seas were a virtual broth of amino acids; but for some reason, life just hadn't started there.

Needless to say, they didn't have petroleum, either.

By the time the IDE had authorized colonization of thirty planets—and suspected that unauthorized splinter groups had colonized a dozen more—the total without petroleum was up to six. Amalgamated Petroleum set up the same deal with them that they'd developed with Falstaff, and the money started rolling in—from Terra, where the Company sold the grain it had bartered for with its oil.

Because, you see, it turned out that petroleum is cheaper to ship than most cargoes, since it requires less handling—at least, the way Amalgamated Petroleum did it. The ships didn't even have to land, just sent scoop-ships down to suck in vapor and chill it into liquid. Sure, the re-action mass still cost an arm and a leg, but a tanker is a tanker, and when the oil had been delivered to Falstaff, they flushed out the tanks, relined them, and filled them with grain. Terra's always hungry, and it has far more people than it can support by itself, especially since they've turned so much farmland into housing towers—so the petroleum companies traded oil for wheat and corn, then sold the grain on Terra for a good profit. Plus, each shipload of oil always cost a bit more than the official price of the wheat and corn, so Falstaff gradually ran up a good, substantial debt that it would be able to pay when its gross national product was big enough—in a century or two. Meantime, there would be constant payments coming in.

So the oil companies had found another bonanza—but they did some more math, and found out that they could load even more cheaply if their ships could pump up liquid instead of scooping and chilling vapor.

"But that doesn't make sense," Susanne objected.

"Yeah," Marty seconded. "It's got to take a lot more reaction mass for a ship to come down to the surface and take off again, than for it just to dip into the cloud layers."

"Right enough," Chovy said, "if all you're thinking of is one pass through the atmosphere. But you can't take just one, of course—you have to take three or four. Hundred. Because, you see, when you get done condensing the vapor into liquid, it doesn't take up much room in your tanks. Not to mention the energy it costs you to do the condensing. No, all things considered, it's cheaper to just go into orbit and let them bring up a hose."

"A hose thousands of kilometers long?" Lacey said with skepticism.

"It's a *big* hose," Chovy explained, "and it stays there all the time, going from a sea or ocean to an orbital loading platform. If a tanker wants gasoline, he goes to the one over the eastern ocean; if he wants heating oil, he goes to the one over our heads right now. Here, have a look." He turned the car toward the pier and it rolled out along the plasticrete. We could hear the surf rolling heavily to either side of us, and see it, too, because only one or two ships were moored to the docks that ran out from the pier like right-angled branches on a tree.

"What do the ships carry?" I asked.

"Everything people need at the other work-site towns," Chovy said. "Grain, water, a little meat, vitamins—we import them, or make them, here at Aphrodite, and ship them out to all the folk around the planet who need 'em. Somebody has to take care of the pumping stations, you know. But the biggest cargo is oxygen."

"Oxygen?" I stared.

"And nitrogen, too," Chovy confirmed. "We make 'em here in Aphrodite—that's where I work, the oxy plant—and ship 'em out. Not too tough—the pumping stations are all located on the shorelines, of course."

"I should think that would be rather dangerous," Larry stated.

"Isn't it just! You've never heard of safeguards and fail-safes until you see the 'cautions they take loading and unloading that stuff, nor a more cautious breed of men than the sailors."

"But why don't you just send it by rocket?" Marty asked.

"Cost, Jack." Chovy shrugged. "Costs less to use boats. Shipping is still the cheapest shipping, here—'specially when you can actually sail your freighters. We use wind power for that job—no chance of sparks."

Lacey shuddered. "Just think what would happen if one of your tankers sprang a leak, and somebody did strike a spark!"

"We do," Chovy assured her, rather grimly. "We definitely do."

"You seem to know a lot about this," Lacey said.

"This kind of history, we're taught in school," Chovy said. "Little things like the Roman Republic and Magna Carta and the Charter of Human Rights, no—but the chronicles of petroleum, yes."

I frowned at his profile. "But if they're not taught, how come you know about them?"

Chovy pulled the car around at the end of the pier, and we had a clear view out over the gulf. "There it is," he said easily, pointing.

We looked.

If I'd been in Nebraska, I would have thought it was a tornado. Out there where the horizon seemed to curve, there was a long, narrow tube running up from the surface—and up, and up, and up. It didn't disappear into a big cloud overhead—it just disappeared, period: dwindled into a line, then a trace, then wasn't there at all.

"A sky-stalk," I breathed. "How big is it?"

"Only ten meters wide," Chovy said, "but it's twenty-five thousand kilometers long."

Marty gulped.

"How can it hold together?" I asked. "It's own weight should be enough to tear it apart!"

Chovy shrugged. "I can't tell you the details, Jack, but I know the outside is steel mesh, and the inside is some sort of flexible plastic that's fantastically strong. What's in between, I don't know—but there's plenty of it."

"What's on the other end?" Susanne asked.

"A space station," Chovy answered. "An orbital platform in a geostationary orbit, big enough to moor two ships at a time and let 'em pump."

I stared at the narrow tube stretching up forever. "So a ship can just dock at the station and hook up to the tube and fill itself to nearly bursting?"

"In less than a day," Chovy confirmed.

I could feel my eyes trying to pop out of my head, something like the feeling I got the first time I looked at Susanne, but I couldn't help it. "And there's one of these over each body of . . . liquid?"

"One for each kind of petroleum fraction," Chovy confirmed.

"Think of the labor that took!" I gasped.

"Couldn't it do a lot of damage if that bottom end got loose?" Susanne asked.

"To what?" Chovy said. "They brought it down out there, where there's nothing to hit but oil—and if they churned up a lot of that, so what? It's just fall back into the drink. Same thing if it got loose today—nothing to hit, as long as the ships stay away—which they do, they do."

"But it doesn't get loose," Larry said.

"Too right it doesn't! What good would it do sucking air, hey? No, it's moored right and tight to the bottom, believe it, and the intakes are round the sides."

"Right at the bottom?" Marty asked.

"Right at—so the pressure of the liquid helps push it up to the platform."

"That must have taken a fantastic amount of money to build," I said.

"Oh, believe it did, Jack," Chovy said softly. "The oil companies on good old polluted Terra calculated the cost, found out the capital was too much for any one of them, got government permission to form a limited-purpose cartel—and Amalgamated Petroleum was born."

"That's the Company?"

"Believe it is—and it's bound and determined to get back every shekel and a hundred more for each, no matter what it has to do."

I glanced at him out of the corner of my eye, noticing that he'd started looking awfully grim all of a sudden.

"But how did they condense all that vapor into liquid?" Marty asked. He had a sharp-eyed look to him that I'd only noticed once or twice before—and whenever he'd had it, I'd heard jokes about the subject the next day. "And how do they *keep* it all from evaporating again?"

"By cooling it all down," Chovy explained.

"All?" Marty looked like an owl, his eyes were so wide. "A whole planetary atmosphere? What did they use—an ocean of dry ice?"

"Not a bit," said Chovy. "They moved the planet."

The inside of the car was awfully quiet.

Then Marty said, "I think I sense a punch line coming. Okay, I'll play straight man: 'How do you move a planet?' "

"Very slowly," Chovy said.

"I knew it," Marty said.

"No, really," Chovy said. "I had this in tenth grade science, just before they kicked us out of school."

"You were kicked out of school?" Susanne asked, wide-eyed.

"Oh, they called it graduation," Chovy said, a little nettled, "but it came to the same thing—anybody who wanted more schooling was just out of luck."

"In tenth grade," Marty said, "I didn't know too many boys who wanted to stay in school."

"That's because they had to, bucko. You just see how many want it when they can't have it . . . Anyway, Amalgamated moved the planet. I'm a little fuzzy on how, but I think that, when they pooled their money, they had enough to be able to manufacture some quantum black holes . . ."

I nodded. I'd heard of the process—it had to be carried out in space, of course, well away from any planet—and it consisted of tying two starship engines with H-space convertors back to back and running them both at constant acceleration. They stay in place, since they're balancing each other out—so they're trying to pull H-space into normal space, and the result is a knot in the space-time fabric, a very deep but very small gravity well. Voila! You have a singularity. Of course, you lose the engines—we think. Nobody can see inside to say for sure. Then, there's the little question of what happens when they run out of fuel—and the answer is that the singularity disappears. So do the engines. So they have to calculate the amount of fuel very nicely, to make sure they don't leave a menace to navigation lying around—or in this case, a rock that will pull the planet too far. "A *bunch* of them, you say?"

"Six," Chovy said, "manufactured right there in space, around the planet's orbit, with each one a little farther away from Centauri—and slowly, ever so slowly, New Venus began to move away from its sun. Then they made more holes, and the planet moved farther out, and they made more holes . . ."

"And finally it was all the way out where it is now," Lacey said, trying to sound bored.

Chovy nodded. "It took fifty years and a lot of earthquakes, but what the hey, nobody was living here; and a kilometer at a time, it moved out of its place, expanding its orbit, until it was a full AU away from Alpha Centauri. The climate cooled down—and the rains began."

"Of course!" Marty lifted his head, the slow grin spreading. "It was vapor—cool it down, and it condenses."

"You catch it quick, bawcock. Not that it stayed liquid, not at first. For a year or so, the droplets turned right back into vapor as soon as they hit the rock below—it was as hot as a stove top, after all. But awhile later, the drops began to stay liquid. That was when the Company brought in gangs of men to supervise the caterpillar-treaded robots that arranged the dikes and canals and dams and levees and sluice gates, to channel each rain into a different lowland—because it was fractional distillation, you see; the cooler it got, the lower grade the liquid. The dams channeled each grade of petroleum product into a different geological basin. A geologist kept track of the quality of the distillate, and told the crews when it was time to shift the barriers to form a new channel—so we wound up with the Ocean of Gasoline, the Great Kerosene Lake, the Gulf of Oil, and so on."

"How could they do all that without starting a fire and sending the whole planet up in one mammoth explosion?" Marty asked.

Chovy shrugged. "Simple—the planet didn't have any oxygen. After all, it didn't have any plant life—too hot. And no liquid; everything was vapor. Kinda like the original Venus, that way. Okay, so solar radiation broke apart molecules in the stratosphere, and liberated a little bit of O_2—and O_1, for that matter; but the next passing ship would ignite a flare that would use it up. No, it didn't burn up more than a fraction of a percent—we're talking about a whole atmosphere of petroleum vapor, here. When it had all rained out, the only gas left was a little free nitrogen. Then the company manufactured helium out in space and pumped it down here, to hold the volatiles down."

"So the geography is geology," I inferred.

Chovy nodded approval. "Good. I'll remember that one. Yes, we wound up with a Bay of Benzene, and an Ocean of Gasoline separated by a huge dam from the Ocean of Diesel Fuel, and a mammoth tar pit—christened La Brea, for some reason."

"I might know why," Larry said with hauteur.

"Would you truly?" Chovy drawled.

I figured an interruption was in order. "They also wound up with a permanent labor force?"

"Oh, yes," Chovy said softly. "Done looking at the unnatural wonder? I'll show you where the labor force lives."

"I'd like that," Susanne said, and that decided the matter. Just for form's sake, though, I asked the others, "Seen enough here, folks?"

"Of course," Lacey said. "What else is there to see but that mammoth tube?"

Chovy had already turned the car and was rolling back along the pier, so it didn't really matter that the others mumbled agreement.

Susanne gazed at the bleakness outside the window and murmured, "It's hard to believe people choose to stay here."

"Hard enough," Chovy said, his voice flat. "Too hard, because they don't. There isn't a one of 'em wouldn't go back to Terra tomorrow, if he had the cash for the ticket."

"But I thought they paid you well!" Lacey said, startled.

"Right—they did." And Chovy went on to explain that the original crew was paid scandalously high wages to make them willing to give up the comforts of Terra for ten-hour days inside pressure suits, breathing canned oxygen—there wasn't any free oxygen, of course, or the whole planet would have gone up in smoke with the first lightning stroke. There wasn't any water, either; every drop had to be shipped in from the moon, which was fortunately mostly ice. So the Company had to provide air and water—but that was all right; it had to provide food and living quarters, too. Pretty nice living quarters, at least at first—and the food was good, by cafeteria standards. They had to do everything they could to persuade people to work under such unholy conditions—especially since the temperature was pretty hot at first, though it did cool down to something bearable. But after the rain had stopped falling, the Company offered them wages they couldn't refuse, to stay on. About two-thirds of the men accepted, and the Company shipped the others home, then brought out a number of new hands, again at huge wages on five-year contracts . . .

All women.

And a few preachers.

Then the Company saw to their work force's mental health by providing recreational facilities—3DT theaters, and sports arenas, and bars, and gambling casinos.

The miners started spending a quarter of their paychecks, between their own amusements and dating the new supply of women.

Then the Company started charging for the food.

It had originally supplied chow in mess halls, of course—but who wanted to eat institutionalized mess when they'd decided to stay a few more years? So gradually, the mess halls were phased out, and the restaurants and supermarkets phased in. That was when the miners found out how much food could cost, when it all had to be imported.

Some of them decided marriage would be cheaper than dating, and settled down.

"That's where." Chovy pointed through the windshield.

Suddenly, there were houses ahead—small, square boxes, painted in soft pastels, seeming to defy the barren beige all about them.

"This is where the workers live," Chovy said.

"But didn't the Company provide housing?" Susanne asked.

"Oh, you *have* read a history book, then!"

Susanne blushed. "Same as you—in school."

"A bit higher school, I'll wager, but no more fact in the

textbooks than the Company wants. How much did they give us—a paragraph?"

"Four," Susanne admitted.

Chovy nodded, steering smoothly past the quiet little houses lining the road. "Well, they told you the start of the story, but not its end. The Company provided housing, right enough, and still does—if you want a bunk in a barracks. Of course, that's for beginners—after a couple of raises, they put you in an apartment with three other blokes. Which is all well and good if you get along with each other, and are young and single—but when our grandsires got married, it was another matter."

"Of course," Susanne murmured.

"There speaks an honest woman," Chovy said with warmth. "And right, too—within the year, an apartment in the company's barracks wasn't good enough any more, so they took out loans and built their own minidomes—"

"And they had mortgages," Susanne said.

"Too right. Then the kids came, and they found out that they couldn't save anything, what with the high cost of living. Sure, their paychecks were gargantuan, by Terran standards—but so were the prices; and workers who'd been willing to put up with Spartan living conditions for themselves, found that they wanted something better for their spouses and children—in fact, the best possible. Which meant—"

"They weren't visitors," Susanne said.

Chovy nodded. "They were immigrants."

"Or to put it another way," Marty said, "they were stuck."

Lacey looked daggers at him, but Chovy nodded. "Don't mind putting a fine point on it, do you, Jack? But you're right, and if they were immigrants, they had to live by the law of the land."

"And who made the laws?" I asked, already knowing the answer.

"The Company, of course," Chovy said, with the contempt the question deserved. "All this time, they'd been working for the Company, and the Company had been making the rules. Even their leisure time had been spent in Company barracks, or Company recreation halls and bars—so the Company was the government."

As he explained it, the ones who accepted the fact that they weren't going to see Terra again, or at least not until the kids were grown, started wanting to have some voice in local politics—and found they couldn't. There wasn't any town government—just a Company executive. And, of course, Company police. The only good thing about it was that there weren't any tax collectors. How could there be, when the Company collected all the money and just paid wages and salaries? In fact, in some ways, it was a lot like socialism, where the government owned all the industry and distribution—except that *this* government was out to make a profit.

They provided all the necessary social services, of course—hospitals, doctors, roads, transportation, schools, and all that. Of course, if you wanted the better hospital, or personal attention from the doctor, or marriage counseling, or better teachers, you had to go to the private-practice sector. There was the public school for the workers, and for lower- and middle-management, and a private school for the upper management. Same thing for the doctors—if you wanted a human instead of a robot, you had to pay.

All in all, it was a real sweet system—if you were top management.

"Couldn't the union do something about it?" Larry asked.

"Shhh!" Chovy glanced around melodramatically. "Mind your mouth, Jack! No dirty words here, please—I run a clean cab!"

"Dirty words?" Larry flared, but Lacey put her hand on his and said, "This car isn't really bugged, is it?"

"Not that I know of, but I thought I'd make the point."

"Unions are illegal, of course," Lacey inferred.

Chovy nodded. "So is idle chitchat about unions—and *speeches* about unions are worse. But books about unions are the worst thing of all."

"Not to mention books about exploitation of labor," I inferred, "or about class conflict?"

Chovy was still nodding. "Or criminals, unless they are shown as being totally evil and always die gruesome deaths at the end. In fact, there isn't much freedom of the press, or freedom of speech, at all. There is freedom of religion, but the preachers' sermons are under the same censorship as any other speeches—and more than one preacher has wound up in jail because of it."

"These houses have domes over them," Marty pointed out.

Everyone looked. Sure enough, each house had a clear dome, like the glass over a serving dish—and it didn't just cover the house, it covered a few hundred square meters of very green lawn.

"This is where the senior workers live," Chovy explained, "the skilled tradesmen and the foremen."

"But those first houses we saw?" Lacey was staring out the side with wide, almost horrified, eyes. "Aren't they airtight?"

"Oh, they keep the air in, right enough," Chovy said. "All the houses had to, or the Company wouldn't have had any workers left. Of course, they could let the house have a few leaks and put a dome over it, if they wanted a bit of a yard for the kid to play in. Not too big a dome, of course, because the Company allotted them just so much air per week. Sure, they could have extra—if they paid for it. Some of them did; it was a status symbol, having a bigger dome. Management had big domes indeed, and you could tell how high up the ladder a man was by the size of his geodesic—and the size of the house inside it, of course, but it was the ratio of lawn to house that was the real status symbol. The top kick, the managing director, only had a twenty-room house, nothing palatial—but his garden was a virtual park, and his dome was two hundred meters across."

A slow-moving vehicle turned the corner ahead of us and came trundling toward us. It was a tank truck, with a very thick hose coiled on a reel at the back.

"An oil truck?" Marty stared. "Of course, I should have realized. What else would you heat your houses with?"

"Geothermal," Chovy said immediately, "when there's any need for heat, which is only a few weeks out of the year. We don't burn oil, Jack. We don't burn *anything*."

"Not even if the fire's locked up tight inside a furnace?"

"What's inside can come out," Chovy said.

Marty got that faraway look in his eye that meant he was working up a new joke. Before he could let it out, I said quickly, "So what *is* in the truck?"

"Water," Chovy said. "The nice man comes around and fills your tank once a month."

"What happens if you run out before the end of the month?" Lacey asked.

"You stay dirty," Chovy answered.

The cab was awfully quiet for a minute. Then Susanne said, "What do you drink?"

"Whatever you can," Chovy said. "There's always cola—if you have the cash."

"Speaking of cash," I said, "what happens if you can't pay for the tankful of water?"

Chovy turned around and flashed me a grin. "Why, then, you owe the Company. No shame in that, Jack—everybody owes the Company. More and more, all the time."

We were quiet again. Then Marty quoted, "He who dies, pays all debts."

"Not here," Chovy said. "When you die, your kids inherit whatever debts you didn't manage to pay before you died."

"Can't you borrow from somebody else besides the Company?" Larry asked.

"Wrong." Chovy shook his head. "Very wrong. This poor bloke already owes half his hide to the Company, and you want to take what he's got that was going to pay for the other half? Very wrong, Jack. Nobody borrows here— except from the Company. You have to do that, or you wouldn't have food to eat."

"Where do you shop?" I had a hollow feeling in my belly.

"The Company store," Chovy said. "They're all Company stores."

"So," Susanne said, "You're born into debt . . ."

"And you die in debt," Chovy finished. "And you live in debt, or you don't live at all. Welcome to life on New Venus."

Even Marty wasn't up to giving a fanfare.

Finally, to break the silence, I said, "You know, there's something I don't see here."

"There's an awful lot I don't see," Lacey said angrily. "But what are *you* missing, Ramou?"

"Posters," I said. "Handbills. Billboards. Anything advertising the Star Co— the Star Repertory Theater, performing in its gala opening."

I glanced at their faces. They were all wide-eyed in horror.

It was Marty who voiced it. "You don't suppose nobody knows we're coming, do you?"

12

"Do you suppose anyone knew we were coming?" I ventured.

Barry's face was grim—or at least his eyes were; his mouth and nose were hidden by his breathing mask. He had been seized by the same apprehension, but both of us had hesitated to voice it, as if the mere saying of it might have made it come true. Now, though, the fear was in the open, and we had to deal with it. "We must find Publius and discuss the issue," he said, his voice coming flat and muffled through the breather.

"How are we to find him?" I wondered.

"Easily enough," Barry said. "There can't be all that many hotels in so rudimentary a town."

I looked around me at the bleakness and devastation of graded and rammed earth and low, beige and gray buildings, slightly relieved by garish shop signs. Oh, some of the stores had been cast in pastels, but time and ultraviolet had softened and leached the color till it was almost indistinguishable from the rest. We were looking at downtown Aphrodite, capital of New Venus—and a very negative tribute to the goddess of beauty it was. "In fact," I murmured, "I can't think there would be even one hotel. Who would wish to visit here if he did not have to?"

"Ah, but we must consider those who *must* visit," Barry said, smiling. "After all, Amalgamated Petroleum has many outlying offices; surely their executives must need to attend conferences with the central management now and again."

"But why?" I said. "With visiphones . . ."

"For the impact of personal confrontation." Barry turned to me, the smile still in place. "Surely a man dedicated to live theater could understand that better than any. For personal confrontation, inspiration, and intimidation, and for the ceremonies of power."

"Also for security," I amended, "if they don't want some enthusiastic teenager eavesdropping electronically on their plans for dealing with labor."

Barry nodded. "No doubt. So I would be surprised if the Company did not have some accommodation for visiting executives—which is, I trust, willing to take the occasional tourist from Terra."

"Tourist?" I wrinkled my nose at the scent of gasoline fumes that managed to penetrate through my breathing mask—spray suspended in the helium, no doubt. "Who would want to visit this barren—"

"Now, now, my good Horace," Barry reminded me, "we are guests, of a sort."

I sighed. "I shall try to remember, Barry. Now, where is this hotel?"

We had asked the cabbie to drop us in the center of town, so that we could wander about a bit and get the feel of the locale—get lost and find our way home, as it were. We had managed to become lost excellently, but we were doing rather poorly at finding our way home.

"I haven't the faintest," he replied, "but I do see a phone."

I looked up and saw the screen fastened to the side of a tavern, with a sign above it that read, "If you can't make it in on time, *phone*!" Pleasant chaps.

Barry stepped up, fed in his credit card, and waited while a mellow synthesized voice advised him, "Processing." Just in case he couldn't hear, it flashed the words on the screen, too. Then they were suddenly replaced by a sign saying "Dial," and the voice said, "Please dial your call," in the event that Barry could not read.

That meant that it had cleared his credit card for use. I had a brief but dizzying vision of electronic impulses corresponding to his credit number, spinning through the fibers of the information network of New Venus, then flashing out across the void to a central computer register on Terra . . . No, of course not. There was no faster-than-light radio; the credit check would have taken three weeks en route to Terra, just as we had, then taken another three weeks for the confirmation to return—and that only if there happened to be a spaceship leaving, one that could take a recording of the transaction. By radio itself, the signal would have taken four years each way, for a total of eight. No, New Venus must have had a complete copy of the credit data base from Terra, updated periodically.

"Information, please," Barry said.

"Information," the mellifluous voice replied. "How may we help you?"

"Hotels, please," Barry said.

"The Cosmos Hotel," the computer said as the name appeared in tinted letters on the screen. "12-34561."

Barry waited.

"The Cosmos Hotel," the voice said again. "12-34561."

Barry stared, surprised.

"Is there only the one?" I asked.

Before Barry could answer, the voice asked, "Will there be anything more, sir?"

"There are no other hotels?" Barry asked, then remembered that computers analyze syntax, not inflection, "Are there no other hotels?"

"None, sir. Shall I connect you to the Cosmos?"

"Yes, if you would be so kind," Barry answered.

I caught myself wondering if the computer would also

record the conversation, and decided I was becoming paranoid.

A face appeared on the screen, a polite mask with a frame of auburn hair about it. "Hotel Cosmos."

"I wish to speak with Mr. Publius Promo," Barry told the mask.

The face only smiled back for a second, its eyes never leaving Barry's face, then abruptly said, "He is not in, sir. Would you care to leave a message?"

I realized, with a shock, that the polite mask was only that—a mask, a computer-generated picture of a face, seeming more real than the actuality. It had no need to look up information; it had only needed to search its memory, which had taken less than a second.

"Yes, please," Barry said. "Ask him to contact Mr. Barry Tallendar at the starship *Cotton Blossom.*"

"Yes, sir. Will that be all?"

"Yes, thank you."

"Thank you for calling the Hotel Cosmos, sir." And the screen went blank.

Barry turned away from the phone. "Well, he's not in his room. Where would you think to look for him?"

"In the taverns, of course," I answered. "Where else?"

Barry looked startled for a moment, then nodded. "Of course. Why did I not think of that? Come, Horace. Let us see if we can find a tavern."

We found one. We found several. We found many. There were a very great number of taverns.

Barry was beginning to look gaunt and weary as we came out of the fifteenth house of alcoholic refreshment, and I confess that I was not feeling terribly spry myself. All that walking had been bad enough—though not outrageous, for men used to navigating Manhattan. What truly wore us out was the ladies parading for temperance.

"Is the poison washed out!"

Barry and I had looked up and back, startled.

There they were, frowsy housewives in shapeless dresses with trumpets and drums, beating up a racket and blaring most ferociously—and off-key; I winced visibly. I assumed their instruments had some symbolic significance—that was the only reason I could imagine for not using electronic keyboards that would, at least, have had accurate pitch. But no, the trumpets shrilled, and the bass drum battered our ears. They were gathered around a huge wheeled vehicle with a shape like a pregnant cucumber, and a sign on the side that proclaimed H_2O DELIVERIES. A man slunk out of the cab and caught the nozzle of a huge hose as he passed, very quickly, and almost ran to the nearest building, where he fastened the hose to a coupling in the wall and leaned back in relief.

Now the good ladies did use electronics, or at least their leader did. "Climb on the water wagon!" she bellowed through an amplified megaphone—and, yes, she really did yell, into an instrument that was amplifying her voice—yell, when all she had to do was turn up the volume. As it was, she accomplished nothing but a horrifying distortion of her voice that rendered her words almost incomprehensible.

"Are you whited in the wash?" she bellowed. "Have you flushed out the booze? Or do you have a wife and children at home, waiting for your paycheck? Hard-hearted heathens!"

Barry winced; I was afraid I must have, also.

"You there!" The harpy pounced with avarice. "You men!"

We looked around; surely she must have been addressing someone else. But no, the street was empty except for Barry and myself. I was sure there had been a score of men walking about only moments before.

"Where is your wife!" The harridan's forefinger stabbed out at me.

"Which one?" Barry asked, wide-eyed.

"Bigamy!" one of the other women shouted.

The harridan turned on me. "How many poor girls have you despoiled, deceiver?"

"None," I said. "At least, they weren't poor when I left them."

"So you thought to buy their virtue, did you? Whoremaster!"

"No, husband," I said imperturbably, "and only once. Though I will admit to the occasional liaison before I met her."

"Poor, naive girls whom you despoiled and threw away!"

"A few years older than me, actually, and quite sophisticated."

"And you threw them away!"

"No, actually, they broke up with me, though they were quite gentle about it—all except my wife."

"Because you were a slave to demon rum!" the fishwife orated, raising her right arm on high as if to smite the evildoer. "A worthless drone made useless by the devil gin!"

"Wrong again," I said, fighting down my irritation. "I rarely overindulge, and never on working days."

Disappointed, she turned to Barry. "And where are *your* wives?"

"All back on Terra," Barry said, with imperturbable poise, "and all collecting alimony."

Well. Now I knew what had happened to all that money he had earned in his prime.

The harridan opened her mouth, but Barry forestalled her. "My habits are temperate; I drink, but rarely in excess."

"Rarely!" she trumpeted. "That means you do get drunk! How often is 'rarely,' sinner? How many women have you left in poverty because you were so sodden with drink that you couldn't earn a living?"

"None," Barry assured her. "As I've told you, they all

take alimony, though none of them really needs it—and all three chose divorce, though I didn't wish it."

"No doubt because you were enslaved to the demon!"

"Not unless you're counting work as a demon. In fact, that was their cause for complaint, all three—that I spent to much time earning, and too little with them."

"Deserter!" the ringleader cried. "Abandoner!" But doubt was beginning to shadow her face.

Barry ignored the accusation. "As to the frequency of 'rarely,' I exercise moderation in all things—including moderation."

"How can you moderate moderation!" the harridan fairly screeched.

"By occasional excesses. It restores a sense of balance to a disciplined life."

"You're talking nonsense!" the woman orated, and turned to her followers. "Sisters! His brain is a sponge soaked in alcohol! So thoroughly soaked that he cannot make sense! Exhort them, admonish them!" Then she turned back to the two of us and began to chant, "Climb! Climb! Climb on the water wagon!"

The ladies behind her took it up:

> "Water wagon! Water wagon!
> Climb on the wagon!
> Throw away the booze,
> Pull on your shoes!
> Go out and earn a life
> For your children and your wife!"

The chap with the nozzle unscrewed it from the connection on the shop front, nerved himself with a shudder, and dashed back to the shelter of his cab. The drum on the back revolved slowly, winding up the hose. The nozzle thrashed to and fro like a cobra looking for a choice morsel, and one of the women had to jump out of its way. "Brute!" she shouted at the driver. "Trying to strike a poor, defenseless housewife with the end of your great long thrasher!"

But the driver had made it back to the shelter of his cab, and the truck rumbled with menace as it heaved itself into motion. The women sidestepped deftly and followed after it, shouting and banging. The leader looked back for a parting shot at Barry and myself. "Go home to your wives and your families, slackers!" But she had to turn away and hurry to catch up with her mob, as the truck pulled away. The last of the women followed it around the corner, though we could still hear their chanting and thumping— and we found ourselves facing the blank, bleak face of another tavern. With one accord, we dashed into it as if to a haven in a storm.

We came in, shuddering. "What was all that about?" Barry wondered.

"Apparently, the ladies have taken exception to their husbands' frequenting of establishments like this one," I guessed, "though if they behave like that at home, I don't wonder the poor men would rather spend their time in bars. At least in here there is peace and fellowship."

Barry turned to me with pursed lips. "That's right, you did know what it was to always come home to an argument, didn't you?"

I looked away.

Quickly, he said, "No, no, I know you never spoke of it, and won't to this day—but I knew as well as you did, I'm afraid. I was quite relieved when she left you—though heaven knows she had no cause."

"I had become rather inattentive," I admitted.

"Who wouldn't, with a harridan like that?" He held up a palm. "No, no, old chap, no offense intended; sorry about the insult to your former lady. And perhaps I wrong these possibly-worthy housewives; I seem to remember that men who feel trapped into a bleak existence of unremitting toil tend toward alcoholism."

I nodded. "It was endemic on the American frontier, as well as in the mill towns—and if the man became so incapacitated as to be unable to work, his wife and children fell into utter poverty. I seem to have read somewhere that a woman's only protection was a sober, hardworking man, which was why the Ladies' Temperance Union gained so many adherents and thrived for so long."

Barry nodded. "Though one wonders if they wouldn't have done better to make their homes and themselves so pleasant that their husbands would have felt they were worth all that work."

"I seem to remember the argument that such efforts constituted expoitation of women," I demurred, though not with much conviction. "Why were they clustered around that huge truck, though?"

"I noticed the sign on the side," Barry said. "I believe that truly was a water wagon—or its modern equivalent. But why was it going about making deliveries?"

"No doubt we'll discover that in time." I sighed. "Perhaps municipal plumbing isn't all that it should be." My eyes suddenly lost focus as I contemplated a thought. "On Terra, when petroleum was scarce, water ran through the city pipes, but oil was delivered by truck. You don't suppose . . . ?"

"Perhaps," Barry mused. "But it does seem odd that a tavern should be concerned about its water supply."

"It may be that the bartenders know better than to sample their own product," I conjectured. "After all, they know what is in it."

Reminded of our whereabouts, we looked around us. It seemed just like any other tavern—dim and dingy, with a row of recreational machines against the far wall. The air reeked of stale beer. The atmosphere of taverns will always be the same, I fear—one of the enduring characteristics of mankind, I reflected as I surveyed the room.

Then my head stopped turning, and my eyes focused on

a face. I felt as if that face had just jumped closer to fill my
field of vision. It was a somber face, a hangdog face, a
woeful and woebegone face, as crestfallen as I'd ever
seen—and at the moment, it seemed to have fallen into
the mug of dark liquid in front of it. Bitter, I judged
by the color, and of strong alcoholic content, as I judged by
the heaviness of his eyelids and the slight swaying in his
seat.

I nudged Barry. "I think I have discovered the reason for
our lack of publicity."

He turned, and his breath hissed out in a sigh of satisfaction. "Indeed, it would seem to have been drowned in
beer."

Then we were moving forward together, splitting to go
around to opposite sides of the table, and sitting in the
chairs to either side of the face, that lugubrious face with
the gaze sunk deep into its glass of bitter. It was much gone
to flesh, flesh that sagged into jowls. The chin sagged, too,
into a double or more—unshaven, at the moment. The eyes
seemed too small for all that skin.

Barry reached out and gently removed the glass from the
hand. The fold of mouth opened to let out a cry and glared
up at him—then turned ash pale, and the eyes suddenly
seemed of a size with the face. "M-Mr. Tallendar!"

"I was 'Barry' on Terra, and I'm still 'Barry' here," my
friend said gently.

"Of—of course, Mr. . . . Barry!"

"I am delighted to see you again, Publius," Barry said,
still gently.

"Uh—same here, Mr. Tal—Barry! But, uh, I uh, wasn't,
uh, expecting you . . ."

Certainly not, I reflected grimly; but Barry was more so-
licitous. "We had a sudden change of plans, due to the efforts of Elector Rudders. He worked up enough sentiment
among the electors so that they were on the verge of passing a law that would have prevented our emigrating to

bring the benefits of culture to the heathen of the frontier planets—so my brother Valdor fought a delaying action while we moved our departure date up a bit. Of course, we'll understand if it is impossible for us to open before our scheduled playing date—but I was rather hoping to be able to move the opening up somewhat."

"Uh ... yeah, sure, Mr. ... Barry!" Publius was regaining some poise, but he still looked fearful—and quite bleary.

"I was rather disappointed to see no trace of publicity announcing our arrival," Barry said, still gently, "though I suppose that might have been premature, with opening night still a month away."

"Uhhhh ... yeah! Premature!" Publius nodded vigorously.

Barry took hold of his forearm, and his voice rang with the echo of steel. "Publius—have you placed an order for posters?"

Publius hung his head.

"Publius," Barry said, "have you rented a theater?"

He was about to go on, but I touched his elbow. Barry looked and saw that Publius's shoulders were shaking. "It's horrible, Mr. Tallendar! The ignorance in which this planet is sunk! They're uncultured, that's what they are, totally uncultured, swine sunk in darkness, that's what, and they don't give a fig about art or poetry, they don't even dream of pulling themselves up, they're just know-nothings full of turpitude and proud of their heathenry!"

"From that," I said, "I would gather that you've had no success."

But Barry, kindly again, said, "Come, man, pull yourself together and tell us the worst of it!"

"They won't let us play," Publius blubbered.

"Won't let us play!" we both cried, horrified.

"Well, they'll have to, at least for one performance," Publius amended. He pulled a sheet of paper out of his inner pocket and unfolded it on the table. Craning my neck, I could make out an official seal under some signatures at the bottom. "I got it in writing—oh, they were overjoyed at first! 'Culture for the people,' they said. 'That should keep them quiet for a spell!' And I got them to sign this before the enthusiasm wore off, says we have the privilege of performing in public in the city of Aphrodite—but it doesn't say where, nor how often! Then just today, they called me in and told me they'd changed their minds . . ."

"Just today?" Barry looked up at me, frowning. "How long ago was this?"

"Two hours."

The same thought leaped to both our minds, I'm sure, for Barry's eyes must have been a reflection of my own—that the courier ship that had passed us had indeed carried a private message from the LORDS party to their members here—of whom management was no doubt inclusive. Rudders had anticipated us, had sent word that we weren't to be allowed to perform. Would our whole tour be blockaded thus? For surely, while we tarried on New Venus battling bureaucracy for access to an audience, Rudders' couriers were speeding through the void to bear the same message to all the colony planets.

There had to be another explanation. Barry turned to Publius. "Why?"

"I can't say." Publius looked down into his drink, a fat tear forming at the inner corner of his eye. "I only know that every poster I paste up gets torn down; every merchant I ask to display our bill in his window refuses. Of course, they're all Company stores."

"Then why don't you try non-Company stores?" I asked.

"There aren't any. Even the bartenders won't let me post bills!"

"Though they don't mind letting you run one up." I watched as he tipped his mug to drain the last drop; the bill must have been gigantic.

Right on cue, the waiter came up with a tumbler full of a clear fluid.

"I think we could do with one of those, too." Barry glanced at me; I nodded. "Each," he said to the waiter. "But you might put a little vermouth in it."

The waiter nodded and turned away, and Barry turned back to Publius just as he set the glass down and asked, hoping not to hear the answer we suspected, "Why are they so intent on stopping us?"

Publius drew circles in the moisture on the table. "I can only guess, Mr. Tallendar."

"Then do," Barry urged. "Conjecture for us."

Publius looked up into his eyes, suddenly earnest. "It's ideas, you see, Mr. Tallendar. You can't do a play without ideas—no one will come to see it."

"Yes, that's true," I said. "If it's all froth and no substance, the audience will feel cheated. Even the most superficial farce has to offer some insights into human character, or the word will get around, and the audience won't come."

Publius nodded, making his jowls quiver. "That's right, Mr. Burbage, that's right! But if there's ideas, you see, they might be ideas that the management doesn't want labor to hear—maybe heretical notions about individuality or human rights, or even some nonsense about people wanting a voice in their own government. At the worst, it might make them think—and you never can tell what may happen when people begin to think for themselves." He glanced about furtively, then leaned close—Barry winced at the reek—and confided, "Then there's the union."

"Union?" I frowned. "Surely there are no unions on this planet; they must be illegal!"

"Shhh! Not so loud." Publius glanced about frantically, but no one seemed to be listening. He relaxed and leaned closer, confiding, "Illegal it is, but it's there nonetheless."

My eyes widened as I realized the implications. On a

company world, in which management is government, then surely a union must be a subversive organization.

"All well and true," Barry said, "but why should the union not want us seen?"

"A man came up to me when I'd been here a week," Publius said. I wasn't clear as to whether he meant on New Venus a week, or in that bar for a week, the more so as he went on: "He came up and sat beside me as I was drinking and hissed at me that this 'thee-yater' was just a capitalist plot to rob the poor working man of a few more of his hard-earned BTUs."

"Not really!" I said, but Publius nodded, with a sardonic smile.

"Surely you can place broadcast advertisements," Barry protested. "Surely this benighted planet does have 3DT!"

"Oh, they have it, all right," Publius said, "but the network's run by the Company, too—everything is, here—so they won't touch anything that's not approved by the censors."

"The very censorship that we fled Terra to escape!" Barry said in disgust.

"The urge toward total control festers eternally in the insecure breast," I replied, then turned to Publius. "Why, then, are we being allowed to perform at all?"

"Because they gave permission in writing before Rudders' message reached them," Barry said, "and perhaps also because trying to shut us down would be too obvious a contradiction of free enterprise, which is the cornerstone of their philosophy—or, rather, of the philosophical system to which they pay lip service. It is far less troublesome to let us perform, but virtually guarantee that we shall have no audience."

"I see." I nodded. "In that manner, they preserve the appearance of free enterprise, without risking the substance."

"Well put," Barry agreed. "Then, too, if the show folds and we are all stranded here without the price of the fuel we need to lift off, the Company will have the benefit of a few more unwilling workers."

I sat rigid, chilled by the thought of spending my declining days on so barren and bleak a dust ball, dipping oil— not to mention the fact that I was far too old for the arduous manual-labor positions that would be all that would be available to a newcomer without status. "Surely it will not come to that!"

"Oh, certainly not!" Barry waved the thought away. "Valdor and I had anticipated that we would operate at a loss for the first season, possibly even for the second—so I came well equipped with sufficient funds to buy enough fuel to lift off of a dozen planets."

"Your power plant is fusion, right?" Publius asked.

"Of course." Barry frowned. "Aren't they all?"

"Then it needs water for its raw fuel."

"Certainly, water, which is broken down into oxygen for breathing, and hydrogen for fusion—water, which is in copious supply on any Terrestrial world, in teeming abund—" Barry's voice ran down as he realized the implications of what he was saying.

Publius nodded. "New Venus isn't all that Earth-like, Mr. Tallendar. There's no natural water; they have to synthesize it all, or import it from the asteroids."

"Alpha Centauri has asteroids?" I asked.

"No, but Proxima does, and it's only a short haul, in H-space. But the water's expensive."

"Yes, I see that it would be." For the first time, Barry looked worried. "That could throw off our financial planning a bit. Oh, no, not enough to keep us on New Venus . . ."

"But management doesn't know that," I interpreted.

"Let us not seek to enlighten them, then." Barry stirred restlessly. "But let us do all we can to attract a large crowd—in spite of their discouragements."

"I'll get full houses for you, Mr. Tallendar," Publius promised. "I don't know how, but I'll do it."

"So good of you," Barry murmured. "Speaking of the house, Mr. Promo, I don't suppose you've rented a theater? Or some kind of performance space, at least?"

Publius lapsed into another fit of gloom. "They're all owned by the Company, Mr. Tallendar." He gazed down into his glass again, shoulders shaking.

"Come, man, buck up!" Barry slapped him on the back. "It's just red tape, after all! What did they say?"

"Not a word." Publius gasped and lifted his head, blinking away tears. "They won't even talk to me. Mr. Tallendar, and that's the truth! Insisted on talking to you, in person!"

Barry gazed at him for a long moment, then sighed. "Ah, the price of fame! Well then, I shall talk with them, Publius. Who are 'they'?"

"The city fathers," Publius said. "The planetary government. Which, on a planet that's just one big company town, means: the management."

13

"The management," as it eventuated, was a committee.

"Of course," Barry murmured to me as we rode up in the lift—the old-fashioned kind, in which the car rode on a hydraulic column. The colony planets tend to have more primitive technology, since they lack the capacity for producing spare parts for sophisticated machines—and New Venus certainly did not lack for hydraulic fluid.

"Why 'of course'?" I asked, somewhat nettled. "They could at least accord us a single individual to speak with!"

"Ah, but a committee is far more intimidating," Barry reminded me, "and makes it possible for no single person to have to accept the responsibility, should anything go wrong."

I felt anger beginning to rise. "They will not find we are easily intimidated!"

"To be sure, they will not," Barry agreed, "but we must be courteous, my good Horace. After all, we *are* guests."

"True." I sighed and did not state the obvious—that the committee had the authority to refuse us an opportunity to perform. "Still, it would be much more effective to deal with a single person."

"And I don't doubt that we shall," Barry assured me, "though not until we have run the gamut of the committee's interrogation."

He was right, of course. He must have picked up some hints of business procedure from Valdor. What the true purposes of the Committee on Cultural Resources were, I can only conjecture—giving junior executives a feeling of importance, or an opportunity to curry favor with the upper management wives, or a sinecure for executives who had already reached a dead end in the Company, or for those who had been passed over for promotion and needed the illusion of importance without the substance—it would have been difficult to say. Their real purpose was plain—to impress the famous visitors from off-planet with their own importance, to make clear in their own minds that they were more important than two famous actors, to make clear to us where the true power lay, and to make absolutely certain that we would not present any hazard to the Company or the existing social order. Barry bore it all with stoic grace, smiling where necessary, looking deeply serious when appropriate, and flattering their miniscule egos, never too obviously, whenever the opportunity presented itself. The upshot of it all was their reluctant approval—I rather thought they overdid the reluctance—and their assigning of us to the civil servant who was in charge of actually getting things done.

"The *high school*?" I said, as soon as the lift doors had closed behind us. "Why on earth would they assign us to the director of the high school?"

"You heard their rationale," Barry sighed. "Their primary concern is the welfare of their children and youth . . ."

"Also incidentally insuring that the adults are not exposed to rebellious notions," I clarified, "since if our plays cannot be presented due to ideas that are questionable for young people, they also cannot be seen by their parents."

"Of course," Barry said, "they could arrange separate performances, to which youths are not admitted—but I am certain they have their reasons for not wishing to do so."

"Yes," I said darkly, "and you and I both know what those reasons are. Barry, this is unabashed censorship!"

"It is," Barry admitted, "but let us try to see the issue

from their point of view. In fact, let us see the issue from the point of view they claim, which is even more demanding than the one they actually hold: that they do not wish to have their young people exposed to ideas that might trouble them, frighten them, or reinforce antisocial impulses—and who would be more aware of what is good and bad for youth than the director of the high school? Especially since, as senior education official, he is also director of all the schools. It is simply that his office is at the high school."

"Wonderful," I grumbled.

"Now, Horace," Barry soothed, "look on the bright side. If he is a dedicated official who is sincerely devoted to the welfare and mental enrichment of his students, he could welcome us with open arms, as the greatest cultural resource ever made available to him."

"In which case, he will no doubt wish us to delete only the more scurrilous lines and omit *Didn't He Ramble?*" I muttered. "Of course, he could be a self-serving career bureaucrat whose only true dedication is to himself and his own advancement, and his interest in his students *might* be limited to keeping them off the streets and teaching them to submit to authority—but let us not consider that."

"Why, as you say, old chap," Barry murmured. "I shan't."

The taxi driver of course had no need for directions; everyone in town knew where the high school was.

"There is only the one?" Barry asked.

"Course, mister," the driver answered. "If you'd wanted the academy, you would've said 'the academy.' "

Which left me wondering what the academy was.

I might have been only well known within the trade, and to the truly dedicated theatergoers—but Barry had been a star, and was still famous, and was certainly deserving of

honor. He was certainly *not* deserving of arriving at the
school unheralded, with no one waiting to welcome him,
nor of having to walk in unannounced like any common
salesman or deliveryman.

On the other hand, give them their due; perhaps they
could not believe that a truly famous person would come to
their out-of-the-way school; perhaps they believed it was all
a hoax.

Or perhaps the committee had not phoned ahead and told
them of our arrival—but I don't believe that for a second.
I believe, quite thoroughly, that the director knew Barry
was on his way over and chose to make him go through
channels like any common deliveryman, to make clear that
here, at least, Barry was not important, and the director
was.

I could see that Barry knew this, too, by the curl of his
lip and the set of his jaw; but all he said was, "Shall we enter, Horace?"

We went inside; the door hissed shut behind us, and the
lock cycled through. The inner door opened, and we took
off our breathers as we stepped in, slipping them into our
inner pockets.

A sign glared at us, fixed to a pillar directly in front of
the door:

ALL VISITORS MUST REGISTER AT FRONT DESK.

As if they hadn't known we were coming! But one look
at Barry's face, and I held my peace. He stood a moment,
very still, staring at the sign, then turned away to search the
lobby for the front desk, his face immobile.

An electronic tone sounded.

Instant babble! A horde of noise, remotely identifiable as
comprising youthful voices, assaulted our ears. A second
later, their bodies assaulted our space. We had to step back
against the pillar to avoid being crushed; even as it was,
one young man with a pompadour and some very colorful

clothing jostled me as he passed, snarling, "Outa the way, duffer!"

I pulled myself very upright, feeling my face grow hot. Barry's hand fastened on my shoulder. "Steady, old fellow, steady! After all, they're too young to remember you as Morty the Milkman."

I tried to allow for their ignorance, though from the look of them, I couldn't allow for much innocence. We took our station in the lee side of the pillar, letting it break the flow for us, and waited it out as teenagers streamed past on each side of us, reuniting in a single flow a meter beyond.

Then another tone sounded and, as suddenly as it had begun, the flood was over. A few stragglers sprinted by, late for class; then the hallway was clear.

Barry stepped away from the pillar, a hard glint in his eye. "Come, Horace. Let us comply with regulations."

Apparently, during the barrage, he had identified the front desk, for he stepped over to a long, high counter without the slightest hesitation and waited for the old dragon behind it to look up and inquire as to our business.

And waited.

And waited.

A pretty young thing in a cheerleader's uniform bustled in behind the counter and handed a cube to the old dragon. "Here's batch file on the freshman boys, Ms. Turpentine." Of her uniform, the less said, the better—because the less is what it was.

The old dragon gave her a curt nod, stuffed the cube into the ROM slot, and fixed her gaze on her screen.

The cheerleader sat down behind the other desk, its surface strewn with hard copies and cubes.

I stared. What could they be thinking of, using students as office help?

Barry must have had a similar reaction, but he recovered more quickly than I and cleared his throat.

The PYT looked up. "Did you need something?"

"I would like to speak to the secretary," Barry said.

"I'm the secretary."

Barry stared. "A student, the school secretary?!"

A ripple of annoyance passed across her face, leaving it as expressionless as before. "I'm the *morning* secretary."

"Morning?" I realized I was staring and gave myself a shake. "What do you do during the afternoons?"

"I go to class, of course! Literature, math, history, science, and phys ed. I just get one hour of credit for being secretary—and a paycheck, of course. The director calls it maximal utilization of personnel resources."

"Fascinating," I breathed. "What do the students who go to school all day learn?"

"Oh, the same, of course, plus electives. I have to give up my electives for this job."

I couldn't help wondering what the electives were. Household Maintenance? 3DT Appreciation? Contemporary Verse and Music? But I forebore to ask, saying only, "Your uniform . . ."

"Oh, this?" She gave it a scrap of a glance, which was appropriate. "I didn't design it. Now come on, tell me whatever you have in mind! I've got a lot to do."

I wondered if learning manners was on her list, but Barry managed to absorb the shock and be all urbane politeness again. I wondered if he was regretting leaving his milieu, but he showed no sign of sensing the humiliation. "We have come to see the director."

She glanced at a smaller screen inset on her desk top. "Do you have an appointment?"

"I assume so; my name is Barry Tallendar."

She shook her head. "Doesn't say so here."

Barry took a deep breath. "We were referred to him by the Committee on Cultural Affairs."

She frowned, but touched a key on her desk. "Ms. Turpentine, do you know anything about the cultural committee sending someone over to talk to Mr. Seeholder?"

Her voice repeated, echolike, over Ms. Turpentine's desk. The old battle-ax looked up, pressed another key, and said, "Oh, yes, Flippie, they called over twenty minutes ago, said for the director to squeeze him in. I asked what about, and they said he knew."

Flippie looked up at us with a dubious frown. "Well, I guess you can go in." She turned back to her desk.

"*Thank* you," Barry breathed. "In where?"

She looked up, annoyed, and pointed at a door to our right, opposite the lobby. "In there."

"In there" turned out to be a warren of offices that must surely have been laid out by a drunken rat on an off day. Several cold glances speared us as we wandered from one waiting room to another, accidentally stumbling into several cubicles inhabited by people gazing at screens, then backing out again. Barry said nothing, but he was growing more pale, and his face more taut, the farther we went.

Finally, we stumbled into the last waiting room. It was not large, but the carpet was thick and the lighting was muted. There was a secretary off to the side—it was typical of the colony planets that they had as a matter of course what would have been the highest order of luxury on Terra: a live receptionist. On the frontier, people were cheaper than machines.

But this one might as well have been a machine, for all the courtesy she gave us. No, let me amend that—I've encountered machines that were far more accommodating. She gave us a disinterested glance and pointed to a few straight chairs lined up against the wall. "Sit down. It'll be a while."

We sat.

I suppose my mounting anger must have been showing in the color of my face, because Barry leaned over to me and said, "Remember, Horace, we need his approval."

I nearly exploded—but with a supreme effort, I mastered my anger and began to breathe slowly and steadily. Barry was right—we were in no position to stalk out in high dudgeon. I glanced at Barry's profile, though, and from the speculative look on his face, I thought he might be toying with various possibilities of revenge.

We waited an hour.

Finally, Mr. Seeholder must have been satisfied that he had asserted his own importance sufficiently, and had cowed his guests plentifully, for he finally came out of his office. He was short, plump, and bullet-headed, with a fringe of fuzz around a bald pate. I noted it carefully—the fashion had once had a brief vogue among midlevel managers; leaving the bald spot had supposedly proved that they were too busy to have hair-restoration treatments, thereby testifying to their importance.

He ignored us.

He ignored us, and stepped over to his secretary. "Ms. Chainsaw, have those people the committee sent over arrived yet?"

"Yes, sir." She didn't bat an eye—apparently she had been through this before. Moreover, she relished it. "They're waiting, right over there." She pointed.

Seeholder turned and feigned surprise. "Gentlemen! A pleasure to see you! You're the actors, I gather?"

Ms. Chainsaw did a double take, which was satisfying—then gave us a glare, which was not. Were these people so benighted as to equate theater with vice?

They were.

I could only compare this travesty of a reception by a small-town petty official with the courtesy lavished upon us when we had called on Barry's brother, Valdor Tallendar, who was a billionaire several times over and one of the most important men in the whole of the Terran Sphere. Perhaps it was because he knew he was truly important, so did not need to emphasize it—whereas Seeholder secretly suspected that he was truly insignificant, therefore feeling the need to be so rude and treat famous men so shabbily.

But Mr. Seeholder was giving each of our hands a quick squeeze and dropping them as quickly as he could. "Come on, let me show you my school!"

"I don't think . . ." Barry began.

"But you really must!" A hint of iron in the tone, then Seeholder was all affability again as he stepped in front of us, beckoning.

We followed grimly, though outwardly smiling. The quid pro quo was clear—if we did not listen to Seeholder boast about his little school, he would not give us the permission we needed to perform. I took another deep, even breath and followed.

But my mood was not helped by hearing Flippie mutter to Turpentine, as we passed them, "Silly old geezers!" I lost the rest of the remark, but vowed that Valdor would not. Even if Barry was too much the gentleman to ask his brother to intervene, I was determined that I would not be—for the first time in my life. I would write to Valdor that very evening and tell him in detail how his brother had been slighted. I would be very surprised if, in a year or so, Seeholder did not find himself back in the classroom, and Flippie studying nothing more than the beans in the cafeteria pot. The mills of the tycoons grind slowly, but grind they do, and the grist rues the day it saw the stone.

Meanwhile, though, we had to see the school.

We saw it all—the swimming pool, the indoor track, the outdoor track, the boys' gymnasium, the wrestling room, the boxing room, the football room, the weight-lifting room, the cafeteria, the girls' gymnasium, the squash court, the aerobics studio, the cheerleaders' room, and the Grand Gymnasium.

"That's where you'll be performing, by the way," Seeholder said as we started out of the huge athletic chamber.

Barry stopped. "Don't you have a theater?"

Seeholder shook his head. "No money for nonessentials,

Mr. Tallendar. We have to answer to the Company—no extraneous expenditures."

"But surely an auditorium . . ."

"No need. We can hold assemblies in the gym just fine. Students sit on the bleachers, and we have a portable stage we can rig up. It'll do you folks great, no problem."

Barry swallowed and remembered to flatter where he could. "You must be very proud of your young athletes."

"Winners, every one of 'em." Seeholder nodded, almost visibly expanding. "Beat every other team on the planet, every sport."

"Other teams?" Barry frowned. "I should have thought this was the only school."

"No. There are a host of boondock towns here, to service the loading siphons. Four or five of 'em band together to run a high school—not much, really, but enough for the basics: football, baseball, basketball, swimming. We beat 'em hands down, of course . . ." A shadow crossed his face. ". . . except for the academy. But you don't dare win against the managers' sons—fact of life. Now, let me show you the karate dojo . . ."

He also showed us the snack bar, the electronics shop, the metals shop, the housepainting shop, the plastics shop, the small engines shop, the large engines shop, the football field, the soccer field, the baseball stadium, the skating rink—all indoor, of course, since breathers encumbered athletic prowess.

Seeholder expanded visibly as he proudly paraded his domain before us, rattling on about the virtues of each specialized facility and its vital importance to the training of young bodies and the formation of character, and the channeling of youthful energies into constructive pursuits, so that they would grow up to be dependable, productive members of society. In fact, he rattled on so long that I began to hear a humming in my ears, rather like that made by a swarm of bees, and had to concentrate to hear his words through the buzzing, or at least their gist.

Finally, he said, "Well! You've seen all the sights! Let's go and talk now, shall we?"

"It is very impressive," Barry commented, though he didn't say in what way.

The director nodded, satisfied, and I could have sworn his chest expanded an inch or two more. "It's a very clean school," he said. "It's a very clean, safe school. There's no fighting, and we have a huge janitorial staff."

"Of vital importance to the learning environment," Barry murmured. "Might we see a classroom? You know, one in which books are discussed and lectures given?"

Seeholder gave us a peculiar look, as if there were something wrong with our minds. "Sure, if you really want to. But there's not much to see."

There wasn't. We stepped in just past the doorway, and the teacher looked up inquisitively. Seeholder signed to him, and he turned back to his students, who had begun to mutter with alarm—or perhaps it was excitement; after all, we were an interruption in the routine. "Okay, class, now simmer down. You've all seen the director before, and guests aren't all that surprising." And to the buxom tow-headed wench who had begun primping, "Save it, Suzie—they don't have a 3DT camera with them."

She lapsed into a disappointed pout. I thought his advice was well placed, all things considered, though erroneous, under the circumstances—but he apparently hadn't been informed of those circumstances.

"Physics class," Seeholder muttered to us.

I blinked, looking about in surprise. There was nothing to mark this as a science room—only the usual array of data cube racks with screens and readers nearby, a video pickup over the teacher's desk with a projector aimed at the screen built into the wall behind him, and row after row of student desks in timeless array. I leaned over to Seeholder and whispered, "I take it the laboratory is a separate room."

He gave me another of his peculiar looks. "Sure, we've got a chemistry lab next door—but what's that got to do with physics?"

So. There were no laboratory facilities for physics.

Not that they were needed, if I were to judge by the content that the teacher was patiently explaining as he went back to the lecture we had interrupted.

"But I don't see any pole," the student objected.

"You can't see them, but they're there." The teacher held a bar magnet under the video pickup that projected it onto the wall behind him, five times life size. "Now, let's say the south pole of the magnet is a girl, and the north pole is a boy . . ."

"And they're gonna have little magnets?" another student suggested, and was answered with a huge hoot of laughter from his contemporaries.

The teacher took it without batting an eye, waited for his laughs, then spoke up as soon as the laughter had passed its crest—and won my instant admiration for his professionalism. "That's next week's lesson." He put a second bar magnet onto the screen. "So if you put the north pole of one magnet next to the south pole of another magnet, what's going to happen?"

"They're gonna grab each other!" the class card yelped, and the class went into howls of laughter again—and once more, the teacher waited till the laughter had just passed its crest before he said, "Quite right."

The laughter stopped, and the teacher let the magnets go. They jumped together, and the class hooted its approval, with a variety of ribald comments.

The teacher let them pass and slacken, then said, "So opposite poles attract each other. Of course, it was just puppy love, so they broke up." He pulled the two magnets apart, then turned one of them around and asked, "Now, what will happen if we put two south poles together?"

"Nothing much," one girl opined.

Another asked, "Do they both like the same north pole?"

"Of course," the class card said. "They've got the hots for Santa Claus!"

When the laughter had died again, the girl said, "Then they'll claw each other's eyes out."

"Well, not quite that drastic." The teacher released the magnets, and they sprang apart.

The students stared, riveted—except for two at the side, who were trying to smile politely, but who had the glazed look to the eyes that denoted chronic boredom at hearing something they already knew. Between them was a lad with the most elaborate pompadour in the class, yawning ostentatiously, fidgeting, and hissing remarks at the other two, who did their best to ignore him, but looked pained; one frankly looked scared. So much for the "safe school."

Two more at the other side were fighting a losing battle at keeping their eyes open, and three at the back had given in.

Then the class card demanded, "Hey! How'd you do that?"

"I didn't," the teacher said. "The magnets did. Now, what happens if I put two north poles together?"

There was a brief silence, then a nervous giggle.

"Just to save you asking," he said, "they're both after the same south pole."

"Hot for penguins, eh?" the class card quipped.

One of the other boys said, "They'll pound the hell out of each other."

"No," the teacher said, "they're both black belts." And he let go of the two magnets.

They pushed each other apart, of course.

A couple of people oohed and aahed, but they shut up at the first glance from their peers.

"That's the other part of the law of magnetism," the teacher said. "Like poles repel."

"Unless they like each other too much," one of the other boys said, and the class howled.

While the teacher waited for the yuks to subside, I surveyed the class, noting that the two fighting sleep had come awake at the oohs and aahs, and were looking about them, wondering what they had missed. The pompadour was hissing steadily into the frightened boy's ear, whose face was turning very pale.

The teacher sighed. "Slade, as long as Mr. Seeholder's right here, why don't you just walk over to him and sign in for your usual stint at the office."

The pompadour looked up, affected a casual yawn, unfolded himself from his seat, and strolled over to the director, raising a hand in casual salute.

Seeholder met him with a stony glance. "You know where the detention room is, Slade. Why don't you just toddle on down there?"

The pompadour tossed a lazy grin back at his classmates and sauntered on down the hall.

"Well, that's enough," Seeholder turned to the teacher. "Thanks for letting us watch."

"Any time," the teacher said with a sketchy salute, and Seeholder turned away, leading us out.

"A very talented teacher," Barry commented.

Seeholder nodded. "He keeps 'em quiet."

"But that Slade chap is obviously a habitual troublemaker . . ."

Seeholder looked up, startled and suspicious. "How'd you know that?"

"Why, by the teacher's attitude and word choice," Barry said, surprised. "He is clearly disrupting the class continually—he doesn't want to learn, doesn't want to be in class, and is making it difficult for others to learn. If he is such a chronic problem, why not simply expel him?"

"Expel him?" Seeholder winced, looking at Barry as if he had just uttered the foulest of heresies. "No, no! As long as you've got him in school, there's a chance he'll learn something!"

"But he doesn't," Barry said, frowning. "He clearly has no wish to, and is only making learning more difficult for his classmates."

Seeholder glanced at him suspiciously. "Laymen don't usually notice such things, and certainly not so quickly—but look at this: If we kick him out of school, he'll just go making trouble outside, where it's harder to keep track of him, right?"

"I suppose so," Barry said slowly.

"Well, then!" Seeholder said with finality. "It's better to keep him off the streets. Come on, let's go to my office and talk."

"Yer lunch money or yer life!"

I looked up, startled—a hulking, pompadoured chap had backed a smaller boy with tousled, mousy hair into a corner.

"Aw, come on, Billy, I only have enough for myself, I . . . Ow!"

Billy had just slapped the other boy's head. "Come on, come on, fork up, you little grease ball!"

"But Billy . . . *Uh!*" The smaller boy folded around a fist in his belly, his eyes bulging.

"Director . . ." I said, "over there."

Seeholder looked; then his eyes bulged in fury. "Billy!"

The bigger boy jumped as if he'd heard a shot, then turned slowly and slouched toward Seeholder with an insolent grin.

"Detention," Seeholder snapped. "I'll tell you how long your suspension is sometime after school."

The youth sneered and started to saunter away.

"And I'll tell the youth foreman," Seeholder said. "He told me he needs a gang to clear a yeast tank."

The kid hesitated for just a second, then lounged on by, but a bit too casually now.

The director transferred his glower to the smaller boy. "What are you staring at, Farnholm? Hurry up, you're late for class!"

The boy swallowed and dashed away.

"Surely he could have used a bit of reassurance," I protested.

"Namby-pamby pantywaist like that? Doesn't deserve any pity," Seeholder growled. "Take that Billy, now—he may be a pain, but at least he's a man!"

"I thought there was no fighting in your school," Barry noted.

"Sure." Seeholder looked up in surprise. "That wasn't fighting. Farnholm didn't hit back even once!"

And he led us on toward his office, while I silently noted that his statement was accurate—technically, what we had seen was a beating, not a fight.

It was also we who had called it to Seeholder's attention—he apparently hadn't noticed. I wondered how many incidents like that went on every day, ones that never came to the attention of either the administration or the teachers. I had no doubt that some of the bullies had become very skilled at striking blows where the teachers couldn't see.

We marched into Seeholder's office. The secretary looked up in surprise, then went back to her work, apparently disinterested. Seeholder marched on through the door, then swung around the broad expanse of desk and sat down and leaned back in the leather swivel chair—synthetic, I'm sure, but almost indistinguishable from the real thing. "Okay, make your pitch."

Barry frowned. "I beg your pardon?"

"Your pitch, your spiel," Seeholder said impatiently. "What kind of trash are you trying to foist off on my kids?"

Barry reddened. "No 'trash' at all, Mr. Seeholder, but a new play by one of Terra's most respected authors of musical theater."

"Oh, so we get his rejects, huh? Who is it?"

"Vagrants from Vega," Barry said, with a touch of frost, "by Cant and Arbuthnot."

"Oh, yeah, I've heard of them. Cant's the one who writes those sexy plays that make adultery look like small potatoes, isn't he?"

"He has written some comedies that are termed 'bedroom farces,' yes," Barry said, "but they show would-be adulterers as ridiculous people who never receive the gratifications they pursue."

"Yes, but in the process, they make adultery look like something that's a lot of fun and okay to do. You side with the adulterer and start rooting for him." Seeholder shook his head. "No, that's out. What else have you got?"

Barry reined in his temper—I could tell because he mustered a polite smile—and said, *"Filters and Phyltres,* by Swathe."

"Oh, the one that shows the hero defying authority and getting away with it?"

"It depicts the classical Romantic struggle of the individual against the institution," Barry said slowly.

"Same thing. And the heroine's a whore, and the hero's got a social disease."

"The heroine has had an affair or two in her past," Barry said, "which scarcely constitutes prostitution . . ."

"No, but it makes her a whore."

". . . and the hero is suffering from consumption, which is definitely not sexually transmitted."

"That's what the whore dies from in that opera, isn't it? The one with the camelias," Seeholder said.

"Certainly an interesting digest of *La Traviata,"* I mused.

"Look," Seeholder said, "we don't want our people even

knowing about that kind of thing, let alone seeing it. What else have you got?"

"Backer's *Didn't He Ramble*—a classic from the mid–twentieth century."

Seeholder stared. "Not the one that takes place in a converted whorehouse!"

"Yes, that's the one," Barry sighed.

Seeholder shook his head. "If you don't have anything better than that to offer, you can just go right back to that trash heap you call Manhattan!"

From the look on his face, I could see that Barry was sorely tempted—but he must have done his mental arithmetic and realized just how much of his brother's money he would have wasted, because he said, "Perhaps you could indicate the kind of content you would find acceptable. For example, what kind of plays does your Drama Club produce?"

"Drama Club?" Seeholder stared. "You don't think we'd waste money on frills like that, do you? This is a frontier planet, mister—we can't waste time or cash on extras like that!"

Barry stared. "Don't you have any arts program at all?"

"Oh, yeah, sure! We've got the best marching band on the planet! Even the academy can't touch 'em!" Seeholder glowed with pride.

"Yes, the academy," Barry mused. "I've heard that mentioned before. Exactly what is the academy?"

Seeholder made a dismissive gesture. "The fancy private school where the managers send their kids. Costs an arm and a leg, I can tell you. Ten years I've been saving, and I'll just barely be ready next year, when my boy starts going there."

"Your son?" I stared. "You mean you're not even sending your own son to your own high school?"

"Of course not! Be very bad for him, attending the same

school his father runs! Besides, I want to make sure he can get into any college on Terra that he wants."

"But doesn't this high school prepare its graduates for college?"

"Oh, sure! They get out with a high school diploma, after all."

"You don't feel your son would be adequately prepared here, though?"

"Look," Seeholder said impatiently, "only a handful of the students here even *want* to go to college. Most of 'em don't even wanna be here, and it's all we can do to keep them in through tenth grade. The ones with really great grades, or really great athletic records, get to stay on to graduate, but that's only ten percent."

Barry frowned. "Then those first two years must be very difficult for the few who really do want to learn. They must find it devilishly hard to concentrate on their classes, when they're in there with so many students who are threatening them and sneering at them."

"Intimidation and threats are against the rules!" Seeholder snapped.

"I see." Barry rubbed his nose. "But how do the teachers know when students have been making threatening remarks?"

"Why, the students who have been threatened come and tell them!"

"Doesn't that open them to reprisals from the bullies?" Barry asked.

"I told you—fighting is strictly against the rules! We catch 'em at it, we suspend 'em!"

"I had in mind beatings that might happen on the way home," Barry said slowly.

"Well, of course," Seeholder said, "we can't be responsible for things that happen off school property. Besides, if a kid can't take care of himself, he's got it coming, if you ask me."

"But it certainly must make it difficult for him to concentrate on his studies," Barry said.

"We haven't noticed the problem."

"No," I said slowly, "I don't suppose you have."

Seeholder flushed. "Anyway, it hardly ever happens."

"But couldn't you prevent it by having separate classes for those who really do want to learn?" Barry asked. "Even a whole sequence of classes—a real college-preparatory curriculum?"

"Hell, no!" Seeholder scoffed. "That's old-fashioned."

Old-fashioned? My mind reeled with a sudden vision of schools run according to the dictates of fashion. Did the educators read the teachers' journals in hopes of spotting the new trend? How high was mathematics going to be worn this year? Would literature have a peplum, or a scalloped border? I realized a sudden gold mine of possibilities in the notion of high school principals constantly alert to the fashion news, straining to be the first on their planet with the new fad. The ideas was fraught with possibilities, and all of them made me shudder.

"But students who have the potential for college work need special advising, special methods of teaching," Barry argued.

"What are you, an elitist?" Seeholder glared at him suspiciously.

"No, only an interested bystander." Barry capitulated with a sigh. "And I take it you have no arts program."

"Like I told you, we don't have time for frills."

I ached to correct his grammar, but I managed to keep my lips closed.

"But there must be something you can recommend as an indication of the kind of content you approve," Barry said. "What are your students studying in literature class?"

"Well." Seeholder leaned back in his chair. "Now that you mention it, the juniors are studying Shakespeare this year. *All* year—the teachers have to explain all the strange words, of course."

"Of course," Barry murmured, with a look of trepidation. "May I ask which play they are studying?"

"Macbeth."

"Why, what an amazing coincidence," Barry breathed, through parched lips.

14

So it was to be *Macbeth*. Barry was generous when he presented the issue to the Star Company—he tried to make the government's logic clear. That was rather difficult, since the government didn't have much logic, but Barry tried to infer as much as he could from Seeholder's curt comments.

Of course, his fellow artists didn't let him explain anything before they reacted; their motto might have been, "Never in accuracy, but always in haste." The announcement was barely made before they felt the need to comment.

"But I thought you said we weren't going to do *Mac*—the Scottish play, after all!" Marnie snapped.

"No, I merely postponed rehearsal," Barry said wearily. "It would seem that my reasons for wishing to present it were more accurate than I knew."

"But why do we have to?" Larry demanded.

"Because the Committee for Cultural Affairs, represented by Director of Schools Seeholder, has politely banned all the other plays in our repertory."

"I wouldn't have said 'politely,' " I amended.

"But that's censorship!" Lacey sputtered.

"Absolute and total," I assured her. "If you think the Company's management exceeds its rights, you are welcome to appeal to the government and file suit."

"But the Company *is* the government! The whole planet is just one big company town!"

"Makes the enforcement of civil liberties difficult, doesn't it?" I tried to look sympathetic.

"Be generous, people," Barry sighed. "No one ever does anything without a reason, though they may not always know what that reason is."

"And that reason is frequently a bad reason, and the action resulting from it, evil," Winston reminded him.

"Not in their own minds, Winston. In their own minds, they merely have goals that conflict with ours."

"Only conflicting goals?" Merlo demanded, pop-eyed. "You can explain something as evil as censorship in terms of nothing but conflicting goals?"

"I can, I'm afraid; it doesn't seem evil to them, any more than the Catholic church thought it was evil to try to prevent the Bible from being published in English, or the women's rights movement saw anything wrong in their campaign against pornography. In fact, as I've grown older, I've realized that nearly every special-interest group has some literature that it discourages and thinks should not be published."

" 'Nearly'?" Susanne frowned. "Which groups don't have something they want to ban?"

"The Civil Liberties Union," Barry said. "They merely think that some books should not be read. They wouldn't dream of attempting to stop their being published, of course."

"Oh, come now, Barry!" Ogden huffed. "You can't mean that these silly provincial managers actually have good and moral reasons for forbidding us to present such excellent plays to their workers!"

"Unfortunately, morality does seem to be their main concern," Barry lamented.

"At least, so they claim," I qualified. "That doesn't mean there aren't stronger and wronger reasons underlying the ones they acknowledge."

"But who are these managers?" Marnie demanded. "Did they talk to you themselves?"

"At first, yes," Barry said, "in the communal persona of the Committee for Cultural Affairs."

"Though they didn't go into the specifics," I amended. "They left that to Director of Schools Seeholder."

Larry frowned. "Why?"

"Oh, really, Mr. Rash!" Marnie said, exasperated. "Why does any committee let an underling act as its mouthpiece?"

"Oh. Of course," Larry said slowly, though he obviously didn't understand at all.

"A committee," Winston explained, "is a group of people gathered together to avoid responsibility. In this case, they have allotted that commodity to an officeholder, so that they will not have to be tarred with the brush of censorship."

Ramou frowned. "Then he's a fool to take it!"

"Not if he is ambitious, and needs their favor," Winston replied. "Also, he may enjoy the additional power thus gained, and feel the responsibility is a small price to pay. Indeed, as director of schools, he must be quite accustomed to complaints and accusations."

"Oh, be fair, Winston," Barry said irritably. "They may be sincere. Misguided, but sincere." He turned to the company at large again. "It is not management alone who opposes us, but the leaders of the people themselves, according to Publius. He conjectures that the good folk of New Venus, as represented by their covert union, have no use for the silliness of a musical comedy. For our part, we can say with certainty that the managers of the Company won't hear of anything so blatantly immoral as *Didn't He Ramble*."

"Immoral?" Marty stared. *"What's immoral?"*

"It takes place in a converted bordello," Barry said, looking very weary, "and it's made quite clear that Bonnie is sleeping with a man to whom she is not married."

"A man who just happens to be the boss." Lacey frowned. "You don't suppose that hits a little too close to home for them, do you, Mr. Tallendar?"

Barry looked up in surprise. "Yes, quite possibly, Ms. Lark. An excellent insight."

Lacey didn't say anything in reply, but she seemed to glow. Marnie frowned at her, looking quite annoyed; I suspect she understood neither the reference, nor Lacey's manner of inference.

"But," Winston said, "it then follows that the managers would see themselves as analogous to the older brother, and the laborers the younger."

Barry held himself still, but a smile glowed on his face. "My thought exactly, Winston. Yes, I think they were aware of the parallel."

"But the boss wins!" Ramou objected.

"Exactly," Barry agreed. "The boss wins—but the subordinate did rebel. New Venus's good managers do not wish to see even that much illicit activity."

"But surely it is the right of the people to see into the governmental process," Charlie Publican objected.

"Perhaps—but labor doesn't have a right to question management." Marnie had finally caught the drift of the conversation. She turned a gimlet glare on Barry. "At least, in the opinion of management."

Barry let it slide right by him. "And on New Venus, management *is* the government—so *Didn't He Ramble* is out."

"And the Scottish play is in?" Marty stared. "An earl kills a king, and the king's son pulls some dissatisfied nobleman together to mount a rebellion, and the people flock to his banner, and *that's* not revolutionary?"

"No, it's a classic."

Charlie Publican looked up at Marty, interested. "A novel interpretation, young man."

"And one which has hopefully eluded the good managers

of Amalgamated Petroleum," Barry said. "It is taught in the schools, it is Literature with a captial 'L,' so it must necessarily be a harmless and boring cultural artifact. Therefore they will allow us to perform it."

"Well." Marnie stood, gathering the aura of charisma around her like a pet cobra coiling to strike. "Let us see if we can keep it from being boring, shall we?"

The company answered with a shout of approval.

It had taken an hour to go through customs to get back to the ship, and it took another hour the next morning, when Susanne and I ushered Ogden through to see that doctor.

"No excuses this time, Mr. Wellesley," Susanne told him firmly. "You have to see that doctor, and you really should have seen him as soon as we landed, yesterday!"

"I couldn't have, even then," Ogden grumbled. "Not without waiting two hours to go through customs. Really, this is insupportable! Surely you are not going to drag me through that interminable delay just to have a flesh-and-blood doctor tell me exactly the same thing that the robo-doc said."

Susanne turned on the charm. "But you know we can't have you going about without your floater unless a real doctor says so, Mr. Wellesley, and we do so need you for the performance—no one else could possibly be as effective a King Duncan as you, and I'd be most horribly upset if anything happened to you from overexerting yourself, and . . ."

"Enough, enough, my dear!" Ogden held up a hand. "Flattery will get you . . . well, cooperation, at least. But really, if we're concerned about my heart, can't this customs agent expedite us at all? The frustration is elevating my blood pressure!"

"I'll try." Susanne turned and advanced on the customs agent, all girlish charm and undulating rhythms. "I'm sorry to seem impatient, sir, but Mr. Wellesley had a heart attack during lift-off, and we've made an appointment at the clinic, and they're so overloaded that it's absolutely vital that we be there on time, and . . ."

She went on, and the customs agent gave her a look that was slowly turning into euphoria until he glanced over her shoulder and saw me, with my hands in my jacket pockets, grinning like a shark that's waiting for somebody to fall overboard. The smile vanished; he cleared his throat as he looked down at his papers, said, "Yeah, that's all right," hit them with the stamp, and handed them back to Ogden, glancing nervously at me.

"Oh, that was *so* good of you!" Susanne gushed.

He looked surprised, the smile came back, and he was about to ask her for a date when he noticed me grinning again. The smile disappeared like a thief hit with a searchlight; he cleared his throat nervously and nodded toward the gate. "Glad to help, lady. You can go on through, now."

At least Ogden waited until we were twenty feet past the gate before he began grumbling, "Insupportable indeed! Absolutely insupportable!"

Susanne just smiled and held the outer door for him.

If Ogden thought customs was insupportable, he should have thought about himself. It took me and a husky orderly, both, to get him off that floater and onto the examination table. "Dratted floater," he muttered as he settled down, with Susanne cushioning his descent. "Completely lost muscle tone; no exercise, not even from walking . . ."

Never mind that most of the exercise he usually got was bending his elbow.

The doctor said as much, and it was definitely not what Ogden wanted to hear. "You were very fortunate, Mr. Wellesley," he said as he handed him the hard copy from the physical analyzers. "Lift-off from a gravity well as deep as Terra's could have killed you—but you only sustained a mild shock. I'm not quite sure how, but I do know that if you don't get some exercise and stop drinking, the next one *will* kill you—or the one after that."

"Stop drinking?" Ogden bleated. "Doctor, you can't be serious!" But you could see in his eyes that he'd been expecting it.

"I've never been more serious in your life," the doctor assured him, "a life which won't be long, if you keep it marinated with alcohol."

"I am not sure," Ogden groaned, "that a life without alcohol is a life worth living."

"It's either that, or stay on New Venus and stop traveling and playing in your shows." There was a hint of contempt in the last phrase.

Ogden frowned. "That, of course, is not even open to consideration, doctor. For me to give up the theater would be to give up life."

"Which is exactly what you will do, if you don't stop drinking," the doctor said with finality.

Ogden grumbled about it all the way back to the spaceport, all the way through customs, and all the way back to the ship. I think the agent may have passed us through a little faster, just to be rid of his griping. By the time we escorted him back through the air lock, even Susanne's monumental patience was wearing thin.

We stopped by his cabin door. "In you go, Mr. Wellesley," Susanne said. "You might want to rest now."

"Yes, that was a rather strenuous excursion," Ogden agreed. "No, my dear, you don't need to come in. The good doctor—though what's good about him, I can't guess!—has not only certified me as being fit enough to walk, but has even commanded it, under the guise of mandating exercise. I can clamber into my bunk by myself, now."

"If you say so." Susanne's brow wrinkled with concern.

"But please be careful. We *do* want you to stay with us awhile longer, Mr. Wellesley."

"If it were not for your own gentle presence, I am not at all certain that I should wish to, without strong drink," Ogden said.

"You don't mean that," Susanne stated flatly. "If you did, you wouldn't let me go to all this trouble trying to lengthen your stay."

Ogden looked up, startled, then frowned. "I'm sorry if you find me troublesome, my dear."

Susanne melted—not that she'd been all that much frozen to begin with. She touched his cheek gently and said, "I'd go to twice the amount of trouble without batting an eye, for an old dear like you, Mr. Wellesley—so please don't drink, eh?"

"Well . . . for your sake . . ." he grumbled, and trundled on through the door.

As we turned away, Susanne was muttering, "I've *got* to keep him away from alcohol! I've just *got* to!"

"More to the point," I said, "you have to keep alcohol away from him!"

There was a muffled bellow behind us, like the sound of a mortally wounded buffalo.

Susanne whirled, eyes wide with shock. "Mr. Wellesley!"

"Is perfectly all right." I took her by the elbow and started guiding her away again.

"When he made a noise like *that*? What could have *happened* to him?"

"He just found out that his beverage dispenser won't give him cocktails anymore," I said. "I set it up with Merlo—while we were gone, he rigged the machine so it won't give him anything but warm milk, tea, and decaffeinated coffee. Under those circumstances, how do you *think* he would sound?"

* * *

Ogden was right about one thing—the time we lost going through customs every day really was insupportable. Barry decreed that everyone was confined to the ship until we were ready to move into the Grand Gymnasium, whereupon he would rent hotel rooms for us all.

But he had to make an exception for Merlo and me. After all, we did have to do a "site survey," as Merlo called it: taking a preliminary look at the theater—or in this case, as Merlo called it, the "playing space." We had to check out sight lines, acoustics, where we could plug in our equipment, whether they had enough power for all our gear, where we could mount our lights, and a host of other details. So we waded through customs again, and we both brought book ROMs this time—we were beginning to wise up. Then we hopped a cab, came to the high school, looked, saw, and were conquered.

"This is where we're going to perform?" I stared around in dismay at the Grand Gymnasium.

"I told you we might have to play in gymnasiums, Ramou." Merlo sighed.

"This isn't a gym—it's a spaceship hangar! What do they need all this room for—a dozen games at once?"

"For lots of spectators, and a marching band, and cheerleaders, and, oh, yes, the players." Merlo shook his head. "Besides, when you play air hockey on ground-effect shoes, you need a lot of room."

"Ridiculous," I grumbled.

"Look, Ramou, just because your idea of space demands is based on a karate dojo . . ."

A tall, burly man in an athletic jacket ambled over to us, tossing a puck in his left hand as he reached out with the right. "Hi! I'm Rocco Lambert, the phys ed director. You must be the men from the acting company."

I frowned. You couldn't pin it down, no sarcasm on any single syllable, but somehow Lambert managed to imply a fine contempt for us and for theater. Or was I inferring it?

But Merlo was shaking his hand, and from the frozen grins on both their faces, I could guess they were playing the old game of squeeze-the-hand, trying to determine social status according to who could mash whose hand. The whole ritual made me impatient; somehow I'd always thought that when men grew up, they left childish games behind. But as I grew up myself, I saw that the petty competitions survived as rituals of competitive life. I began to realize that those little struggles, like the enthusiasm for competitive sports, weren't really childish at all, but adult rituals to which children were introduced and guided early on. The male of the species is built to battle other males—it goes back to the apes and way before them, for whatever reason. We demonstrate our civilization by sublimating that drive into games, in which the risks are controlled and the likelihood of injury minimized. The man who cheers at a football game is a living testament to evolution, and the dominance games that men live by all their lives are just part of the animal nature that still pervades all but two of our drives. Boys are little men, not the other way around; it's just that they're more obvious, more open, and more honest about it than their elders are.

So I took Lambert's hand, adjusted my pressure to equal his, and answered his smile with a question. "Mind if I do a few exercises while I'm here? We don't get much room on shipboard."

The grin widened. "Sure, go ahead."

I slipped off my shoes and stepped onto the floor. It was good, very good, firm but not hard, just the thing to run on all day without getting shin splints. Then, while my boss chatted with the coach, I ran through my warm-ups, did a few flips, tried a few falls and bounced up—yes, it was a good floor—and noticed out of the corner of my eye that, more and more, the coach's eye was on me rather than on Merlo.

Damn, it felt good! The exercises, I mean, though knowing the coach was watching didn't hurt any, either. I hadn't realized how much I had missed being able to really move.

I kept it down to fifteen minutes, then picked up my shoes and padded down to the other end of the gym after them.

It was a long way.

As I came up to them, Merlo was saying, "Well, there sure are enough power drops, but are you certain the total power supply will be up to our equipments' demands?"

"I wouldn't worry about it," the coach said easily. "We can generate enough air to flood this floor *and* keep the second-half shoes charging, all while we're flooding this place with light and running a full PA system. But if you have any doubts, you might want to check with maintenance."

Merlo nodded. "Think I'll give them a call, though it does sound like enough." He glanced up at me. "Have a good time?"

I nodded, still breathing hard. "Just great." I turned to the coach. "Thanks a lot."

"My pleasure. Looks like you'd be more at home in the dojo, though."

So he'd recognized the moves. I'd been pretty sure he would. I grinned and said, "I am, but I'll take what I can get."

"Well, we've got a dojo, too. Want a quick match?"

My grin widened. "I'd love it."

As we left the school, Merlo said through his breather, "You could have let those kids win a few, at least."

I shook my head with decision. "No, Merlo. You don't let anybody win in martial arts. It's wrong—and if they figure out what you're doing, it's an insult."

"Yeah, I know—" Merlo sighed, "—but couldn't you have gone easy on the coach?"

"Why? He didn't go easy on me." I rubbed my bruises reflectively. "Anyway, if you tallied up points, he won."

"I know." Merlo sighed. "That's why he let every kid in his class have a try at you."

I nodded. "It's only polite. A strange black belt comes to visit, you accord him the honor."

Merlo frowned at me. "You told him you were a black belt?"

"Hell, no. I didn't need to."

"Anyway you say." Merlo shook his head. "Hope you feel like you accomplished something."

"Oh, yes," I said softly. "Oh, yes."

"Friday night?" I stared at Barry in horror. "They want us to perform in five days?"

"I'm afraid so, Horace." Barry sighed. "The logic, such as it is, is that as long as we're here, we might as well be working."

"Don't they realize that rehearsal is work? Even harder work than performing?"

"I did attempt to point that out to Seeholder," Barry said. "The message struck his ear and bounced off his preconceptions. As far as he is concerned, acting is nothing but playing—after all, that's what the word means, doesn't it? 'Strolling players.' No, he can't see any reason why we can't all just step out on the boards tonight."

"To what," I said, "do we owe the courtesy of not having to do just that?"

"The high school students have school the next day, and presumably have to do homework, then be abed by ten."

"Praise heaven for the tunnel vision of the provincial," I sighed. "I take it the gentleman believes that students will constitute the bulk of our audience?"

"It was unspoken—but yes, I perceive that he does," Barry said. "After all, why should anyone have to witness something so boring as a Shakespearean performance if he doesn't have to?"

The sword broke.

The sword broke, and the pointed end went flipping over and over into the wings. Everyone froze, then Lacey saw it coming toward her and jumped aside with a squeal. She looked up, pale-faced, and saw me running toward her. The paleness flushed into the red of anger, and she turned on me. "Honestly, Ramou! How could you make a sword that could break like that? Don't you know somebody could get hurt?"

"Hey, don't . . ." I swallowed the 'look at me' and substituted, ". . . worry, Lacey. It was a fluke."

"You're not supposed to let flukes happen!" Lacey blazed. "Any prop man worth his salt would have made that blade out of a material that couldn't snap! What were you thinking of?"

"Experimenting, no doubt." Marnie advanced on me, her face grim. "I understand, young man—everyone needs to learn his trade some time. But other people's wounds are not your laboratory!"

"I—I'm sorry, Ms. Lulala," I managed. Inside, I was raging—at Merlo.

Until he stepped between me and Marnie. "What the hell? Why are you taking the rap for me, Ramou?"

I stood silent, every muscle stiff.

"For you?" Marnie spun to face him. "How is this your fault, Merlo?"

"Because I'm the one who chose the prop swords and bought them, back in New York," Merlo answered. "We need real metal ones, so it'll sound like a sword fight instead of a game of jackstraws. Okay, so we got a defective one in the batch. There was no way to know that. After all, they've all been used before."

"For what—crowbars?" Marnie snapped. "You're supposed to give us props that are one hundred percent safe, Merlo Hertz!"

"There ain't no such beast as a 'sure thing,' " Merlo said right back, beginning to sound angry himself. "I do the best I can, but you all know stages are dangerous places."

"Yes, especially when you're in charge of them!" Marnie snapped back. "That is exactly why we cannot take any more risks than are absolutely necessary! You test each of those swords, Merlo Hertz, and test them *personally*!"

"Oh, I'll test 'em, all right—but even that's no guarantee." Merlo's eyes narrowed. "They're only metal, after all. They're safe as anything, fight after fight, but the metal gets more and more brittle inside, until finally they snap."

" 'Finally'? Just how old *are* these weapons, anyway?"

"Only three years—and they've only been used in two productions." Merlo frowned. "*The Merry Wives of Windsor* and *King Lear.*"

"*Windsor* and *Lear*? You mean you gave us swords that were only intended as ornaments?"

"No, not just for dress." Merlo looked offended. "There're a couple of sword fights in *Lear*."

"Yes, but they're short and sweet, and nothing remotely like the ones in this play! I don't know how you could be so blind!"

"I told you, it was just an accident!" Merlo snapped. "A thousand-to-one shot! I can't hedge the odds any better than that!"

"Oh, so it's not your fault at all, eh? Is that why you hid behind your apprentice here?"

"He didn't hide," I said quickly. "He stepped up and took the blame."

"Yes, but only after you had tried to hog it!" Marnie snapped at me, then turned on Merlo again. "Do you teach all your staff to take your blame?"

"No." Merlo frowned at me. "He did it because he's loyal."

"Loyal?" Marnie exclaimed in disbelief, and turned a contemptuous, pitying glance on me. "Oh, my dear! You have a very great deal to learn!"

"What he's learned is just fine," Merlo retorted, "as long as he's dealing with honorable people." He turned to me. "That was it, wasn't it, Ramou? You figured I was your boss, so you owed me total loyalty?"

"Not because you were my boss," I qualified. "Because I took you as my teacher."

Merlo's face softened just a little. "So because you had committed yourself to me, you felt you had to defend me?"

"No," I said, "but you don't put blame on your friends."

"Even if it means getting stuck with it yourself, eh?" Marnie shook her head. "Yes, you have a *great* deal to learn."

I decided I didn't want her for a teacher.

She turned her look of annoyance back to my boss. "Very well, I suppose rehearsals can proceed. But don't let it happen again, Merlo."

"I didn't 'let it happen' this time," he snapped. "Don't let the part go to your head, Marnie."

She turned on him, chin lifted and nostrils flaring, but Barry spoke up then. "Scarcely much chance of anyone getting too far into character, with only two days till opening."

Marnie's and Merlo's gazes unlocked and faltered for a second.

"We really must make every minute count," Barry said, moving away from them, "especially when we're almost done with the last act. Right, then, we'll take it from the final sword stroke—without blades, if you please. Macbeth falls behind the upper platform—down, if you will, Winston . . ."

Winston obligingly dropped down behind the top. I saw Ramou start and step forward, then halt himself; I gather he wasn't accustomed to stage falls. By his standards, no doubt, Winston should have fractured his coccyx. In point of fact, the actor's fall had a great deal in common with the martial artist's—but it was far more vivid.

". . . then MacDuff chops his head off, so . . . !" Barry pantomimed swinging a sword down, and Ramou winced again. He was the only one of us, of course, to whom edged weapons were real. I stepped over to him and muttered, "Don't worry—by the time the blade falls, Winston will have rolled under the top platform."

"Unless something goes wrong," Ramou muttered back, "and maybe Winston's a little slow in rolling, and Barry slips at the same time, and I know those blades are so blunt they couldn't cut butter, but they're *heavy*!"

"Winston and Barry know their trade." I glanced at him anxiously. "Don't fret so, Ramou."

"I won't," he said. "I'll build a chopping block into the set back there, instead."

Barry was waving to Larry, down below. "The sword blow will be the cue for your entrance."

Larry led his troops on and turned to Charlie. "I would the friends we miss were safe arrived."

"Some must go off: and yet, by these I see, so great a day as this is cheaply bought," Charlie answered.

"As you say that, you mount the platforms to the top level," Barry said. "That's right . . . Now turn to look out over the battlefield . . ."

"Otherwise known as the audience," Winston rumbled, *sotto voce*.

"Then comes MacDuff." Barry stepped out, holding the model of Winston's head. "Hail king! For so thou art . . ."

Lacey gave a little shriek, and Susanne clapped a hand over her mouth. Even Marnie gasped.

"Why, thanks," Merlo said. "Didn't know it looked that real."

"It is also positively ghastly!" Marnie turned on him. "Really, Merlo, did you have to use so much blood?"

Merlo shrugged. "We have to at least nod to realism."

"I see no reason why!" Marnie retorted. "Even if we did, surely an actual beheaded head would have less blood, not more."

Merlo shook his head. "More. I looked it up."

Marnie stared. "What sort of reference work would have *that* kind of information?"

"The Hollywood makeup and prop manuals."

"Hollywood. I might have known," Marnie said with a curled lip. This, from the woman who had made several hundred thousands playing vampire villainesses on 3DT, though with never an award nomination—which may have explained her attitude.

"I must say, I sympathize." Barry looked away from the head, his mouth working. "Couldn't you, ah, stylize it a bit, Merlo? After all, it *is* Shakespeare—not Ibsen."

"Or the Grand Guignol," Winston pointed out—but he was gazing at the head with morbid fascination. "Amazing . . ."

"Yes, well, I don't think we really need such a *memento mori* on hand all the time." Barry tossed the head to Merlo. "Give that thing a decent burial, will you? Or at least a less grisly paint scheme—and a box to keep it in, on the prop table."

"S'awright," Merlo grated in basso, and relayed the head to Ramou. "See what you can do, assistant. Maybe they'll like your aesthetics better than mine."

Ramou caught the head and nodded.

"And not too Japanese," Merlo added.

"I do not long for all one sees that's Japanese," Ogden rumbled, with a faraway look in his eye.

"Gilbert and Sullivan next season, perhaps, Ogden," Barry said. "For now, let's work our way on to the tea break, shall we?"

"Tea break?" Ramou frowned up at me.

"Just wait," I advised him.

". . . to see us crowned at Scone!" Larry blared triumphantly.

"For what is tea without a scone?" I muttered, and Ramou winced.

"And, curtain!" Barry declared, then looked about at them. "Not bad, not bad at all! Blocked the last four acts in three hours. Now we'll run it this afternoon, and we'll be in amazingly good shape for only the second day of rehearsal."

"But amazingly bad shape, for only two days till opening," Marnie said acidly. "I suppose you'll want to rehearse us again after dinner, Barry."

"If he doesn't, we'll insist," Winston said grimly. "I don't know about you, my dear, but I would rather lose sleep than face an audience unprepared."

"But how can you possibly be anything else, under conditions like these!" Marnie cried, tears in her eyes.

"By gifted improvisations and sheer brazen nerve," Ogden rumbled. "That's what got us through *Lewis and Clark* in Omaha, forty years ago. We murdered the script, of course, but the audience never knew it."

"These people will have *read* this play!"

"High school students?" Ogden stared, totally dumbfounded. "Come now, my dear! You must be confusing fantasy with reality!"

"I didn't think high school was all that long ago for you, Ms. Lulala," Lacey said sweetly.

Marnie turned slowly and fixed her with a long, cold look, but her tone was all forced sweetness. "Quite right, my dear. What *was* I thinking of? Surely no one will notice if we rewrite the Bard a bit."

"Nonetheless, we might want to have a fail-safe system," Barry said, a musing look coming over his face. He turned to Merlo. "You don't suppose you could concoct some sort of prompting machine, do you?"

Merlo's eyes clicked over into faraway-gaze mode. "Now that you mention it, the idea does have possibilities . . ."

"We'd have to feed the script in as computer text." Ramou's gaze had gone into the fifth dimension, too. "And we'd have to couple it to a vocoder . . ."

"Yes, and give everyone a hidden earphone."

Everyone turned in surprise, for it was neither Merlo nor Ramou who had spoken, but Charlie Publican.

"Didn't know you knew electronics," Merlo said slowly.

Charlie shrugged. "A little bit of everything—some computer programming, some nuclear physics, some music composition, some theory of aesthetics . . ."

"A regular Renaissance man," Marnie said with sarcasm.

"No, I'm afraid I'm not much of an athlete."

"So how are you going to set up the earphones?" Ramou asked.

"With a microchip that combines an FM receiver with a transducer. Then we'll tape it behind the ear with a dab of adhesive."

"Glue?" Marnie said, as if she'd just bitten an apple and found a worm. "Never! Not on *my* skin!"

"Robex should prove adequate," I pointed out.

Charlie looked up in surprise.

"It's a skin putty," Merlo explained. "We use it for prosthetics in makeup. It sticks like iron to an electromagnet, and loosens up just like turning off the power—only instead of turning a switch, you swab on a solvent."

"Ah!" Charlie's face lit up. "A miracle material! So we'll have to design our earphones to be immune to the solvent . . ."

"Yes, well, I'm sure it's a fascinating topic," Barry said firmly, "and I encourage the three of you to discuss it into the ground and work out all the difficulties—which, I think, is the signal for us all to break for dinner. Back in an hour, my friends—we've no time to lose."

"Perhaps we shouldn't dine," I noted. "The others can eat when they're offstage."

"A point, but I'd like to enjoy my last chance to eat sitting down. I hope you will all enjoy it, too, my friends—it will probably be the last dinner break we will take until the show has opened. Good appetite."

The sword broke again.

Macbeth and MacDuff were in the middle of their final duel. The movements were choreographed as precisely as a ballet. MacDuff swung up with his great two-handed broadsword, Macbeth swung down—and with a crack like a gunshot, MacDuff's sword broke in half. The pointed end went spinning off into the wings, straight toward Marnie and Susanne, who were standing there watching. Marnie gave a shriek and leaped aside, yanking Susanne with her, and the blade hit the floor, clattering, right where they had been standing.

Ramou was there beside Susanne, magically, it seemed. "Are you all right?"

Susanne looked up, ashen-faced, but Marnie snapped, "Yes, no thanks to your chowderheaded boss!" She blazed into full fury. "Merlo Hertz! I *told* you those swords weren't safe!"

"Yeah, you sure did." Merlo knelt to pick up the tip of the blade—his new flexible cast gave him much more ease of movement, but he was taking entirely too much advantage of it. He frowned at the break, inspecting it closely. "Must have been a flaw in the metal."

"You cheese-headed Neanderthal, do you realize you just came within an ace of killing us? You need your wits checked!"

"You checked yours at the door," he shot back. "If you'd spend half as much time working on your character as you do trying to tell me how to aim my lights, you might actually learn how to act!"

"Learn how to act! Why, you peasant scoundrel, if you really had a smidgen of talent in design, you never would have had to learn how to pilot a spaceship!"

Merlo reddened. "Smidgen of talent? You should know!"

"Yes, my record speaks for me—and so does yours!"

Before Merlo could respond, Susanne said, "That was quick thinking, Ms. Lulala." She was ashen-faced—but not too shaken to keep from trying to pour oil on the waters.

"Sheer reflexes, dear," Marnie assured her. Then, to Merlo, who was red-faced but no doubt biting his tongue, "Flaw? The flaw was in you, not the sword! Whatever possessed you to bring a prop that could be lethal?"

Merlo's eyes flashed, and he opened his mouth for an acid comeback, but Ramou was there before him. "It was my responsibility, Ms. Lulala. I'm prop master." But he looked torn.

Susanne looked up at him, startled and apprehensive, but Merlo snapped, "Yeah, you put the swords on the prop table—but I bought 'em! Don't claim any more blame than is due you, Ramou."

"Let the blame rest for a few minutes." Barry came up beside them. "It was obviously a fluke, a rare event. The flaw was in the metal, not in Merlo."

"Nonetheless," Marnie snapped, "it was his responsibility to provide safe properties." She wasn't about to let a perfectly good reason for blaming go without a fight.

"Marnie—" Barry sighed, "—you know that no sword fight onstage can ever be totally safe. *Almost* totally safe, perhaps, but there is always a margin for error."

"Well, that's true," Marnie said grudgingly, "but there's no reason to make that margin any wider than it has to be."

"We were speaking of stage properties, not word processors," I reminded her.

"The only typing you've done is in your casting, Horace," she retorted. "Can't you do anything to make this idiot provide us with safe props?"

"Oh, we'll make 'em safe," Merlo growled. "Next rehearsal. Ramou and I will duel with every single one of 'em, and after that, I'll resurface them, just to be sure."

"You could make new ones," Barry suggested.

"New? Please, Barry!" Marnie rolled her eyes up. "Bad enough we must work with antiques that this incompetent selected—if you let him make them afresh, they're bound to be twice as dangerous!"

"Not unless I sharpened them as much as your tongue," Merlo returned.

"We need an edge on the competition, not on each other," Barry interjected.

"Competition?" Marnie stared at him, wide-eyed, and Merlo spun to face him. *"What* competition?"

"Seeholder and his management," Barry returned. "They are in competition with you two to see who can ruin this production most quickly. Might we return to rehearsal now?"

15

Merlo woke me at six, after four hours' sleep. "Go kill the rooster yourself," I groaned.

"Come on, kid!" Merlo clapped his hands. "Move-in today. The actors go to the hotel, and the set goes to the theater—well, the playing space, anyway."

"Just great." I cranked myself upright in bed, an inch at a time. "And just how are we going to get it there? Carry it?"

"That's the first item on the agenda—finding a truck."

"Truck?" I looked up, squinting against the light he'd turned on. "Wait a minute, I might have a lead." I reached out for my shirt, fumbled in the pocket, and pulled out the business card the cabbie had given me when he had brought us back to the terminal. I shoved myself to my feet, stepped over to the desk, and punched for an outside radiophone connection. Then I punched in the number, checked the screen to verify it—I wasn't too sure of my reading, so early—then punched "Enter." The number disappeared, and the word RINGING appeared—I don't know why, the sound's more like a chirp. I let it ring. And chirp. And warble.

Suddenly, the screen went black, and Chovy's voice grumbled, "I'm not turning on the flaming light at a time like this. Who the hell is calling when any decent man is still abed?"

"It's Ramou Lazarian," I said, "the guy you took for a tour with the pretty actresses the other day."

"You don't need a cab so early!"

"Three of them," I said, "but I suspect Horace has already called one of your buddies about that. What we need, Chovy, is a truck. Got anything handy?"

There was a considerable silence—almost a minute—then Chovy said, wide awake and very interested, "A lorry? Yeah, it might be possible, mate. Let me call around and see what I can find. What's your code?"

I gave him the string of numbers and signed off. I looked up at Merlo, but he was already grinning. "Unless I miss my guess, we've got transport."

"Yeah," I agreed. "I think Chovy knows the angles."

Turned out he knew the whole geometry book. An hour later, he pulled up at our loading door with not just a truck, but a whole crew, too.

It cost us a fortune to have that set moved. Chovy wouldn't let us into the truck, and he'd hired a buddy to stay inside with him and load the set pieces, costumes, and props. Of course, the truck couldn't quite get close enough for its tailgate to meet the hatch door—there was a meter's space between them—so Chovy had hired two more guys to take the units from Merlo and me and pass them into the truck.

"But that's ridiculous!" I protested. "We can get them far enough for you guys in the . . ."

I stopped and looked down at Merlo's hand on my shoulder. "It's okay, Ramou," he told me. "Believe me—it's okay."

Chovy nodded, grinning. "Now there's a chap who knows the world. Just pass it over, mate."

I clamped my jaw shut and helped Merlo pass the stair unit out. As we turned back to pick up the next unit, I hissed, "*Why*, Merlo?"

"Union jurisdiction," he explained in a low tone. "They may be illegal here, but the unions are as alive as they ever were on Terra, and if we want to get anything done, we deal with them on their own terms. Also, if I want to keep my IATSE membership, I've got to support the locals."

"*What* locals?" I said. "All they have here are petroleum handlers!"

"And truckers," he reminded me. "Truckers are teamsters."

I stared at him a minute, then nodded reluctantly. "Okay, so we have to deal with the teamsters. I take it Chovy and his buddy inside the truck are them. But why the two guys in the middle?"

"Because the set units are passing over solid ground," Merlo said, "which is neither teamsters' jurisdiction, nor IATSE's—it's stevedores'. Just haul, Ramou. You'll understand after you've joined up."

"If I ever do," I grumbled. "So if Chovy could have backed the truck close enough for its tailgate to actually touch the hatch rim, we wouldn't have to pay those two stevedores?"

"Of course not. Why do you think he made sure he couldn't get close enough? Okay, lift!"

I lifted.

It griped me, but it did go fast. We had the set loaded and out while the actors were still swearing at their alarm clocks.

Marnie looked about her and wrinkled her nose. "*This* is a *hotel*?"

"It is the only one in town, Marnie," I whispered, leaning close to her ear. "And I don't doubt that, by New Venus's standards, it is quite luxurious."

"Well . . . if you say so, Horace." It was quite a concession, for her, but the memory of our last two-hour bout with customs was fresh in her mind—and the more fresh because the second hour was doubtless due to her own tantrums. She loathed being in a position in which she could not fly into a rage with impunity about anything that took her notice—so she accepted the hotel, albeit ungraciously. "It should be minimally comfortable." But she glared about her at the deep-pile carpet with armchairs and table lamps as islands of light in a sea of subdued illumination. Everything was synthetic, of course; there was no shortage of petroleum, but also no local supply of wood or fiber. By Terran standards, it was Spartan.

Barry turned to address us all. "Aboard ship, there are more cabins than people, so everyone has had his or her own chamber. Here, however, we have to pay for every room, and we have developed a need to economize—nothing drastic, I assure you, but necessary nonetheless . . ."

We older actors all nodded with understanding, but the young folk exchanged puzzled glances. To them, being stranded in the boondocks was something mentioned only in history books, and those not of the sort used in classrooms.

"Accordingly," Barry went on, "though the more mature actors shall each have a room to themselves, we shall ask those of you who are younger to double up."

Instant consternation. Lacey glared, reddening with outrage; Larry turned pale, and Marty glanced at him uneasily.

"Ah, Barry," I said, "perhaps we should set an example by bunking in together."

Barry looked up in surprise, then nodded with a smile of gratitude. "Thank you, Horace. Yes, I think that would be apropos. Surely, Ms. Lark, if we two old troupers can forego the privilege of our position, you cannot take offense."

"Oh, yes I can!" Lacey snapped. "If you think for a minute that I'm going to share a room with that . . . that *cow* . . ." She pointed at Susanne.

For an instant, hurt showed in Susanne's face. Then anger replaced it, and she snapped, "No one asked you, Lacey—and no one will!"

"Oh, he was going to, right enough! After all, we're both

female and young, so we should be roommates—right, Mr. Tallendar?"

"It was logical." Barry seemed rather casual about the whole thing. "However, if you insist on private accommodations, Ms. Lark, I'm sure you'll be welcome to the single that Horace has just given up."

She stared, taken aback by his ready acquiescence—too ready, certainly.

Grudy Drury reached out to pat Susanne's hand. "That's all right, dear. You can share with me."

Susanne flashed her a look of gratitude, and I could see by Ramou's face that he would have liked to have made the same invitation. So would Larry and Marty, though they hid it better. Training has *some* advantages.

Lacey didn't notice; her brow was furrowed, and you could see that she was still wondering why Barry had not only surrendered the point so easily, but also not taken offense at her impertinence.

"I suppose I could bunk in with Publius," Ogden offered, entirely too easily. Susanne glanced at him with concern, but Publius was looking surprised and gratified, and Barry was nodding. "Very good of you to offer, Ogden. Publius, if you have no objection . . . ? Excellent. Now, are there any other volunteers?"

"I volunteer for a single," Larry said immediately. "Surely you can't expect me to share accommodations with either of these two clowns."

Ramou flashed him a glare, but Marty only grinned. "Hey! Thanks for the compliment, Larry!"

Larry opened his mouth for a scathing retort, but Barry's words came first. "If you wish, Mr. Rash. Mr. Kemp, might I suggest that the two of you last named consider cohabiting?"

"Hey, okay with me." Marty glanced at Ramou. "How about you?"

Ramou nodded. "Sounds good. You got the cards?"

Marty grinned, producing a deck and executing a shuffle that was pure sleight of hand, ending with the cards cascading from one hand to the other, landing in perfect order.

Ramou stared. "I don't know if I want to play with *you.*"

"We could go partners in bridge," Marty offered, "if anybody else thinks they stand a chance." He looked around at the older actors. "Anyone want to lose some money? The game starts as soon as we unpack."

"I might try that," Merlo said slowly.

Ogden nodded. "So will I—if one of you has a bottle."

"Deal me in," Susanne said immediately.

Ogden sighed. "My dear, you trust me not at all."

"Oh, yes she does," Marty countered. "She trusts you to drink every drop in every glass you can lay your hand on."

"Accordingly," Barry said, "I will ask you all to abstain until we have completed our opening performance. Now if you would follow the porter, please?"

We all set off after the floating platform that was piled high with our luggage.

"Hey, Ramou, this isn't bad!" Marty looked around at our cubicle.

I nodded. "Only a little larger than our cabins aboard the *Cotton Blossom.* Of course, there're two people in it instead of one, but it's big enough for two of us."

It was. The beds were singles, but there was a half-meter space between them, and a meter on either side. The table was in the corner by the window—a tight fit, but possible.

"Only two chairs," Marty said. "The game will have to be BYOC as well as B."

" 'Bring your own chair and bottle,' " I interpreted. I opened a closet. "Little cramped in here, Mar—"

A muffled yell came through the door. Marty looked up at me in surprise. As its echoes were dying, it was answered by a shriek of pure rage, likewise muffled by the walls.

"What in unholy hell was *that*?" Marty asked.

"Larry and Lacey," I said with a grin. "They just found out how small the singles are."

By the time we'd finished checking in and unpacking, Chovy called to say customs had finally finished going over every nut and bolt, or at least every cavity and hidden crevice. Merlo told him to meet us at the high school, collected me, and we hopped a cab.

Since we'd hired Chovy to drive the truck, now we were stuck with an even younger friend of his, Hoby. Hoby had a fine disregard for both traffic laws and Newton's laws. We peeled ourselves off the windows, took ourselves out the door joint by quaking joint, and paid him off with a large tip not to come back. Then we went over to the truck.

It wasn't very long before I was mighty glad to have those stevedores Chovy had hired—because, of course, they hadn't planned the Grand Gymnasium with road shows in mind. They hadn't planned it for much of anything else to be moved in, either, except a visiting team—so there was a door, but it was only a meter wide, and it led down into the locker rooms. Chovy had had to back the truck up to the loading dock, which opened into the utilities room, which had a door into a corridor. So the stevedores had to carry every load half the length of the school to get to the Grand Gym. It wasn't quite as bad as it sounded—they'd brought their own floater. Still, that was a lot of hauling.

We found most of the set piled just inside the gym door. I stared in surprise, then sidled over to my boss and muttered, "Thought the stevedores couldn't set foot inside the theater."

"Yeah," Merlo said, "but this is no theater." He looked up as the floater drifted in with the final load. "Thanks, guys."

"Just part of the job," one of the men grunted as he hauled the big platform in.

Chovy sauntered up behind him, hands in his jacket pockets, grin on his face. "All unloaded, Merlo."

"Yeah. Thanks, Chovy." Merlo shook his hand, and I caught the glitter of a five-kwaher note in the middle of the handshake. "You boys available when we need to move out?"

Chovy's hand slid smoothly back into his pocket, and the easy grin widened. "Sure, Merlo. Glad to help." He nodded to me. "Thanks for putting me on to him, Ramou."

I swallowed and shrugged. "Like you said, Chovy—glad to help." I shook with him, too, and noticed that Merlo was busy giving his paper-holding handshake to each of the stevedores, who were grinning and also telling him they were glad to help and would be glad to come back.

Then the three of them were strolling away, comparing reminiscences of high school days as they looked at the nostalgic sights around them, and Merlo nodded complacently and said to me, "Good contact you made there, Ramou."

I swallowed and shrugged again. "Pure luck, Merlo. Like they said—glad to help."

We had just finished laying the light rails down when a short, bald guy came storming up to us. He wore a business *complet* and definitely needed to lose some weight. "Just what the hell do you two think you're doing?"

Merlo looked up in surprise. "Who're you?"

"I'm Seeholder, and this is my school! What do you think you're doing to my floor?"

"Laying the rails," Merlo said slowly.

"Not right on my floor, you don't! We just had it refinished last summer!"

I looked up, frowning. It was spring on this planet; the year was almost over.

"Cost us a hundred kwahers!" Seeholder snapped. "No *way* are you going to put a single scratch on it!"

"No, we're not," Merlo said slowly. "The rails have rubber feet."

"Rubber feet? The whole damn thing better be rubber! Or you put pads under 'em! Heat-proof pads, mister! I don't want any holes where you've melted my varnish!"

The synthetic coating we call "varnish" doesn't melt until a thousand degrees Kelvin, and the light rails never got above a hundred. I bit my lip, though, and let Merlo do the talking. But I could feel the old eager smile tugging at the corners of my mouth.

"Okay, pads." Merlo sighed. "Ramou, go get the asbestos strips, will you?" He pointed at the pile of scenery units in the corner. "We brought along plenty."

Seeholder stared at the mountain of gleaming white. "You're gonna stand *that* stuff on my floor?"

"It won't even mar the finish," Merlo assured him. "It's just foam. Very strong foam, but just foam."

"I want pads under it!"

Merlo nodded. "Will do. I brought along plenty."

"Then why weren't you laying them down under your rails?" Seeholder shot back.

"Because there is no *way* the rails could damage your floor, even as much as a gym shoe," Merlo sighed.

Seeholder gave him a narrow glare. "I don't like your attitude, mister!"

I was back with the pads by this time, and I couldn't help it—the smile lazed loose, and I looked up, bright and eager.

Seeholder noted, and his face turned into a mask. He turned to face me, feet apart, hands hanging loose, every muscle tense. He wasn't any taller than me, but he was six inches wider in the shoulders. He might have been a tough opponent ten years earlier, but he'd been sticking to his desk too long—now, he just looked like a bowling pin waiting for a ball to knock his feet out from under him.

Of course, I didn't kid myself. Never underestimate an

opponent; pride goeth before the fall—and before the broken bone, too. For all I knew, he could have been a black belt, too.

Merlo gave me a warning glance, then turned back to Seeholder. "How long have you been running this school?"

That pulled his attention; Seeholder scowled at him. "Ten years. What difference does that make?"

"Sounds like you know your job," Merlo commented.

"You damn well bet I know my job!"

"Well, I've been putting up sets for fifteen years," Merlo said, "and I know *my* job. I've never seen any damage from light rails in all that time—they don't carry enough power, and they don't get hot enough. Damage *to* them, maybe—but never damage *from* them."

A crack of uncertainty appeared in the armor of Seeholder's hostility. "I want pads under 'em anyway!"

"Pads there will be," Merlo promised. "Come on, Ramou. I'll lift, you slip the pad in."

"And don't think you're going to go hanging any of your damn lights on any of my bars, either!" Seeholder pointed up at the pipes that supported his climbing ropes and backboards and air-hockey goals.

"Wouldn't think of it," Merlo assured him. "They're too far away. We brought our own booms."

"Booms?" Seeholder glared like a mother bear defending her cubs. "What's a boom?"

"A big long pipe," Merlo explained. "Ramou, bring us a boom."

Now, the bases on those things are *heavy*—they have to be, to make sure the weight of the lights doesn't topple 'em—so the usual way of moving them is to pull the pole down sixty degrees and roll the base along the floor. I could just hear what Seeholder would say about that, though, so I slung a pad over my shoulder and picked up the pole by the pipe, right next to the base, and brought it over.

"You're going to put *that* on my floor?" Seeholder yelped.

"It's rubber," Merlo assured him, "and we'll put a pad under it, too."

"Damn *right* you'll put a pad under it!" Seeholder glared at the long pole in my hand. "Stand that up."

I flipped the pad down, lowered the base carefully onto it, and stood it up. Then I stepped back, flexing my arm—it was a little stiff from all that weight.

Seeholder looked up at the length of the pole. "How many lights are you going to put on this thing?"

"Sixteen," Merlo said.

"*Sixteen!* It'll fall over!"

"It's weighted," I pointed out.

"It can't be weighted *that* much!" Seeholder stepped up and wrapped his hands around it. "Not the way your kid carried it over here!" He lifted.

It was very gratifying to see his biceps bulge, the veins stand out on his temples, and his eyes widen as the implications hit him. He did manage to get it off the ground, I'll say that for him. Of course, he was at a bad angle.

"Besides," Merlo said, "it has a gyroscope built in; that's why the base is a meter high. Not turned on yet, of course, or Ramou wouldn't have been able to tilt it."

That saved Seeholder's face, a little. He put down the pole and turned back to us, narrow-eyed. "All right, I can't really complain—but if it does fall over, I'll have your hide!"

"The horns go with it," I told him.

This time the glance was pure venom, and he spun on his heel and stalked away.

I rounded on my boss. "Why did you let him push you around like that, Merlo? You should have told him to go push his grade book and leave the skilled stuff alone!"

"Because it's his gym, and we need it," Merlo said, his tone absolutely level. "I wouldn't want to bet that he couldn't have us shut down in an instant. We're guests, Ramou, no matter how much we're paying—and if we aren't *good* guests, we won't be invited back when we want to play New Venus again."

"I can't dream of ever wanting to play New Venus again," I grumbled. "Couldn't he think of being a good host?"

"We weren't invited," Merlo said simply. "Now, the cables have to go up the wall, to the press box; that's where they told us to set up the surveillance camera for our lighting cues. Then the light board and scene boards plug in back there . . ."

We were just attaching the control cables to the camera as the actors began to drift in, looking about them and standing stock still in horror. Then the gestures began, and I could almost hear them exclaiming in dismay and demanding to know how they were supposed to play in a barn like this.

"Almost" because the press box was soundproof. Why, I don't know. "What was this box built for, Merlo?"

"Putting in 3DT camera controls and audio boards, when there's a game," Merlo answered. "High school sports are very big, on a planet like this."

I nodded. "Makes sense—there's no college on New Venus, and I can't see the Company putting out the money for a professional team."

Merlo looked up with interest. "Where'd you learn all that?"

"Chovy. He's a font of information. So if all they do up here is set up cameras and controls, why do they call it a 'press box'? What are they pressing, anyway?"

"Dunno." Merlo shrugged. "I used to think it was like a penalty box, where they put players who have been naughty boys—'press' short for 'impressed,' meaning 'pushed into'—but I had to set up lights in a field house once, and the engineers there said no."

I frowned. "Don't they call news reporters 'press'?"

Merlo nodded. "Way back in the dark ages, they used to make hard copies with a gadget that actually pressed the letters onto the paper. They called 'em 'newspapers'—so news reporters were 'the press.' "

"Maybe they put news reporters up here?" I ventured.

"Why?" Merlo said simply. "Who'd put stories about sports events in a newscast, when the games have programs of their own? No, the term just doesn't make any sense, Ramou, but we're stuck with it." He stood up, stretched, and pulled up a high-backed stool. "Okay. Let's go back down to the control boards and check out our systems."

And the light show began.

"Barry, I've heard of actors having to perform in a barn," Marnie said, "but this is a rocket hangar! Honestly, what could you have been thinking of!"

"Nothing at all," Barry said grimly. "The committee did my thinking for me. We play here, or nowhere."

"Why did you even consider coming to this pestiferous hole!"

"Because we needed a short trip to accustom everyone to space travel—" Barry sighed, "—and if we made planetfall, the landing had to pay for itself. *Quid est*—or there will be no quid at all." He turned to me. "Ramou, will you run down to whatever room Grudy has assigned the spear carriers? I'd like you to make certain they're cooperating with her."

"Yes, sir," I said, "but what authority do I have if they're not?"

"A good point—we need a stage manager," Barry said, "and Merlo is stuck in the booth. Horace, will you take charge of the position for this production?"

"Of course, Barry." And that easily, Horace became stage

manager as well as supporting actor. I found out later that
the stage manager belongs to Actors' Equity, the actors' union, so that he can take bit parts when he needs to. Of
course, his part was considerably more than a bit, so obviously Barry wasn't expecting the stage to need much managing.

And the biggest task, they were leaving to me. "I hereby
appoint you assistant stage manager, Ramou," Horace told
me, "with full authority over the extras—not that I expect
you to need to pull rank."

"No, sir." I grinned. "How does this work with Equity?"

"You're drafted," Horace said simply. "It's not unknown
for a man to have dual union membership, and you're still
working on your points for both unions in any case."

"And his competence," Larry sniffed.

"That will do, Larry, or I'll delegate him authority over
all male members of the cast under the age of thirty."

Larry paled. Marty grinned.

"Now, go take care of your new charges, Ramou," Horace said.

"Yes, sir," I said, and headed for the locker room.

"Extras?" Winston frowned. "I wasn't aware we had
hired extras, Barry."

"Oh, yes, Winston, for the army. We had planned to, all
along—and a local boy, to play MacDuff's son. We found
an energetic lad who proved to be a quick study."

"So easily?" Winston said, surprised. He turned to me.
"How, Horace?"

"Ramou found a cab driver who has a little brother—the
driver for the young folk, 'Chovy' is his name."

"Isn't he the one who found them transport for the scenery?"

"Ah, I see you're alert as always, Winston. Yes, Chovy
seems to be taking care of us quite nicely." I smiled. "He

told Ramou that if he needs anything, he is just to call for 'Uncle Chovy . . .' "

"Or if he's short on time, to just cry 'uncle,' " Winston said with a wry grimace. "Odd how the oldest jokes go wherever there are people, isn't it, Horace?"

"Merely part of the cultural tradition that binds the human race together, Winston," I assured him, and to Barry, "Perhaps Shakespeare will play here better than we thought."

16

We had to dress in the locker room, of course—a gymnasium has no dressing rooms. We were each assigned an archaic thumbprint lock, and we impressed our prints on them immediately; we heeded the sign on the wall that advised us that, if any of our valuables were lost to theft, it was due to our own failing, and the school could not be responsible.

"How absurd, Horace!" Ogden protested.

I could only nod in agreement. "Surely burglars could not open a thumbprint lock!"

"I think that's rather the point of it," Winston put in. "So long as the lock is on and fastened, the students have nothing to fear."

"Except for management deciding to search their lockers." Marty pointed to the slot in the center of the thumb patch. "See that? The coach just has to stick a key in, and bingo! Lock's open!"

"Yes, I seem to remember something of the sort from my dim youth," Winston agreed. "Surely no one could open it without the key."

"Oh, couldn't they?" Larry pulled a slender instrument out of his pocket, stuck it in the nearest lock—and it sprang open.

We all stared—except Marty. He only sighed. "Showing off again, huh, Larry?"

"Just because you have no technical skills, Marty, is no

reason to denigrate those of us who have." Larry opened the door and wrinkled his nose. "Athletic shoes, gym clothes . . . singularly unimaginative student, here."

"Larry!" I cried, shocked. "That is someone else's personal property!"

"And very uninteresting it is, too." Larry shut the door and stuck his pick in the next lock. "Let's see if his neighbor has a bit more imagination."

"Let us see if you can discover a notion of ethics! How did you ever develop such a criminal trait?"

"I worked one summer for a locksmith." Larry rifled through the locker's contents. "Well, now! This fellow, at least, has a pornographic magazine secreted away!"

"Larry, *stop* that!" I cried. "You have absolutely no right to go peering into other people's personal—"

"This one has a small bottle." Larry had opened another locker, and another. "Aha! A packet of tobacco! And they had the gall to tell me it was a criminal offense!"

"I have no doubt it is, and we should report it instantly." I went along behind him, slamming locker doors. "However, if we were to do so, we might find ourselves up on charges of burglary! Larry, *stop* it!"

"Barry will take a very dim view of this, if he learns of it," Winston said, "and you may be sure there are those among us who would tell him."

Larry paused.

"And tell Ramou, too," Marty said. "I happen to know his roommate. He has a very old-fashioned sense of honor."

"My amusements have nothing to do with him!"

"I don't know if he'd see it that way. After all, we're all from the same company, so your reputation affects his."

"It most certainly affects Barry's." Winston stepped up behind Larry—very closely behind. "We really must ask you to desist."

"Yes, we truly must." Ogden stepped close, towering over the slight young man.

"For the last time, Larry, please!" I stepped quite close on his other side.

"Oh, very well, Mr. Burbage!" Larry slammed the last door shut and jammed the pick back into his pocket. "I can see there will be no chance of fun in *your* presence!"

"We are here to work, not to amuse ourselves," Winston said severely. "Acting can be immensely satisfying, young man—but only after the tedium and stress of rehearsal is done. If you wish to 'have fun,' I suggest you discover a rich uncle and do your best to ingratiate yourself, for there are very few gainful occupations that consist of play."

"Hey, I thought we were players," Marty protested, taking the pressure off Larry for a moment.

"Quite so—which is to say that we are the only human beings for whom play is work," Winston rejoined.

I couldn't quite agree with him. When all is going well in a comedy, the line between play and work blurs to the point that the distinction ceases. In drama, of course, it is quite another matter—and as Winston had pointed out, rehearsals are simply work, plain and simple. Satisfying work, when all goes well—but it frequently doesn't.

Then, of course, there are tragedies—such as the Scottish play. I could only hope that it would not prove to be too tragic, indeed.

It didn't take much to find my recruits—all I had to do was follow the racket. It was just good-humored guffawing and loud voices, punctuated by Grudy's shrilling. It was coming from the dojo, so I swung in and felt right at home.

"Yes, it *is* necessary for you to wear hose." The poor old lady was beginning to wear thin. "Now do be good boys and pull them on! I've a costume of my own to don, you know."

" 'S all right, love—we'll be there on time," said a cheerful basso that had dropped a few down its gullet. "Why the tin hat?"

I stepped over, trying not to grin too hard. "Barry wants to start running in fifteen minutes, Grudy!"

"Oh! Ramou! Thank heaven!"

"No, thank Horace. He just assigned me to take care of this mob."

"Oh, izzsat so, mate?" the basso said, not so cheerful any more.

I turned toward the voice and found myself staring at an acre of chest. I followed it up to the hard grin and said, "Yeah. I'm supposed to tell you guys where to go."

"Suppose we tell you where to go first, eh, Jack?" said a shorter version of the same with a low baritone and a hard face. Hard arms and shoulders, too—since he didn't have his shirt on, it wasn't hard to tell.

"Don't think you know your way around," I said cheerfully.

"Know our way around!" a high baritone bleated, coming in on the giant's other side. "Who went to this flaming high school and who didn't, eh?"

"It's not a high school now," I said. "It's a theater."

"Yeah, and we're being paid to walk into our old gym and look like an army." Chovy stepped up beside me, turning to face Tall and Wide. "This's Ramou, Bolo. Don't give him a hard time—he's got trouble enough, trying to ride herd on us lot."

"Does he now?" Bolo said easily. He didn't want to let it go.

Neither did I, but Barry needed us in fifteen. "Hey, I didn't ask for the job," I said. "I know, don't tell me—neither did you. But you took it, so . . ." I raised my voice. ". . . everybody into costume, okay?"

Bolo didn't budge. "After you."

"Good idea." I turned to Grudy, who was looking very nervous. "Got my costume, Grudy?"

"Yes, dear." She pulled a hanger off a rack.

"You'll look ver-r-r-y pret-ty in it, 'dear,' " Bolo mimicked.

I felt the frisson of anger tingling all over my skin—but I remembered the rules Sensei taught me, so I let it wash over me and dwindle away.

Grudy handed me the costume. "Suspenders for the hose, and wrap the thongs from the sandals around your legs in diagonals that crisscross."

"Will do. Don't they need you in the ladies' now?"

"Why . . . yes, thank you, Ramou." And she moved toward the door, glancing back at me anxiously.

She didn't need to worry. "Okay." I turned back to Bolo and kicked off my trousers. "You pull the hose on all the way, but don't let 'em bind your toes too tight." I'd been through this yesterday, fortunately, when the company had run a dress rehearsal aboard ship.

"Stockings, eh?" Bolo said. "Pretty, pretty."

"Glad you think so. Try 'em on."

"*Me* wear stockings? Don't make me laugh, chum!"

"I didn't know you could," I said, and reached up to clap him on the shoulder. "Look, Bolo, it's really simple—you put on the hose, or you're fired."

His grin turned nasty, and he knocked my hand off—or would have, if I hadn't seen it coming and yanked it away. "If you fire me, chum, you'd better not step outside."

"You're fired." I headed for the door. "I'm stepping outside."

The extras whooped and followed along.

But Bolo didn't. "Why bother?" he called. "We're right here in a dojo."

I turned on my heel and came right back. "Good point. Step back, folks—give us room."

Where was Chovy all this time? Leaning back against the wall and looking interested, that's where. Fine friend he was—to either of us.

"Watch out, Bolo," somebody said. "He's the one threw every kid in karate class the other day."

"Yeah, you told me," Bolo said. "But how is he on street fighting?"

I managed to keep the laugh down. You don't get very far in martial arts before you learn not to boast about it—and Bolo obviously didn't know much about karate, if he could even ask the question. Of course, he didn't know about my scurrilous past, either.

I know. A black belt isn't supposed to let himself get pushed into a fight if he can walk away from it. But Bolo had just made it clear I couldn't walk—and besides, this wasn't a *real* fight, just a social one.

So it behooved me to put it on that basis. I stepped onto the red rug, paced over to the far side, turned back, and beckoned to him. He grinned, shucked his jacket, and leaped onto the mat.

I bowed.

He threw back his head and laughed.

Well, I'd made the terms clear. But I didn't fall into guard stance, I just ambled two steps closer to him—all the time remembering that Barry wanted these apes onstage in fifteen minutes. Ten, now. I didn't have time for a long, drawn-out bout—but I couldn't embarrass Bolo too badly, either. It would be a tough balancing act.

Bolo stepped a little closer and taunted, "Why don't you throw a punch, big black belt?"

"Because," I said, "I'm not the challenger here. You get first kick."

He didn't bite. "Oh, no, after you!"

Well, at least he knew something. "No, I insist."

"Be my guest."

"Fine." I spun on my heel and headed for the costume racks. "Since we're not going to fight, let's get into costume."

"Hold on there," Bolo snarled. I heard his feet pounding

up behind me, and whirled about just as he reached for my shoulder. He hesitated, disconcerted to see my face again, then snarled and jabbed with his left.

I took the punch on my shoulder, rolling with it. It hurt, but not enough to complain about, so I just grinned and said, "Thanks."

"Thanks?" His face was a study in consternation.

"For making it self-defense."

He stared at me, wondering if it was a joke, realized it wasn't, snarled, and jabbed again.

I caught it, spun, locked his elbow, and pressed down just enough to make him squawk with surprise. Then I released the hold and leaped back. "So that's street fighting, huh?"

He bellowed and came in, foot and fist.

I ducked the fist, let the foot glance off my hip as I was stepping back, then kept on stepping, faster and faster. He followed, jabbing with that left; I took it on the shoulder, on the arm, on the chest, but I wouldn't let him hit the face, and he knew it was a matter of what I would and wouldn't allow, too. Knew that I wasn't letting him get that right fist in—and he was getting frustrated and very angry. "Stand still, Chicken Little!"

When he was going fast enough, I paused just long enough for him to follow up with that right, fast and hard. But I wasn't there anymore, I was catching that right wrist and whirling in to throw him over my shoulder. He was just the right size for it, and he landed with a very satisfying thump. No damage, of course—I pulled up on his arm just enough to cushion his fall—but he looked very disoriented for a minute.

The onlookers howled.

Since he was down anyway, I locked his elbow against my leg and pushed back—again, just enough to let him know I could have broken his arm if I'd wanted to, and to weaken his right a little; now both arms were under strength. Then I let go and jumped back.

It had been fun at first, but I was beginning to feel bad now. It was too easy, and I was cursing myself for a bully. Never mind that Bolo had picked the fight, or that the rest of them had probably put him up to it, one way or another—I was so far past him in ability that it was really unfair.

But I had to let him save face, which would maybe also salve my conscience. He clambered to his feet, shaking his head and glaring at me, hunched over like a bull, fists in close to his chest.

Then, suddenly, he charged me.

Maybe it made sense, in a way—using his bulk to flatten me. But he was too easy to dodge . . .

So I didn't.

Well, I did move a little—I had to make it look good. But I made sure I was slow, just slow enough so that he hit me a glancing blow, and I went flying. Okay, I jumped a little. I rolled to my feet right away, of course, to see him bearing down on me again.

Then it came to me in a flash. I stepped aside just enough to punch him in the head as he went by. An instant later, his shoulder caught me, and I went flying again. I rolled and came up, and Bolo was coming back cautiously, shaking his head to try to clear it, hunched over, guard up. He stepped in and let go with both fists at my midriff, like trip-hammers. I gave way just enough to keep it from hurting too badly, and slammed my right into his face.

He straightened up, fast, his eyes glazing.

He really didn't need it, but I stepped in and let him have a shot in the chin.

The crowd was going mad.

Bolo toppled like a pine tree—it was all I could do to keep from yelling, *"Tiiimmmberrrr!"*—straight into the arms of his backup group. While they worked him over with a towel and a bucket, Chovy stepped up to me with an approving nod. "Nicely done, Ramou, nicely done!"

"Thanks," I said sourly. "They were laying for me, huh?"

Chovy shrugged. "They figured you'd be the one sent to ride herd on them. How'd you guess?"

"Because they brought a bucket, sponge, and towel." I turned away so he wouldn't see my face work.

Not quite fast enough, though. "No fun?" he said softly.

I shook my head, straightening up before I turned back to him. "The tough ones on New Venus just aren't up to the tough ones on Terra, Chovy. Sorry, but that's the way it is."

"'S all right, mate," he said, with an appraising gleam in his eye. "I told 'em it was right bad manners—and it was, considering you lot are our guests. But there's some as won't listen to the voice of experience, eh?"

"I take it Bolo graduated a few years behind you?"

"Right, except 'graduated' wouldn't quite be the term I'd use." He reached out to touch my cheek with a thumb. "Nice bruise coming there."

"That's all right, I'll be wearing makeup." At his look of alarm, I said, "No, not you guys. I've just got a couple of lines, that's all. Even *I'm* not dumb enough to try to tell these apes to put on lipstick."

"Never seen an ape," Chovy said slowly, "just pictures—but I'll take it as a compliment."

"It is, in its way," I said.

Chovy nodded. "Well, then, tell 'em what you will, mate. I don't think they'll give you any argument now."

I nodded, took a deep breath, and stepped out.

I went over to Bolo. His friends looked up in alarm and tried to close ranks around him, but I was already right next to him. He was on his feet, very groggy, but he recognized me, and his face went blank.

"You're a tough one," I said. "Gave me a rough time, I don't mind telling you."

His face thawed a little.

"Wish I could ask you out for a drink right now," I said,

"but we're due on stage in five minutes. Think you can get into costume?"

Bolo nodded slowly, then smiled just a little. "Yeah. Sure, mate. Costume it is. Which one's mine?"

I met Marty coming down the stairs as I was coming up. "At last!" he said. "Barry's getting antsy, Ramou. What kept you?" Then he got a good look at my face and said, "Oh." And, "No time for makeup, huh?"

"Not yet," I said. "Go tell Barry we'll be right there, okay?"

"Sure." He turned away, then glanced back at me uncertainly. "You sure you're okay, Ramou?"

"Oh, yeah," I said. "Just had to establish my authority, like Horace said to do. Takes a little time, though. Go tell Barry, huh?"

Marty grinned. "Wish I had your talent, Ramou." Then he turned and was gone, while I wondered what he meant.

I led my troops out onto the gym floor into the middle of the set. They stared at the platforms and stairs, making noises like, "Hey, superlative!" and "This is amazing!" Not quite in those words, of course.

All except Bolo. He was staring around the rest of the gym through his bruises, with a faraway look in his eye. Something about him plucked at my empathy. I sidled over to him and murmured, "Lot of great memories, huh?"

He nodded, eyes still on the bleachers and the equipment. "Best part of my life, mate. Best part of my life. All downhill from there. Ruddy bastards! To build us up so high, then drop us down so hard!"

Something connected. "They didn't kick you out after tenth grade."

"Oh, they let us stay in school, right enough—'cause we were the best at air hockey, and they wanted to see us play. So they led us up to thinking there was a future for us, then gave us a piece of paper, a pat on the head, and a job pumping oil!"

"Yeah," I said. "It's outrageous for the best years of your life to be over before you're twenty-one."

"What've I got to look forward to now?" he growled.

"It's not that far to Terra," I said. "Save your money. Don't get married. Buy your ticket to where there's some opportunity."

He finally realized who was talking to him and looked down, amazed. Then his face darkened. "What business of yours is it, anyway?"

"None," I said, "and all. Everyone's pain is mine, and mine is theirs—because I'm human."

"You won't last long that way," he snorted.

I nodded. "I know. Bad habit—I should break it. So should you. Make yourself a chance."

"Did you?" he sneered.

"No," I said. "I lucked into it—after I got to New York."

He shook his head impatiently. "I don't need New York. New Venus is enough—if I didn't have to be a pump-humper!"

"Then get that ticket to Terra," I said, "and go to college. Come back in management."

He stared at me. Then he said, "I wanted to be an air-hockey champ, bo!"

"Then be it," I said. "Start a team. Get the other men who used to be BMOCs. Do it through the Company—they must have a recreation program. But even if you don't, at least you had your days of glory. I didn't. You were lucky."

He gave me a long, brooding look. Then he said, "Might be as you're the lucky one, mate. Happen as your days of glory could be ahead."

I smiled. "Thanks. I hope so. I'm sure as hell going to work at it."

He finally smiled, too. "You've got the shoulders for it, bo."

"Come on," I said. "Time for work."

"If you can call this work," he snorted, but he turned back and came along with me—and do you know, I never had another bit of trouble out of him. Or any of the other extras, either. Funny thing about that.

We strolled up as Horace was trying to call the boys to order and getting red in the face about it. "Gentlemen, *gentlemen!* Will you come to order, please? We really must give you your blocking! Ramou? Has anyone seen Ramou?"

"Right here, Horace." I held up a hand. "Where do we go first?"

"Ramou! Thank heavens!" Horace sighed. "Take them around stage left, will you? You know the blocking."

I nodded and headed stage left, beckoning my little army. "Come on, guys."

I watched Ramou and his squadron troop off, then turned to call to Barry, "We can begin now!"

"Very good." Barry looked around at the whole company. "Pay attention, please, friends. This will be our dress rehearsal. Mind you, we will still have a runthrough with principals tomorrow, and time to work through a few trouble spots, but this will be our only opportunity for a full rehearsal with all the extras—they have jobs, from which the Company has graciously not released them—so they have to be at work tomorrow and cannot stay with us past midnight. Therefore, this will be the last chance to run the full show in this space. So do your best, and if you blow a line or two, just cover for one another, will you? I know it's been horrible having to prepare this play in so short a time, but you've all been splendid about it, and I want to thank you deeply."

"We have not all been splendid," I muttered to Winston. "There are one or two among us who have been protesting every inch of the way."

"Well, Horace, you know that, and I know that," Winston answered, equally low-voiced, "but I'm sure Marnie and Larry do not."

"Let us begin, then!" Barry cried. "Merlo, the heath, please?"

Before our eyes, the castle changed to a blasted heath with a huge rock outcropping. I heard some murmurs of amazement from the far side of the stage, where Ramou and his extras watched.

"Very good!" Barry turned away toward the wings, calling, "Grudy?"

Grudy came out on top of the rock—or perhaps I should say that the first witch did. She looked so ugly and malevolent that I could scarcely believe it was my old friend. I reflected, not for the first time, that Grudy had not chosen the branch of the field best suited to her talents.

"When shall we three meet again?" she shrilled, and we were off.

It was a disaster. I mean, it was the first play I'd ever been in, and even *I* could tell it was a disaster. Susanne and Lacey stumbled over their lines—they got them, but they stumbled—Banquo and Macbeth came on from opposite sides when they were supposed to be together, I was running around onstage correcting my extras and trying to herd them more or less in the same direction, and Larry dropped so many lines I almost tripped over them. Chovy's kid brother got his lines right as MacDuff Junior, but when the murderers came after him, he resisted so well that Charlie went around hopping on a wounded shin and I took a black eye before I finally hissed, "Look, kid, we're supposed to win this one, get it?"

"I thought I was supposed to fight back," he whispered.

"Yeah, but not for real. Now lie down and play dead, or I'll tell that big old guy with the crown to come sit on you."

He played dead. Fast. I didn't blame him; the idea of Ogden sitting on me would have made *me* drop dead, too.

Then there was the little matter of Burnham Wood.

"A tree?" Laro demanded—but quietly. "I gotta carry a bloomin' *tree*?"

"Just a few branches," I said, "and they're fake, so they won't trigger your hay fever."

"What's hay fever?"

"Nothing compared to what you're going to get if you don't pick up that flaming branch!" I was beginning to catch on to their slang. "It's supposed to be camouflage, see? Soldiers have been using it forever! The marines used it in World War II, back on Terra! Hunters use it, to catch deer! You're going to use it, or you're going to catch a pink slip!"

"No need to go torching, Ramou," Laro grumbled. "I'm going."

They just barely made it onstage in time. Of course, there were three bushes that made it all the way to the battlements, and one that started climbing the platforms, before Malcolm called them to lay aside their greenery and come out fighting like humans, but I was sure Marnie was offstage taking notes about those little details.

Then we got to the battle.

I was coaching Malcolm's army, and Horace was advising Macbeth's forces on the other side of the stage. We both knew the blocking, but getting it across to our eager but raw recruits was another matter.

"Enter upstage right," Horace was telling his troops, "and cross downstage left. Stop in center stage and exchange a few blows and blocks with the enemy."

They stared at him in blank incomprehension.

"Not real blows, mind you!" he hastened to add.

They still didn't look as if they understood much.

I was a little more direct. "You come in down there, around that low platform," I told them, "and go running diagonally across the stage, toward that curtain that's supposed to represent the sky, all the way across to the other side of the stage."

"So we come out at the back on the other side," Chovy clarified.

"Right. But when you get to the middle, you're going to meet a bunch of other guys in red coming toward you. You stop and swing at them—but make sure you don't connect; those blades are plastic, but they could still hurt. They'll swing at you, so you block and swing from another direction. Then you, Laro, fall down—you, too, Peppo. The other guys will run past you. Bolo and Chovy, you two pick up Laro and carry him off. Mozz and Cal, you guys carry Peppo off. When you're out of sight of the audience, everybody get back on your feet and ask Horace what to do—he's the old guy who's about my height. Everybody got it?"

"Sure." Laro grinned. "We charge out, knock down, and drag out."

"Right," I said. "Now get out there!"

Everything went fine, except that one of Horace's boys apparently hadn't understood that bit about not really connecting on the blows with his billhook; he caught Mozz right over the head. The plastic helmet soaked up most of the blow, but there was enough left to hurt, and Mozz took exception to it. He took exception so hard that Bolo and Hilber eventually had to pick up Mozz and the overeager attacker and actually carry them off, still trying to fight. In the fracas, Cal really did get knocked down, so there was nobody left to carry Mozz off—but that was okay, since he hadn't fallen. Chovy and Laro carried Cal out, and the other corpse got up and made it offstage on his own.

They came off to see Horace standing there covering his eyes with his hand, but he gamely smiled up at them, took a breath, and said, "Right, lads. Now, for the next pass . . ."

That was pretty much the tone of it—the blocking for the battle was basically right, except for the wrong people getting knocked down and the draggers becoming draggees, on every fight. Nothing really bad—until the last tableau, where everybody's supposed to end up in a circle and slam their pole-arms down to form a sort of upside-down funnel. They were a bit too far apart, so instead of all those poles stopping each other, they all came down and met on top of Borny's head. He went down, for real, and it took Susanne five minutes to bring him to offstage. He woke up talking about hazard pay, saw who was ministering to him, and grabbed for her. I intercepted the pass and told him that if he could still go after Susanne, he wasn't really all that badly hurt, but she made me call an ambulance for him anyway; she wanted an X-ray, just to be sure. Borny tried to shrug it off as sissy stuff, but Susanne turned on the charm and he got into the medi-van, even though she had to stay for notes.

But that's getting ahead of the story. There was still the little matter of the swords.

MacDuff swung down, Macbeth swung up, and everybody winced. But the two swords clanged like gongs and bounced off each other. We stared and all held our breaths. Then Macbeth chopped overhand, and MacDuff chopped sideways, and the two blades crashed against each other again—and we all winced and ducked. But amazingly, the swords held, and the two knights backed off and started whirling their swords around in circles.

"What's everybody ducking for?" Chovy wanted to know.

"Those swords have a track record of breaking," I advised. "Keep your head down."

"You're kidding," Chovy said, staring at the two swords just as they came together with a crash like a meteor striking a hull. Both swords broke across, and the tips went pinwheeling off into the wings.

"Heads up!" Horace shouted.

"Get down!" I yelped.

Somehow, all the extras managed to follow both directions as Macbeth's blade bounced off the masking flat and clattered to the floor, taking a piece out of Seeholder's expensive finish job. "Oh, hell," I said, turning gray at the thought of the look on his face.

The other one hit the backing flat point first, went right on through, and had enough energy left over to hit the upstage light boom. It swayed, it tipped, but it righted itself—and the sword tip clattered down onto Larry's helmet. He yelped and fainted dead away.

"Larry!" Susanne dashed over to him and started checking his vital signs. It was almost enough to distract me from the battle royal that was about to erupt—but not quite.

Lacey stood by and stared, looking stunned.

"Why, you arrogant, vegetable-headed imbecile!" Marnie advanced on Merlo like the *Victory* rounding on the French fleet. "Do you want to kill us all? What do you think you've *done* to that poor boy?"

"Absolutely nothing." Merlo met her advance with a stony glare. "The force was spent by the time it hit him, and his helmet was more than strong enough to ward it off."

"He's lying there unconscious on the floor! That could have been any one of us! It could have been *me*!"

"Oh, we were all braced for it." Merlo wasn't about to give up a good fight, even if he was in the wrong. "Nobody was hurt, were they? We all knew enough to duck."

The extras looked up, wide-eyed, and Bolo snapped, "*We* didn't!"

"You stay out of this!" Marnie flared at him, then turned back to Merlo.

Bolo's face darkened, "Now, look . . ."

"Good idea." I touched his arm. "Just watch. Best performance you'll ever get, and you're getting paid to watch it. But whatever you do, don't get caught in the middle."

"Anyone so incompetent as to furnish breaking swords ought to be fired on a moment's notice!" Marnie raged. "A second's inattention, and one of us might have been skewered!"

"Not as far up as those swords flew," Merlo retorted. "I know you're high and mighty, Marnie, but you're not *that* lofty."

"No, nor as high as your opinion of yourself! Where did you learn your blacksmithing—the Hammerhand Toy Company?"

"Thought that was where you got your wardrobe. Sorry, Grudy—I was talking about her street clothes."

"Whereas you would never be caught dead in anything but corduroy and denim! Which is exactly what you're going to be, if you're too close during that fight scene some night!"

"Good point. What were you hanging around for, anyway—hoping to see some blood?"

"The only blood I long for is yours! Oh, it's all well and good for you—you're over there by your board, thirty meters away from all this! If anybody is hit by flying metal, it's not going to be *you*!"

"Yes, but it might be someone in the audience." Barry finally stepped in, looking rather severe. "I'm afraid the period of experimentation is over, Merlo. We must have swords that won't break."

Merlo sighed, deflated. "Yeah, I know. Ramou and I will run back to the ship and make new ones out of the safety formula. Sorry, Barry—but they should have worked, damn it!"

"Two hours in customs, each way?" Horace stepped up. "And they close down at midnight; it's thirteen o'clock now. Even if they rush you through, you will have to sleep on the ship, and will barely be on time for rehearsal tomorrow morning."

"Uh, boss?" I said.

"Not now, Ramou," Merlo said, and turned to Horace.

"I brought 'em with me."

Merlo looked up, startled. "You went ahead and made 'em after I told you not to?"

"Well, yeah." I shrugged. "I mean, you told me to be ready for anything."

He just gave me a very long look before he said, "Yeah, I guess I did. Thanks, Ramou."

But Chovy was holding Macbeth's sword tip and hilt, gazing at the break with a very thoughtful look. "You didn't buy them with these drips of welding wire on the flat surfaces, did you?"

"Huh?" Merlo looked up, startled. "Well, no, I didn't. I used a spot welder to decorate 'em."

"That's your problem, then. The welding ruined the temper—made the metal crystallize just enough."

Merlo stared. "How the hell would *you* know?"

"I started out in maintenance." Chovy flashed him a grin. "Welding's one of the things I did. Made that mistake back in school—trying to weld an impact plate back together. It split on the first strike, and the teacher had to explain the hard facts to me."

Merlo just stared at him. Then he turned to me. "Anything else your encyclopedic friend over here can tell us about how to fix our problems?"

"You know how to get Larry to finish memorizing his lines by tomorrow?" I asked Chovy.

A slow grin spread over his face. "Happen I do, mate—but I don't think it's legal, even here."

"Yeah, I thought of that, too," I admitted, "but Barry wouldn't let me. How about running me back to the hotel, so I can pick up the swords?"

Later, as we waited in the dawn light for Chovy and his buddies to bring up the cabs, Horace sighed. "Oh, well—there's an old tradition in the theater, Ramou, that if you have a bad dress rehearsal, you'll have a good opening night."

"Really?" I asked, relieved. "Then our first performance ought to be a real work of art."

17

I woke up as I was snapping bolt-upright in bed, with the thought chilling through me that tonight was opening—and we weren't anywhere near ready. "Oh, well, bad dress, good performance," I growled to myself as I rolled out of bed and pulled on my trousers. Quietly, so as not to wake Marty. It reminded me of Horace's tiptoeing around, when I'd been a guest on his couch; I wondered if he was awake yet. Probably, even though the poor old guy needed his sleep more than I did. I'd noticed, though, that he usually couldn't sleep past six; they say age does that to you.

Today was an exception, of course, because we'd stayed up all night in the gym; the coach had to have it back for classes at eight A.M.—so we had rehearsed until six, running everything except the battle scenes again and again. Eyelids grew heavy and people grew glum; movements became slower and slower, and the sword fights deteriorated into slow-motion pantomimes. By the time Barry told us we could quit, it was all we could do to drag ourselves back into the cabs.

The alarm chimed—high noon. I hit its "off" button and told it, "You're a little late." But at least I wasn't—six hours' sleep—Barry had insisted—and I was ready to meet Charlie Publican for one more try at getting our homemade prompting machine ready. I felt logy and gritty, but I could function. I grabbed my shirt and headed for the door.

"It's no use, Charlie." I sighed half an hour later, in the improvised electronics shop he'd set up on top of the table in his room. If the hotel ever found out about it, they'd probably raise hell—but they wouldn't find out; Charlie had put up a mar-proof board, and all our instruments stood on that. The board folded into suitcase size; I had a notion Charlie was used to doing clandestine work—probably in cheap hotels, or a faculty office.

"Never give up hope, lad," Charlie consoled me. "We have it broadcasting the lines that we feed in from the ROM cube; it only needs to do it reliably."

"Yeah, but if the actors can't depend on it, it's worse than useless," I pointed out.

"Pity." Charlie sighed. "Another twenty-four hours, and we might have it debugged and on line—but we don't have twenty-four."

"No, we've got about two, till we have to show up for rehearsal. Good thing Marty and the girls memorized their lines as soon as they were assigned."

"Yes, and that the old-pro contingent had theirs memorized from previous productions," Charlie agreed. "That leaves only Larry."

"I wish it did," I sighed, "but he's still with us."

"Don't fret, lad—I told him last night that the prompter might not be ready on time. Presumably, he was up half the night cramming."

I frowned at him. "You talk like it was an exam."

" 'As if it were,' Ramou, not 'like it was.' And yes, it is an examination—of the worst sort: in front of an audience."

"That's one way of looking at it," I admitted. "If we ever get this thing working, Charlie, you ought to patent it."

"You, lad—it's as much your work as mine, and more, since you came up with the original idea. I don't need the money, and I'm not about to go back to Terra to collect it in any case."

That reminded me of the bridges we had burned behind

us. "I don't think any of us will, Charlie—unless we can be sure Rudders would call off his dogs. No point in going back to an arrest. Come on, time to go."

"Then we'd best tidy up," Charlie said. "Wouldn't want to startle the chambermaid, now would we?"

Five minutes later, the prompter was stowed in a suitcase along with the work-top and the tools, the table top was pristine and unmarked—and Charlie and I were going out the door and heading for the theater. Excuse me—for the lobby.

I was back at the old stand, administering coffee and doughnuts to hung over actors—only this time they were hung over with exhaustion, not booze. Except Ogden, that is. Susanne was giving him her best glare, but it bounced right off the alcoholic miasma that surrounded him. She couldn't figure out where he was getting it.

I could, though—the same place I'd gotten the coffee and doughnuts. I decided I'd have to ask Chovy how much Ogden was paying him, then see if I couldn't pay more to have our friendly local declare that his sources had suddenly and literally dried up.

Barry came into the hotel lobby last of all; I think he'd had to shoo Marnie and Larry out of their respective rooms. He accepted a cup of coffee and sat down, carefully. "All right, friends," he said. "We will be in the gymnasium at three o'clock; the coach feels that he absolutely cannot cancel classes to allow us to rehearse."

There were rumbles of anger throughout, but none with much conviction; we were all too tired.

"The gym isn't really necessary for this morning, though," Barry went on. "I'm satisfied that we all know our blocking and can cover for whatever little slips we make. However, I'm not quite so sanguine about the lines; we all seem to have them fairly well, but 'fairly well' isn't enough, in front of an audience. Accordingly, we will spend the time in a line run. Fire them off as quickly as you can, please, and don't try for interpretation or characterization; we—"

"We know what a line run is, Barry," Marnie groaned.

Anger sparked in Barry's eye, and I realized he was running on fumes, too—but all he said was, "A matter of phasing us in to the morning's work, my dear. I merely wished to recapitulate."

"Not in public!" Marnie snapped.

We all looked up at her, startled.

"Is it so odd that I would attempt a witticism?" she demanded, then held up a hand to forestall Marty. "I know, I know—some can tell them, and some cannot."

"And some can't hear them." Marty grinned. "Which is all of us, right now. Sorry, Ms. Lulala. I'm too tired to laugh."

"As long as you can remember your lines." She sighed. "Very well, Barry. If we finish this two-hour play in fifty-five minutes, can we have the second hour for sleep?"

"An excellent idea." Barry nodded. "Grudy, would you lead?"

"Whenshallwethreemeetagain," Grudy shot out, and we were off running into the wildest, rattling spin-through of MacScottish that Shakespeare ever dreamed of.

MacDuff swung up, Macbeth swung down, and we all held our breaths. The two swords cracked together, then rebounded off one another, ringing like bells; the actors had to swing around with their blades to keep them under control. "Very good, Merlo," Winston said, looking a little dazed.

"Yes, indeed," Barry agreed, "though the elasticity will take some getting used to. Still, it should prove a delight. I can begin to conceive all manner of effects it might produce."

"Please!" Marnie begged. "Not in this production!"

"No, no, certainly not, Marnie," Barry said quickly. "Not when we're about to open. But don't you think the swords have possibilities, Winston?"

"Oh, undoubtedly—and without question, a superior formula for a stage sword. Certainly a better tone than the iron ones, and I don't doubt they'll hold up."

"A triumph, Merlo," Barry concurred.

Marnie gave him a glare of irritation.

"Hey, it was Ramou's doing." Merlo had to be the most generous man I'd ever met, with everybody except Marnie. "I don't know where he got that formula, but it's a honey."

"Not terribly well tried, then." Barry turned to me, looking concerned.

"Oh, I wouldn't say that," I told him. "I learned about it in Materials Science—even us EE boys had to take it, 'cause there are so many formulas that affect current flow now."

Marnie eyed the new swords warily. "What are they made of?"

"A complex alloy of silicon compounds," I said.

"Silicon?" Marnie stared at me. "You made them out of *glass*?"

"A sophisticated ceramic," I answered. "They use it for the outer skins of ships that have to go through atmosphere. It rings just like steel."

"But it will *shatter*!"

"Not a bit," I assured her. "See, just think of it as being a frozen liquid . . ."

"Not ice! Ice shatters, too!"

". . . like iron. Only with iron, we beat the hell out of it and add bits of other elements, and come up with fantastic alloys that won't bend or break."

Marnie's eyes narrowed. "You're not trying to tell me you can do the same thing with glass!"

"More like pottery." I took a deep breath, reining in my temper.

"*Pottery*? I'm going to trust my life to a *clay pot*?"

Fortunately, I still was still holding my breath. I let it out gently and tried a different tack. "Well, if it's only clay, it can't hurt you if it breaks, can it?"

"Broken vases can cut!" she snapped.

I nodded. "And if clay can be made hard enough to cut, it can also be made strong enough and resilient enough so that it won't break. But it still rings like . . ." I bit off "crystal goblet" just in time and substituted, "Quasimodo's bell—and it won't melt even in the middle of a blast furnace."

I didn't tell her that modern ceramics weren't clay—she wasn't the kind who could understand anything outside her own experience.

Still, the compound out of which I'd had the Constructor craft the sword bore about as much resemblance to clay as a blade of grass does to a bamboo pole. I mean, they're both *basically* the same, aren't they? Both grasses—and technically, just different varieties of the same thing. Of course, there are so many differences piled on top of that basic sameness that they look totally different and don't behave at all alike, but those are just details.

"Well, I'm delighted to hear they can stand the heat." Marnie scowled, hands on hips. "But I'm a bit more concerned about their breaking, young man."

"Not to worry," I told her. "There've been the occasional crash landings—and the steel inside the ship has bent, the plastics have broken, but the tiles made out of this formula never even cracked. That's why I thought it would be good for these swords. I'll admit I didn't know about the ringing, though." I threw that in because I could see she needed something to feel superior about. From her viewpoint, there was a definite chance that I knew something she couldn't even begin to understand, and that made her feel intimidated.

"Very fortunate, I'd say," Winston held up his blade,

scrutinizing it. "Well, if it can take a spaceship crash, it ought to withstand the worst we can give it, eh, Barry?"

Marnie eyed me askance, and coldly. "How do we *know* it won't break? It's still very much of an experiment, in this application. You just made this up, didn't you?"

"No," Merlo said. "It's been used for—"

"The outside of spaceships, I know." Marnie's lip curled. "But has it been used for swords before?"

"Well . . ." I said.

"Of course not," Merlo snapped.

"Well, then." Marnie leaned back, preening herself. "We don't know it won't be worse than the iron ones, do we?"

"All right, we'll test it." Merlo sighed. "Just to be safe, one more collision."

"Yes, quite so," Barry said slowly, "but I'd like to see what Ramou can do with it." He held his sword out, pommel first, to me.

"Hey, I'm not all that strong," I protested.

Susanne went into a coughing fit.

"Perhaps." Barry looked pretty skeptical himself. "But you do know how to concentrate what force you do apply. Give it a go, will you, Ramou?"

"I think I'd better take the other one." Merlo plucked the blade from Winston, looking a little nervous. "But if we're going to treat it as something potentially dangerous, let's use all due precautions. Do we have chest protectors and masks, Winston?"

"Of course." The Mordant Emperor grinned. "I never travel without my kit."

"Could we borrow it, please?"

We could. In ten minutes, Winston had delivered the "kit" and was helping me into my chest protector. "You've used these before, Ramou?"

"Something like 'em," I admitted. "We ran more to bamboo, where I was trained."

Winston raised his eyebrows in surprise, then stepped

back. "I really believe Barry and I should make the experiment—after all, we are the ones who will be wielding these weapons in the actual duel."

Merlo looked thoughtful, but I said, "We want to test them under maximum conditions, Mr. Carlton."

"Maximum?" Winston frowned. "Are you implying that you can strike so much harder than I can?"

I stilled the tip of my sword on the floor, me glowering down at it. The conflict between truth and modesty had me again.

Merlo saw. "Yes, he can," he assured Winston. "Besides, it's the tech man's job to make sure the props are sound, before he lets the actors have them."

"But I'm quite sure—"

"Marnie isn't," Merlo reminded him, "and it's her hide as much as either of yours. Okay, everyone get way back, now. Heads up!"

They got. With that huge cavernous gymnasium, they could get a long way, and they did.

"Okay, Ramou," Merlo said quietly.

"Real, or looking good?" I asked.

"Showy," he answered, "but with everything you've got."

I brought it up from the subbasement, and I brought it up hard and fast. There was a huge *clang*! Then I was standing there looking down at my sword again, its point on the floor. It was whole.

"What made that noise?" Susanne was asking.

Marnie cried, "Are we to believe he swung?"

They were putting it on. I remembered the tale of the sword master who moved so fast nobody saw him, but I never really believed that. Besides, I wasn't a master in that Way.

"He swung," Marty assured her. "You must have blinked at the wrong moment."

Marnie turned on him, angry, but Merlo said, "My blade's still there. Intact."

She turned back, staring at the two swords. Then she said, "I don't believe it."

"Slower this time, Ramou," Merlo said. "Now!"

I saw him swing out of the corner of my eye and brought my blade up to meet his. It was beautiful—two matching arcs, exactly opposed. The swords met and bounced off each other. I used the bounce to return to guard.

Marnie was staring.

"That the kind of sound you wanted?" I asked Merlo.

"Just fine," he assured me, "but I'd scarcely say the durability's been fully tested. Let's make it a real bout, Ramou. Five minutes."

"En garde!" Winston called.

It wasn't my style or my language, but I knew what it meant. I was still on guard. Merlo swung his sword up to cross mine. Winston stepped in and whisked his toothpick up, separating our blades, and we started chopping.

"Remember!" Barry cried. "Not real! For show!"

So he had heard me ask. I nodded to show I'd heard, blocked Merlo's slash, then whirled my blade around to come in low. I deliberately went slowly, but not quite enough—he just barely got his sword down to block mine. They rang like hammer and anvil, and I stepped back to whirl around full circle and come in with a horizontal cut at belt height.

"Wonderful!" Winston cried.

Merlo stepped back and met my roundhouse with one of his own, then guided his sword on the rebound to chop in low. I swung and blocked it, then hopped over my sword and swung it up for a vertical blow.

"Can't either of them hit the other?" Marnie exclaimed in scorn.

"That's not their purpose just now, young lady," Ogden

rumbled. "They're testing the mettle of the swords, not of each other."

"But I thought they were glass!" she protested.

Ogden shrugged. "It looks like metal, it sounds like metal, it behaves like metal . . ."

I thought it was nice of him to cover for her lack of vocabulary.

Merlo's sword was coming right at my sinuses, and I didn't feel like trusting to that flimsy wire mask Winston had given me. I dropped to one knee, swinging up overhand, and my sword chimed against his. He swung down at me, just as he should have, but I had baited the trap, and I wasn't about to be there when I sprang it. I leaped out of the crouch and back, and let his blade crack into the platform beneath us. It left a scar, but the sword stayed whole. I timed my swing so it would reach while his blade was still down, but he ducked under it and came up from below. I met his cut backhanded, and . . .

"Time!" Winston called.

We dropped our points, and Merlo took off his mask, panting, sweating, and smiling. "We ought to do that more often, Ramou! I need the exercise."

"As do we all." Barry turned to face the full company. "Fencing practice for all men, and for those ladies who wish it, at four P.M., as soon as we are back aboard ship, and until our next planetfall. Winston, will you oversee the sessions?"

"Glad to—but I'd like young Lazarian to show us a few of those movements he used today," Winston said, with a devilish grin. "It's a style I don't know."

Larry stared, scandalized.

I shrugged. "I was making it up as I went along, Mr. Carlton. You said to be showy."

"Then let's see if you can remember it long enough to teach the rest of us, eh? And perhaps show us the discipline they came from." He turned to Merlo. "I think these new swords will be just what we need, Merlo. Don't you, Marnie?" He turned the full strength of his diabolical beam on her.

Marnie glared at him and clipped out the words syllable by syllable. "Why, yes, Winston—I think they've proved durable. But let's see how they wear, shall we?"

Merlo turned away to hide his sigh.

I came back early from dinner, figuring to get into my costume and makeup before my bravos arrived; it would be bad enough listening to their wisecracks when they saw me in lipstick and rouge, without having to suffer the extra lines they could come up with while I was putting it on.

Besides, I just couldn't sit still.

I came through the door and stopped dead still.

The intruder looked up with a polite smile, one hand still on the locker. He was tall, dark-complexioned, and black-haired—and he was wearing a gray business *complet*.

I went cold with the anger of invaded territory. "Excuse me, but I'll have to ask you to leave."

"Isn't this the men's room?" he asked.

"No, it's the locker room—ordinarily. But right now, it's a dressing room for a troupe of actors." I nodded at the portable makeup table that almost filled the center aisle between the lockers and the showers.

"Oh." He glanced at it. "I see. Sorry about the mistake."

"Don't mention it." I stepped aside and watched him as he brushed past me and out. I was memorizing every feature of his face, because this was the first time I'd seen him up close—but I was sure I'd seen him before, on Terra. He was the man in gray who'd been in the mob that watched the reporter ambush us, watched the gang that jumped us on our way home, and tried to serve the restraining order on us as we were trying to take off.

I know—gray suits all look alike. I could be making a very simple mistake.

But I was sure I wasn't. It wasn't a matter of recognizing a face in the background of a photo—it was remembering a face I'd seen stare right at me, alive.

His footsteps faded away up the stairs. I hurried over to check the locker he'd had his hand on, but it was securely fastened shut. So was the one next to it, and the one next to that.

But just to be safe, I checked every locker in the place.

So it was opening night, and I was running around frantically from the boys' locker room to the door of the girls' locker room, the stage in the Grand Gym to the tech booth in the press box. "Everything going okay? Only an hour till curtain!"

Why they called it "curtain" was a mystery to me—this was a medieval set, none of the windows had any hangings. The closest they came was the tapestries on the walls of Castle Macbeth, but we didn't bring those up until Scene Two.

Of course Merlo told me, while we were wiring things up, that way back in the old, old days, the actors used to hide the set from the audience by an actual, genuine, gigantic piece of drapery. Then, when it was time for the show to begin, they'd raise it up, revealing the set, like a picture inside the frame of the proscenium.

Then the picture came to life.

It must have been magical, especially back then in those primitive times. I mean, Merlo says this started in the 1600s and went all the way into the 1900s. I can imagine what it must have been like—sitting there in the theater, the lights suddenly going out all around you, then this streak of light appearing in front of you, widening until it showed you a living picture . . . It must have really seemed magical, to people who'd never seen much theater. Maybe even to people who'd seen a lot; maybe it always had a tinge of the enchanted.

Then the electricians gave the actors so much control over light that they started the show just by bringing up the lights—and of course, nowadays, we make the set glow into existence, too. Even so, I guess the term stuck. We didn't have a curtain anymore, but Merlo had told me I was supposed to keep everybody notified as to how long it was till "curtain," and that it still meant the beginning of the play, so "curtain" it was, and I was keeping everybody posted.

Every ten minutes.

"An hour?" Marnie shrilled from inside that mysterious country where no man has gone before. "Why in heaven's name are you bothering us so early, you blithering idiot? Grudy! Where is Grudy! The fit on this costume is abominable!"

"Yes, Ramou, stop blithering," Lacey's voice snapped. "Susanne! Fasten my seam, will you? Why in heaven's name did Grudy put the press joint up the back?"

I took the hint and ducked into the boys' locker room. "An hour till curtain!"

"Idle down, Ramou," Marty said with a grin. "We've got plenty of time."

"Yes, quite impossible," Larry snapped. "Don't be any more of a fool than you have to be, Ramou."

Before I could reply, Horace's hand was on my shoulder, and he was saying, "Really, Ramou, you're already in costume and makeup, and we truly do have more than an adequate amount of time to prepare. Why don't you run a check on the tech systems?"

"Yeah, sure, Horace, great idea!" And I was out the door and up the stairs.

"Ramou's having his first-opening-night jitters, eh?" Barry asked from his seat at the portable makeup table.

"In spades," I confirmed as I sat down beside him. "I don't know whether he's more excited or more frightened."

I chuckled and shook my head. "He actually asked if makeup was really necessary."

"Of course it is," Barry said. "It gives us something to do for the hour before the show."

"Well, will you look at that!"

I turned to Charlie Publican. He stood before his open locker in makeup, frowning and holding up a needle.

"Where did that come from, Charlie?" Winston asked.

"My tights." Charlie laid it carefully aside and pulled on the article in question. "If I hadn't happened to notice it, I would have had a very unpleasant surprise."

Winston stared, appalled. So did I.

Then I turned on Larry. "Now, this has gone positively far enough! It's one thing to go opening lockers and rifling through them, young man, but to try to inflict pain on your fellows, as a practical joke, is completely unacceptable!"

"What? You don't think *I* . . . ?" Larry looked up, completely taken aback. Then his face darkened. "Now, see here, Mr. Burbage! I might practice a harmless prank now and then, but certainly nothing of *that* sort! What would make you think I would?"

"Your general level of interpersonal interaction with the other members of this company," I snapped, stepping closer, "coupled with the fact that only you, among us all, knows how to pick locks!"

"I didn't do it!" Larry looked up at Winston, who was crowding him from the other side. "I didn't, I tell you! If I had intended that, would I have let you see that I could open locks? Come to that, whoever did, obviously didn't let the ability show! Any of you might have done it!"

I was about to press the point when Charlie intervened. "Gentlemen, gentlemen!" he said softly. "It's over and done with, and no one hurt. It's really not worth your emotion— and we do have a play to do."

I frowned, reminded of the overwhelming concern of the evening. "Quite so—and tensions run high on opening night." I stepped back to my own locker. "But if there is the slightest sign of any further prank, Larry, you may be sure it will not be so easily resolved!"

I dashed into the tech booth. "Everything okay?"

"You've asked that five times," Merlo said, "and we've checked both boards three times. Yes, everything's okay, Ramou—except you. Calm down."

I stilled, then sank down on a stool, looking up at the camera monitor, which showed me an expanse of gym floor with the stage we'd set up, as seen from the side and above. Then I went rigid. "The bleachers! They still haven't pulled 'em out!"

"They got the ones at the end." Merlo pointed. "Then they went away—must have been time for their after-dinner coffee break."

"Coffee break? At this time of night? Let's hope it wasn't quitting time!"

"No, I asked Seeholder who was going to lock up, and he told me they had a night-time custodian—so there's a night shift."

"You better get 'em back here to open up the bleachers on each side!"

"If they haven't come back by quarter after, I will." Merlo gave me a wide grin. "I told you, relax. You're looking for things to worry about."

I sat rigid for a minute, then sagged as if the air were going out of me. "I suppose I'm being an idiot—but I'm so *excited*, damn it!"

"Enjoy it," Merlo advised. "Concentrate on how you're feeling and do the best you can to remember it. It's a once-in-a-lifetime experience, Ramou."

I looked up in shock. "Why? You don't think we're going to have dozens of opening nights?"

"Sure. Hundreds." Merlo grinned, leaning back. "But every one of us only has one *first* opening night. No other one will ever be quite the same. Just as much fun, some of 'em, but never the same fun. Go check on the extras, will you, Ramou?"

"No prompter?" Lacey fairly screamed. She was pale with rage—or was it fear?

"Please be calm, Ms. Lark," Horace said. "The new system that Ramou and Charles are developing still isn't quite ready."

"Ready or not, I'll take it!"

"You wouldn't want it," I told her. "It's liable to give you the middle of a sentence without the beginning or the end. We'll get it working eventually, but this was just too little notice."

"But I've only had three days to practice this part!"

"You have had the script for a month," Horace pointed out gently. I admired his self-restraint.

"Well, yes, and I know I've got it memorized—but that's in a room by myself, not in front of an audience! I still needed prompting this afternoon!"

"There were a great many distractions during rehearsal," Horace reminded her.

"And there won't be this evening? Heaven only knows what those yokels are going to do! They could heckle, they could hiss and boo, they could laugh at the tragic lines—"

"But at least we will be proceeding through the play nonstop."

"I *hope* I won't stop! What am I going to do if I blank?"

"Cover," Horace said simply. "Ad lib. Or do what actors have done for centuries—find a reason to go over to the wings, where one of your fellow actors will be holding the book, and hiss 'Line!' "

"But that'll pick up on the PA system!"

"Oh, let your mind be easy on that score. We won't have a PA system."

Lacey stared at him, turning light blue. Larry erupted.

"No PA? In a cavern like this one? Impossible! Incompetent!"

"Why not?" Marty asked, looking nervous.

"Because," I said, "the school won't let us tie our body mikes into their system."

"For heavens' sake, *why*?" Even Susanne had a case of incipient panic.

"They say it's because their PA is hooked into their main computer, and who knows what viruses our nasty unhygienic equipment might have? After all, who knows where it's been?"

"They're afraid we'll contaminate them?" Larry cried in outrage.

"Sure. After all, that's what they're afraid of from us in every other way, isn't it? That we'll contaminate their teenagers' pristine minds, not to mention their sterile community."

"Sterile!" Larry spluttered. "Haven't they seen the discontent seething under their noses? Don't they know how much bitterness is welling up in the workers?"

"If they don't look at it, it isn't there," Ogden rumbled.

"But what's the matter with our own amplification system?" Lacey turned on me.

I shrugged. "We thought we'd be tying into the school's system."

Lacey fixed me with a beady eye. "So you didn't bring our system?"

I nodded, feeling sheepish. "After all, they told us we could when we made the site survey . . ."

"Shouldn't have given them time to change their minds," Ogden huffed.

"I'm afraid we did need a few days' rehearsal, Ogden," Horace demurred.

Lacey turned on Horace. "Oh, that's just great! That's really reassuring, Horace! Nobody will hear me call for a line, because nobody will hear me, period! How am I supposed to make these rubes listen without a PA system?"

"Project," Horace said simply. I could see his temper was wearing thin. "Use the fullness of your natural voice."

Ogden frowned down at Lacey from all the majesty of his somewhat unsteady height. "Don't see what all the fuss is about, myself. If the audience is farther away, you project more loudly, that's all."

"Fifty meters?" Lacey shrilled.

"Fifty, or a hundred." Ogden scowled. "Any actor worth his pay should be able to fill a space this size with his voice—especially since there are bleachers on each side of us; if they can't hear, they can move closer." He looked up, blinking. "Or was anyone thinking there would be a full house tonight?"

"It would take the whole town to fill *this* house," Marty muttered.

Horace added, "If it was good enough for Thespis, Ms. Lark, it should be good enough for you."

"Thespis was trained for it!"

"And so were you," Horace reminded her, "or so it said on your list of credits."

"Well, yes—but I was trained to fill a five-hundred-seat theater, not a barn like this, with the acoustics of a racetrack!"

Horace nodded. "The simile is apt; Thespis had to make his voice heard in an open-air amphitheater."

"Yes, an amphitheater that was semicircular and concave! An amphitheater that just happened to reflect his voice back to everybody who hadn't heard it the first time!"

"Ah, you did learn some theater history, at least," Horace said.

"It's been done without that, Ms. Lark," Ogden added. "The tale is told of Winston Churchill, that he was addressing a vast crowd in the open air, when the microphone went dead. Those farther away from him could see his lips moving, but could not make out the words and began to protest. The grumbling spread until the whole crowd was rumbling."

We young sprouts were hanging on his words, in spite of ourselves. "What happened?" Larry asked.

"Churchill raised his hand for silence. When the crowd had quieted, he flourished the microphone overhead and, with a dramatic gesture, flung it to the ground, where it shattered into a thousand pieces. Then he gripped his lapel and thundered, 'Now that mechanical contrivances have failed us, we shall fall back on Mother Nature!' "

Susanne gave a little, half-disbelieving laugh, and Marty grinned slowly.

"Surely that's not true!" Lacey protested.

Ogden shrugged. "Have you ever seen a film of the great orator, Ms. Lark, or heard one of his recordings?"

"Of course," she snapped.

"Then you may say for yourself. I do not know whether the tale is true or not, but I do not find it hard to believe."

Horace seized his opportunity. "And you will not be in the open air, Ms. Lark. This enclosed gymnasium we are in will echo the sound back and forth quite nicely. There may be a few dead spots here and there, and the resonance may blur our phonemes a bit—but as long as we speak slowly and distinctly, there is no reason why the audience should not hear us. They'll surround us on all three sides, after all."

"Oh, it's well and good for you to make it sound so easy—but you haven't ever done it!"

Horace frowned slightly. "Whatever makes you say that?"

"Because you . . ." Lacey swallowed the rest of the words, reddening. "You mean you *have* performed in a barn like this before? Without a microphone?"

"Quite similar. It was a handball court in Lima, Peru— well, not handball, actually, but a rather more energetic version of the game called high-a-lie, presumably because it is played in an antigravity chamber, in free-fall, and the players have to make the ball rise high to lie right for their shots. They had the antigrav turned off, of course, but we were down at the bottom of a well, surrounded by hard plasticrete walls, and we had to make our voices rise up to the people seated above. It was no mean feat, I can tell you, but we managed it."

She was wide-eyed, hanging on his every word. "And the audience understood you?"

"They laughed in all the right places," Horace affirmed. "Of course, they laughed in some rather odd ones, too, when someone turned on the antigravity by accident—at least, I *think* it was by accident. But the spectators were quite considerate about hauling us in over the rail to safety, until the malfunction could be rectified."

"What an impossible story!"

"Yes." Horace nodded. "That is how you can be sure it is true. If I had made it up, it would certainly have been more plausible."

She glanced at him uncertainly and said, "Then you're sure they'll be able to hear us?"

"If you project from the diaphragm, my dear, without shouting—yes. Would you have any doubt that an opera diva could fill this hall with sound?"

"Well, of course ... I mean, her training ..." Lacey stopped, looking shamefaced. "Then I can, too, can't I?"

"Yes, indeed." Horace beamed like a fond uncle. "Mind you, you shouldn't have to—but since you must, you will."

She smiled, amused and relieved. "Thank you, Mr. Burbage. You've made me feel a lot better."

"My pleasure. Now be off with you for warm-ups, my dear."

She turned away, and so did Horace. His face was immobile; he didn't say a word. But he took a deep, deep breath, and let it out in a gust.

"Just opening-night jitters?" I ventured.

"Presumably," Horace said. "I only hope she won't be that way for every opening night. Time for places, Ramou. Summon your minions."

But before I could get away, Susanne came dashing back, her face white. "Ramou! They haven't opened the side bleachers! Only the ones at the end—and they're only half full!"

I looked up, startled, and Horace's face was a study. Then it set into grim and purposeful lines. "Come along, Ramou. We must discover the meaning of this."

It only took a few steps; we could hear the argument before we got there. For the first time since I'd known him, Barry Tallendar was raising his voice, and he wasn't projecting.

"Very well, I can understand only opening as much seating as is apt to be used," he snapped, "but why the *end* ones?"

Seeholder frowned. "Because the audience is supposed to sit in front of the stage, isn't it? I don't see what your problem is, mister."

"The audience sits in front of a 3DT screen, not a theater! We have staged this play in three-quarter arena, since we knew we were unlikely to find a proscenium—and the style is better suited to Shakespeare's plays anyway; it corresponds to the conditions of his original theater! The audience is supposed to sit on all three sides!"

"Well, they're not." Seeholder's eyes narrowed. "The custodians rolled out the bleachers before they went off duty, and there's only one old man left on shift. We're not opening any more bleachers unless those fill up—and the teachers have already called roll; we know all the English classes are here already."

"English classes?" Marnie gasped, appalled.

" 'Course. That's why we wanted you to put on this show—so they'd get motivated about Shakespeare."

"You mean they were *required* to come?" Barry's voice was grim.

"Yeah, and they're not very happy about giving up their Friday night, I can tell you. You better do a good job, mister, or you're going to have a lot of angry people out there."

"Surely you haven't barred adults from coming!"

"No, but who would want to?" Seeholder shrugged. "Shakespeare is boring. Look, you better start pretty soon, or they'll tear the place apart."

As if on cue, a roar that was half cheer, half rebuke, came from the far end of the gymnasium.

"Oh, my heavens." Horace gripped Barry's arm and pulled him away. "Oh, my aching drum! Come, Barry, let us get this performance started, before we discover something else that has gone wrong!"

18

"Mr. Ogden! You promised!"

I turned fast and saw Susanne and Ogden wrestling over a small bottle.

"Just a little bracer, my dear," Ogden panted, "to put me in shape for performance."

"The shape it will put you in is flat on your back! Ramou, *help* me!"

I reached out and grabbed the bottle, twisting it against Ogden's thumb. He hung on with a death grip—he may have been getting feeble, but all his strength went into holding fast to that bottle. His arm stayed rigidly bent, pulling against mine like a stone statue's, while he pleaded, "Young man, surely you can understand! There are times when only the taste of strong drink can nerve a man to do what he has to do!"

"Maybe," I said, "but this isn't one of those times." Frankly, I didn't believe a word of it.

It was a genuine predicament—if I applied real force, I'd hurt the poor old guy, certainly strain a muscle, maybe even tear a ligament. Fortunately, just then, Horace came up. "What's the matter?" He hissed. "Surely you know you're making enough noise to . . . ah!" He saw the bottle in Ogden's hand.

"Only a small nip," Ogden pleaded, "just enough to get one in the mood, so to . . ."

"To slow down one's reflexes and make one late on

one's cues!" Horace laid his hand over the current issue. "Really, Ogden! It's not at all fair to your fellow actors!"

"We could let you have a drink after curtain call," I bargained.

"A very small one!" Susanne snapped, then suddenly turned tender and teary-eyed. "Oh, Mr. Wellesley, you really are an old dear, and we'd be lost without you—so you really mustn't, mustn't drink!"

"Well—since you are so concerned," Ogden grumbled, and his hold on the bottle loosened just enough.

I twisted it out of his hand like white lightning, and Horace crowed in a whisper, "Well done, old friend!"

"Oh, yes, very well done!" Susanne reached up on tiptoe to plant a kiss on his cheek. "Oh, thank you very much, Mr. Wellesley!"

"Curtain!" I whispered, looking out toward the stage.

"Oh, yes!" Susanne turned away—and Ogden reached out to give her retreating backside a delicate pinch. She yelped and whirled back, red-faced. "*Mister* Wellesley! I thought you were a gentleman!"

"Just for luck, my dear," Ogden assured her—but I noticed that he didn't say whose luck, or in what. I started toward my little army, then hesitated, glancing back at Ogden.

Horace leaned close to me and muttered, "You may entrust him to my care, Ramou. I shall see that he makes his entrance in no worse shape than he is in already. Do go take care of your extras."

"Thanks, Horace," I said gratefully, and hurried off to my rowdy group, who were getting more and more rowdy by the second, with stage fright.

Unfortunately, the damage had already been done before Susanne caught Ogden; I could see it would be quite a chore getting him onstage on cue, and an even greater chore trying to act with him. I took firm hold of his arm and turned him to face the stage.

The lights went down—or off, I should say; why should a school waste money on dimmers for the gymnasium? The audience quieted—more out of surprise than anticipation, I suspect—and Merlo brought up the special spotlight on Grudy, crouched atop the highest platform, which had somehow turned into a crag under Merlo's virtuoso playing of the scene board. She cackled, high and long, then called out, "When shall we three meet again, in fire, thunder, or in rain?"

The light came up on the second level, where Susanne swayed in an invitation to damnation, answering, "When the hurly-burly's done, when the battle's lost and won!"

But her line was drowned out in a storm of whistles.

Barry plucked at his doublet nervously, watching from offstage. "Perhaps the choice of a young and seductive witch was not for the best . . ."

The third special came up on Lacey, trying her best to outdo Susanne in voluptuousness. She did well enough; she, too, was greeted by a torrent of whistles. Her line was lost in the midst of them. Grudy and Susanne came down to join her as they recited their lines; at last, the three turned in a circle in a travesty of a gavotte, chanting,

> "Fair is foul, and foul is fair;
> Hover through the fog and filthy air!"

Then they split, shrieking, and ran off, Susanne up the stairway, Grudy off right, Lacey off left, and the soldiers began to straggle on, hauling the bloody sergeant.

A chorus of booing echoed through the gym.

Lacey came off, livid. "How dare they! Those boorish little twerps! How dare they boo us!"

"Don't fret, dear," Grudy assured her. "They were booing your exit, not your acting. The way you and Susanne were gyrating, they were hoping to watch you all night."

Lacey stared, startled; then she smiled. "And more and more of us as the evening went on, eh?"

"Don't oblige them," Susanne advised.

"Don't worry, darling, I won't—and next time, think up your own variations on the bump and grind, will you?"

"My own! Why, you little thief! I was doing that move two days before you began it!"

"Pretty good, for only a five-day rehearsal period," Merlo hissed from the board. "Quiet down, would you, ladies? We've got a scene onstage!"

Ramou was shooing his extras out, hissing, "You've just been through a battle! Look strung out! Look paranoid! Look *tired*, at least!"

I watched him anxiously, wondering how he would fare. His first entrance in front of an actual audience was bound to be hard enough, but an audience that was booing . . .

I stepped out, and terror hit. I looked up, and there they were—there seemed to be a solid wall of them, sweeping up from right in front of my feet to way over my head, and all of them were yelling "Booooo!" and "Bring back the girls!"

I tell you, I've known fear, often and sharp—but it was always something in the background, something I could shove out of the way. After all, it was just fear of getting hurt, and I've done that time and again, and always walked away. But this was fear of . . . I don't know what. When the individual stands alone in front of the mob, stark panic hits, the certainty that they're going to get you, descend on you, annihilate you . . .

Maybe. All I really knew right then was that I was paralyzed, that every inch of me was sodden with fear.

Then a hand fell on my shoulder, and Marty's voice whispered in my ear, "Don't let 'em get to you, Ramou.

They can't do anything—and they're really hoping you'll astound them. They're just an audience."

I almost sagged with relief, just knowing that I wasn't out there alone. I stole a quick glance at Marty, and almost jumped—he wore a bloody bandage around his head, with trickles of crimson over his forehead and down his cheeks. It took me a second to remember that the "blood" was glycerine, and his scalp was unscratched under the bandage.

Everything clicked back into perspective suddenly—but the audience was still there.

Then a wall moved between me and them, and a voice hissed, "Hey, Ramou! Where'd you say we were supposed to go?"

I looked up; the voice was Bolo, come to the rescue. Suddenly, I couldn't afford to be frozen; I had to supply answers, give directions. They were depending on me.

"Over to the other side of the stage, Bolo," I hissed. "Help me with Marty."

He stuck a hand under Marty's armpit, and Marty obligingly slumped between us, but still bore most of his own weight, limping very believably. We paced down left with him, and I stole a quick glance at the audience again. They were just an audience now, a small mass of people way far away at the long end of a very large gym.

And there was a man in gray right smack dab in the middle of them.

Then I had to look away to see where we were going. I couldn't take time for a long look—but I knew he was there and I knew he was the guy who had been in the locker room. I didn't have a chance to look for him again until the end of the show—but I didn't need to.

Ogden started to follow them, but I held up a hand to restrain him. He blinked down at it owlishly, as if wondering what it was doing there, and my heart sank; the bottle we wrested away from him had not been his only supply. Ap-

parently he had outbidden Ramou for Chovy's services—
though I wouldn't have put it past our enterprising young
local to have taken money from both. I waited for the extras to settle down, trying to look depressed, while isolated
laughs of disbelief echoed from the audience, followed by
shouts of, "Hey, Bolo! I like your tin suit!" and, "Chovy,
mate! How's the stockings feel?"

But I must admit those voices came thin and strained—
they *were* a long way away.

When enough time had elapsed, I took my hand away
from Ogden's chest and nodded. He moved nobly if somewhat unsteadily out onstage, flanked by two of the local
boys. As the nearest one passed me, I hissed, "If he starts
to tilt, push him back upright."

I could hear Ogden's opening line, "What bloody man is
that? He can report, as seemeth by his plight, of the revolt
the newest state." But I could also hear a puzzled rumble
from the other end of the gym. Apparently the sophomores
did not understand Elizabethan English. "Break a leg, Mr.
Kemp," I hissed as Marty passed me.

"Did you say that to Merlo, too?" he whispered nervously, then stepped out to proclaim, "God save the king!"

The rumbling from the far end of the gym was a little
louder now.

It had grown to a steady, muted sound like distant surf,
punctuated by an occasional erratic clinking, before the
scene had finished. Ogden came back in a suitably royal
rage. "Why, those insubordinate, immature yokels! Those
unsophisticated, uncultured boors! What the blazes was that
clinking?"

"Soft-drink bottles, rolling down the steps of the aisles,"
I told him grimly.

"Pop bottles! I haven't heard that since we played North
Platte forty years ago!"

"No doubt the source of the original colonists." He was
right; I knew I had heard it before.

"They won't stop talking long enough to listen to us!" Marty, for once, was not laughing.

"They will listen to *me*, or no mystic fourth wall ever imagined will protect them!" Marnie snapped, and strode onto the stage, every inch a queen, pacing with nervousness, the note in her hand—but nonetheless, she found some believable motivation to look up and glare at the audience, as if Lady Macbeth were defying destiny itself. The young folk out there actually did throttle back to a dull roar. I scarcely blamed them; if Marnie looked at me with that much venom, I would have become very still, too.

Satisfied, Marnie turned, stopped pacing, and began to read the note in her hand. "They met me in the day of success; and I have learned by the perfectest report, they have more in them than mortal knowledge."

The dull roar grew sharper.

So did Marnie's tone. "Glamis thou art, and Cawdor, and shalt be what thou art promised; yet I do fear thy nature; it is too full of the milk of human kindness to catch the nearest way . . ."

The roar grew.

Marnie reddened. "Hie thee hither, that I may pour the spirits in thine ear . . ."

I knew what she was doing wrong, of course—what they had all been doing wrong. I'm sure Ogden would have realized it if he had been sober, but the rest of them were simply too young—they were used to real theaters with excellent acoustics, and 3DT studios with sensitive microphones—or, if they had toured before, were accustomed to body mikes and amplifying systems.

I, however, had begun with a struggling summer company in a tent and, moreover, one that had been forced to tour as a condition of its government grant, but had been too poor for such luxuries as amplifying systems. I knew why the audience was so restive, and how to cure it.

So, when the moment came, I entered, bowed, and blasted

out so loudly as to make those distant ceiling girders ring, "THE KING COMES HERE TONIGHT."

The audience fell totally silent.

Marnie looked at me in shock, wondering why I had blared like a trumpet. Then I saw understanding come into her eyes, and she belted back at me, "THOU ART MAD TO SAY IT! IS NOT THY MASTER WITH HIM?" as well as the finest pop-song singer ever heard.

"SO PLEASE YOU, IT IS TRUE," I thundered, and went on to bellow at her how one of the soldiers had sped on ahead to bring just that much news and no more.

She kindly belted back, "GIVE HIM TENDING; HE BRINGS GREAT NEWS." Then I bowed, turned, and left.

Behind me, I could hear Marnie soliloquizing with all the subtlety and confidentiality of a trombone in mating season.

But the audience was quiet. They could finally hear.

"A hit, a palpable hit," Winston whispered, grinning at me with delight.

"I'll settle for being able to finish the play," I hissed back.

He whisper-chuckled like a snake in hysterics, then stepped past me onto the stage, roaring, "MY DEAREST LOVE, DUNCAN COMES HERE TONIGHT!"

Beside me, Lacey stared, pale as milk. "I can't possibly do that!"

"Of course you can," I whispered. " 'Pack your tones against your belt,' as the old Elizabethan actors used to say. Bring it up from your diaphragm, but keep your throat relaxed, as if it were the most natural thing in the world to utter secrets at a hundred decibels. After all, you're on as a witch next, and if you can't let yourself go and rock the rafters with your cackling in that sort of part, when can you?"

The absurdity of the question didn't seem to reach her; certainly she made no attempt at the further absurdity of the answer, but only developed a gleam in her eye and said,

"You're right, Mr. Burbage. If I want to steal a scene by sheer volume, I'll never have a better chance."

Well, that wasn't quite how I would have thought of it—but anything to motivate her to blast like a typhoon. . . .

Which gave me an idea. I sidled over next to Susanne and whispered, "Lacey may try to steal the scene by simply outshouting you."

Susanne was looking just as aghast as Lacey had, but my jibe brought the color back to her face and determination to her lip. "She'll get nodes on her vocal folds, Mr. Burbage. If that phony thinks she can drown *me* out, she'd better look to her hearing aid!"

So they went on determined to compete for sheer volume. I wasn't too worried—I was certain they were both alert to the dangers of shouting. They would project, not blast—but project more loudly than any drill sergeant in an open field.

Winston came off, and I grinned at him, whispering, "What's your motivation?"

"To be heard," he muttered back.

"But what of subtlety? Nuance? Interpretation?"

"What of characterization?" he rejoined. "It's nothing but a bellowing contest out there. At least the younger folk are proving they know how to project."

I didn't tell him that I included him as one of the "younger folk" I hadn't been sure of. Perhaps I should have, though—the comment about age might have done him a world of good.

The audience had begun talking among themselves again—after all, most of them were merely in their teens—and a steady hum had arisen from the distant bleachers. However, it was nowhere nearly as loud as the dull roar had been. Many of them were, I think, actually becoming interested in the story that was unfolding on stage. No doubt it was a surprise to them.

Then the three witches began again, and the hum lessened and shifted higher in pitch. The boys had stopped gossiping to watch Lacey and Susanne move about, and the girls had started exclaiming to each other about the shamelessness and lewdness of those hussies onstage, and about anyone's being able to be beautiful with as many false appliances as the younger witches were doubtless using. The only things false about Lacey and Susanne, of course, were their eyelashes and face paint—but the teenage morsels couldn't know that—and didn't want to.

The witches were well worth the watching—they were dancing about the cauldron, with some movements that I doubted Shakespeare had ever thought of. For that matter, neither had Barry.

A high-pitched retching echoed from the audience—the local girls, with a legitimate excuse for expressing their opinion of this imported competition. It was nice to know they were paying attention. On the other hand, with all three ladies blaring away at their maximum volume, there wasn't a corner of the gymnasium that wasn't ringing with their chant. I was gratified to notice that Grudy's voice was louder than either of the younger ladies. Experience will always tell, and loudly, too.

Toward the end of Act II, I had happened to glance up through the gap between the leg curtain and the return flat, at the audience—not to count them, of course; that would have been bad luck. I caught a fleeting glimpse of a figure in gray against that darkness, but thought nothing of it at the time; I was far more interested in the impression that, where there had before been only a small black mass of people more or less centered against the lighter darkness of the bleachers, they had now, amoebalike, spread to engulf almost all of the seating.

By the middle of Act III, I was certain of it.

"Surely the audience has not grown!" I whispered to Barry.

He looked up, startled, then smiled slowly. "Do you know, Horace, I do believe they have."

"But *how*?" I hissed.

"No doubt some freshmen have been sent to notify the truants that they are actually missing an exciting show. Let us hope the newcomers mentioned the fact to their parents."

They had. During the intermission, the harried and elderly custodian actually had to come out and turn a key, causing the side bleachers to glide out from the walls.

"We have them!" Barry crowed in the locker room, as exultant as any air-hockey coach. "But don't let up, good friends! You will have audience near the stage, but the youngsters at the far end still need to hear you! And with so many bodies soaking up sound, the acoustic situation may be even worse!"

"Just how many of them are out there, Barry?" Ogden asked.

"Publius says he has sold a thousand tickets at the box office—and they are still streaming in."

"For *Shakespeare*?" Lacey was completely amazed. "Why?"

"The excitement of live theater, child." Marnie no doubt meant it as withering scorn, but she was too elated for the comment to emerge as anything but an insight.

"The Bard speaks to all cultures and all ages," Ogden pontificated, "provided they can see his stories come alive on the stage, not have to labor through an alien vocabulary on the printed page."

Barry nodded. "They are following the story line from the action they see, even if they miss many of the words. Congratulations, friends. You are reaching them!"

"But *how*?" Larry seemed completely at a loss. "Characterization, interpretation, concentration—it's all swallowed up in the sheer need to be heard!"

"Nonetheless, the characters are emerging," Winston said, his eyes glowing. "Our concentration is definitely beginning to develop. The interaction with the audience does it, my lad. There is something about knowing that the people out there appreciate what you are doing that makes the character come alive within you in a way nothing else can!"

Ramou came hurrying in, passing out inch-wide wafers. "Body mikes, Mister Tallendar! Chovy sent somebody to rustle up a sound system, and Charlie got it set up and working!"

A cheer went up from the whole company.

"Pity." Marnie sighed. "I was almost looking forward to straining my corset in this delightfully new way."

"I wasn't." Lacey rubbed her throat. "I wasn't sure I could keep it up for another hour."

"Praise heaven, you should not have to," Barry said, but Ogden reached over and knocked on the nearest seat.

"It's as close as we can come to knocking on wood. Hopefully, St. Vidicon will keep our microphones working—but if Finagle should triumph, be ready to project again."

"The caution is well taken," Barry agreed. "Something so quickly set up, may just as quickly fail. We should have *some* respite, though."

Chovy came running in, grinning from ear to ear, and Ramou looked up. "What did Publius say?"

"He says to hold the curtain!" Chovy exulted. "They're still pouring in!"

Another cheer made the walls ring.

As it died, I developed a suspicion. "Did you have anything to do with this?"

Chovy shrugged modestly. "Had a few lads in the audience, ready to take word to some more lads outside, that's all. Each one told ten, and each of them called up ten more—you know how word gets around."

"Apparently not as well as you do." Barry exhaled.

"Young man, when this is over, I don't suppose you would be interested in a position as a publicist?"

"What, traipsing from planet to planet?" Chovy's grin vanished. "Thanks for the sweet word, mate, but I couldn't think of it. This is my world here, and my people and my work. It's my life, is all."

"Can't see that working in an oxygen plant on a boondock planet is much of a future," Larry muttered, so low that only Winston and I could hear him, and that only because we were right next to him. My own inclinations agreed with his—but there was some quality in Chovy's tone, some earnestness, that I had never seen in him before. I stared at him, startled, and saw an iron determination there for just a second, before he masked it with his customary, devil-may-care grin. For some reason, it seized my spinal column with chills and gave my vitals a stab of foreboding.

But Barry was saying, "Back up onstage, friends! We must be ready for Publius's signal! Chovy, if you would be good enough to continue as courier . . . ?"

"Ramou won't let me, in costume," Chovy answered, "but I've got a cousin running for us. Little scaper, still in school."

Which meant that he knew these halls very well and would no doubt be an extremely efficient channel of communication.

"Thank you!" Barry turned to us all, eyes gleaming. "Once more unto the breach, dear friends, once more!"

"Wrong play," Larry muttered, but even he couldn't make it sound like the sneer he intended. We all streamed out the door, eager for action.

Boy, did we have action! I mean, I had it bad enough, trying to argue my superannuated juvenile delinquents into their camouflage outfits—branches tied to their helmets, tabards of leaves. Out on stage, Winston and the ladies were having a field day.

Horace told me it was a very appreciative audience. Winston told me they cheered damn near every line—and when the witches were on, I could hear the whistling and stamping all the way down to the locker rooms. I had to come up and see it, risking leaving my gang to Chovy's tender mercies.

They really loved the drunken porter. I mean, the way Marty was playing it, it would have gotten laughs without any words at all—but why the audience roared with mirth when he greeted the equivocator, I couldn't tell. It was the line about not being able to equivocate between God and the devil—and come to think of it, maybe the roars weren't entirely amused. They sure were approving, though. They booed the murderers with a ferocity I couldn't believe, and when Banquo called, "Fly, good Fleance, fly!" and rolled over dead, I thought the audience was going to come give him a hero's funeral right then and there. So I wasn't too surprised that they really loved the banquet scene—why, I don't know, but every time Macbeth looked up and saw Banquo's ghost, the audience howled their approval. When Lady Macbeth cried, "Stay not upon the order of your going!" and chased the barons out, she was met with a roar that rocked the set.

Susanne was bright-eyed and breathless. "They love us! They really love us!"

"It's not us, dearie," Lacey said sourly. "It's a couple of hussies who happen to look like us, and who they think are available. When you go out the stage door tonight, keep a hand on your girdle."

But I think she was missing the point—because it was the ghosts the people were cheering, not the witches. I glanced at Horace and I saw the first lines of concern etching his face. I was beginning to feel that way, too—they were cheering all the wrong lines. I mean, sure, they were

great poetry—but "Who would have thought the old man
had so much blood in him?" shouldn't have rated howls of
anger, and "All the perfumes of Arabia will not sweeten
this little hand" sure as hell shouldn't have brought down
the house. Looking back on it, I began to realize that, when
Charlie and Marty and I had entered as murderers the second time, the boos and hisses had been entirely too
energetic—and when we had mimed stabbing Chovy's little
brother and Lacey, I'd thought the audience was going to
charge the stage. I mean, it was getting scary.

I felt a little better when I heard all the isolated yells of
commiseration for MacDuff's sorrow, but the howls of approval when he determined on revenge sounded all too
much like a pack of baying wolves for my comfort.

"Tomorrow, and tomorrow, and tomorrow" had always
seemed dumb to me, in English class—why call it great poetry, when all it did was repeat the same word? But it really
reached these people. "All our yesterdays have lighted fools
the way to dusty death" drew an angry chorus of agreement
that rang off the rafters, and set me to wondering:

Why agreement?

Apparently, this audience seemed to know what Macbeth
was feeling—from personal experience. At least, they em-
pathized with his depression at the end of the play. But I
couldn't help wondering if the way they cheered when he
said, "At least we'll die with harness on our back!" wasn't
more what they wished they could do, not what they'd already been through. Maybe it was the way Winston charged
off, brandishing his broadsword—or maybe they felt he was
going out to do their chopping for them. Horace told me
later that that's a perfectly legitimate purpose in theater—
that if the hero slays the villain, he's vicariously slaying the
bad guy for them, so the people in the audience won't feel
the need to go out slaying their own enemies; it's called the
"catharsis hypothesis." But the idea rang hollow to me—
because the audience wasn't ringing hollow at all. They

were totally sincere, every one of them. They sounded like a crowd of sports fans following the cheerleader—only these fans were working themselves up to running down there and playing the game on their own.

I hoped they'd wait till after the curtain call.

Then my boys were coming up with their camouflage, and the sentry was telling Macbeth he'd seen a walking forest, and Macbeth remembered the witches telling him he wouldn't be killed until Birnham Wood came to Dunsinane—and the audience was cheering the wood. You could almost see my boys swell with enthusiasm, and I forgot my worries about the audience's verve long enough to worry about my army's. I wasn't supposed to be out onstage for every sally and clash, but I was this time, making sure that none of those halberds or pikes was really being used. These boys were really getting into the spirit of the thing, and I was afraid they might really come out for blood. The audience sure seemed ready to.

Then the army's fight was over, my boys were off the stage, and I was wiping sweat off my brow, letting myself begin to feel relief—until the roars damn near deafened me. I turned around to see Winston and Barry battling it out with their broadswords and caught my breath, crossing my fingers, and hoping that the St. Vidicon I didn't believe in would keep Finagle from letting those swords break. My fellow actors were alert and stiff in the wings, staring at the stage, and I could tell each one of them had the same apprehensions I did. We held our breaths and got ready to duck.

Of course, the audience didn't know it might be the Target for Today. They were cheering and hollering and having themselves a fine old time. They were rooting for MacDuff now, where a few minutes before, they'd been cheering Macbeth out of the doldrums. I wished they would make up their minds.

Then Winston fell, Barry chopped down with a very

solid thunk, and the audience went wild. Every one of us actors went limp with relief—the swords had held.

Larry came out to pronounce Malcolm's victory, and the audience quieted down to hear him. But when Barry came out with Winston's head, the hooting and clamoring went on for three or four minutes. In the wings, Winston turned ashen. I heard him muttering, over and over again, "It's not me, it's the character."

Finally, the audience quieted down long enough for MacDuff to announce Macbeth's death, and for Malcolm to invite everybody to come see his coronation, and I thought the audience was ready to take him up on it. The cheers had slackened just a little bit when the witches came out to start looting the dead soldiers, and the audience booed them so loudly and vociferously that they got offstage fast. Susanne was pale, and really scared, as she came running off. "Ramou! What's the matter with them?"

"Live theater," I said, for want of anything else, and the stage lights went down. The audience yelled and applauded like a thunderstorm. The lights came up again, and Horace herded us all onstage—except me; I was too busy herding my extras. We all got out there and took a bow—but the applause kept up full strength, with yells and whistles of approval, so we bowed again. And again. And again. And again, facing that sea of sweating, feverish, wild-eyed faces, every single one of them aglow with the excitement of having seen a really dramatic production of one of humanity's really great plays, with famous actors in the starring roles, right there in front of them, in the same room, alive.

Except one. There was only one face that wasn't smiling, and it was right there in the front row, about fifteen meters away from me on the stage right side:

Seeholder. With his face drawn and pale, his eyes huge and angry—and scared.

I knew how he felt.

19

The stage lights went down, the houselights went on, but the sound from the audience didn't fade a bit—it just changed quality. The cheers and whistles tapered off, to be replaced by the rumble of a couple of thousand audience members discussing the play—and they sounded enthusiastic. Furiously enthusiastic.

Backstage, we were just plain enthusiastic, and for once, nobody was furious at anybody else. Lacey was actually hugging Susanne, Larry was wearing a grin that outshone Marty's and was thumping him on the shoulder, and Marnie was disappearing into Barry's arms. He let her go, and Merlo quit hugging Grudy long enough to squeeze Marnie and give her a big fat kiss on the cheek. Ogden was grinning from ear to ear, clapping Horace on the shoulder.

Charlie was standing back, watching everyone else with a quiet smile. I felt a stab of pity for him, then realized that he was enjoying watching everybody else's delight. He also seemed to yearn for the closeness we all had—or maybe I was just reading that in. One way or another, though, at least he was enough part of us to be able to be there to bask in our hilarity.

No wonder he'd made a good bartender.

"Did you hear that applause?"

"Eh? What say? I'm a little deaf at the moment."

"They loved us! They were eating us up!"

"We had 'em in the palms of our hands!"

"They wanted to swallow us whole!"

"They couldn't get enough of us!"

But Horace came plowing through their jubilation like a surfer on the run from a tidal wave. "Quickly! Quickly! Into street clothes! Off with your makeup! Grudy, pack the costumes! Merlo, pack the staging equipment! Ramou, help him!"

"Why so agitated, Horace?" Winston asked.

Marnie cried, "Horace! You could at least wait for the celebration to calm a little!"

But Horace was herding people toward the locker rooms. "Yes, yes, it was very wonderful, but we really must take off our makeup and costumes! After all, we can't start the party until we're home, can we?"

"Party? Hey!" Larry whooped and disappeared down the stairs as if he'd been dropped into the ocean.

"You mean Mr. Tallendar's laid on a party? Let me at it!" Marty shot after Larry.

"Whiskey!" Ogden disappeared after them with less speed but just as much verve.

"I'm ready to dance the night out!"

Lacey headed for the stairs, arm in arm with Susanne, who was saying, "I'll match you partner for partner!"

But Winston lingered. "Why such a rush, Horace? I'm sure I'm as anxious to celebrate as anyone else—but it isn't characteristic of you."

"Why, Winston." Barry looked nervous, too. "Didn't the crowd's reaction seem a bit unusually strong to you?"

"Almost frightening in its intensity, yes," Winston answered. "I put it down to their delight in their first live performance, coupled with my long absence from a live audience."

"It was a bit more than that," Barry said. "Exactly what, I don't know—but we are strangers in town, and I'd prefer not to tempt the fates."

"Back to the hotel, then?"

"I think we'd best plan on the ship," Horace said. "Did you see Mr. Seeholder's face?"

"The funereal gentleman in the front row? Who is he?"

"Our friendly neighborhood censor—and he was not pleased."

"Censor?" Winston frowned. "What problem could he have with Shakespeare? I mean, you even talked Marnie into cutting the 'unsex me here' sequence! Admittedly, it was appropriate, in view of her interpretation of the character, but still . . ."

"I have a notion Seeholder's discontent had nothing to do with the sexual references in the play," Barry said, white-lipped, "and everything to do with the way the audience cheered the slaying of a tyrant."

"Oh." Winston lifted his head, finally understanding. "He *is* authority, isn't he?"

"Yes, and of the lowest rank; he may fear his superiors' displeasure."

"But really! What legitimate complaint—"

"It doesn't have to be legitimate." Horace cut him off. "As long as we're within his jurisdiction, we're his logical scapegoats. I would really prefer to be on our ship with the engines warmed."

"Surely you don't think he would attempt to incarcerate us!"

"I will be delighted to be proved paranoid and over-reactant," Horace said, "tomorrow. But tonight, I would prefer to laugh at my own weaknesses in the ship's lounge."

"I agree," Barry said, "Please, Winston!"

"Now you have *me* worried." Winston turned away to the stairs. "I'll try to hurry the younger generation."

"Thank you, Winston!" Barry turned away to Merlo. "Merlo, pack up the . . . Oh, I see you've noticed."

Merlo and I had the light rails disconnected and lined up

for packing. Merlo was coiling the cables, and I was lugging the lighting board toward the door.

"Ramou!" Horace called.

I turned back. "Yeah, Horace?"

"Do you suppose you could persuade that local friend of yours to have taxis waiting for the whole company?"

"The way we've been tipping, I expect he'll jump at it." I turned to the stairway, but Chovy and his boys were already coming up, faces scrubbed and back in their work clothes. "Hey, Chovy!"

"Ramou! One hell of a performance!" Chovy slapped me on the shoulder, grinning from ear to ear. "Never knew that play had so much power!"

There was something odd about the way he said it, but I didn't have time to worry about it now. "Chovy, we've developed a sudden yearning to get back to our sweet old ship. Think you can line up taxis for us all?"

"Easiest thing in the world, mate!" Chovy waved a hand at the set. "How's about all of this?"

"Back into the truck and out to the ship!"

"That's two loads; we'd better work fast." Chovy turned to his boys. "Hey, mates! All this stuff into the truck!"

"No, leave the set," Horace said. "It's just extruded foam, and we can always buy more of the sludge it's made of—it's cheap enough. Just bring the light rails, the board, and the properties."

"One load, then." Chovy called, "Leave the big stuff, mates! We'll come back and pitch it for them!"

Horace stared. "Why, how thoughtful of you, Chovy!"

"My pleasure, Mr. Burbage. Anything for a guest."

"And anything for a considerate host." Horace reached for his currency wallet.

Chovy waved it away, but his hand got caught on a large-denomination bill that Horace was pulling out. "*I* should pay *you*, Mr. Burbage, for the blast this performance's been. Likely the only time in my life I'll ever be on a stage. Thanks awfully." And he strolled away to exhort his crew.

Horace stared after him. "Did I miss something there?"

"If you did, so did I, and I have a hunch I'm glad I did." I picked up the lighting board again. "Should I bother taking off my makeup, Horace?"

"Oh, yes, Ramou! Only an amateur would wear his makeup outside the theater!" Then Horace checked himself. "No, I'm speaking automatically, aren't I? You're only going to be seen between the gym and the truck—then you'll be riding out to the spaceport instantly. And this is an emergency, after all. Yes, don't bother to take off your makeup."

So it really was an emergency; he'd finally come right out and said it. I wasn't sure why, but I wasn't about to doubt him.

We finished packing up, but when I tried to climb into the truck, Bolo waved me away. "The cabs are just about to pull out, Ramou. You go ride in comfort; we'll come along to help unload at the ship."

"Uh—thanks, Bolo." Not that the truck's cab was any hardship—but Susanne and Lacey were in the taxi, and I wasn't about to argue. I did kind of wonder why Bolo needed all the extras along—there wasn't that much to unload. But they were all piling into the back of the truck as I was turning away, and I was in no mood for debate. I hurried over to the cabs and caught the last one.

Of course, it was the one with the other junior members of the company—and driven by Chovy. He wasn't about to waste a chance at some time with Susanne and Lacey, either. "Glad to have you aboard, Ramou! Everyone present or accounted for?"

"You'd know that better than I would," I returned. "How about Grudy and Merlo?"

"The old dame went in the second cab, with some shrill protests, I might add." He pushed the stick, and the cab glided away from the high school.

"She didn't want to be separated from her costumes," Lacey explained. "Couldn't you have reasoned with these musclemen, Ramou?"

"Costume chests are safely stowed in the truck," I assured her. "I'm the one who sent Grudy back to the cab—no sense a nice old lady like her thumping along a route of potholes in the back of a truck. I mean, no cushions—and we won't even talk about seat belts."

"There *are* more pleasant topics of conversation," Susanne agreed.

Chovy swung down a street, and we all looked up at a distant roaring noise. It was too dark to see past the next streetlight, though. "What's that, Chovy?" I asked.

"Oh, just some late revelers out celebrating," he said easily.

"Celebrating what?" Lacey frowned.

"Celebrating you, lass. You've kicked off quite a spree."

We sure had. Chovy had to slow way down—people were out dancing in the streets, and he had to wait for them to move aside. The air was filled with shouts of joy and howls of mirth. They were wearing their ordinary, everyday working clothes, but they had pinned on brightly colored ribbons by way of adornment.

"What is it—Mardi Gras?" Marty asked, staring out the window.

"Something like that. Your play was a rare treat, you know."

"*Macb*—the Scottish play? A kickoff for a festival?" I protested.

"I thought the play had a curse on it!" Larry said.

"No curse for us, chum—just great good news." Chovy came to a stop and waited for a particularly dense throng of people. When they didn't disperse, he pushed a switch and called, "Hey, you lot! Out of the way."

They didn't pay him the slightest bit of attention.

"Lowbrows," Chovy snorted, and turned the car ninety

degrees. "Let's see if we can find some clear space a block over."

"They're getting kind of close," Susanne said nervously.

"As long as there's an alley," Chovy said easily, and the car glided down the narrow way.

"Why is that bus parked across the street?" Lacey asked as we came out.

"To stop cars." As good as his word, Chovy stopped, then pressed his mike switch. "Let me by, mates!"

"Oh, yeah?" A big man stepped up beside him, bellowing loudly enough to be heard through the window. He had half a dozen men behind him, and another half dozen coming up on the other side.

The girls glanced around nervously and sidled up against Larry and me. Not much use—we were looking kind of nervous ourselves. I mean, I don't mind being outnumbered, but a dozen to one is pretty long odds when you're hemmed in by other passengers. "Who says?" the big man demanded, peering through the window. "Oh, it's you, Chovy! What, and the actor people? Sure, sure!" He waved at the bus, bawling, "Let 'em by, Rudy!"

Sure enough, the bus eased back.

"Thanks, mate!" Chovy called, and eased past. The bus glided back into place behind him, and he picked up speed.

"What was that all about?" Marty asked nervously.

"Barricade," Chovy said unhelpfully, then added, "If you're going to let people dance in the streets, you have to block off traffic, you know."

That made sense—but it wasn't exactly satisfying.

There were sharp cracking sounds off to our right, toward the center of the city, then a huge explosion that left echoes reverberating around.

Susanne all but jumped into my lap. "What was that?"

"Noise makers," Chovy explained, entirely too readily. "Can't have firecrackers on a petroleum world, y'know—so we make do with light shows, and boxes that belt out the sounds."

Which explained why a sheet of light brightened the sky over that way, then faded.

"If I didn't know better," Marty said, "I'd think we were driving through a revolution."

"It can't be," Larry said. "The people aren't throwing paving stones."

I decided not to remind him that the streets of Aphrodite were made of poured plasticrete.

Finally, we saw the spaceport terminal gliding past us on our left.

"Why aren't we going in through customs?" Lacey asked, frowning.

"You kidding?" Chovy said. "You folks are the people of the hour. Nobody would think of trying to slow you down tonight—not after *that* performance! You rate first-class treatment in every way tonight, you do!"

Well, that was more than enough for Lacey and Larry; they sat up a little straighter in their seats, and you could fairly see them preening.

The gates to the field swam out of the darkness at us— but if we were such big heroes, how come there was a uniformed cop stepping out in front?

"Got to have a guard," Chovy explained, "or there would be no point to customs."

Well, that made sense. But Marty asked, "So how come he's carrying a bolt thrower?"

The big energy gun did look kind of mean.

"Wouldn't you?" Chovy said, as if that settled it.

Susanne turned half-around, looking back through the window at the bright lights coming right up behind us. "What's that truck doing crowding us?"

"Just next in line, love," Chovy said. "That's the boys with your costumes and props, y'know."

The cop hulked awfully menacingly for an honor guard,

as he came up near the cab. "Taxis at the terminal, kid. What are you trying to pull?"

A dark shape rose up behind him, and a hand the size of a dinner plate clamped down on his shoulder. The cop yowled. I recognized the hold—somebody who knew something was hitting a pressure point. The cop half turned, his mouth wide open yelling, trying to bring his blaster to bear—but somebody else came out of the night to knock it out of his hand. Then two more hid him from our sight. He stopped yelling, and the whole cluster of them moved away.

I was aware of everybody else's eyes on me, but nobody said a word. Me least of all—what could I have said?

Then Bolo was stepping up beside the cab, and his smile was a little on the grim side. "Guard says there's no problem, Chovy. We just had to explain things to him."

I wondered how hard they had needed to explain.

"Right, mate." Chovy gave him the thumb up as a couple of the other boys broke the lock and hauled the gates open. Chovy drove through.

"Rather direct, aren't they?" Lacey was wide-eyed.

"Direct it is," Chovy said. "Why shilly-shally around, eh? Here you are, folks."

The *Cotton Blossom* towered beside us. We got out, thinking that our battered old spaceship had never looked so good.

"Thanks, Chovy." I gave him whatever money I had left in my wallet—after all, this shore leave was over, and payday was due. "You've been a great host."

"It's easy, with guests like you." Chovy waved and closed the door. We turned away toward the boarding ramp, but Susanne glanced back with a frown. "Strange—he's driving back toward the spaceport."

"Probably checking to see if anyone needs a ride back into town," Lacey said. "After all, why go back empty, when he could have a paying fare?"

"I suppose so," Susanne said dubiously, but she went on up the ramp.

I knew how she felt—there was something odd about this whole thing. I mean, I liked thinking that the audience loved our show so much that they'd roll out the red carpet for us—but this seemed a little too much. Maybe a lot too much. Besides, that carpet would have been nicer coming in.

Horace was standing there by the hatch, checking us off on his noteboard. "Ramou—rear guard, as always. Nobody lagging?"

"None that I could see."

"Good, because if we've left anyone behind, we will not be able to come back to pick them up." Horace tucked the minimal computer under his arm and turned up the companionway. "According to my tally, we have everybody. Thank you for being shepherd, my boy."

"Hey, at least I feel useful. Anything else I can do—like maybe check the staterooms?"

"Yes, do, please. Then I believe Captain McLeod wants you on the bridge."

"McLeod!" I slapped my forehead. "I don't have the right reflexes yet." I headed for the nearest intercom, hit the "talk" button, and said, "Ensign Lazarian aboard and reporting for duty."

"Good to hear you, Number Three." McLeod's voice was a tinny rattle over the tiny speaker. "Check the passengers and report to the bridge."

"Yes, sir!" I hurried off to the lift, reflecting that it was kind of confusing, changing jobs as I came on board. Fun, though—in its way. Being third officer was kind of a kick, especially when I was talking to Larry.

I checked to see that Marnie was still bubbling, that Larry was going to stay in his acceleration couch, that Susanne had all her straps in the right places, that Ogden had nothing stronger than water in his hand, and that everybody was webbed in. Then I reported to the bridge.

As I came in, I saw a professional-looking face on the screen. Behind him was the Company's logo. He looked a little harried, but he was delivering the news reports with the proper aplomb. "There is, of course, no cause for concern."

I stared. What was wrong?

"Citizens are asked to clear the streets," the smooth voice went on, "and not interfere with Company security officers in the execution of their duties. Reports of street violence are false."

"What reports?" I asked.

"We seem to have triggered an armed insurrection," Barry said, his face taut and pale. "Workers have erected barricades and stormed the main utility plant, the 3DT station, the oxygen factory, and the management complex."

The announcer's picture turned into jagged streaks; the sound was covered by a roar of static. Then a harsh voice overrode the white noise, saying, "Two hundred-odd Company security men have joined the rebellion! Most of the rest are standing at their posts with their arms crossed, refusing to fire on their fellow workers! Only a hundred or so are fighting it out with our men, trying to keep us out of the management complex! We have the power plant, and we've almost broken through to the 3DT studio and the oxygen plant!"

"We didn't see any of that!" I cried.

"Disappointed at missing the show?" Merlo asked.

"Apparently there was a confrontation with energy weapons," Horace said, "and stray oxygen went up in flames for half a kilometer all around the city center. It died out within seconds, of course—as soon as all the oxygen was gone, there could be no more fire—but it lasted long enough for the rebels to take one of the 3DT stations, which they apparently do not know how to operate properly."

"But we were out there!"

"It would seem our faithful Chovy made certain we would all be driven back along a route that avoided the worst of the violence," Barry noted.

"Considerate of him," Horace said.

Another voice burst in, filled with static, loud and harsh. "The Company goons at headquarters are battling it out with our brave fighters, but they're losing ground fast. We should be inside the building in ten minutes."

The audio hash cut out, the picture settled down, and the announcer was saying, "The only disorder is excessive celebration, due to the unsettling performance paraded by the shameless troupe of off-planet actors."

"What?" I bleated, but Merlo shushed me, then turned back to the screen, where the announcer was saying, "Director of Schools Seeholder has condemned the actors for their outrageous behavior."

His picture was replaced by Seeholder's, standing right outside the gym, obviously fighting for self-control. "Sacrilege!" he was saying. "To twist the words of the greatest poet of the English language, just to titillate the masses, was totally irresponsible."

"Twist?" Barry stared as if he couldn't believe his ears.

"The lines they added were scandalous!"

"We did it line for line as it came from the Bard," Horace snapped, "except for the ones *he* made us cut."

But Barry lifted his head, eyes widening with understanding. "He doesn't know the real play! He only knows what he read in high school!"

And the high school version, of course, had been suitably censored to prevent scandal—and to suit the Company's liking.

"Are you taking action against them?" a disembodied, professional voice asked.

"I certainly am! I've asked the management to issue a warrant for their arrest!"

"*All* of them?"

"The whole gang!"

"But . . . on what charge?"

"Importing inflammatory ideas! And incendiary artifacts, too—we have reason to believe they smuggled in some tobacco lighters!"

"That's it!" McLeod hit the talk button. "*Cotton Blossom* to ground control. That ship from Orbit Three just landed, didn't it?"

"Well, uh . . ." Ground Control stalled.

"Then the orbit's free, so we'll use it to take off. Nice of you to agree, ground control. So long!"

"But wait!" Ground Control squawked. "They're issuing a warrant for your arrest! I just saw it on the news!"

"No, you saw Seeholder asking for one. Wish I could wait to find out if they give it to him, but we have a performance date to catch."

"You smuggled in matches!"

"Surely we didn't!" Barry exclaimed.

I groaned.

Barry turned to me. "You know something about this, Ramou? Tell me at once!"

"Not 'know,' " I said, "but I can guess. Remember how Larry tried to bring in cigarettes?"

"Don't tell me he found a way!"

"I wondered why he was looking so pleased with himself yesterday morning," Horace said, thin-lipped. "And where you bring cigarettes, of course, you must bring lighters—mustn't you?"

"But what are they using them for?"

Static burst on our ears again, and the announcer's picture turned into jagged streaks as the harsh voice told us, "Rebels have captured an oxygen freighter just off Aphrodite! They've opened the petcocks and made a gigantic oxygen spill! The breath of life is lying all over the Aphrodite harbor, and a kilometer out to sea! Our men are standing on

the docks with matches! Management, surrender, or they'll
strike a light that will be seen all the way to Terra!"

"This really *is* a revolution!" Horace gasped—but he had
to shout to be heard over the rumble of the warming engines.

"*Cotton Blossom*, turn off those engines!" Ground Control
squawked. "We've just had word from the chief executive
officer! You may not, repeat not, lift off! Any attempt to do
so will be an act of treason against the government of New
Venus! You will not be allowed to make planetfall on any
other colony world! Douse those engines! If I see so much
as a flicker from the power meter on your launch cradle, I'll
call for a cannon and hole you amidships! You're under arrest! Repeat, you are under arrest! Power down and wait for
Company security to take you into custody!"

"He can't think we really will, can he?" I asked, incredulous.

"No," Horace said, "but he has to make his position
clear for the record, or he will be fired."

"You can't . . . uhhhhh!" There was a confused assortment of cracks and dull thuds from the loudspeaker; then a
new voice said, "Orbit Three? Right as rain, mate. Have a
good trip!"

McLeod hit the button, and the ship roared beneath us.
For a few minutes, we were too busy—trying to keep our
faces from melting into our seat backs—to be able to talk;
but when the acceleration was over, I leaned forward and
hit the key for Susanne's cabin. "Susanne, please check on
Ogden! No grounds for concern—just routine." Then I
swung back to the communicator. "Chovy?"

"No, I'm his uncle," Ground Control answered.

Another voice chimed in. "*This* is Chovy, mate. But
don't worry, my uncle is ground control for the New Venus
Provisional Urban Revolutionary Government Executive, so
you're clear with the new bosses—and just in case we

don't last, you have a great case to keep you clear with any other planetary authorities you meet. You are recording this, aren't you?"

I stared at Ramou, who stared back at me, dumbstruck.

"We are recording, aren't we?" I finally asked.

Ramou gulped and nodded.

"You might reassure him on the point," I said.

"Uh, yeah!" Ramou turned back to the audio pickup. "Good to hear you, Chovy. Uh, what's the New Venus Provisional Urban Revolutionary Government Executive?"

"New PURGE," Chovy shortened it helpfully. "You might've heard about the union, mate?"

"Uh, yeah! But I kinda thought they were part of the establishment."

"They were. We're not them. We're a bunch of disaffected members who realized the union was playing footsy with management, so we started our own new and very secret organization."

"Young Turks," Barry muttered.

"Not all young," Chovy corrected. "The top folks are in their fifties and sixties; I'm just a low-ranker. There're a lot of us, mates."

"Including your uncle," Ramou said.

"Also my aunt," Chovy corroborated, "and my mother and father, and my sisters and big brother. It's the new family business, you might say."

"Talk about a grand opening," Ramou muttered. "Widespread, huh?"

"Oh, very. Been going for fifty years, we have—and had everything set up for a coup. Frustrating as hell, though—the kindling and wood were all laid, but we didn't have a match."

"A catalyst." My mouth was suddenly dry.

"Or a trigger. Right. Some event that would set the whole population howling for management's blood."

"Macbeth?" Ramou bleated.

"There *is* a curse on the play," I reminded him.

"Only for management," Chovy said. "But then, they're the ones who tried to censor it, right? And we made sure the people on the street knew all about that, too—we had an agent in Seeholder's office. Wasn't a young buck in Aphrodite wasn't out for his blood . . . Anyway, we passed the word that you were going to be showing folk how to fight back, through your play."

Barry groaned, his head sinking into his hand.

"So they were prepared to perceive a revolutionary message," I said, my mouth turned to cotton.

"You mean they only heard what they were expecting?" Ramou asked.

"Every bit, mate. Old Shakespeare maybe knew that, when you were talking about tearing down a tyrant king, it was dangerous stuff—but old Jamie his king didn't, did he? I mean, whether a king's good or bad kind of has something to do with whether or not he's on your side. So when MacDuff said, 'Bleed, bleed, poor country! Great tyranny! The title is afeared!' our folk knew they were really talking about the Company."

"I don't think Shakespeare . . ." I gasped.

But Chovy wasn't done. "Of course, we pushed it a bit, by having our boys shout slogans when they were attacking the castle."

"I wondered about that 'Purge the tyrants!' line," Ramou said. "Publicity for your organization, huh?"

"No, the signal for the uprising," Chovy said. "The word went out all through your audience—as soon as you finished your bows, they were to grab up their sticks and start hunting the Company."

"Sticks?" Ramou stared. "Against ray guns and energy weapons? What kind of sticks could do you any good there?"

"Matchsticks," Chovy said. "We really didn't need the

ones your friend distributed with the cigarettes he was selling for a kwaher a pack . . ."

"A what?!"

"Oh, he had buyers," Chovy said. "Worth more than
gold, here. But we had half a dozen crews ready to take
over their oxygen freighters, so they're sitting in ports right
now, spreading oxygen all over the docks and standing
there with matches in their hands."

"Talk about a strike . . ." Ramou murmured.

"It's all over but the shouting," Chovy assured us. "We
kidnapped the vice CEO on his way out of the Grand Gym,
and our boys are breaking through into the CEO's office
even as we speak. The rest of the managers are all tied up,
as they've claimed to be whenever we've had a complaint
for the last ten years—so don't worry about a bad recco
keeping you from landing on your next planet."

I glanced at Barry and Ramou, then at McLeod. He nodded. "So there isn't any warrant?"

We heard a loud ripping sound, and Chovy said, "Not a
bit, lads. Be off with you now, and have a good trip. Give
my love to the ladies."

"Will do, Chovy," Ramou answered. "And, uh, thanks
for everything."

"You're welcome, mate. Come back any time."

Barry shook his head silently.

McLeod hit the button, and we swung out of orbit and
off toward the stars.

"One could wish them luck," I said quietly.

"Yes, and I do," Barry said. "However, you'll pardon me
for feeling used—and somewhat badly."

"They did not *make* us perform, Barry," I reminded him,
"and it was the Company itself that made us do *Macbeth*."

"They must not have known about the curse on the
play." Barry sighed.

"They do now," Merlo said.

20

Barry stepped up onto a chair and called out over the hub-bub, "A moment's silence, my friends, please!"

It took a while for the laughter and the excited chatter to die. All were enjoying themselves—Marnie actually engaged in civil, even animated, discourse with Winston, and lowering herself to exchange kind words with Merlo and Grudy. Ogden lounged in a huge chair, quietly and happily absorbing an increasing amount of alcohol, and Susanne was only occasionally sparing him an anxious glance, between dances. Everyone was in high spirits and higher voice, so it did take a while before they all quieted. But quiet they did, though the raucous battering that the younger generation is pleased to call "music" did continue for several minutes, until Ramou went over and killed the power. He'd been dying to do that for some time, to judge by his face—he'd had to stand by watching Susanne dancing with Larry while Lacey danced with Marty, and what they called dancing could have inflamed a stick of wood, if it had been male. Ramou had definitely been the odd man out, and smoldering through it, even though what Marty called dancing was absolutely hilarious to watch.

"Hey, Ramou, put it back on!"

"Just because you weren't—"

"What do you think you're doing, Lazarian?" Larry bristled.

Ramou stood quietly, letting only a glint of satisfaction

show, folding his arms and nodding to Barry. "Listen to the boss, folks, okay?"

Reluctantly and sulkily, they all turned to give Barry their attention.

"The ghost shall walk!" he proclaimed. "Our endeavors have netted us a huge profit!"

Everyone cheered, and Publius stood below Barry, beaming around at the crowd, thumbs hooked into his suspenders. Then Marnie demanded, "How? With only one performance and almost no publicity?"

"Our friends on the Revolutionary Committee seem to have taken care of that last item," Barry explained, "directing word of mouth with almost military efficiency. And our nemesis, the management, in their efforts to control us, actually cut our costs to the bone. They supplied us a theater, after all, and were not able to collect rent—and with all the failings of the Grand Gymnasium, it seems to have held an inordinate number of people: two thousand in just one house! And in the last-minute rush, we were not able to prorate standing room, so everyone paid full fare. Thus we have paid for our transportation, hotel, food, and port fees, and still have two thousand kwahers, five hundred fifty-seven BTUs profit!"

The cheer rattled the walls.

When we had stopped, Barry went on. "We shall calculate shares, and tomorrow shall be payday! Party well, my friends—you have earned it!"

They cheered again, and the partying broke out anew. Ramou punched the music back on, then leaped out onto the floor too quickly for Larry to prevent him—though it was Lacey who came out to dance with him first, and Marty paired up with Susanne. Larry stood by, smoldering and waiting for the next number. I reflected that we really should hire a third young artist—perhaps a female comic.

Marnie immediately launched into conversation again, somewhat loudly and stridently. "But really, those poor souls! The conditions they lived in were abominable! And so far from a decent couturier! They were quite right to rebel!"

"Quite so," I said, though I disagreed as to the specific causes.

"What'll they choose for their monument to the revolution?" Merlo wondered. "An actor holding a sword?"

"I should think an eternal flame would be more appropriate," Grudy demurred, "considering the circumstances."

"I hope they have succeeded." I sighed. "In fact, I feel rather badly that we couldn't stay to help resolve the conflagration we apparently kindled with our incendiary remarks."

Marnie blanched, and Winston said sternly, "Our business is drama, Horace, not politics. Our purpose is to reflect life and to comment upon it, not to interact with it."

"Brecht didn't think so," Merlo muttered.

"No, nor did Clifford Odets—but they sought only to preach, not to practice," Barry pointed out. "They made great theater out of political issues—but when all is said and done, they were still professionals of the stage, not of government."

"True," I sighed. "But can we thereby disown our responsibility for the effects of our work?"

"The only effects we cause," Winston said, "are laughter, tears, and, if we are fortunate, a greater understanding of human life."

"Understanding, yes," I agreed, "but acceptance? Ah, not always!"

"Nor should it be," Winston rejoined. "If the understanding we give makes people less willing to suffer abuse, have we not done good work?"

"Ah," I murmured, "but if they shed blood in their resistance, what then?"

"Why, then," Barry said, clapping us both on our shoulders, "we must play for them again, and seek to make them abhor bloodshed—but just now, gentlemen, we must celebrate our survival. Come! The punch bowl awaits!"

About the Author

CHRISTOPHER STASHEFF spent his early childhood in Mount Vernon, New York, but spent the rest of his formative years in Ann Arbor, Michigan. He has always had difficulty distinguishing fantasy from reality and has tried to compromise by teaching college. When teaching proved too real, he gave it up in favor of writing full-time. He tends to pre-script his life but can't understand why other people never get their lines right. This causes a fair amount of misunderstanding with his wife and four children. He writes novels because it's the only way he can be the director, the designer, and all the actors, too.

Now available in bookstores everywhere . . .

THE WITCH DOCTOR

by

Christopher Stasheff

Published in hardcover by Del Rey Books.

Read on for the opening chapter of
THE WITCH DOCTOR . . .

1

What can you say about a friend who leaves town without telling you?

I mean, I left Matt sitting there in the coffee shop trying to translate that gobbledygook parchment of his, and when I came back after class, he was gone. I asked if anybody'd seen him go, but nobody had—just that, when they'd looked up, he'd been gone.

That was no big deal, of course—I didn't own Matt, and he was a big boy. If he wanted to go take a hike, that was his business. But he'd left that damn parchment behind, and ever since he'd found it, he'd handled it as if it were the crown jewels—so he sure as hell wouldn't have just left it on the table in a busy coffee shop. Somebody could have thrown it in the wastebasket without looking. He was just lucky it was still there when I got back. So I picked it up and put it in my notebook. "Tell him I've got his parchment," I told Alice.

She nodded without looking up from the coffee she was pouring. "Sure thing, Saul. If you see him first, tell him he forgot to pay his bill this morning."

"Saul" is me. Matt claimed I'd been enlightened, so he called me "Paul." I went along—it was okay as an in-joke, and it was funny the first time. After that, I suffered through it—from Matt. Not from anyone else. "Saul" is me. I just keep a wary eye for teenagers with slingshots who also play harp.

"Will do," I said, and went out the door—but it nagged at me—especially since I had never known Matt to forget to pay Alice before. Forget to put on his socks, maybe, but not to pay his tab.

When I got back to my apartment, I took out his mystical manuscript and looked at it. Matt thought it was parchment, but I didn't think he was any judge of sheepskins. He certainly hadn't gotten his. Well, okay, he had two of them, but they hadn't given him the third degree yet—and wouldn't, the way he was hung up on that untranslatable bit of doggerel. Oh, sure, maybe he was right, maybe it *was* a long-lost document that would establish his reputation as a scholar and shoot him up to full professor overnight—but maybe the moon is made of calcified green cheese, too.

Me, I was working on my second M.A.—anything to justify staying around campus. Matt had gone on for his doctorate, but I couldn't stay interested in any one subject that long. They all began to seem kind of silly, the way the professors were so fanatical about the smallest details.

By that standard, Matt was a born professor, all right. He just spun his wheels, trying to translate a parchment that he thought was six hundred years old but was written in a language nobody had ever heard of. I looked it over, shook my head, and put it back in the notebook. He'd show up looking for it sooner or later.

But he didn't. He didn't show up at all.

After a couple of days, I developed a gnawing uncertainty about his having left town—maybe he had just disappeared. I know, I know, I was letting my imagination run away with me, but I couldn't squelch the thought.

So what do you do when a friend disappears?

You have to find out whether or not to worry.

The first day, I was only a little concerned, especially after I went back to the coffee shop, and they said he hadn't been in looking for his damn parchment. The second day, I started getting worried—it was midnight and he hadn't

334

shown up at the coffeehouse. Then I began $\ldots$
he'd forgotten to eat again and blacked ou $\ldots$
around to his apartment to tell him off.

He lived in one of those old one-family houses $\ldots$
been converted into five apartments, if you want to $\ldots$
them that—a nine-by-twelve living room with a kitchene $\ldots$
wall, and a cubbyhole for a bedroom. I knocked, but he
didn't answer. I knocked again. Then I waited a good long
time before I knocked a third time. Still no answer. At three
A.M., when the neighbor came out and yelled at me to stop
knocking so hard, I really got worried—and the next day,
when nobody answered, I figured, Okay, third time's the
charm—so I went outside, glanced around to make sure nobody was looking, and quietly crawled in the back window.
Matt really ought to lock up at night; I've always told him
so.

I had to crawl across the table—Matt liked to eat and
write by natural light—and stepped into a mess.

Look, I've got a pretty strong stomach, and Matt was
never big on housekeeping. A high stack of dishes with
mold on them, I could have understood—but wall-to-wall
spiderwebs? No way. How could he live like that? I mean,
it wasn't just spiderwebs in the corners—it was spiderwebs
choking the furniture! I couldn't have sat down without getting caught in dusty silk! And the proprietors were still
there, too —little brown ones, medium-sized gray ones, and
a huge male-eater with a body the size of a quarter and red
markings like a big wide grin on the underside of its abdomen, sitting in the middle of a web six feet wide that was
stretched across the archway to the bed nook.

Then the sun came out from behind a cloud, its light
struck through the window for about half a minute—and I
stood spellbound. Lit from the back and side like that, the
huge web seemed to glow, every tendril bright. It was beautiful.

the light went away, and it was ʾnin-laden debris.

ʾhat had attracted all these eight-ʾ ʾust have been a bumper year for flies. *just* maybe, they'd decided to declare war on the ʾckroaches that infested the place. If so, more ʾʾto them. I decided not to go spider hunting, after all. Besides, I didn't have time—I had to find Matt.

The strange thing was, I'd been in that apartment just three days before, and there hadn't been a single strand of spider silk in sight. Okay, so they're hard to see—but three days just isn't time enough for that much decoration.

I stepped up to the archway, nerving myself to sweep that web aside and swat its builder—but the sun came out again, and the golden cartwheel was so damned beautiful I just couldn't bring myself to do it. Besides, I didn't really need to —I could look through it, and the bedroom sure didn't have any place that was out of sight. Room enough for a bed, a dresser, a tin wardrobe, and scarcely an inch more. The bed was rumpled, but Matt wasn't in it.

I turned around, frowning, and scanned the place again. I wouldn't say there was no sign of Matt—as I told you, he wasn't big on housekeeping, and there were stacks of books everywhere, nicely webbed at the moment—but the pile of dirty dishes was no higher than it had been, and he himself sure wasn't there.

I stepped out into the hall and closed the door behind me, chewing it over. No matter how I sliced it, it came out the same—Matt had left town.

Why so suddenly?

Death in the family. Or close to it. What else could it be?

So I went back to my apartment and started research. One of the handy things about having some training in scholarship, is that you know how to find information. I knew what town Matt came from—Separ City, New Jersey—and I knew how to call long-distance information.

"Mantrell," I told the operator.

"There are three, sir. Which one did you want?"

I racked my brains. Had Matt ever said anything about his parents' names? Then I remembered, once, that there had been a "junior" attached to him. "Matthew."

"We have a Mateo."

"Yeah, that's it." It was a good guess, anyway.

"One moment, please."

The vocodered voice gave me the number. I wrote it down, hung up, picked up, and punched in. Six rings, and I found myself hoping nobody would answer.

" 'Allo?"

I hadn't known his parents were immigrants. His mother sounded nice.

"I'm calling for Matthew Mantrell," I said. "Junior."

"Mateo? Ees not 'ere."

"Just went out for a minute?" I was surprised at the surge of relief I felt.

"No, no! Ees away—college!"

My spirits took the express elevator down. "Okay. I'll try him there. Thanks, Mrs. Mantrell."

"Ees okay. You tell him call home, si?"

"Si," I agreed. "Good-bye." I hung up, hoping I would see him indeed.

So. He hadn't gone home.

Then where?

I know I should have forgotten about it, shoved it to the back of my mind, and just contented myself with being really mad at him. What was the big deal, anyway?

The big deal was that Matt was the only real friend I had, at the moment—maybe the only one I'd ever had, really. I mean, I hadn't known Matt all that long; but four years seems like a long time, to me. Four years, going on five—but who's counting?

It's not as if I'd ever had all that many friends. Let me see, there was Jory in first grade, and Luke, and Ray—and all the rest of the boys in the class, I suppose. Then it was down to Luke and Ray in second grade, 'cause Jory moved away—but the rest of the kids began to cool off. My wild stories, I guess. Then Ray moved, too, so it was just Luke and me in third grade—and Luke eased up, 'cause he wanted to play with the other kids. Me, I didn't want to play, I was clumsy—I just wanted to tell stories, but the other kids didn't want to hear about brave knights rescuing fair damsels. So from fourth grade on, I was on decent terms with the rest of the kids, but nothing more. Then, along about junior high, nobody wanted to be caught talking to me, because the "in" crowd decided I was weird.

What can I say? I was. I mean, a thirteen-year-old boy who doesn't like baseball and loves reading poetry—what can *you* say? By local standards, anyway. And in junior high, local standards are everything. Made me miserable, but what could I do?

Find out what they thought made a good man, of course. I watched and found out real quick that the popular guys weren't afraid to fight, and they won more fights than they lost. That seemed to go with being good at sports. So I figured that if I could learn how to fight, I could be good at sports, too. A karate school had just opened up in town, so I heckled Mom until she finally took me, just to shut me up. I had to get a paper route to pay for it, though.

It only took six months before I stopped losing fights. When school started again in the fall, and the boys started working out their ranking system by the usual round of bouts, I started winning a few—and all of a sudden, the other guys got chummy. I warmed to it for a little while, but it revolted me, too. I knew them for what they were now, and I stopped caring about them.

It felt good. Besides, I'd connected with karate—and from it, I got interested in the Far East.

One of the teachers told me I should try not to sound so hostile and sarcastic all the time.

Sarcastic? Who, me?

So I learned to paste on the smile and sound cheerful.

Didn't work. The other kids could tell. All I succeeded in doing was acting phony.

Why bother?

Of course, things picked up a little in high school, because there was a literary magazine, and a drama club, so I got back onto civil terms with some of the other kids. Not the "in" crowd, of course, but they bored me, so I didn't care. Much.

So all in all, I wasn't really prepared for college. Academically, sure—but socially? I mean, I hadn't had a real friend in ten years—and all of a sudden, I had a dozen. Not close friends, of course, but people who smiled and sat down in my booth at the coffee shop.

Who can blame me if I didn't do any homework?

My profs, that's who. And the registrar, who sent me the little pink slip with the word *probation* worked in there. And my academic counselor, who pointed out that I was earning a quick exit visa from the Land of Friendship. So I declared an English major, where at least half of the homework was reading the books I'd already read for recreation—Twain, and Dickens, and Melville. I discovered Fielding, and Chaucer, and Joyce, and had more fun. Of course, I had to take a grammar course and write term papers, so I learned how to sneak in a few hours at the library. I didn't take any honors, but I stayed in.

Then I discovered philosophy, and found out that I actually *wanted* to go to the library. I started studying without realizing it—it was so much fun, such a colossal, idiotic, senseless puzzle. Nobody had any good answers to the big questions, but at least they were asking.

My answers? I was looking for them. That was enough.

So I studied for fun, and almost learned how to party. Never got very good at it, but I tried—and by my senior year, I even had a couple of friends who trusted me enough to tell me their troubles.

Not that I ever told them mine, of course. I tried once or twice, but stopped when I saw the eyes glaze. I figured out that most people want to talk, but they don't want to listen. It followed from that, logically, that what they liked about me was that I listened, but didn't talk. So I didn't. I got a reputation for being the strong and silent type, just by keeping my mouth shut. I also found out, by overhearing at a party, that they thought I was the Angry Young Man.

I thought that one over and decided they were right. I was angry about people. Even the ones I liked, mostly. They wanted to take, but they didn't want to give. They cared about fighting, but they didn't care about brains. They spent their time trying to get from one another, and they didn't care about why they were here.

Oh, don't get me wrong—they were good people. But they didn't care about me, really. I was a convenience.

Except for Matt.

Matt was already working on his M.A. when I met him, and by the time I graduated, he was making good progress on his Ph.D.

So what was I going to do when I got my degree? Leave town, and the one good friend I had? Not to mention the only three girls who'd ever thought I was human.

No way.

So I started work on my master's. Physics, of course.

How come? From literature and philosophy?

Because I took "Intro to Asia" for a freshman distribution requirement, and found out about zen—and learned about Shrödinger's Cat in "History of Science." Put the two together, and it made a lot of sense.

Don't ask. You had to be there.

Then Matt ran into a snag on his doctoral dissertation. Do you know what it's like to see a real friend deteriorating in front of your eyes? He found that scrap of parchment, then got hung up trying to translate it. Wasn't in any known language, so it had to be a prank. I mean, that's obvious, right? Not even logic—just common sense.

Matt didn't have any.

Now, don't get me wrong. Matt's my friend, and I think the world of the guy, but I'm realistic about him, too. He was something of a compulsive, and something of an idealist, as well—to the point of . . . Well, you know the difference between fantasy and reality? Matt didn't. Not always, anyway.

No, he was convinced that parchment was a real, authentic, historical document, and he wasted half his last year trying to decipher it. I was getting real worried about him—losing weight, bags under his eyes, drawn and pale . . . Matt, not me. I didn't have any spare weight to lose. Him, he was the credulous type—one of the kind that's born every minute. I'm one of the other kind, two born for every one of him. I mean, I wouldn't believe it was April if I didn't see the calendar. Forget about that robin pecking at the window, and the buds on the trees. If I don't see it in black and white, it's Nature pulling a fast one. Maybe a thaw.

So he had disappeared.

I thought about calling the police, but I remembered they couldn't do anything—Matt was a grown man, and there hadn't been any bloodstains in his apartment. Besides, I hadn't been on terribly good terms with the local constables ever since that year I was experimenting with recreational chemicals.

Still, I gave it a try. I actually went into the police station—me, with my long hair and beard. Nobody gave me more than a casual glance, but my back still prickled—probably from an early memory, a very early memory, of my father saying something about "the pigs" loving to beat on anybody who didn't have a crew cut. Of course, that was long ago, in 1968, and I was so little that all I remember of him was a big, tall pair of blue jeans with a tie-dyed T-shirt and a lot of hair at the top. I hated that memory for ten years, because it was all I knew of him until Mom decided to get in touch with him again, and I found out he wasn't really the ogre I figured he must have been, to have left Mom and me that way. Found out it wasn't all his idea, either. And I had a basis for understanding him—by that time, I had begun to know what it was like to have all the other kids put you down.

"I'm sorry, kid," he told me once. "I didn't know alienation was hereditary."

Of course, it wasn't—just the personality traits that led to it. I wouldn't say I ever loved him, but at least I warmed to him some. He had shaved and gotten a haircut, even a three-piece suit, by then, but it didn't fool anybody for very long. Especially me. Maybe that's why I wear chambray and blue jeans. And long hair, and a beard—like my early memories of him.

And early memories stay with you longest and deepest, so I really felt as if I were walking into the lion's den.

The cop at the desk looked up as I approached. "Can I help you?"

About then, he could have helped me out of there, and I might have needed it—but I said, "I hope so. A friend of mine. He's disappeared."

Right away, he looked grave. "Did he leave any message?"

I thought of the parchment, but what good is writing you can't read? Besides, he wasn't the one who wrote it. "Not a word."

He frowned. "But he was over twenty-one?"

"Yeah," I admitted.

"Any reason to think there might have been foul play?"

Now, that question sent the icicle skittering down my spine. Not that the idea hadn't been there, lurking at the back of my dread, mind you—but I had worked real hard not to put words to it. Now that the sergeant had, I couldn't ignore it any more. "Not really," I admitted. "It's just not like him to pick up and pack out like that."

"It happens," the sergeant sighed. "People just get fed up with life and take off. We'll post his name and watch for him, and let you know if we find out anything—but that's all we can do."

I'd been pretty sure of that. "Thanks," I said. "He's Matt Mantrell. Matthew. And I'm—"

"Saul Bremener." He kept his eyes on the form he was filling in. "Three-ten North Thirteenth Street. We'll let you know if we hear anything."

My stomach went hollow, and my skin crawled. It doesn't always help your morale, finding out that the cops know you by name. "Uh . . . thanks," I croaked.

"Don't mention it." He looked up. "Have a good day, Mr. Bremener—and don't take any wooden cigarettes, okay?"

"Wooden," I agreed, and turned numbly about and drifted out of that den of doom. So they remembered my little experiments. It makes one wonder.

The sunlight and morning air braced me, in spite of the lack of sleep. I decided they were nice guys, after all— they'd left me alone until they could see if it was a passing fad, or something permanent. Passing, in my case. So it was smart—they'd saved taxpayers' money and my reputation. I wondered if there was anything written about me anywhere.

Probably. Somewhere. I mean, they had to have something to do during the slow season. I began to sympathize with Matt—maybe blowing town suddenly wouldn't be such a bad idea.

Get real, I told myself sternly. Where else would I find such sympathetic cops?

Back to the search. Maybe *they* couldn't do anything of-ficially, but *I* wasn't official.

So I searched high and low, called the last girl Matt had been seen with—back when I was a junior—and started getting baggy eyes myself. Finally, I took a few slugs of Pepto-Bismol as a preventative, screwed my disgust to the nausea point, and went back into his apartment.

I scolded myself for not having moved that table; just lucky Matt hadn't left anything on it. I laid my notebook down on the desk next to the phone and gave a quick look at the table, the kitchenette counter, and the miniature sofa. Nothing there but dust and spider silk.

Then I went through that apartment inch by inch, clearing webs and squashing spiders. Or trying to, anyway—I must have been dealing with a new and mutant breed. Those little bug-eaters were fast! Especially the big fat one—I took my eyes off it for a second to glance at the arachnid next door, and when I glanced back, it wasn't there any more.

It wasn't the only thing that wasn't there—neither was any sign of where Matt might be. I mean, *nothing*—until I turned and looked at the kitchenette table and saw the parchment.

I stared. Then I closed my eyes, shook my head, and stared again. It was still there. I could have sworn I'd put it back in my notebook—so I picked up the notebook and checked. Yep, the piece of sheepskin was still in it, all right.

That gave me pause. Practically a freeze, really, while I thought unprintable thoughts. Finally, slowly, I looked up and checked again.

It was on the table.

I looked down at the notebook, real fast, but not fast enough—it was back between the lined sheets. I held my head still and flicked a glance over to the table, but it must have read my mind, 'cause it was there by the time I looked. Then I laid down the notebook, real carefully, and stepped back, so I could see both the notebook and the table at the same time.

They each had a parchment.

Well, that settled that. I gave up and brought the notebook over to the table. I set it down beside the parchment. Yep, they were both still there—Matt's parchment in my notebook, and a brand-new one where none had ever been before. At least, a few minutes before—I had checked the table as I crawled across it. I frowned, taking a closer look at the new parchment.

It was written in runes, and the "paper" was genuine sheepskin, all right.

How come runes?

Because runes are magical.

I tried to ignore the prickling at the base of my skull and told myself sternly that runes were just ordinary, everyday letters in somebody else's language. Okay, so it was an old language, and a lot of the items written in it had been ceremonial, which was why they had been preserved—but that didn't mean they were magical. I mean, the people who wrote them may have *thought* they could work magic—but that was just superstition.

But it was also something that made the scholar in me sit up brightly and smack his lips. I mean, literature had been one of my undergraduate majors—justified an extra year on campus, right there—and although it wasn't my main field anymore, I was still interested. I'd learned at least a little bit about those old symbols—and I knew Matt had a book around here that explained the rest. I hunted around until I found it, blew the dust and webbing off, and sat down to study. I looked up each rune and wrote its Roman-letter equivalent just above it. I tried pencil first, but it just skittered off that slick surface, so I had to use a felt pen. After all, this couldn't really be anything old, could it?

After three letters, I leaned back to see if it made a word. H-e-y.

I recoiled and glared down at it. How dare it sound like English!

Just a coincidence. I went to work on the next word.

P-a-u-l.

I sat very still, my glance riveted to those runes. "Hey, Paul"? Who in the ninth century knew my name?

Then a thought skipped through, and I took a closer look at the parchment. I mean, the material itself. It was new, brand-new, fresh off the sheep, compared to Matt's parchment, which was brittle and yellow—several years old, at least. Something inside me whispered *centuries*, but I resolutely ignored it and went on to the next word.

I wrote the Roman letters above the runes, refusing to be sidetracked, resisting the temptation to pronounce the words they formed, until I had all the symbols converted—though something inside me was adding them up as I went along, and whispering a very nasty suspicion to me. But as long as I had another rune to look up, I could ignore it—even after I'd already learned all the runes again and was looking each one up very deliberately, telling myself it was just to make sure I hadn't made a mistake.

Finally, though, I had written down all the letter equivalents and I couldn't put it off any longer. I stayed hunched over the parchment, my hands spread flat on the table, trying to grip into the plywood as I read the translated words.

H-e-y P-a-ul g-e-t i-n t-o-u-c-h I-v-e l-o-s-t y-o-u-r a-d-d-r-e-s-s.

Or, to give it the proper emphatic delivery: *"Hey, Paul! Get in touch! I've lost your address!"*

I could almost hear Matt's voice saying those words, and I swear my nails bit into the plywood. What kind of a lousy joke was this? Friend? You call that a friend? First he leaves town without a word, and then he sends me *this*?

I was just realizing that he couldn't have sent it, when I felt the pain in the back of my hand.

"Damn!" I snatched it back, saw the little red dot in the

346

center, then the big fat spider standing there with that big wide grin painted on its abdomen, and so help me, it was laughing at me. Anger churned up, but the room was already getting fuzzy. Still, I tried to hang on to that anger, tried to lift a hand to swat—the blasted thing had no *right* to. . .

But before I could even finish the thought, the haze thickened, wrapped itself around me like a cool blanket, rolled itself up, and bore me away to someplace dim and distant, and I almost managed to stay conscious.